M. ANDERSON

The Lord of Long Shadows

Knights of the Fallen Realm - Book 1

First published by Anderson Books 2019

Copyright © 2019 by M. Anderson

This novel is entirely a work of fiction. The names, characters and incidents portrayed in it are the work of the author's imagination. Any resemblance to actual persons, living or dead, events or localities is entirely coincidental.

First edition

ISBN: 978-1-7331908-0-0

Cover art by E Book Launch
Editing by S. Jean Brenner

This book was professionally typeset on Reedsy.
Find out more at reedsy.com

For Sarah

Thank you for always being my biggest supporter and advocate.
None of this would have happened without you.

1

Prologue

The boy had been up for three hours by the time the sun's rays began to paint the western tower in warmth and light. It was an important day, and nervousness for the afternoon's ceremony had left his mind far too occupied for sleep or dreams. Four years of menial tasks, endless training drills, and dealing with harsh orders barked from unforgiving masters had led to this day. The rest of the empire would keep on bustling as it always did. For them it was just another day, but for the boy, there had never been a more important one.

Now the sun had risen, the boy could leave his chambers with no need to dodge the monastery's night-guard. Jumping up from his cot, he gathered his belongings and took one last look at his humble abode. It wasn't much; a thin cot on the stone ground, a small chest, and a window, but for the past four years it had been home. Not anymore though. After today, he would earn his place with his brothers and sisters. He took one final moment to compose himself and arrange the tangle of black hair atop his head into something that looked like a hair-style and closed the door on his room.

As the boy rushed down the spiral stairs (four hundred and sixty seven of them - he had counted) he passed other initiates who paid him little mind. They would have been up for hours now, attending to their morning duties. There was a small part of the boy that would miss his chores. There was peace in the simplicity of honest work, or at least that's what Ser Rahlven had told him. The boy had always been suspicious that the proverb was a ruse, designed to trick initiates into complaining less. Where proverbs did not quiet wagging tongues, however, Ser Rahlven's thin wooden rod got the job done. The boy had avoided it by keeping his head down, his mouth shut, and focusing on his chores.

As he reached the bottom of the western tower the boy spilled out onto the courtyard, barely able to contain his glee. The training yards were empty and quiet, but after breakfast it would fill with the sound of young men and women training in sword, lance, and bow. At this point he could complete his training exercises in his sleep. No more wooden practice swords after today, the boy thought to himself with a grin.

The sounds of the city spilled over the tops of the high eastern wall. Unlike the monastery where the boy lived, Rakara, Capital of the Aquillonian Empire, never slept. Already the desperate cries of hawkers selling their goods echoed in from the Low End, and the distant thunder of legionnaires marching in the streets rattled over the ancient stones of the monastery. The boy had given thought to joining a legion once, before he conscripted with the order. As a poor boy on the streets of Rakara, all he wanted was to serve a greater cause, and an escape. The legion would have provided that, but even in the slums, tales of the legion's corruption had reached him. The order was a harder path, but he thought it was a more righteous one. He had seen enough crime in the slums.

Reaching the main barracks, the boy stopped for a moment to compose himself. It may have been his ascension day, but if he burst into his master's study like a gleeful hooligan, the consequences would be less than pleasant. The boy put his disheveled robes and practice sword into a more orderly state and went up the stairs and to the left, where his master's door stood ajar.

This was unusual. The boy had never known his master to leave his door open, but he was too distracted to put much thought into it. The boy walked through, checking his emotions and his wide grin at the door.

He had always liked his master's study. It was a high, circular chamber with ornate bookshelves spanning the length of the walls. Behind a great desk with an ever burning lantern, a small terrace opened out onto Rakara. Even from the door, the boy could see the city gleaming like a thousand jewels in the morning sunlight. The boy had never stepped outside the walls of Rakara, and before conscripting with the order, he had never been outside the slums. From up here though, the city didn't seem so bad.

Ser Ecklan, the boy's master, was nearly shouting in the middle of a heated conversation with a strange man. The man wore long, flowing, blue robes and gripped a gnarled staff in his left hand. He didn't look older than Ser Ecklan, but there was something strange about him. Long gray hair parted in the front, and cascaded unchecked down his shoulders, and there was a wild light which burned in his green eyes. Ser Ecklan was shouting at him, waving a scroll in his left hand.

"Why didn't you come to us sooner, Fallstaff? Do you have any idea how many lives this delay will cost?" Ser Ecklan thundered. He had a deep, booming voice that commanded attention, even when he wasn't furious.

"I came as a courtesy to you, old friend. You cannot win the war that is to come. Flee while you can, and your life may yet be spared," Fallstaff said. His voice was thin and wiry.

"You know I will not do that. None of us will. We took an oath to defend the Empire. And what of the Eastern Watch? What of your oath?"

"The Eastern Watch are making our own preparations at Sanctum. We will not be on the losing side of a war we cannot win. The Watch must rescind our oath, with much regret of course."

"Then get out, you coward. Run while you can, because if I survive this, I'm coming for you. All of you." Ser Ecklan was fuming and seemed ready to boil over.

"You won't survive it, and you're a fool Ecklan," Fallstaff said. "I don't have time for this. I have to go. It begins." With that, Fallstaff mumbled something and his image vanished. Ecklan turned to the boy.

"What are you doing here, boy? That wasn't meant for you to hear."

"What was he talking about master? What war?"

"There's no time to explain. I have to take this to the high council across town. You're with me." As Ecklan spoke, an explosion rocked the city behind him, knocking him and the boy flat. Once they had picked themselves up, the boy wandered over to the terrace and looked out onto a city in flames.

The center of the city was obliterated, and in its place a massive ring of energy hovered above the devastation. The portal was black as night and seemed to suck in the light around it, and even the sun's rays seemed to bend to avoid it.

Ecklan stood and came to the boy's side. A chorus of terrified screams danced on the wind and fires raged unchecked across the city. The boy looked up and saw that Ecklan's face had gone white as plaster, and his old brown eyes were wide with horror. The boy knew all that Ecklan had witnessed in his years as a knight of the order, but this was clearly something he had never seen, and that scared the boy more than anything.

From the center of the ring, a deep rumbling sound of rolling thunder came, and out of the noise a voice boomed over the center of the city.

"Behold for the reckoning comes. Bow before the righteous hand of the gods. I am justice, come down on swift wings upon the wicked. Witness me and despair!"

It took only moments to see from where the voice had come. A tall, black lion came striding out of the portal. He walked on his paws like a man, and shining, golden armor covered him. He was massive, at least the height of three buildings. His eyes were a deep burning red, and gleamed with malice, and he clutched a wicked scythe in his left paw.

A wave of legionnaire had arrived and charged at him, but his cut through them as though they were stalks of wheat. From behind him, thousands of smaller humanoid lions sprang into action out of the portal, rushing into the streets as a tide of devastation.

Ser Ecklan and the boy stood in a moment of stunned silence, and then the moment passed. Ecklan turned to the boy.

"Come with me, we have a new mission." His voice had a grim finality.

"But what about the high council?" the boy asked.

"I'm fairly sure they're aware of the problem by now," the old knight said with a dark chuckle. "Falstaff may have been a coward, but he's right, this is a battle we won't win. But there may be hope yet. Step lively!"

The boy followed Ecklan, who was quick despite his age, and they raced out of his chambers and down into the courtyard. The center of the training yard had exploded into motion as knights armed themselves for battle. Ecklan paid them no mind and kept running, taking turn after turn until he arrived at the main hall. Just as they entered the doors, and he shut them behind, an explosion from the courtyard rattled the doors and the sounds of battle began to rage.

"We have to go back! We have to fight!" the boy protested.

"Listen to me boy, this fight is already over. All your brothers and sisters can do is buy us time. Don't spit on their sacrifice by wasting it."

The boy rankled at running away, but he followed his master without further question. After a dizzying series of twists and turns they arrived at the ceremonial chamber of the order. The boy's eyes widened when he realized where they were. The chamber only had one purpose.

Ecklan walked to the end of the room and opened a stone receptacle and removed a small vial. Inside a glowing red liquid sloshed.

"Wait, are we going to... now?" the boy asked.

"There is no time. I'm sorry I can't do this the proper way, but we just don't have the luxury of standing on ceremony. Drink up."

The boy took the vial and looked at it. He had been working towards this for so long, and now it was here, but the event seemed insignificant in the face of the devastation outside.

"Get to it boy. The order needs every knight it can get right now. Stop your dallying and do your duty. You've trained for this, now come on."

The boy gripped the vial and drank the liquid. A rush of energy flowed through him and all at once a thousand memories flowed through him. They weren't his memories, but he felt as though he had lived them all. It was dizzying, and he gripped his head. Once he had recovered, he looked at Ecklan.

"Now kneel. We can at least do this properly," Ecklan said. The sounds of battle were dying in the courtyard, and the boy had a feeling that it wasn't because the order was winning. He kneeled and felt Ecklan's sword pressed against his shoulder.

"You are one of us, part of our living history. You knelt a boy, now rise a man. Rise and be counted among us." The boy rose, and he wanted to feel pride, but there was only terror, tugging at his gut like a knife.

"Well, now that you're one of us, I'm giving you your first mission."

Eckland walked over to the stone receptacle and turned over the scroll he had been holding. He found a quill on a nearby desk, and he scribbled something on the back of the scroll. He then rolled it up and put it in a leather tube and handed it to the boy.

"Now listen to me boy. Once news of this attack spreads, every legion will muster and return to fight, and most of them will make it. But the tenth is deployed in the Eastern Marches, and it will take them a while to muster out of that gods forsaken jungle. Get there and deliver this message, before they can get too far."

"But doesn't the empire need all the legions to fight? I don't understand." Despite being knighted moments ago, and his years of training, he was no less of a scared boy and he didn't feel ready for this.

"The empire will fall before the month is out. Nothing can stop that. But if we can get the tenth legion, at least, to hide and form a resistance, we may stand a chance at winning the long game. I know the praetorian who commands that legion. He's a stubborn old bird, but once he reads what's on that scroll, he won't give you any guff about it. Now we need to go before whatever those things are realize they haven't killed everyone yet."

The boy followed Eckland back out into the main hall, but stopped short of it.

In a steaming hole where the door leading into the courtyard used to be, the great black lion stood with a cruel smile carved on his face. He was somehow smaller now, but still twice the height of a man. His scythe was dripping red and all around his soldiers surrounded him, blocking any exit.

"Ah, I see we haven't found the last of them. Come thralls, and meet the blade of a just god!" The black lion's voice was deep and rich, but riddled with anger and madness.

Ecklan turned to the boy.

"Take this," he handed the boy his sword. It was heavy and he tried to refuse, but Ecklan shook his head. "Go boy. I will buy you have much time as I can. Get out through the sewers. You know where the back up into the cellar of this building?"

The boy nodded.

"Get to the tenth. Stop for nothing, and help no one, no matter what you see. We don't know what these things are, or what form they could take. Get to the tenth. Aquillon depends on it."

The boy tried to protest, but Ecklan shoved him through the door into the hall and slammed it shut. The boy felt the sting of tears in his eyes, but he knew he couldn't waste time. As formidable as Ecklan was, it wouldn't be long before they were through the door and on his trail. He shut the cross-bar lock and ran down the hall toward the cellar door. He pulled it open, and rushed down the stairs.

Near the back of the cellar was an old sewer grate. The boy had used it a time or two to escape the monastery and roam the streets at night. He tucked his master's sword into his belt and found an old potato sack to put the tube in, and a few provisions. He took one last look at the stairs and hesitated, but another explosion from above snapped him back into reality. He turned and fled into the night-filled sewer tunnel, leaving his world behind. His mind was a flood of panic and fear, but he knew two things as certainly as he knew anything.

He would find the tenth legion.

And then he was coming back.

2

The Door Out of Time

A lex Winters walked down the sidewalk silently cursing her
job.

"Two lousy hours. A forty-five-minute walk for two
hours," she said to herself, muttering and flailing her arms about
wildly. The wind howled around her and she clutched at her jacket.
It was a long hike back to her trailer in the woods. Just a few more
weeks and she'd have the money to buy that shiny red Camaro that
she'd been eyeing for months at Big Al's Used Kar Kingdom (though
from the spelling she didn't imagine she would enjoy meeting Big Al).

A fresh gust of icy wind assaulted her, snatching her hat up, and
sending her blonde hair up with it. Alex ran down the street frantically
chasing it. She loved that hat; it was one of the few things she still
owned that reminded her of life before her dad died. It was a red ball
cap with faded letters that used to read 'Fenway'. She sprinted down
the road following it and lunged, barely catching it before it wafted
over the bridge and into the racing, dark waters of the river below.

Alex clutched the hat to her chest and smiled.

She was eight, and the day was gorgeous, the perfect day for a baseball game. There wasn't a cloud in the sky and the sun beamed down, showering Boston in warmth.

"Where are we going?" she asked him.

Her dad said nothing, refusing to tell her where they were going until they rounded the corner and she saw the stadium. As Alex walked into the stadium, the cool breeze surrounded her and the summer sun shining off of the field was dazzling. The Fenway Frank her dad bought her after the game tasted better than anything she had ever eaten, and to celebrate the Sox victory, he got her the hat, and they all took a picture with Wally, the Green Monster, who she found insanely terrifying.

A drop of freezing rain cut her memory short, hitting her in the center of her forehead. Alex looked up at the sky.

"Really?!"

The sky did not respond, except to send more rain down as Alex ran. The rainfall was a cold and unrelenting onslaught, coming all at once in a deluge and it seemed the perfect way to end Alex's miserable evening. She began to sprint down the road, only stopping to put her thumb out to a few passing cars, but it looked like they were in no mood to take in soken strangers. Cars passed her by at top speed, one dousing her with a nearby puddle.

By the time Alex was within sight of her mobile home, she was a drowned, chattering mess. The temperature seemed scarcely above freezing and each blast of wind was a fresh assault on her body. Her fingers and toes were numb and she couldn't think about anything other than home, and warmth. Alex could see the dim lights of her trailer through the woods from the road. The warm, cozy house was so close.

It wasn't much to speak of, just a doublewide trailer she rented from a local businessman. When she arrived three years ago, most people wouldn't rent to a seventeen-year-old orphan from nowhere with no credit. Her landlord, a laxidasical retiree named Bob, didn't seem to mind though, as long as her rent check wasn't late. Alex had a feeling he might have been trying to do her a favor, but she couldn't complain either way. Bob was the closest thing in town Alex had to a friend, and he only came over once a month to collect his check and grumble about how she needed to be doing more with her life than working at that "lousy diner".

Alex had made efforts over the past three years to make it more like a home and succeeded in most respects. She adorned the walls with an odd collection of t-shirts from Boston area sports teams, or punk rock bands, whichever showed up at Goodwill. Aside from a small collection of work uniforms and a few outfits the only thing remotely personal were bent photos of her and her dad at Fenway Park, Gillette Stadium, and TD Garden. When she left Boston they were the only things she had taken. Being the daughter of a warehouse worker didn't afford many luxuries, but her dad always found a way to take her to a few games a year.

The trailer wasn't fancy, but to a twenty-year-old orphan, it was what it needed to be - a cozy place on cold nights. And right now it was a hot shower and a warm bed.

As she crossed the street, something caught the corner of her eye and she wished it hadn't. Living outside town in the woods had its share of benefits (reasonable neighbors, great stars, quiet, etc.) but it also meant she had to stay on guard. She twisted to see where the motion was and saw three figures struggling in the rain. When she focused, however, she saw two men attacking an older-looking man.

Alex took one last glance at her trailer, wishing that she was the type of person who could walk away. Unfortunately, her father hadn't raised that kind of daughter. When other kids got grounded for picking fights with the school bully, Alex got an ice cream sundae and a big hug. Still, sometimes being the girl who looks away was easier, especially on a frigid April night in a downpour of freezing rain.

"Hey!" she said.

Alex shouted at them and they turned to look at her, then went back to beating up the old man. From what she could make out, it was two punks, probably teenagers. Bands of them roamed the woods outside town getting into all sorts of trouble. A few of them tried to set in on Alex once, but she was happy enough to teach them a lesson in personal property and manners. The punks left her alone after that.

Alex approached them at a run and stopped about fifteen feet ahead of them.

"Hey, idiots! Get away from him," she shouted at them.

As she got closer, they turned and Alex realized they weren't teenagers. They were large men in dark coats, inexplicably sporting sunglasses. The elderly man they held looked two punches away from not waking up again. Blood streamed out of a busted lip, and both his eyelids were bruised and swollen shut. Alex wasn't sure if he had any teeth to begin with, but he didn't now. He was wearing the typical homeless man ensemble - a ratty jacket with a hoodie underneath, gloves, pants two sizes too big, and boots that looked like they had been fished out of the river. Even through the rain, his stench of old cabbage and rotten potatoes with a healthy dose of body odor overwhelmed her.

"Back away, little girl. Not your business." The one who spoke was taller than the other but had no more defined features than his partner. He talked with a thick accent that Alex couldn't recognize.

"Maybe not, but I'm nosy. Personal quirk. Now get out of here, before I call the cops!" She brandished her cellphone as a prop to help her bluff. The cop (there was only one) wouldn't come this far out of town, especially to help a drifter, and her phone hadn't had minutes on it in a year. She held her breath, hoping the bluff would work.

The two goons dropped the old man from their grasp and turned towards her. They were big, burly men, but to Alex's relief, they didn't appear armed (aside from their lamp-shade sized fists, anyway). As they moved closer, Alex slowly began to realize she had bitten off a bit more than she could chew. Her dad had given her lessons in basic hand-to-hand which was fine for teenage punks, and the odd drunken idiot outside the diner, but the two mammoth gangsters were another matter entirely.

The goons flashed gold-toothed smiles that showed lazy dental hygiene more than intimidation . These were smiles she had seen before in her life; smiles of evil men who enjoyed hurting people. If they were smiling for other reasons, Alex didn't want to think about it.

"This will be fun," one said to the other, with a short chuckle. As they moved closer, Alex felt a rush of energy within her. It was odd, like a high-octane mixture of adrenaline and caffeine. Her brain seemed to rewire itself and suddenly everything was moving slower and was easier to concentrate and block out the rain, the cold - everything but the threat.

The taller one moved in first and swung a clumsy, undisciplined punch at her. His jab told her everything she needed to know about her opponent. These were the type of men who were not good at fighting and had gotten by their whole lives by being bigger than everybody else. Bullies.

Alex easily sidestepped the blow, as if she was a half-step ahead of it, and caught his arm in a hold. The dodge felt odd to her, as if someone else was moving her. She bent his arm backward and applied pressure until she heard bone snapping, then she let go. Alex knew she didn't have the strength to do what she had just done, but she decided to let it go for the moment. If this was some sort of divine kung-fu intervention, she wasn't about to start complaining, under the circumstances.

The big one tumbled to the ground, screaming in pain and cursing at her in a creative set of adjectives. Once he recovered from his stupor, the smaller thug moved towards her. This was probably the first time in his whole life someone had fought back, and it was taking a while for his brain to comprehend it.

His attack was no more graceful than his partners; he quickly met the end of Alex's knee in his ribcage and a popping sound told her ears that his ribs had cracked. He backed away into the darkness, and helped his friend, who was still nursing his broken arm, to his feet. As they hobbled off into the rainy night, the bigger one shot a death-stare back at Alex, but she merely stuck her tongue out at him.

As quickly as the rush of energy had come, it was gone, and Alex collected herself for a moment and caught her breath. Her head began to spin as though blood was rushing to it, and she felt a massive headache coming on. She tried to focus on the situation at hand.

Alex shifted her attention to the old man. He was sitting on the side of the street, his eyes staring away blankly into the night. His eyes finally found hers and he mouthed something, but Alex couldn't understand the words. She turned to look up the highway and see if any cars were coming that she could flag down to call an ambulance, but the street was deserted.

By the time she turned back to him, he had vanished. Startled, Alex glanced around but there was no sign of him. She doubted that he had summoned his inner track star under the circumstances, but he was nowhere to be found. Alex looked around the area for a moment, but there was to be no trace of the man, not even his blood on the road.

She would have stayed to ponder the mystery longer but the adrenaline from fighting and the strange surge of energy had worn off and she was losing sensation in most of her body. Running across the road and down the path that led to her trailer, she sprinted across the threshold and slammed the door shut.

With no hesitation, she stripped off her clothes and turned the shower on as hot as possible. Steam from the water quickly fogged up the bathroom, and it was a warm embrace on her chilled skin.

After she had gotten out and changed into fresh clothes, the bizarre nature of the incident washed over her and she felt as though she had more questions than answers. The old man made sense; homeless people often squatted in the forest surrounding the town. The goons made less sense. Despite being clumsy idiots, they were too well dressed to be simple thugs, and unless the town and its population of two hundred and eight had a large, under-reported infestation of the mafia, nothing else made any sense. There was to be no reason for them to be doing anything on that road that night, much less committing felony assault.

The events of the evening took their toll on Alex and sleep washed over her like a wave, drowsiness pulling at her eyelids. Alex sat down on the couch and slumped over, as the world slowly faded to black.

Alex's dreams that night were strange and terrifying. She saw large beasts moving around a glade in the woods. A black lion spoke to a crowd of other strange creatures and roared at them. A great golden ox sat on a throne and responded, followed by a huge woman with seven heads and a huge swarm of flies that moved and whispered as one being.

Alex knew eating questionable, leftover burritos for dinner before her shift had been a very poor choice.

Her burrito nightmare continued and none of it made any more sense but then, without warning it vanished, and the old man from the night before appeared. Or at least she thought it was him.

He had striking black hair, and wore different clothing; long, flowing blue robes and he looked a little less like something had run him over. He stood before a massive tower on a silent plateau and smiled at her in a knowing, sad way, mouthing the same words he had before his disappearance. This time she understood him.

"I'm sorry," he said.

Though Alex couldn't hear him, she was sure that was what he was saying. Before she could ask him for what, the dream broke off. She sat up, drenched in sweat, her heartbeat thundering in her chest.

"Get it together, Alex," she told herself. As she shook off the remnants of sleep, she looked over at her alarm clock.

6:15 AM, the clock reported in cheerful, glowing red numerals.

She tried repeatedly to fall back to sleep, with little success. After an hour she got up, made coffee and turned on the TV. Hopefully, the infomercials would be boring enough to clear the jitters out. After the tenth *Shamwow* commercial, she didn't feel better and wasn't tempted to buy one.

"Better go for a run," she said to herself.

Just hearing her own voice made things seem a little better like she was back in the real world, free of burrito dreams, the evil zoo, and vanishing old men.

A run always cleared Alex's head.

"Concentrate on the run Alex, and the rest will take care of itself," her dad said. The harbor breeze shifted through Alex's hair and the chill of the sea air nibbled at her cheeks. It was five thirty and she had a high school final that day.

"Dad, I need to be studying right now," Alex insisted.

"First," he said, "math is stupid and I don't see why they force you poor children to study it. And second, just go running with your old man and I'm sure you'll do fine."

"That's all easy for you to say. You don't have to deal with Mrs. Kowalski's death stares if you flunk her exam." She tried to land a playful jab on his arm, but he was too quick, and had already taken off down the street. As Alex chased him she felt the stress melt away as the pure adrenaline of the run took over.

Alex smiled at the memory as she put on her running outfit - a pair of shorts that cut off above the knee, an aged but resilient pair of Nikes, a tank-top with a jacket, and her red hat. She grabbed her old iPod, blasted punk rock, and she was ready to go. She opened the door and took a step out.

The rain had let up by now and through the trees around her trailer the first glimmers of morning light danced in the dewy treetops like a kaleidoscope. It was still cold, but the rain had cleaned the world and everything had a fresh smell to it. Alex jogged up to the road and began her run.

There was still no sign of the old man from the night before, but she tried her best not to think about it. From the old man vanishing, to the strange surge of energy, to the meeting of evil zoo animals in her dream, it had been an evening she'd just as soon forget. She wanted the world to go back to the same, boring one she was used to. In the years since her dad died, she clung to whatever was stable and predictable.

As she ran up the road, the familiar sounds of *The Dead Kennedys* blared in her ears and she was starting to feel better. She rounded a bend and ran across another bridge and glanced down at the water. The cold morning air and the gleam of the sun's rays off the water reminded her of Boston Harbor, and early morning runs with her dad.

Without realizing it she felt the sting of tears burning her cheeks in the frigid morning air. It had been several years since her dad's death, but she hadn't really gotten over it. She'd been bounced from a few foster homes before just running away and stowing onboard the first freight train out of Boston. Everything there reminded her of her dad and she had to get somewhere else. Somewhere nothing was familiar and nobody knew her. Northern Michigan had fit the bill nicely.

It wasn't long before Alex was nearing the end of her running trail and she saw her trailer through the woods.

Turning off the main road, Alex ran down the path to her trailer. There was a hazy fog in the air that seemed a bit unusual for this time of year, but *Blitzkrieg Bop* was blaring in Alex's ears and she wasn't paying attention to much else. As she fidgeted with her keys to open the door, a small halo of translucent runes and a ring of energy surrounded the door. Small symbols in a language began to appear until they completed an archway above her door, but between the *Ramones* punk anthem booming at full volume and her irritation with her keys, she didn't notice it and pushed open the finicky door and walked inside.

Alex put her foot down where the floor should have been, but found nothing. The rush of air surrounded her as she began to freefall through an endless void of night and starts. The cosmos spun around her as she tumbled through the abyss so far that it was impossible to get her bearings. By the time her senses returned to her, all she could see was the dark sea towards which she was barreling headfirst. Alex hit the water and blacked out.

3

The Red Fleet

lex returned to consciousness. Oxygen exploded in her lungs like cold fire and she swam. The raging sea threw her about as easy as it would a weather buoy and she struggled to avoid being swept under in the swell. The water was freezing and each new wave was a dark sea-monster threatening to swaller her under, and it took all of her strength just to stay afloat. Alex searched for any sign of coast, her mind in survival mode. The how and where of her arrival would have to wait.

Alex peered at the dim outline of the beach but it seemed too for her to swim. She might have been able to do it in a calmer sea that was twenty degrees warmer, but the cold had already sapped her strength. Besides, she saw a large outcropping of rocks that looked like a reef jutting out of the ocean between her and the seashore. As the waves pounded them, her vision cleared, and she saw ruins, extending hundreds of feet out of the water.

Where am I?

That would have to wait.

Turning the other direction, a single glimmer of light caught here eye. It illuminated an old-style ship, with twin masts and a thick hull, like the ones that took tourists out for pirate cruises in Boston Harbour. The masts creaked in the wind and on deck dozens of men moved about frantically, tying down things and securing the deck. Alex swam towards the ship without hesitation. There was no time to wonder why a colonial style vessel was floating several hundred feet away, or who was on board. Whether they were friendly or not, it beat swimming. She knew she was fighting a battle that the sea would win, sooner rather than later.

She approached the side of the mysterious ship, letting a scream tear from her chest as loud as she could muster, hoping someone would hear her. Massive waves crashed without mercy against the hull and it was all she could do to keep from being crushed underneath it. After several minutes, a rope ladder dropped into the water. She swam towards it with the last bit of her strength. The ladder lifted Alex from the ocean, and she breathed a sigh of relief.

Alex's victorious feeling of not drowning was short lived. As the rope stopped her near the railing, she felt rough hands grasp her arms and throw her onto the deck like cargo, deposited with a thud. Alex glanced around, and she realized large men in red pantaloons and open shirts were surrounding her, gripping swords. The men had grim faces, free of any humor or warmth. Alex waited for one to make a move, counting them in her head. The odds didn't appear good, and besides, even if she could fend one off, each one looked as massive as the next.

After a long, tense silence, a man approached her, parting the crowd as he did. It surprised Alex to see he was shorter than the rest by at least a foot, although the look on his face was no less cruel. As she stared at them, she marveled at how off the mark the pirates at Disneyland had been. The smaller man studied Alex with eyes colder than the water still dripping off her body, like a hawk looking at a fish.

"It seems the Lady of the Deep has given us a gift. Or perhaps it's one of those rats from the coast, come fishin' where she had no business?" His words dripped with contempt and arrogance.

A voice from the back cried out.

"Who gets her?"

Alex gulped at the possible meanings of the word "get" in a pirate's vocabulary.

"No one," the short man said with a tone of finality, "she's a pretty young thing with some fire in her eyes. She'll make a fine prize at auction when we put into port." He brandished his sword and the rest of the pirates receded.

A fire was burning in Alex's gut. How were there people like this anywhere in the world? Nobody was selling her, much less the *Muppet Treasure Island's* ugly stunt doubles.

"I'm not going anywhere or being sold, you pig!" Alex snapped at them as her face flushed red with indignation. She realized it wasn't the best time to speak up but controlling her temper had never been in Alex's wheelhouse. She felt the stiff side of a boot in her ribs and an explosion of pain.

"I'd keep further commentary to yourself, Miss, unless you want me to let the boys sample the goods before they're brought to market." The captain let his threat linger in the air like a dagger around her throat and she stayed silent. Turning to two of his men, the captain whispered something to them and waved the rest of his men back to work.

The pirates carried Alex off-deck and below to a long hallway which led to a small area below deck filled with dank cells, she could only figure to be a brig (did they call it a brig on a ship?) The men opened the door and threw her inside. Alex landed on some rotting hay which looked like the closest thing to a bed. It didn't feel like a bed, but she did her best to make herself comfortable as the storm raged outside, and the looming specter of fear crept up in the shadows.

Alex sat for a while, contemplating the events that had led up to her being in a brig on a pirate ship in a strange sea while nursing bruised ribs. Nothing made sense. Was this more of the burrito dream? The only connection she could make was to the old man. Alex had saved him only to have him show up in dreams apologizing.

"For this." A raspy voice from the darkness of the other cell spoke, answering her unasked question.

"Excuse me?" Alex asked, but her voice was hoarse from shouting in the sea.

"I was apologizing for this," the voice said. A figure rose from the shadows and approached the bars of his cell.

"You!" Alex leapt and slammed against the bars, swinging wild punches at him. She knew she couldn't hit him but just trying made her feel better. "What did you do? I saved you and you pay me back by dropping me in the middle of the ocean? I almost drowned and then get captured by pirates, who will sell me to God knows who!"

"Well you see..." he began.

Alex interjected before he could continue. "Never mind all that. Where am I? What kind of place still has pirates? Also, who are you?" Alex stopped and realized she had been asking questions so fast she wasn't sure a human's ears could have comprehended them. She paused, even though every fiber of her being wanted to throttle the old man instead of listening to him.

"Your concerns are understandable, and I apologized," he said with emphasis, sounding almost hurt that his apology was not enough. "I guess I should start with where." He hesitated and looked around. "I have brought you here, to Aquillon, my home. The land you come from is one of many..." his voice trailed off and his image flickered.

"Wait, are you even here?" Alex asked, her voice shaking with anger.

"Yes and no. I am projecting myself, but that's not important! I have little time." As he replied, he looked around nervously.

"Seriously? You rip me out of my life and drop me here, in the ocean, and you're not even here?" Alex was so angry she was almost shouting.

"Teleportation between worlds is an inexact science, to begin with; I did the best I could. I'm sorry the location was... less than ideal," he replied, continuing to glance all around him.

"Forget your apologies! Why. Did. You. Bring. Me. Here?"

"I believe you are the one that can save this world," he answered. "There is something within you. You must unlock it."

"No, no, no. Don't you go putting that on me. I don't know anything about this world, or what it needs saving from. Put. Me. Back!"

"I'm afraid I used all of my power to bring you here. There is no going back, at least not yet." The image flickered out again as the old man continued glancing behind him. "They've found me. I... I have to go. There is a friend of mine in a village close to here; he goes by Thistle. Find him, he can help. I've opened the cage and put the pirates to sleep, but it won't last long. You must not be here when they wake up; the Red Fleet will not take kindly to losing a prisoner."

The images flickered and grew more translucent, and the sound of his voice began to fade.

The old man's last words were an echo. "Find Thistle."

True to his word, however, the gate on her cell opened of its own volition. Alex didn't wait to find out if the pirates were asleep, she couldn't afford to. She snuck down the hall and poked her head out onto the deck. She stepped over several pirates who were drooling all over the deck in a comatose slumber. Darting past them, she found a small rowboat tied to the side of the ship. She untied the various ropes and cords that held it alongside and the boat fell down and hit the ocean with a splash. She almost leaped overboard, but turned stopped when she saw the sword of one of the pirates glinting. She knelt down and relieved him of it. Alex had taken a year of fencing in high school and figured the principles were about the same. One just had to know where the sharp end went.

Alex spent several minutes exploring boxes which mostly seemed to be pickles or fish, but she eventually found a rope ladder.

"Eureka!" she said with a smile to herself and lowered herself into the rowboat and kicked off the side of the ship. She rowed with all of her strength and breathed easier once there was some distance between her and the ship. The sea had calmed down somewhat, though the rain persisted. Turning towards the shore, Alex realized she now had a different problem. The ruins she had spotted earlier jutted out of the ocean like the fangs of a sea monster and whirling eddies pulled the water towards them.

Turning her boat towards the ruins she rowed on, hoping to avoid the swirling currents that would crush her and her tiny boat on the ruins. Alex glanced over the side of her boat and could have sworn she saw a shadow moving beneath the waves but ignored it. If this world had evil pirates, it most likely had evil mermaids too. She was close to the ruins now and as she felt the water pulling her boat towards death, and her heart began to pound with panic.

"Breathe Alex. You watched Dad... you can do this," she said to herself..

Alex had always liked the sea and boats. Her dad had taken her boating on Lake Superior once as a kid, but the past twenty-four hours were poisoning her opinion on the subject. Alex looked at the rocky wall of the ruin she was being pulled towards and got an idea. She figured if it worked in white-water rafting it would probably work here too. Or she would drown and die in evil pirate land.

Alex turned the boat to face the oncoming rocks and extended an oar, bracing herself. Moments before the impact, she stretched out with an oar with all of her strength and used the momentum of the current to push off of the rock wall of the decaying structure.

Alex breathed a deep sigh of relief as her little craft shot clear of the eddies, and, more importantly, the ruins. She got a better look at them as she rowed away. The ruins were beautiful and sad like time had forgotten them. Ornate, carved designs extended up into the steel-colored sky. Barnacles encrusted much of them, and ancient stone figures silently watched her pass. Alex wondered what their story was, or how far down the ruins extended into the depths. Alex avoided looking into the water as the shadow beneath the waves grew larger, and she felt more and more like she was being watched.

Turning her attention to much more important matters, she peered at the Red Fleet ship and saw that the crew was waking up. Figures were moving about on deck and she knew it wouldn't be long before they discovered she was no longer a guest aboard their fine vessel. As Alex glanced behind her, she was thrilled to see that the shore was fast approaching.

After what seemed like an eternity, the boat stuck itself in the sand. Alex got out and stretched her legs. It felt good to be back on land. She turned and took in the coastline. To the north and south of her, the coast ran without end, as did the ruins in the water. The soil was a dark gray and a few hundred feet from the water, patches of dark grass grew into thickets of bushes and small trees. Wayward pines blew in the breeze and the sky was still the color of dull metal. The wind howled against her soaked body and the rain stung her face in icy sheets.

After a while of wandering the coast, Alex spotted a rough footpath that lead deeper into a nearby thicket of woods. She wasn't sure where it went and the woods were anything but friendly looking but she knew her friends in red would find her boat sooner or later. While it was a rare position to find herself in, she figured creepy woods beat out angry pirates every day of the week.

4

A Knight of Swine

Alex was wrong.

The woods were way worse.

It had been hours of plodding along into the woodlands and nothing had come of it. Not one house, not one person, not one village. She would have even settled for a charming cottage made of candy with a cannibalistic witch inside. She was hungry, her feet hurt, and even worse, she didn't understand where this Thistle person was. She wasn't even sure if she could trust the old man who sent her here, nevermind this Thistle.

There was something else. The forest seemed off somehow. Alex had grown up outdoors. She loved the woods.

Not these woods though.

The air was thick, but it wasn't the humidity. Everywhere she had seen in the forest looked the same, and there was never a change in the light. She felt like she had been wandering for hours, but she never heard a sound, not even the wind passing through the branches above. And there was the shadow. She couldn't place it; it always looked to be out of reach, like something that lived in the corner of her peripheral vision. She was doing her best to ignore it, but she once again had the same feeling of being watched, only this time it was much stronger.

"Ok, Alex..." It seemed time for a pep talk. "You are in a strange place, full of evil pirates and you're now lost in the woods. You may starve to death. That's the bad stuff." Pause. Wait three seconds and let the overwhelming urge to panic pass. And now lead in with the good. "You have a weapon you might use to chop... wood. And perhaps a slow, drunk pirate. You know who you are looking for. You're wearing your comfy running shoes (a must for surreal out of world experiences) and there's still a solid twenty percent chance this is all a dream and you're just late for work. That's the good stuff."

A sound shook her from her musing and thrust her back into the reality of being lost in creepy woods wearing running shoes and workout pants. A bush several hundred yards from her was rustling and Alex instinctively grabbed her sword as though her brain imagined she might do something useful with it. Crunch. The underbrush cleared. Snag. Something moved closer. Rustle. The sound was closer now. Very close. Squeal. Squeal? Alex preemptively flinched as her fight or flight reflexes began weighing their options.

Before it occurred to Alex what the sound had come from, a dark figure burst through the trees in a bull-rush. Her reflexes kicked in and she sidestepped it easily enough and watched the figure run full-speed into a large tree trunk with a smack that resonated, even in the silent forest. The figure fell over with a thud, and lay still.

After waiting enough time to make sure whatever it was wasn't getting up to say hello, or more probably, "You look appetizing, let me eat you," Alex moved closer to it. She had never been great at containing her curiosity. It relieved her to see legs that looked human and a human-looking torso leading up to the head. When she saw it, Alex screamed and jumped back.

Atop the torso of fairly normal looking (if somewhat plump) man's body was the large, bristly head of a boar, complete with tusks and an overly large snout. Alex's head spun with the contradictory image and her mind didn't seem to know what to make of it.

"Of course there are pig men here. Of course, there are. Why wouldn't the land of evil pirates also contain pig men?" she muttered to herself.

Alex glanced toward the sky as if someone was playing a bad prank on her. Maybe this was a complex reality T.V show with pirates and pig men. She was hoping not since it felt like the writer didn't plan on keeping her character around for the second season at the rate she was going.

"Thistle..." he said with a slight slurred accent which sounded British.

Alex's ears perked up. Finally, she might have caught a break, in the form of an unconscious pig-man, but a break nonetheless. She drew her sword and poked him with the hilt. He stirred.

"Need... Thistle..." he said, groaning.

"That makes two of us, buddy. Can you take me to him?" Alex wasn't entirely sure he would understand, but it was worth a shot.

The strange creature stood up and clutched at his head. A sizable welt was forming, but he seemed to shake it off.

"Thistle..." Alex sounded the syllables out slowly. "Can you... take me... to him?" The pig-man cocked his head and finally nodded, walking slowly back the way he came. Alex followed and poked her head through the underbrush whence the pig-man had come and saw his trail of destruction she could follow. She pointed down the trail.

"Thistle?" Alex said it like a question and received a nod and a snort as a response. Ok, so the pig-man knows where Thistle is. Follow the pig-man.

Following the pig-man was slow going. He stopped every so often to sniff the air, occasionally munch on some shrubs and berries, and at least twice he ran off into the woods squealing, much like he had when he had almost run into Alex. Each time, however, he came back to her, his head lowered as if he knew he had made a mistake and he didn't want to upset her.

By the time they had reached the edge of the forest, which seemed to go on in every direction, Alex was glad to put the place behind her. The edge of the woods opened into a large valley. Spruce and pine trees and rocky outcroppings dotted the landscape, which appeared to be mostly farmland, although it did not appear like anyone used it in years. Snarls of weeds and discarded farming equipment lingered on all of the abandoned fields and scarecrows haunted posts like sad reminders that no one remained. The rain hadn't let up, so Alex hurried along with her new friend toward something that looked like a road.

The road, like everything else, seemed sad and in disrepair. It was mostly old stone, which looked like cobblestone, worn into the ground. Weeds sprouted everywhere. The earth had washed out in some spots, making the ground warped and uneven.

Alex followed the pig-man who seemed relatively sure of his direction now, and she glanced down the road. It occurred to her that she should probably have asked his name, but he had seemed fairly driven to get wherever he was going, and Alex needed to find this Thistle person.

At the center of the valley, a small collection of houses huddled around a large building. Judging from pig-man's direction and the lights in the windows, she guessed that it was his home. She silently hoped the village wasn't full of either pig-men or pirates. Especially pirates.

It was a shorter walk than it looked and after an hour they were on the outskirts of the village. As she studied the buildings, they looked like the buildings at a medieval fair she had been to once. The roofs were thatch over buildings of wood and mortar. The large building in the center seemed to be some kind of church or temple, but the shattered stain glass and boarded up doors were evidence that nobody had used it in a long time, and the smell of mold and decay was everywhere, mixed with the smell of rain. Despite being occupied, the village was doing all it could to look deserted.

As they walked into the center of town, the villagers stared at them, which made sense to Alex; she didn't much look the part of a fifteenth century peasant, and it was possible they didn't see pig-men any more than she did. As soon as they reached the center of town, the pig-man wandered off in a fairly specific direction and Alex followed. Every few steps he stopped and sniffed, then changed direction. Finally, he seemed to find what he was looking for.

In the center of a damp alley, under an awning, a barrel sat with its lid slightly ajar. The pig-man squealed in pure joy and excitement before thrusting his entire head into the barrel. Alex presumed from the crunching and slurping that he had found his favorite snack. She was about to turn and leave him to his snacking when she heard him speak again.

"My thanks, girl. I am in your debt."

Alex turned around in shock. It had been an hour and her brain had adjusted back to normal; she had forgotten entirely that the pig-man could speak.

"You speak?" she asked in an uncertain voice.

"One of a veritable cornucopia of skills I possess," he said with a short bow.

Alex took a moment to process the words. It was hard to get over the disconnect between watching the pig's mouth move and hearing human sounding words.

"And you spent the last hour acting like a bewildered farm animal because?" she asked, trailing off.

"A fair question, from your perspective. I promise I shall tell all! Just as soon as we find something to eat. I haven't had a proper meal in days," he said with gusto.

Alex's eyes glanced at the half-empty barrel and she breathed deeply. "Okay... Well, I'm broke," she said.

The pigman cocked his head to one side, and then continued, "I'm not sure what you mean, but I will gladly pay. It seems the least I can do for escorting me in my state. I shudder to think of the outcome had you not come along."

On the one hand, Alex wasn't sure about accepting anything from strange pigmen, but on the other, she felt as though she would leap mouth first at day-old oatmeal; she was starving. The last thing she had eaten was the questionable burrito from the diner where she worked, and that was at least twelve hours ago, assuming time worked the same on this planet, or wherever she was.

Alex followed the pigman into a nearby building which looked a lot like the place that sold root-beer floats at the medieval fair which they called a tavern. From the smell of things, there would be no root-beer floats. The inside was dark and dimly lit with candles and torches. It didn't appear crowded but Alex figured not too many people had money for drinks given the condition of the village and surrounding farmland. She wondered what had happened to these people.

Alex watched her new friend speak in hushed tones with the bartender who seemed tense at first, but relaxed once the pig-man produced a few coins. He motioned for Alex to join him at a table near the back and she followed. In moments, the bartender brought out two steaming bowls of soup with some dark bread. The soup was a bland, beef stew affair, and the bread could have given rocks a run for their money, but it was the most delicious food Alex had ever had. She scarfed down the entire bowl in minutes and felt a stomach-ache coming on.

When she finished, she looked and saw that the pigman had finished his food. It seemed odd he was eating beef stew, but maybe his digestion was human. Alex had been absent on pigman biology day in school.

"All right, we're not starving. So, what do I call you?" Alex asked him.

"Well, my proper name is Sir Gregory Le'scall," he replied.

"You're a knight?" she asked.

"*Was*, anyway. A long time ago,"

"You're a pig-man and a knight?"

"I wasn't always this way…" he looked annoyed and his snout wrinkled. "The loathsome…" his voice reduced to a whisper, "hand of Four cursed me to be this way. It's why I needed that plant. Keeps me human, at least, mostly . The longer I go without it, the more I turn into what I appear as on top."

"Ok," Alex said, "two things. One, what's the Hand of Four and two, why did it curse you?"

Some villagers gave her poisonous looks and moved far away. The knight's eyes darted nervously around the room before he responded. "First, I wouldn't speak of him too loudly unless you're looking for a quick and painful release from this mortal coil. And he cursed me for not bowing to him. Said I was being pig-headed and, well…" he motioned to his head, "it was never said of him he's without a sense of humor."

"That's terrible. But that still didn't answer my question. What is the… Hand of Four?"

"He's one of the Court of Hours. They rule this world and everyone in it. Are you from so far a place you haven't heard of them?"

"Oh, I'm from far away all right…" Alex trailed off. "Well, Sir Gregory…"

He cut her off. "Please, no one calls me that anymore. I haven't been a knight in many years. My friends just call me Thistle."

"You're kidding..." Alex felt like the bad joke fate was playing on her just got worse. "You're Thistle?"

"Yes, M'lady. My friends call me that after the plant you saw me eating. Not the most dignified moniker I suppose, but it suits me these days."

"But... Thistle was my only... I don't..." Alex said, stammering.

"I'm afraid I have no idea what you're talking about M'lady. What exactly was I supposed to do?"

Alex froze. She couldn't really answer that question. So far, her only lead was to find Thistle, who she now realized was a washed-up old knight, and one-fifth pig. She wanted to throttle whoever was writing the bad joke her life had become. Alex didn't have the slightest idea of how he could help her.

"I just... thought you might be..." she said, trailing off.

"Not one-fifth pig?" He finished her sentence. "I get that a lot."

"No... well... yes. Someone told me to find you."

"Who might tell you to find me? And why?" Thistle seemed as confused as she was.

She told him a slightly less crazy sounding version how she had come to Aquillon. Then she recounted her conversation with the old man and her escape from the Red Fleet. She was hedging her bets against him being a spy or selling her out, which seemed foolish the longer she thought about it, but this was pretty much her only option.

Thistle paused and silently considered her story before responding. "You've made a powerful enemy in the Red Fleet" Thistle said, shaking his head worriedly. "As for the old man, he sounds like a member of the Eastern Watch." Alex stared blankly at him, waiting for him to elaborate. "Ah, you wouldn't know them either. A thousand years ago, during the Fall, the magi of the empire abandoned us and fled across the sea to the Wyld Places. Some say they survived and build up an order called the Eastern Watch, but no one has seen them in a thousand years, and they do not interact with the realm of men, such as it is."

Alex barely understood half of what he said, but she side-step that fact and focused on the things she understood.

"You mean the Court hasn't always been in power?"

"No, not at all. A thousand years ago the empire of humans flourished. Those were the golden days of humanity. Then, without warning, the Demon Lords of the Court of Hours arrived. They struck as lightning; merciless and deadly. The empire put up a fight, but it was nowhere near ready for such an assault. We crumbled against their might and surrendered. We call it the Fall. They've ruled ever since. No one remembers any of it, but we still have our stories. Legends are the prize of the defeated, history is the spoil of the victor."

"Why didn't these demons just kill the humans? Seems like it'd be a lot easier to rule the place," Alex said.

"Some kept us as slaves, others for amusement, others for muscle, and some for food. Mostly they ignore us. They only show up every so often to remind us of our place in things and rub us back in the dirt." There was a bitterness in Thistle's voice. He was a defeated, old, and one-fifth pig, but he hadn't let go of his hatred.

"So, what could I possibly have to do with any of this?" Alex asked, exasperated. The more she found out about this place, the more questions she seemed to have. "And why would these magi have sent me to you?"

"I've never met a magus, well... no one has," Thistle said, sounding even more bitter than before. "If one brought you here it was for good reason. Their order forbids them to use magic in the help of humans."

"But aren't they humans?" Alex asked.

"The magi may have been, once. Now, they're something else. They maintain their elusive ways by not getting involved. They haven't done one thing for us in a thousand years. I imagine they'd have to have a dire reason to break that policy.

Thistle paused and scratched his snout.

"Well, I think we'd best turn in now. Things always look better in the morning, that's what I always say," he said, with a jovial chuckle.

Alex smiled.

"My dad used to say that too. All right, where should we..."

Commotion outside interrupted her thoughts. From beyond the tavern's walls, they heard angry voices and terrified screaming of running villagers. A figure in crimson clothes ran by the window and Alex froze with fear. The Red Fleet had found her.

5

The Lady of Deep Waters

lex would have wondered how they had tracked her down so fast if she had time to think. She would have grabbed her sword and made for an exit if she had time to move. She would have made a plan if she had time. But she didn't.

The village erupted into chaos. Sprinting across the room, the innkeeper barred the door and grabbed a massive club from behind a pillar. The innkeeper was a more formidable man than Alex had taken him for, and she felt better with him in the room. The pirates had already assaulted the front door. It wouldn't hold long.

"All right, Thistle, you're the knight in this situation, what do we do?" Alex asked.

Thistle paused and contemplated the question.

"Run. Yes, run," he said .

Alex could see the fear in his eyes. "Really, we run? What about the villagers? It's our fault these stupid pirates are here!" Alex snapped at him. She realized they outnumbered her, and Thistle was right, but she wasn't about to cut and run, leaving these people to deal with the pirates.

"This village gets raided all the time," Thistle said. "It's just the way of things. Weak preying on the strong. You know how it goes."

"I thought knights were brave! Where's the dash? Where's the debonair?"

"I told you, it's been a long time since I was a knight, and I didn't get by this long by putting my snout where it didn't belong. I'm getting out, and I suggest you do the same. Best of luck though, either way. It's been a pleasure."

And with that, he left. Alex watched him run down a hall and out the back door into an alley. Alex was fuming, but she had bigger problems. The pirates had decided the door would not budge and looked for other points of entry. As soon as Thistle ran out of the back door, Alex heard a cry and several pirates poured in.

Alex was on her feet and armed. The blade seemed balanced in her hand like she had held one all her life. It was odd, but she decided not to question anything that seemed to go her way since everything else wasn't.

The first two pirates rushed into the room. They had gotten no less evil looking or more friendly since she left their company. Various charms and coins hung from all parts of their red clothing. They both had worn, haggard faces, with black teeth filling mouths curled into a snarl. Their smell had also not improved.

"Let's make this easy, girl. You come with us." The one who spoke was more put together than his partner.

Alex paused and feigned like she was thinking about it. "Nope. Counteroffer. I beat you senseless or you leave."

The pirates took time to consider the idea before realizing they didn't like it.

"Fine, the hard way it is. We likes the hard way," the other one said.

They lunged at Alex but their attacks came nowhere close to her. She side-stepped them with little effort and parried their attacks. How was she parrying them? The cutlass was way heavier than her fencing sword. She didn't have time to think about it. Alex responded with a salvo of well-timed attacks that had them on guard. Alex struck and landed a well-timed slash into the smarter one's arm. The pirate howled in pain and dropped his sword.

It took the other one a moment to realize they weren't winning anymore, but that moment was all Alex needed. As one pirate turned to see if his friend was all right, (a noble gesture for a pirate) Alex dropped her sword and snared him in a hold, slamming him to the ground, using his weight against him. The pirate came crashing down and lay still and unmoving where he landed.

Alex looked up as the adrenaline subsided. She noticed the innkeeper and the other patrons looking at her in shock. Alex then realized she was still wearing her running outfit and mused on how ridiculous it looked.

She looked at the innkeeper and said, "I know it's a long shot, but you don't have anything that might fit, do you? I need to get into something more normal looking. You don't know me but..."

The innkeeper smiled at Alex. "Girl, if you're an enemy to the Red Fleet, you're a friend of me and mine. They took my daughter a year come winter. You're about her size and she had some traveling clothes. You're welcome to them."

"What about the rest of them?" Alex asked. The sounds of battle were still raging outside.

"We'll handle them. Your coward of a friend was right, we are used to this, but you've reminded us we don't have to take it anymore. Come on, men! Let's drive these dogs back into the sea!" The innkeeper's voice bellowed as he led the rest of the men out of the tavern, armed with a variety of odd weapon substitutes. As curious as she was to see how one drunk old man planned on implementing a wooden butter knife in battle, Alex took advantage of the time and formulated a plan.

Alex continued upstairs and found the innkeeper's daughter's room. Someone had taken her, just the way the innkeeper said it, and the look of anguish in his eyes made Alex angry. She was still trying to figure out what she was doing in this world, but as an orphan she had seen plenty of broken people kicked around and abused. She wasn't about to let it happen to them if she could help it.

By the time Alex had put on the clothes (a green blouse, some brown pantaloons that cut off around the calf, and a pair of sturdy leather boots), the sounds had died down and the villagers had largely driven back the pirates. Alex walked down-stairs and was almost out the door when it happened.

From every direction, Alex heard rushing water, as if a dam had broken and the entire town was flooding. The water roared outside, but nothing came in. After it subsided, there was an uneasy quiet outside. No villagers. No pirates. Nothing.

"Girl. Come out, or I will drown these thralls."

The voice wasn't human. It was a thousand sounds of shrieks and writhing collided into one another, forming a terrifying concert of discordant words. It was as if a thousand creatures were all crying out at once, and it had somehow made words. Just listening to it hurt Alex's ears.

"First," Alex asked, "what's a thrall, and why do I care if you drown one?"

The voice hissed. "I'm sure they would call themselves human, but our kind would never show them such respect," the voice said.

Well, that's bad, Alex thought. Whatever she was speaking to wasn't human.

"How do I know you aren't bluffing?"

"You don't, but if you don't comply, I will kill these thralls and come in all the same."

"What are you?" Alex's voice was shaking as she asked the question.

"Come and see," was all the voice said.

Alex weighed her options. It was possible the pirates had surrounded the building. If they were bluffing, maybe she could take them. Either way, she didn't think staying in the building was helping anyone; herself included.

"Alright, I'm coming out."

As Alex came out into the village, she saw where the voice had come from. Standing eight or nine feet tall, a massive woman stood in the square. Eels covered the woman head to foot coiling and slithering up and down her body. She wasn't wearing anything, but the eels concealed everything but her hands and feet. Alex stifled a scream and tried to look brave. She doubted it was working.

Soldiers that looked like eels with hands, feet, and legs surrounded the woman. The creatures wore armor made of hardened barnacles and carried whips that sparked. Around her the pirates were groveling, their faces gripped with terror.

The horrible voice began again. Alex couldn't see what made it. It seemed to come from the eel woman, but not from a particular place.

"This was such a simple task... just bring the girl back. Was it so hard, to kill a few villagers and to bring her back?" She seemed to be directing her irritation at one pirate in particular. Alex recognized that it was the captain from the ship.

"My Lady... we..." At first, it seemed like he was stammering from fear, but soon the cause was clear. The woman focused on him and water began to drip from his mouth as he made feeble gasping motions. One by one the other pirates fell over and began gurgling up water. The villagers were all gathered in small huddles around the square, watching in horrified helplessness. After the last pirate had stopped twitching, she spoke again.

"When I heard a single maiden escaped my Red Fleet, I was curious. When I arrived and found it to be true, it intrigued me, but now I don't know." She paused and let a lethal silence settle over the crown. "You don't seem terribly special. Tell me, girl, how did you escape these filthy pirates? It's been ages since anything puzzled me. I must know."

"Listen, eel-face... I'm not telling you anything, you soggy hussie!" Alex said, snarling back at her.

"Such a spirit. You must not be from this province. It's been ages since any thrall spoke to me like that," she said in a bored sounding voice. The woman held up her hand. In the crowd, a woman screamed as water poured out a small girl's mouth. The woman clutched the girl in her arms.

"Please, my lady, not my daughter," the woman begged.

"A pity for this young thrall you felt the need to be so insolent," the eel-woman said.

Alex gritted her teeth. "All right! I'll tell you. Just leave these people be!"

A shimmer of movement across the eels seemed to show that the woman was smiling. The little girl gulped down air and coughed.

"An old man brought me here. He dropped me in the ocean and your Red Fleet scooped me up. He put them to sleep so I could escape. Then I stumbled on this village. Just take me if you must, but leave them alone. These people have suffered enough on my account," Alex resigned herself to whatever unpleasant fate she faced. It wasn't fair the old man dropped her here, and it wasn't fair she was now being captured and would most likely die, but none of that was these people's fault.

The woman paused and motioned, "muradae, take the girl."

41

The eel men ran up alongside her and clamped shackles on her wrists. Alex almost gagged as they grabbed her. They smelled like a fish market in Death Valley in July. Alex's mind was already spinning for a way to escape.

Once she was closer to the woman, the woman spoke again. "Now. As for the rest of these thralls. I will show you the reward for harboring a fugitive of the court! I will take some of your remains to decorate my halls, but the rest of you will stay, and let your corpses mark the fate of those who oppose the Hand of Two!" As she said this, she raised her hand and the entire village collapsed as geysers of water poured from their mouths.

"No!" Alex screamed and struggled against the muradae but the eels tightened their slimy grips on her. "Liar! You said you would leave them alone," she said, screaming at the woman in muted fury. Again, the shimmering of motion in the eels looked something like a smile.

"I promised nothing. Foolish thralls always hear what they wish. The Lady of the Deep Water always keeps a promise made, but we struck no bargain, girl." The woman turned to her eel soldiers. "muradae, we go."

A firebomb of rage exploded in Alex's mind. Anger over her being kidnapped, anger at the monsters who ruled this world, anger over the drowning villagers, and most of all, anger at her own powerlessness. As the rage brewed, she felt a calm pass over her and her skin tingled. All around her she saw strange energy currents slithering through the air like leaves on the wind. The currents seemed familiar to her like they had always been there, and yet she knew she had never seen them before. Alex stopped walking behind the muradae and turned toward the Lady of Deep Waters.

"Hey, eel-face," Alex said. She spoke, but her voice was not hers. It seemed like she was far away, merely a spectator to what her body was doing.

"Stop her!" was the last thing she said.

With a serene calm, as though it was the most natural action in the world, Alex reached out with her mind and sent a wave of energy toward the Hand of Two and her minions. It struck them and pushed them back. The wave of energy shattered through the village, dissolving the muradae closest to the blast, and many others did not stand back up. The Lady herself fell over and for a moment lay still. She stood up with a shriek, and waved her arms while chanting and summoned a massive globe of water behind her, into which she and her remaining soldiers retreated. The globe vanished and the village was still.

And like that, the moment passed. Alex slumped over and clutched at her head. When she opened her eyes, the energy currents had gone and so had the enemies. She saw the wave of destruction that had come from her, and it stunned her. *What did I just do?* Alex wondered. *And how can I do it again?*

The villagers all looked at Alex in silent awe. All at once a wave of cheering erupted, and they surrounded her. She felt herself being hugged by total strangers but she didn't have the heart or the energy to stop them. Looks of joy and happiness had transformed their faces from miserable peasants to people with hope. Alex smiled with them and breathed easy easier for the first time since the old man had dropped her in the ocean.

In the square's corner, she saw Thistle standing against a door, looking as stunned as she felt. It took a while for the villagers to thank her, but eventually, they relented. The innkeeper approached her, as did Thistle.

The innkeeper gave her a warm smile. "Thank you, young miss," he said. "I don't know where you come from, but I hope more of your kind is on the way. All my years, I've never seen one of them laid low. It was a glorious thing and makes my heart have hope again.

Oppression and cruelty is just life here, these last thousand years since the Fall, but not today, thanks to you."

"If I may interject," Thistle mumbled.

Alex scowled at him. "Something to say? Or are you just going to run away again? Alex's voice was an icy accusation mirrored by the frosty look on the innkeeper's face

"I only wish to apologize for my cowardice. It is now clear the Eastern Watch brought you here for a reason, and clear they sent you to me for a reason. From this day forward, I pledge my loyalty and my life to you, until I deliver you to them. Please, accept my pledge, and my apology," he said with a sheepish grin.

"Fine, I'm not in a position to say no to friends. Just don't run off next time."

"You have my sworn word. On my honor." Thistle bowed. "Now allow me to retrieve my things and we should be on our way. It will be a moment until they regroup, but they will return, and we should not be here when they do." Thistle turned to the innkeeper. "I suggest the same to you."

The innkeeper thought for a moment and nodded. "I'm in agreement. We should have left this village months ago. The raids have been increasing year to year, and the Hand of Two will return with a vengeance."

Alex turned to him. "But isn't this your home?"

"Home is a word that has little meaning these days. To be human is to be on the move, always looking for a better life. We live in the ruins of our former lives, scraping out what life we can." His face was a sad tapestry of worn emotion as he spoke, each painful memory a thread worn into a line in his sun-beaten face.

"I see," she said. As an orphan, she could relate to the sentiment. Alex saw herself in these people; kicked around, disregarded and treated as less than human. She felt for them and hoped they'd land on their feet.

She needed answers though, and not just about why she the old man brought her to Aquillon. What was the power she had controlled? It thrilled and frightened her all at once, but mostly, she just wanted to know more. It was the not knowing that scared her most of all.

Thistle was returning, this time equipped in traveling clothes, a sword on his back, and a shield on his arm. It had been some time since the old knight had put on his traveling clothes as they were snug around the stomach.

"Well, what now, Thistle?" Alex asked.

"I saw what you did with those demons, and if the Eastern Watch brought you here, the best thing we can do it get you to them, and soon. But first, we need allies, and I know right where to find them." .

"Where?" Alex asked.

Thistle's voice turned urgent. "Let's just say the demon lords in all of their might didn't destroy every bit of the empire. We have to leave now, though. We need to arrive before their camp moves."

"All right, lead the way then," Alex said.

Alex and Thistle left the village by sundown. Families were gathering by wagons and run-down looking horses. The villagers smiled as Alex passed, but they were sad smiles; smiles of terminal patients at a hospital. Even as she passed them, the look of fear and worry mingled with their smiles. Hope couldn't live that long in a place like this.

"What's this village called, anyway?" Alex asked Thistle.

"Vandlehaven. Why do you ask?"

"Well, it's the first place I've been in Aquillon that's not the inside of a brig or creepy woods. I'd like to remember it."

As they passed onto the Eastern road, Alex looked back and marveled at the strange events of the past twenty four hours. She would be getting off her shift at Joe's Diner right about now and she wondered who would do her side-work, and where they thought she was. Alex wondered if anyone had even called the police, or if they assumed she had just up and quit; another drifter moving on down the road. More than any of that though, she wondered how and if she could ever get back home. Still, her dad had always told her to put one foot in front of the other and a journey would be over before you could blink. Alex hoped that was true.

6

The Eastern Road

A day and a night of hard travel brought no change to the landscape, although the rain lessened as they got farther from the coast. Alex spotted a small outcropping of rocks far enough away from the road to avoid prying eyes.

"That looks like a decent place to make camp," she said.

"Agreed. This isn't a country to be roaming at night," Thistle said.

That night around the fire, Alex pried with questions.

"So are there like, counties or something in Aquillon?"

"I'm not sure what a county is, but we have regions. Each is distinct, and each is ruled by a different hand of the Court."

"What's this one called?"

"We are entering the Lethalan Lowlands, and leaving the Drowned Coast."

"Well, they got the drowned part right, anyway."

As they traveled the next day, Alex took in the scenery. Endless hills and valleys rolled from one into the next, painted with sparse vegetation and small outcroppings of trees. The road they traveled on looked well-traveled and this area of Aquillon seemed more populated than the coastline. Given the coast's dismal weather and pirate infestation, Alex could see why.

Still, the people they passed seemed no happier than the ones she had encountered in Vandlehaven. Everywhere , it seemed, times were hard and there wasn't much happiness anywhere. Alex's life had been tough, but not entirely without fun. This place seemed to be perpetually trapped on a Tuesday afternoon. She tried several times, unsuccessfully, to explain the concept to Thistle.

After his brush with cowardice, Thistle had proven to be a good traveling companion. After a standoff with a few desperados that had been hiding beside the road, she saw his skill with a blade hadn't diminished over the years, even if his physique had.

More than his sword arm though, Alex appreciated Thistle's company. A friend to share the road with made things easier to settle in her head. As the miles snaked by, they traded stories of Alex's world and Aquillon.

"So, you're saying people in your land, Ah'mare'ica' are free to do as they wish?" Thistle asked, with a mournful look in his eyes.

"Pretty much, as long as they pay their taxes and don't break laws." .

"I must admit, I'm envious. No one in Aquillon remembers what that is like."

"Tell me something, Thistle," Alex said after a pause.

"Anything, m'lady."

Alex sighed. "First, stop with that. It's making me think I need to curtsy back at you and I suck at that. Seriously though, why did you come back? You could have left and I wouldn't have had the slightest clue where to look for you. Why stay? I can't imagine I'm the safe bet."

Thistle paused as he chewed a handful of his plant. He had taken a large supply with him before they left, a fact Alex was deeply grateful for as she wasn't looking to add pig herding to her growing list of newly found talents.

"It was something I saw back in Vandlehaven. Not just what you did to the Hand of Two, but before that. You stood up to an impossible enemy and faced certain death or enslavement for people you had never met, even though you knew you couldn't win. That's real courage. It's easy to be brave when you know you will win. Real courage is losing. Real courage is knowing that you're going to get beat and standing up, anyway." Thistle sighed. "When I swore my oath as a knight, I swore to do the same, but I never have. I'm a fraud. I guess I'm hoping that by helping you it'll make up for some good deeds I've left undone. The lives I could have saved."

Alex smiled at him sadly and gave him a reassuring pat on the shoulder. Cheering people up hadn't ever been her thing, but she was starting to like Thistle more and more. As they continued, she looked down the road a way. She sighed and kept putting one foot ahead after the other.

Thistle filled the hours of mundane travel with stories and fables from ages past.

"And in the great war we call The Fall, the noble commanders of the Legions led the final charge against the court, and died to a man."

"So they fought bitterly against all odds to the last man. It reminds me of a poem I read in school, "Charge of the Light Brigade." She taught it to Thistle. It seemed to appeal to his romantic side. He loved it.

"Ours is not to question why, ours is but to do and die. Quite right! I like this poem," He said.

"So, no one's ever tried to resist? In a thousand years?" Alex asked.

"Some have, like the people we are on our way to see, but the Court culled the humans after the Fall. They keep our population regulated, keep us separated. Most people prefer to keep their heads down, miserable but alive. In the days following the Fall, resistance was a popular ideal, but as the years passed and the Court crushed uprising after uprising, people just got tired. Towns started to throw the rabble-rousers out and people taught their children not to resist."

I get that but..." she trailed off, distracted by figures on the road ahead. "Thistle, who are they?"

Alex was pointing a short distance down the road at two large figures walking straight for them. A man and a woman walked in graceful strides down the road. They would have looked normal except for their skin, which was shimmering gold and their eyes which were deep obsidian - an endless night without stars or light. They took in everything and reflected nothing.

"Thistle?" Alex said in a panicked voice.

He paused and looked ahead. Alex noticed his shoulders tightening, and he bared his teeth slightly as he spoke "They are lesser demons, servants of the Hand of Four, who rules this province. Most call them the Golden Host," he paused, spitting on the ground. "Be on your guard. They aren't as violent as the muradae, but they are no less deadly."

The golden figures approached them. They wore flowing white robes that danced cheerfully in the wind. Their faces were masks of serene tranquility, with slightly upturned mouths. Nothing on their faces moved, except for the sea of shimmering gold. Their eyes were even more unsettling up close. They seemed to draw all the light near them in and drew a person's eyes to focus on them. The more Alex tried to look away, the more she was drawn to them.

"Love and serenity be upon thee, traveler, and thee," the woman said. Her mouth did not move to form the words, and yet they came from her. Her voice was smooth and thick as honey and the air around her seemed polluted with an unearthly charm.

Alex felt more relaxed at once. Somewhere in the back of her mind she was screaming at herself to run, but she couldn't seem to break out of the calm stupor that fell over her like a haze.

"Glory to the Lord on High, and peace be upon his children. What brings you to travel his lands?"

Alex felt herself answering, even though she shouldn't have. She tried to fight to urge, but every bone in her body felt inclined to speak.

"We are traveling to meet our friends. We have a long way to go, and we need help," Alex tried to leave out the important details, but she still felt herself giving up too much.

"I see. Poor, weary child. Come with us. We will give you respite against the road and its troubles. Come, stay a while in the house of the Lord on High. Abandon your foolish pursuits and pray for a while with us. The Lord hears and answers all of his flock."

Alex nodded sleepily. The woman was right; she deserved a rest. Why fight against the odds? A long journey sounded tiring and all she wanted was a nap. Maybe the Hand of Four wasn't so bad. It was worth hearing what he had to say. She walked with them and felt calm and peace in the world and breathed easy. She didn't even notice that Thistle wasn't walking beside her.

As Alex followed the paper past a rocky outcropping that flanked the road, she noticed several pebbles falling toward the road, but thought nothing of it. She was too focused on getting to this house and taking her nap.

Above he, Alex heard a warlike cry. She watched Thistle drop, sword first, onto the woman, and Alex jumped back to avoid her falling. The demon shrieked as the sword disappeared inside of her and slumped over. Alex's nostrils burns the acrid scent of a black ooze that snaked out of the demon's body.

It was just enough to wake Alex out of her stupor and she drew her blade quickly. The male demon drew a slender dagger from his robes and hissed, baring fangs at them that had grown out of his mouth. The black in his eyes swirled, and he spoke to them in a much less pleasant voice.

"You defy the will of the Gods! The Lord of Idols will rip you apart on his alter, and consume your flesh for sport," the demon screamed.

Alex figured the woman must have been the talker for a reason.

"Well, maybe so... but you won't be around to see it," Alex said. She looked over at Thistle and they went in for the kill. A series of parrying and dodges later, the demon collapsed on the ground with two swords in his gut, dead. After a moment his corpse bubbled and steamed, finally melting in a pile of liquid gold, which dissolved into the earth.

Alex looked at Thistle with a confused look on her face. "Is that normal?"

"Yes. A lesser demon is only projections of its master's will and power. While the Hand of Four lives, so do his demons. Their essence returns to him when their form dies and they are reborn elsewhere." .

Great, Alex thought, *they reuse and recycle. A win for environmentalists everywhere.*

"We should take care to avoid lesser demons when we can," Thistle said. "If we keep killing their minions, the Hands will take notice, and pursue us, if they aren't already. We can deal with a few lesser demons perhaps, but in greater numbers, we stand no chance."

"No argument here," Alex replied.

They went back to the road and began once again. According to Thistle, they would

arrive at their destination by nightfall, barring any unforeseen encounters.

"So, what exactly did they do and why didn't it work on you?" Alex asked Thistle when they had come far enough down the road for her to collect her thoughts.

"Each of the Hands has a particular corruption they love. The Hand of Four's is vanity. He takes great pride in collecting followers, especially if they abandon their own lives to do so. They would have taken you to his hall in the ruins of Pelor and subjected you to his brainwashing hogwash. The longer a person stays, the less able they are to leave and the more followers the Lord of Idols collects, the stronger he becomes."

"Which is why he turned you into a pig-man for not bowing," Alex said.

"Yes. I suppose I got off lucky. A more violent Hand would have killed me outright. As for why it didn't work on me, well, their charm works best on humans, and my ears are all pig,"

"Better live, to oink another day!" Alex said with a smirk, dodging a playful swipe of Thistle's fist.

By dusk, they had left the main road and were following an old shepherd's path into the hills. The trees were more sparse here and the ones that survived were rugged things, growing out of crevices and cracks. It seemed an apt metaphor of Aquillon to Alex, life growing, despite the harshest conditions.

"So where are you taking me, anyway?" Alex had become so wrapped up in the day's events she hadn't thought to ask.

"I'm sorry I wasn't clear about our destination," Thistle said. "The identity of those I'm bringing you to is a well-guarded secret. A secret that a desperate villager would sell to the wrong people without hesitation. They may hate the Hands, but hate doesn't feed their family, coins do, and the Hands have most of it."

"And these secret people are who exactly?".

"Right, right, sorry. We're traveling to see some old friends of mine, the Old Guard. They're one of the last groups of resistance fighters in Aquillon. Been around since the Fall and before. If anyone knows how to get to the Eastern Watch, they will."

Alex thought about it for a while as they walked deeper into the hills. These men and women had been fighting the Court for a thousand years. A thousand years of being outgunned (so to speak), outnumbered, and probably losing a lot more often than winning. It took real guts to be one. She wasn't sure how the old man thought she could save this world, but she silently added the Old Guard onto her list of people she wanted to help when she mastered this secret Jedi power of hers. Incidentally, it had been easy to explain to Thistle what a Jedi was. Probably because they had swords.

As they walked Alex found herself stumbling more and more, and she found herself more and more grateful to the innkeeper for the boots with every step she took. Shadows painted the landscape in subtle hues of twilight as they walked deeper into the hills. Alex found it beautiful in a quiet, understated way. Thistle's breathing was quick and his gaze dodged nervously around every corner.

"What gives, Ser Porkchop?" Alex asked with her patented cheesy grin.

Thistle shot her a dirty look but relented to a chuckle and a snort when he saw her face.

"I just don't like this time of day," he said. His voice was quiet.

"Care to share with the class?" Alex prodded further.

"This is the hour of the Lord of Long Shadows, Hand of Seven" As he said it, a pall of fear seemed to pass over Thistle. Alex had seen him discuss many members of the Court with nervousness, or even mocking disdain (he referred to the Lord of Idols, Hand of Four as 'the idiotic cow') but even in saying this lord's name, Thistle's face was awash with terror.

"I'm guessing he's extra strength bad, and otherwise evil?" Alex asked.

"He rules the Court. He was the one who united them and led the invasion during the Fall. His power is unmatched, and his cunning is legendary. Each demon lord or lady has a sacred and profane hour in which their power waxes and wanes, respectively. This is his, and it makes any man or woman with good senses a touch nervous. I know it's foolish to fear of a time of day, but I have never enjoyed being out of doors around this hour."

"It's not foolish," Alex reassured him. "I used to be afraid of the dark. Lots of people were. Some still are."

Thistle smiled.

"Thank you, Alex. You seem brave for someone flung so far from her home."

Alex smiled back at him, trying to hide the truth. She was as terrified now as she had been since she arrived. The thought of being connected to all of this, or worse, responsible for dealing with it made her stomach do jumping jacks. For now, she just focused on what she could control, the road ahead of her, which had stopped.

Alex looked up and saw that the path had dead ended into a gullet. She was about to ask Thistle where to go from here when she realized that a rock was pointing an arrow at her.

"Thistle, why is a rock pointing an arrow at me? I'd love an explanation, pretty please," she said in a nervous voice.

"It would seem we've found my friends, or rather they've found us. Perhaps we can..." Someone cut Thistle off with a booming voice.

"Ser Gregory Le'scall! The Old Guard places yer under arrest for crimes against the Aquillonian people. Surrender peacefully an' I will meet ya with justice."

Alex was staring daggers at Thistle.

He stuttered. "I may have forgotten that the circumstances of my departure from their band were somewhat... less than friendly."

The earth shook as a massive tower of a man leapt from the shadows and slammed into the ground feet from Alex. She assumed his clothes were the medieval version of combat fatigues and on his back, a huge battle ax swung menacingly on a large chain. His eyes were blue thunderstorms, and they aimed all their lightning at Thistle. From out of the snarl of a black beard, the rumbling voice spoke again.

"Ya shouldn't 'ave come back."

7

The Old Guard

lex had upgraded to staring swords at Thistle.

"What did you do?" she asked in a low hiss.

"It was so long ago, I'd rather assumed these fellows might have let bygones be bygones," he lowered his head. "It was a miscalculation on my part,".

"You think?"

From out of the gulley, a half-dozen men and women appeared, keeping their weapons trained on Alex and Thistle. Guards approached from the shadows, and tied Alex's hands, and pulled her along with them deeper into the gulley. The ropes were tight and Alex glanced around looking for any path to escape, but she didn't see one.

As Alex looked up, she saw archers surrounded them. Men and women perched on small outcroppings and had she not known what to look for, she would have mistaken them all for rocks. Their skin matched the color of the stone, painted to match their clothes. They blended in almost perfectly.

The large man ahead of them walked up to the rock face and knocked five times in a rhythmic pattern. At that, a handprint appeared on the wall and he promptly planted his hand on it. Alex saw him wince and when he withdrew his hand, she saw a small bloodstain on the stone handprint which vanished as quickly as it had appeared. A grinding sound echoed throughout the gulley and Alex gasped in surprise as a large section of the wall vanished, revealing a set of stone steps leading down into darkness. She looked at Thistle for clarification.

"They're called stone-moots. Ancient magic from before the time of men. The old legions used them as shelters during the Fall."

Alex nodded as they started down the steps. Torches provided dim illumination on the way forward.

It was a long time before they reached the bottom. Alex and Thistle were led down a complex maze of twists and turns that Alex couldn't have remembered if she wanted to. The bottom of the winding stone steps opened into a massive cavern filled with stone structures, illuminated by dozens of large bioluminescent mushrooms. Alex gazed in wonder at the ceiling which extended for what seemed like forever up into the darkness.

Men, women and some children had gathered in what looked like a town square. Some gawked at her, but most were glaring at Thistle. Alex mused that while she had sometimes fallen victim to the abstract concept of guilt by association, this might be the first time someone would find her literally guilty of it. They had stopped now, surrounded by members of the Old Guard and other civilians. The large man spoke again.

"Brothers an' sisters, fate seems ta 'ave delivered us a small victory. This loathsome swine wandered into our camp. What should we do with him?"

"Kill him!"

"Tar and feathers!"

"Stone him!"

"Hey!" Alex yelled at them. "Look, I don't know what he's done, but he's my friend and you're not doing any of that."

The large man regarded her with incredulous eyes. "I hardly think yer in a position ta negotiate. Besides, ya don' even know his crime."

"Well, I'm sure whatever he did allegedly may have been bad, but he deserves none of that. Besides, the Old Guard he told me about wouldn't stand for this mob justice," she said.

Alex worked herself into a temper and realized she was yelling at armed soldiers. Probably not her best move, but Alex's emotions usually won the forty-meter dash to her mouth with her brain finishing second.

The large man paused and Alex waited for him to yell back. Instead, he burst in a deep, rolling, jovial laughter. "Yer a funny little bird, ain't ya? And what makes ya so sure o' his innocence?"

"First, call me a little bird again and you'll be picking your teeth up off the floor shortly after, and second, I never said he was innocent, but he is not going to flung to the mercy of mob justice!"

"Fair enough, my little... friend. I'm no' the one that wants justice, the people are. I am merely the arbiter an' I can find nae reason ta deny them that has legitimate rancor with him. As for what he did, the aforementioned grievance with this swine is well founded. I told him ta guard the western entrance o' a safe house near here. At the first sign o' trouble, he ran an' our position was overrun. Three men died."

Alex glanced over at Thistle, who hung his head, avoiding the accusing eyes of the surrounding mob. His face sullen , and filled with shame.

"Yeah, that sounds like him, but he's changed and he's helping me. Thistle guided me here to see you, that should be proof enough of his character. Cowards don't walk themselves into a noose to help a friend."

"Even if tha' were true, there's still a powerful want ta see some mite o' justice done on his hide. We must punish him," the large man said to the approving roar of the mob.

Alex realized her window for negotiating was closing rapidly. *Think Alex, think.* "Fine, then I challenge you to a trial by combat as his proxy. Or have you become so lawless you would deny this man a fair trial?" she asked, raising an eyebrow and attempting to keep her voice level and confident. She really hoped what she had picked up on medieval society from *Game of Thrones* was accurate.

The big man paused and stroked his beard. "What are the terms?"

"If I win, Thistle stays with me, as punishment, to serve his time. We call it probation where I come from. And you help me get where I'm going."

"An' if we win?" he asked.

"The Guard takes him and do as you will and I join you to try to repay his debts," Alex said. She did her best to ignore the logical side of her brain which was throwing up red flags as fast as it was able about all the ways this plan would end badly.

The big man walked back to a small group who had been watching intently. One young woman with short auburn hair focused her eyes on Thistle; they burned with hatred. The group spoke and seemed in agreement, except for the auburn-haired girl who was shouting angrily and pointing less-than friendly gestures toward Thistle. The big man returned with a smug expression on his face.

"The Guard will no' dishonor the ancient law. We accept an' I will be the proxy champion an' fight on behalf o' the Old Guard."

Alex hoped her gulp wasn't audible. She was mentally kicking herself for being so dumb. *Of course, that would have happened. Who else would they send to fight her but the big, scary, ax-wielding mountain giant? Brilliant plan, Alex.* Now she just had to hope that they wanted her as a recruit and that he just planned on disarming her.

After unbinding her hands, the men and women formed a circle around them.

"According ta the ancient law, ya can choose yer weapon. What'll it be?" the big man asked in a bouncy tone of voice. He seemed to think this wasn't much of a contest, and Alex couldn't blame him.

"I'll stick with the blade I have," Alex said, trying to make her voice feign confidence she didn't have.

"So be it."

The man took several steps back and lifted the ax from his back. It was a wicked thing; four feet of black wrought iron with fangs carved into it, gleaming death in the torchlight. The ax seemed perfectly balanced, and the big man held it in one hand as easily as Alex held her little scimitar. She knew it wouldn't hold up against a strike from that monster, but nothing they would have given her would have, anyway. Her only plan was to be faster.

The big man walked in a circular pattern, and Alex followed his lead. They were both transfixed, watching the other's movement. Again, just as in the village, this seemed more familiar to Alex than it should have. As the adrenaline rushed in, it seemed to her that she had done this before. Her sword arm became more confident, and the scimitar was lighter. Finally, the big man struck with his ax. Alex narrowly dodged the meteor of a strike. She felt the breeze of the axe sailing by her neck and her heart thundered in her chest.

The big man took a minute to remove the ax and Alex saw her opening. Time seemed to slow as her opponent struggled to dislodge his ax and she darted in quickly and made a cut to his upper arm. He groaned, but shook the pain off and swung his fist at her. She narrowly avoided it. Alex had jumped back several feet just as he freed his weapon and swung it at her in savage fury. He was barreling down at her now, slashing left and right in wild patterns, possessed of a blind battle rage that burned in his eyes. At the last moment, before

61

he entered within range of her with his ax, Alex tucked in and rolled between his massive legs. Popping up behind him, she quickly slashed at his back, this time producing a howl of pain.

It was his turn to strike, and he whirled around, seeming to pick up speed as he went. Alex dodged the blade of the ax but caught the handle in her back and she went flying into a rock wall as people moved to get out of her way. Pain exploded in her ribs and back and she took several moments to steady her vision. The familiar warm taste of blood filled her mouth.

She picked herself back up slowly, just in time to roll out from the handle of the ax which slammed dangerously close to her head. The big man had gotten no faster at dislodging his ax and Alex used the time to her advantage. She knew she couldn't beat him by dancing around him all day; eventually, his ax would get lucky and she would get slow.

Alex sprung up onto her feet and somersaulted to the other side of him, wrapping her
hands around his throat before he had time to react, attempting to put him into a sleeper hold. He dropped his ax and thrashed about, Alex hanging on for dear life, but she never let her grip loosen. She felt him slowly going limp on her and finally, he coughed out words.

"Enough! I yield," he said.

Alex let him fall to the floor and collapsed as the adrenaline from the fight wore off. The big man was panting and wheezing but as he looked at her, Alex caught what she hoped was a glimmer of respect. He had the option to a sore loser and order his heavily armed men to kill her, and there wouldn't have been much she could have done about it.

"By... the..." the big man was still having trouble speaking, "ancient laws, the trial by combat is over, an' my arse has been thoroughly handed ta me and so we will consider the matter settled. Thistle will serve his time with ya and have nae further ill will amongst the Old Guard." He seemed to say it more to the surrounding people than to Alex and Thistle. There was some general grumbling about it, but most of them went back to their business. Alex spied the young woman who had been staring Thistle down earlier storming off.

Once most of the Guard had cleared off, the big man looked at her and smiled.

"Nae hard feelings eh? Jus' had ta put on a show for the troops. I would 'ave stopped short o' the blade findin' its mark."

"Could have fooled me," Alex said, looking at him skeptically.

"Where did ya learn such nimble technique? I've never been beaten by someone... like ya before." Alex could sense that he wanted to say girl, but had apparently thought better of it.

"I couldn't say. Just seems to have come... recently," she said.

"Well, come on then. Let's get a drink. I always drink after a fight, win or lose."

Alex wasn't a drinker, but she figured it would be rude to refuse the offer, and even though he'd nearly killed her moments ago, he and his men could do it in a heartbeat if he was so inclined. Besides, she wasn't keen on remaining in the square; she could feel eyes on her from the stone buildings. The men and women weren't happy she had won and she could feel it.

On their way from the main square, the big man introduced himself on the way as Rex Killburn, and Alex returned the courtesy. They walked into one of the stone structures at the edge of the town square. The house had very modest trappings and simple decor. It seemed to fit the image of what Alex imagined the home of a rough frontiersman type man would look like. He sat and offered her a seat and took out a large jug and three glasses.

Alex felt her stomach roll as a black liquid oozed out of the jug.

"I don't mean to be rude, but what on Aquillon is that?" she asked.

"We frontier fighters don't 'ave too many luxuries, including things ya might normally use ta make a bit o' the good stuff. So we get creative. We jus' call it good puddin'. Try some!" He held out the jug and Alex's stomach did another somersault.

She eyed him suspiciously. "Does it taste better than it looks and smells?"

"No' at all, but it'll put yer mind at ease."

Oh well, Alex thought. *When in Rome.*

She took a swig of the stuff and immediately wished she hadn't. It was neither good nor was it pudding. It was like liquid fire going down her throat and it reduced her to a series of coughs, sputters and unmentionable words.

"That's...*poison!*" Alex said as she gagged and slumped into the chair, trying not to fall out. She was light-headed, but after the flavor of bile and the burning sensation passed, she was feeling more relaxed overall.

Rex and Thistle both collapsed into laughter and only quieted when Alex shot them both a lethal look.

"On ta more important things then," Rex said as the quakes of laughter slowly left him. "Why are ya here? Why come all this way an' risk so much?"

Thistle spoke in reply. Rex seemed irritated, but he relented and listened. Thistle told about how they had met (the image of him running squealing through the woods brought Rex to fits) and their encounter with the Lady of Deep Waters in the village, and Alex's strange power.

"Hogswallop! Nae mortal could lay one o' them low, the only one who could be..."

"A magus of the Eastern Watch," Thistle finished his sentence.

64

"Nae one's seen one since the Fall, no' a single, lousy, cowardly one o' the yellow dogs," Rex said, growling. Alex glanced at Thistle.

Thistle replied to her unasked question. "Many feel they abandoned us when we needed them the most. They may not have been entirely human, but most folks thought they owed the empire something. Apparently, they thought differently."

Rex interjected, "The empire gave them shelter an' resources for their studies, in exchange for their loyalty. Then, the minute the demons invaded, they returned to their tower in the Wyld Places as fast as their spells would carry them."

"But how am I involved with them? I'm not a wizard or anything like that. Both my parents aren't from anywhere around here. Human as they come and they're both dead."

Alex stuttered slightly as she talked about her parents. It had been years since she mentioned them to anyone. She felt tears welling in her eyes but held them back.

Thistle looked over at her and put a hand on her shoulder.

"You have my condolences. You might not be a magus, but you are something to them. As I told you back in Vandlehaven, they would not have broken their laws lightly to have brought you here." He turned to Rex. "I know I've no right to ask..."

Rex cut him off. "Ya don',"

"But I beg that you take her to them. She needs answers and we need your resources if we are to make this journey," Thistle said.

"Preposterous, nae one could make it even if we wanted to. And we don'. The Guard has nae interest in the business o' long-dead mystics an' wanderers."

"Rex, we've known each other for a long time. This girl, and whatever secrets she holds, might be the key to bringing the Court down. It has to be worth a shot."

A storm cloud passed over Rex's face. "Nae. My brothers an' sisters will no' die on a fool's errand. We will give ya supplies and ya can be on yer way in the morning," he said and glowered at Thistle as if daring him to press the issue further.

Thistle looked at Alex, but she didn't know what to say. She didn't blame him. If she was in Rex's position, she would have done the same. She didn't even believe that she was anything special, and she had no clue why she was there, so why should he?

Alex opened her mouth to speak, but before she could, a massive quake rocked the cavern.

Rex sprang up and looked outside. "What? Impossible!" He looked at Alex, "It seems you've made friends quickly. The Court has found you again."

"What? How? Those fish things came this far inland?" Alex asked, an edge of panic creeping into her voice.

"Nae." Rex listened to the next strike. "Those are thrall hammers. It seems the Lord of Long Shadows has sent his Pride after ya. We won' 'ave long until the moot cracks. We need to put up our defenses, for what it will matter..." he said, rushing out of the hut.

Alex sprang up to follow him with Thistle in tow behind.

In the village outside, the fighters had assembled, and the children huddled near the back of the cave. Rex was in the center and speaking to his troops.

"We've battled these demons before, and we'll drive them back now. Kyria, lead the old and women an' the children out through the back tunnel. We'll collapse it behind ya." He was speaking to the young woman who had fixed her hateful gaze on Thistle earlier. The girl protested, but Rex quickly silenced her. "This is no' a discussion. It's an order. Now go." She had more to say, but seemed to know it wouldn't matter. The small group followed her to where the cavern ended. She placed her hand on a wall and it again vanished long enough to allow the group and herself through.

Another strike rocked the cavern and Alex narrowly sidestepped a falling rock. She saw a crack in the wall and heard the cries of battle coming from the steps. A force shook the cavern, and the wall fell away. As the dust cleared Alex looked into the opening with horror.

Two large battering rams, held by dozens of men in chains, gleamed in the dim light. Connecting the men were horrifying looking chains that linked every part of their body. They seemed to breathe and move as one living being, and all of them looked exhausted. Sweat covered their bodies and vicious looking lash marks. As the smoke cleared, Alex saw what drove the men on.

In the cave's gloom, a pair of massive lions stood on their hind paws, towering above the slaves. All their features were simultaneously human and animal. Manes of dark fur cascaded down their necks over faces where catlike eyes gleamed with human malice. Large paws with wicked claws held crescent-shaped axes in one hand and massive coiled whips in the other. The lions snarled at the slaves ahead of them, who visibly shuddered and made quick steps to move out of the way. One team put their battering rams down, but the crack of a whip reminded them that their duties had not ended. The creatures advanced into the cavern and even the soldiers seemed unsettled. The Guard held their lines all the same.

The monstrous lions spoke in unison, their voices forming an identical growl, each word dripping with venom and purpose. The blood drained from Alex's face. She knew now that there was a power structure in the Court of Hours, and who was at the top of it. Each movement they made was a firm assertion of power and control. Even though they did not stand much taller than a man, each of them radiated the power of ten. If this was what she felt when she faced two, she could not imagine what an army of them would be like.

"Thralls," the lions said.

Alex remembered that the word was the demon word for humans.

"We outnumber you, and you are without hope. Even though we alone could slay these few laid before our feet, we will spare you in exchange for that female thrall." They lifted their axes and pointed directly at Alex and she had never felt smaller in her life. Whatever power she had against the muradae or the golden host, she had none here.

"Give us a moment ta discuss yer fine, fancy offer," Rex said with a grin.

Rex turned to Thistle. "Do ya really believe she has a chance ta make some difference?"

"I do. I believe the Eastern Watch brought her here for a reason," Thistle said.

"Then take what time our lives will buy an' go." Rex turned to Alex, "I don' know if I trust what he says, but I trust the fire ya showed when ya defended him. I know this is no' yer fight, an' I can't ask you ta take it up in our name."

Alex shook her head. "If I can rid your world of these things, you have my word I'll do it. It's not like I'm going anywhere until I talk to those idiot wizards anyway."

Rex chuckled. "I like ya, Alex o'... well, wherever yer from. Go with the gods, an' may we see each other again in a happier meeting."

"See you around, Rex of the Old Guard," Alex said.

Rex turned back to the demons.

"We 'ave discussed yer appealing offer, an' we 'ave decided that ya may return yer offer ta yer collective arses! Common lads an' ladies, today's a good day ta kill some lions I think. A gold imperial marc ta the first person to kill one; I'm goin' ta make myself a fine coat!"

By the time Alex and Thistle reached the wall, the battle was already raging. The Old Guard was fighting with all their resilience, but from the sound, it didn't seem to be going in their favor. Alex couldn't bring herself to turn around. These people had sacrificed themselves so that Alex could escape. She didn't feel even remotely worthy, but for now, couldn't ponder it. All that mattered now was survival. Otherwise, all of it had been for nothing and she wasn't about to let that happen.

Thistle slid his hand into the slot and the door melted away, revealing a staircase leading upwards towards a lit passageway. Alex paused for a moment, listening to the sounds of the dying battle, and tears stung her eyes for the first time in as many years as she could remember. She made a silent promise to herself, this would be the last time anyone died for her. She would keep this promise, no matter what.

As they ascended, daylight nearly blinded Alex. When the hazy view of the Lowlands returned, it was at the end of a blade. At the other end of the blade stood the auburn haired girl from the caves. Her fiery hair danced in the wind and her green eyes watched them, sharp as the blades she held.

"Sold us down the river huh ol' pigskin? And what's yer new young damsel here got ta do with yer schemin'?" There was a savage light in her eyes, and Alex saw a younger version of herself within them. She saw herself after her dad died in a warehouse fire, when she was seventeen. She saw herself after the owner of the warehouse collected a fat insurance check and laid off all of his workers. She saw herself holding the barrel of a gun at his temple in a car pulled off the side of the road. Alex saw the need for vengeance.

"Look," Alex began. She felt the knife push against her throat. "I know you hate him, and you have no reason to trust me, but Rex did. We wouldn't have been able to get out of here without his blessing to get through that magic stone wall. You know that," Alex was mostly bluffing. She didn't know how they had gotten through, but it sounded good. "They gave their lives to get us out, so we can stand around here all day not trusting each other and wait to see who wins that battle," she said pointing back to the cavern. Alex looked at Kyria's face and she knew she knew the answer to that. "Or, we can get out of here now and I promise they won't have died in vain. Not if there's still air in my lungs. So does he."

Thistle nodded vigorously.

The girl looked unsure of what to do and spoke after some hesitation.

"Fine. I'm no' an eegit. I know what's comin' up tha' tunnel sooner than later. There are some horses an' supplies over yonder. We'll make East, towards Shelhyle, an' maybe we've got a prayer," the girl said. Her face was difficult to read, but her voice was equal parts of sadness and rage.

Alex didn't wait for her to change her mind. The group walked down a hidden footpath to the bottom of the hill. Three horses waited patiently.

"What about the others?" Alex asked.

"They'll hide until the Pride follows us, then make for the nearest village. Gapfallo's only a half a day's march. The civilians can make it there an' take up with our operatives," the girl said.

"All right then, we'll follow your lead. I didn't get your name earlier," Alex said with a friendly tone in her voice, trying to bury at least five percent of the hatchet.

"I'm Kyria," she said, shaking tears out of her eyes. "Kyria Killburn." A shiver of cold rage passed into her voice. "And for yer sake, ya better be worth all this."

8

Premonitions and Portents

The next several days proved to be the hardest since Alex arrived. She had not found the courage to say anything to Kyria since they had retreated from the stone-moot, and Kyria hadn't shown any interest in speaking with her either. The few times Thistle tried to converse with Kyria, she shot him such a withering look, the surrounding plants seemed to shrink.

The horses were agile creatures. It had been years since Alex had ridden a horse, and these seemed friendlier than the ones at the Happy Valley Princess Ranch, where she had first ridden one at her eleventh birthday party. Alex's palomino dodged and scrambled over the rough terrain of the lowlands and it seemed to adjust on its own for the rider's weight. The horse also expected her commands and didn't spook.

Each night they rested in ruins, making a sparse dinner out of trail rations that Kyria had brought along. On the first night, Thistle and Alex speculated on how the Pride had tracked her down. Kyria said nothing.

"I know we haven't been too secretive about our travel, but how would they have known about the stonemoot?" Alex asked. Kyria's eyes drove daggers deeper into Thistle.

"Did you leave anything behind in the village?" Thistle asked. "Anything of personal value?"

Alex thought about it for a moment. She had her hat (miraculously enough) and the sword she had picked up off the pirate, and her clothes. Alex had changed into the traveling clothes at the village but none of those mattered to her so that just left one thing.

"My shoes. They were my favorite running shoes."

"That would make sense then," Thistle said. "The Pride are the most powerful of all the lesser demons. Among their abilities is essence tracking. If they find an item of value to a person, they can sense a part of their soul in it and follow the person that way."

"Tha's why we sleep in ruins," Kyria interjected. "These ruins 'ave stood for a thousand years and they've still got a mess o' memories in them. Like fragments o' the people who lived here. Canno' essence track someone in them; the angry spirits cause too much interference."

Alex let out a nervous gulp nodded and smiled awkwardly back at Kyria. She still hadn't come up with anything to say to her.

The ruins they were sleeping in differed from those Alex had seen from the Eastern Road. As they made camp, she looked around in wonder and awe at the condition of them. Ruins of buildings and walls formed what she imagined was once a small town. Paintings and a language she couldn't read illustrated the walls in vibrant colors, which was surprising given how old the ruins appeared. As the sun set, they cast a vibrant collage of colors over the stones, giving the place an ethereal and forlorn feeling. Alex could almost see the people walking about and performing various chores of daily life. She wondered how the end had come, and did they know it was coming? Would it have mattered? Could they have escaped?

Alex snapped out of her musings and realized it was dark. Everyone had settled into their respective sleeping rolls (which wasn't much more than a blanket). Alex finally decided she had something to say,

"I lost my dad too. When I was seventeen," she said aloud to no one in particular.

"Is tha' supposed ta make me feel better? Or bring him back?" There was wild anger in Kyria's voice, but also sadness and tears.

"No, I just thought... I thought you ought to know. I will keep my promise to you. Their deaths won't be for nothing."

"We 'ave been dyin' for nothing for a thousand years. What's one more death among millions? Why would ya care?" Kyria snapped. Beneath the anger in her voice was a deeper sadness that Alex recognized from her past.

"Because I've cried those tears before," Alex felt the tears coming back again, but this time she didn't hide them. "I can't bring your dad back, but I promise I'll make it mean something."

There was a long pause before Kyria spoke again.

"I believe ya mean that, Alex... I never got yer last name,"

"Winters," Alex said.

"I believe ya mean it, Miss Winters. I no' sure if I'm ready ta trust ya, but my dad did, and I guess for now that'll be enough."

"Thanks, Kyria. I won't let you down." Alex wasn't sure she could keep that promise but just saying the words made her feel more at peace than she had in days. Alex drifted off to sleep from the sounds of Thistle's rhythmic snoring. *Lord*, she thought, *that pig snores loudly...*

Alex had never been much of a dreamer. Not in the metaphorical sense; she wanted to go to college, become a doctor, get that shiny Camaro, but in the literal sense. She almost never dreamed. Until that night.

Alex awakened. She didn't know how, but she knew it was a dream. She stood up, looking around. She was at the edge of a dense forest peering through to a clearing. It was one o'clock in the morning. Nothing about the scene told her this, but she felt it, as much as the night wind blowing in her hair.

In the center of the clearing, a small cottage stood next to a well. Alex felt a sense of deep unease she couldn't place. She walked towards the cottage, even though her heart pounded in her chest and every bone in her body wanted to run away. She listened and heard nothing. A small brook ran nearby but she couldn't hear it. The wind rustled in the trees but it was silent. The entire world was silent. Even breath came out as an inaudible gasp. Alex felt time slowing as if all the world had come to a stop. Then she saw him.

An old man stood at the well, bent over. Aside from large, claw-like hands which gripped the stones of the well, a great cloak shrouded the rest of his body and face. She didn't know how she hadn't noticed him before, and yet, there he was. The man turned to her, but she still couldn't make out his face or any feature of his appearance.

Out of nowhere, a grinding sound like misaligned cogs echoed through the clearing. It was a horrible noise and Alex moved to cover her ears, but her body did not respond to her commands. After a while, she realized that the old man was speaking.

"The sparrow lands in the field, but what use is it to a jackal without teeth?"

"Are you talking to me?" Alex's mouth didn't move, but she thought the words and they became sound.

"Why did the girl choose to come?" the old man asked.

"I didn't choose to come here, I didn't choose any of this," she responded.

"A girl is never without choice. She made hers. Why did she come?"

"I'm telling you old man, I have no clue what you're talking about."

"Flames rise in the east, and in the north, the king of broken crowns takes his throne again. These things will come to pass. Now gaze into infinity and see the blood of time!" As he said this he turned, and she saw under his hood, but a feeling of overwhelming terror engulfed her, and blackness swirled around her. Alex was falling now, falling forever.

Alex woke up screaming, drenched in sweat. Thistle woke up, huffing and grabbing his sword.

"What... what... where's the enemy? I'll run them through," he said while brandishing his weapon about wildly.

"Put tha' away ya eegit," Kyria chastised, "She's jus' woke up screamin.'"

"Ah, well... never too early to prepare for battle I always say!"

Kyria rolled her eyes at him and came over to Alex

"Ya all right then?" she asked.

Alex took a moment to respond and make sure she was back in the real world.

"Yeah, I just had a bad dream," Alex said. She felt her pulse slowly returning to normal. When she looked up, she realized Kyria and Thistle were looking at her like she had sprouted a third arm. "What? Is there a booger on my face?"

"What's a dream?" Kyria asked.

"You know a..." Alex trailed off as she slowly realized that dreams were one of those things that were pretty hard to describe without using the word dream. She explained the idea without sounding too crazy. "You don't have those here?"

"Nae. Nae one does. Some stories the elders used ta tell sound like tha', but they were all about prophecy," Kyria said.

Alex looked over to Thistle, hoping for a dose of his wise swinley knowledge.

Thistle shook his head. "I'm afraid I've never heard of such a thing.

Not since the Fall. What happened in this dream?"

Alex described it. The details were all fresh in her mind. When she finished, Thistle and Kyria exchanged concerned glances.

"Is that bad?" Alex asked.

"My dear, the creature you spoke with was a Hand. The Hand of One, Lord of Awakenings," Thistle replied.

"That crap awakened me all right. Why would a Hand go through the trouble of talking and not threatening me? So far they've all been huge jerks. Besides, none of it made any sense. He was a lunatic."

"It is strange," Thistle said.

"The Lord o' Awakenings has no' been seen since the Fall," Kyria said. "Even the other demon lords o' the Court know little about his comings or goings. He doesn't 'ave lesser demons tha' serve him, an' nae one goes into or comes out o' his corner o' the realm."

"All of that's very fascinating, but what does it have to do with me?" Alex asked.

"Hard to say. You're the first person or demon he's contacted in a thousand years. It confirms at least that your presence here is no accident," Thistle said.

"How so?" Alex asked.

"The Lord of Awakenings is the master of prophecy, and he jealously guards it. Perhaps that's why no one in the realm has dreams. Dreams can contain small amounts of prophecy. Perhaps the Lord of Awakenings wanted to keep those secrets to himself. If he's taken an interest, I would bet my last gold Imperial Marc that your arrival is connected to something larger."

Alex pondered it for a moment. She scowled. As seemed to be the norm, this dream raised more questions than answers. *Typical Aquillon... just typical...* she thought to herself.

They continued to travel for several days, moving in erratic patterns and always sleeping in ruins to throw off the scent of Alex's essence. The group always steered clear of towns, so as not to drag more innocent folk into their troubles. Kyria had spoken more and more and was bordering on friendly. She had even spoken full sentences to Thistle and was threatening to kill him at least sixty-eight percent less than she had been.

All the while, however, Alex couldn't shake the feeling of dread that seemed to follow her every step like a shadow. Ever since the night she had dreamed of the Hand of One, she felt like a pawn on a chessboard, like her actions were being orchestrated or nudged along by forces unmentionable. Alex didn't think it was worth sharing though, as killer demon lions had everyone on edge enough.

That night they made camp outside of a large forest. Deep didn't describe it. The forest seemed to pulse and breathe, reaching out onto the open plain. Dark trees stretched up a hundred feet and or, and from every edge of the woods vines and tangle crept forward like arms extending out of the underbrush. It made the creepy woods of the Drowned Coast look like scenes out of a Disney movie. Alex mentally added it to her list of places never, ever to go. The list had been growing fairly steadily since she got to Aquillon.

Kyria was making camp and took a small package out of her backpack. She dug out a small hole and poured the contents of the package, viscous blue jelly, into the hole and struck a match. Just as Alex was looking at her like she was crazy, she dropped the match and the jelly glowed and radiated heat. There was smoke and the glow was very dim.

"King's Willow, sea water an' mud make... flameless fire," she said, impressed with herself.

Alex was too, but mostly she was just grateful. The warmth of the blue jelly flames washed over her and she sighed happily.

"I figured a fire would do us some good," Kyria said. "We were traveling for a while without much heat ta go on. Feels safe enough here I reckon."

"Thanks. I appreciate it. Makes me feel kind of human again," Alex said.

When she realized both Thistle and Kyria were giving her strange looks, she paused and chuckled sadly. Being human meant very different things to them than it did to her. For her, it was being warm and feeling safe and relaxed. Being human to them was just surviving.

"So then," Thistle said, "Where are we headed? The last few days have been so frantic, I didn't think to ask."

"The Guard 'ave safe houses all over this region. I just needed ta be sure we had thrown the Pride off o' the scent before I took us to one. From there we'll..."

Kyria stopped when she saw the look on Alex's face. Her eyes were wide and straining against the firelight with raw terror, and Alex knew what was behind her. Alex saw them gleaming in the steady glow of the flame-jelly; cat-eyes, small emerald orbs of death and malice. They had snuck up so quietly no one in the party noticed. They were crouched down in attack position, poised to strike. Kyria saw the look on Alex's face and reacted just fast enough to jump out of the way of a massive paw swiping at her. Thistle squealed in alarm and jumped from his cot, drawing his weapon.

In an explosion of motion and fury, the two lions struck from the shadows, swiping and slashing. They were primal forces of death and carnage; each movement an expression of raw power, each swipe was a death sentence for whatever they touched. Fear poured over Alex like a bucket of lightning and she was up in a moment, rolling and evading strikes. Her senses were on edge again, heightened as they had been before, and she felt more alert and ready to respond.

It was instantly clear to Alex that this was not a fight they would win. The only victory could be retreat. Alex barreled deeper into the ruins, the predators hot on her heels, hissing and striking closer and closer. Any strike of their massive paws would have been a kill, and the war ax they swung following each swipe would have done the job equally well.

"What do we do?" Alex asked frantically as she rounded a massive pillar.

"Run," Kyria responded breathlessly, jumping just high enough to evade a low blow from the rear.

"I put that much together! Where?" Alex yelled back.

"We have ta make it into Shelhyle Forest!"

"No! We won't last a day in there!" Thistle shrieked, his voice transfixed with genuine terror and panic.

"We won' last ten minutes out here! They won' follow us in there. It's our only shot!" Kyria yelled.

Alex was less than thrilled that the creepy woods were once again the safe bet, but the prospect of a painful death by lions made her inclined to agree with Kyria. They would be dead inside half an hour if they kept this up.

"I'm with her. Creepy woods over psycho lions!" Alex said back.

"On your heads be it," was all Thistle said.

As they bounded around a corner, they came back to an open space in the ruins and the lions burst in behind them. Alex could barely keep ahead of them as the lions dropped on all fours and nearly doubled. The armor they wore didn't seem to slow them at all, and they struck out easily while they ran. It was a wonder the lions hadn't caught them already.

Looking forward, Thistle, Alex and Kyria saw the treeline and sprinted. The forest was safety, and for now, that would have to do, no matter what other horrible things lurked in the dark shadows beneath the trees. Alex's lungs were on fire, but she dug deep and kept running. Each hiss and snap of a fang behind her fueled her to run faster. She couldn't see the others and was in no position to check on them. The only thing that mattered was running forward and making it to the treeline.

After what seemed like an eternity, Alex ran full force through the treeline and into the forest. Kyria was next, followed by Thistle. He was slower, but he had used the Pride's singular focus on Alex to his advantage and slipped past them at the last moment.

Kyria was right. The moment they had cleared the woods, the lions stopped dead in their

tracks. One panted on its fours, but the other stood on its feet and snarled at them.

"Hide and die, or come out and die thralls, it matters not. It is all the same. You cannot hide from the Lord of Long Shadows! He will find you! His shadow touches and sees all. You will bow before the end!"

As soon as his evil lion monologue had ended, he wandered away in a huff, having

sounded evil enough by his standards. His friend bounded off, but Alex wasn't stupid enough to think the lions had left. She knew they'd be waiting.

The massive fatigue of the sprint finally caught up with her and she collapsed onto her back, breathing deeply. She took more and a few moments to regain her strength and stand up.

Once she had collected herself she looked around and took in the immeasurably dense forest before her. She followed Kyria's lead, and they proceeded deeper into the ocean of trees.

9

Into the Forest of Night

They had only been traveling for a day, stopping every so often to eat rations out of Kyria's pack, but the forest seemed to go on for eternity. The forest was far more massive than it appeared from the outside. Vast trees of all shapes and types reached up and choked the light from the sky, allowing in only minimal glimmers of the sun. Below the dense canopy of a hundred shades of green, a thousand forms of life spread out in every direction.

Alex looked around the forest in wonder. It was like every rainforest on Earth combined into one. The vegetation stretched for miles and miles, painted with deep hues of green. Every color of flower imaginable sprouted out of bushes, trees, and plants from the tallest tree to the ground. From where they stood, the canopy extended up several hundred feet into almost darkness. A small path extended forward away from the treeline they had entered, and it became darker as they went.

Here and there, the odd ruin surfaced in the sea of green, but the forest showed its dominance over any human artifact. It was as if nature had devoured the remnants of human civilization, leaving only trace amounts as a warning to any foolish enough to try again. This was a realm where nature was in control, and Alex was awestruck at the sheer magnitude of its power. She felt the forest was alive, and they were small creatures walking in the realms of giants. All around her the jungle buzzed with life, and the plants seemed to move and shift as they walked.

Around mid-day, they stopped by a stream for water. The stream flowed downhill from a source to the north. They could hear the water rushing, but the vegetation was too thick to peer through. Alex slurped down the water, which tasted better than anything she could remember drinking. It was clear and ice cold, nearly burning her throat as it went down, as if it had come from a spring somewhere nearby. They sat on moss-eaten rocks, taking a short break.

"So why didn't the pride follow us?" Alex asked.

"This is the realm of the Hand of Eleven, Lady of the Wood," Thistle said. "They dare not profane these lands with their steps.".

"Please tell me this means this Hand is the nice one who is waiting just around the next bend with a plate of fresh cookies..." Alex said, trailing off into a dream.

"I'm afraid no," Kyria said with a chuckle. "The Hands 'ave an uneasy truce with each other. After the Fall, the Court divided Aquillon into provinces, one territory for each Hand, no' ta be infringed on by the minions o' another hand. Some are more relaxed about their borders than others, but no' the Lady of the Wood. She tolerates nae trespassers."

"So where does that leave us?" Alex asked.

"Supremely wrung out, should she discover us. Still, better to move in stealth here, than die out there, I suppose," Thistle said.

"Great," Alex said with a groan. She would like to be out of both the frying pan and the fire for once, but no such luck.

"So what do we do from here?" Alex

said, directing her question towards Kyria.

"Try no' ta get lost and make it out alive. We've got two days rations if we're sparin'." She shot a nasty look at Thistle, who had eaten more than his share that morning. "But we need ta get out o' here and ta a safe house.".

"All right, well let's go explore some jungle!" Alex said with a smile and a nervous chuckle, halfheartedly trying to lift the group's spirits.

As they traveled, Alex noted where they had been. She pulled out her sword and was about to notch a tree when she felt Kyria grab her arm.

"This forest is alive. I'm sure ya have felt it."

Alex nodded. She knew she hadn't been crazy for thinking a bush was watching her earlier.

"Each tree is a vein that leads back ta the Lady o' the Wood. Cut one tree, an' every living creature here tha' serves her knows where ya are."

Alex gulped and drew her weapon back, replacing it in her scabbard. *Note to self then... don't mess with...anything.*

The rest of the day proved uneventful. As they broke camp for the night, she couldn't tell if the night had fallen. The darkness in this part of the forest was deep, and seemed to pulse with humidity. She heard creatures creeping about in the underbrush and felt a familiar presence. The shadow in the back of her mind had returned. She remembered it from the woods she had escaped into in the Drowned Coast. Best to ignore it, she decided. Plenty of real things out in this bush that would kill her without her getting jumpy over imagined shadows.

Kyria had started another smokeless fire, though she was careful not to do it on the ground, but rather started it in a skillet from her pack. Alex was grateful Kyria had the foresight to grab their supplies before fleeing the lions. The three sat in silence, the strain of travel wearing into their bones. Alex saw Thistle's eyelids flutter and soon enough he was snoring contently. Sleep soon came like a warm blanket slithering over her. As she began to fall into a deep sleep, the last thing she saw Kyria nodding off too. The sleep felt deeper somehow and even though she wasn't *that* tired; she succumbed to the exhaustion and felt herself slump over.

Thankfully, the night brought no dreams of any sort and seemed to pass as though Alex had closed her eyes for only a moment. As she opened them, however, she questioned whether she might still be dreaming.

Her eyes adjusted well to the light level in the forest, so she was reasonably certain she was looking at a different view than she had gone to sleep to, but that wasn't the pressing concern. The giant plant about to eat her friends was.

Vines had engulfed their campsite in the night and they covered everything. They pulsed and slithered like a thousand snakes all intertwined into one. The vines had almost mummified Thistle and vines covered Kyria, lifting her upwards toward what looked like a huge venus fly trap. Alex nearly gagged at the acrid smell of whatever green goop was oozing from the needle-like spines of the plant's mouth, but her unconcious friends didn't move. She still felt groggy, but she seemed to stay awake somehow. Her mind launched in overdrive. She needed a plan that didn't end with her or her friends turning into plant food.

She struggled to reach her pack, but it was no use. It was too far away, and the plant bound her up to her waist in vines that were tightening by the moment. She looked around to see what she could use.

Bingo!

Alex spotted their campsite, which looked intact, and Kyria's smokeless campfire had come with it. The vines were avoiding the heat of the glowing jelly, and formed a ring of writhing tentacles around it, hissing in its general direction. She could work with that.

She tried to inch herself over towards the campfire, but the vines didn't budge. This would take some doing. Pausing and catch her breath, she summoned enough energy to make a half jump a few inches closer. It wasn't much, and the vines felt like they might try to break her bones if she moved anymore, but it was enough. She reached out and grabbed the tip of the skillet containing the fire. Alex cursed as she grabbed it and the heat of the metal seared her flesh, but it didn't matter; the flytrap had almost gotten to Kyria and Thistle was still fast asleep. She brought the pan down on the vines around her legs

Alex moved it back closer to the coil of vines surrounding her, and heard them hissing and slowly she felt motion (and blood - pins and needles were killing her) return to her legs. Her hand had, mostly, gotten used to the heat, and she brandished the frying pan at the vines, which retreated whenever she got close to them. She grinned, feeling like Rapunzel. Now if she could get her hair to heal people, she'd really be doing well for herself. She settled for the frying pan for now.

Alex ambled across what used to be their campsite and approached the giant pillar of vines wrapped around Kyria. They uncoiled quickly as Alex held the hot metal closer and Kyria fell to the ground with a dull thud. Her eyelids fluttered open, and she was on her feet in a moment, flailing at attackers unseen as she got ahold of her bearings and the bizarre scenario she found herself in.

Kyria looked at Alex. "Where are we?" she asked

"No idea at all," Alex said.

"Killer plants attacking?"

"Yup."

"And yer holding a frying pan filled with flames."

"Yup."

"Well then. I guess things could be..."

Alex thought with a twinge of irritation she might have just been about to say worse. She wasn't sure if things worked the same in Aquillon, but that was never a great phrase to say out loud. *Don't say it*, Alex quietly hoped.

"Worse."

No sooner had she said it, they heard a rustling in the bush behind them where the flytrap had come from. Alex watch as the vines retreated next to the flytrap, reforming as thick tentacles. They flailed about in the air, each tentacle filled with thousands of tiny spines oozing with the same pleasant concoction the flytrap's thorns produced.

Kyria shot a concerned look at Alex who rolled her eyes. "I have got to teach you some things not to say if we get out of this mess alive," Alex muttered.

"On guard!" Alex heard Thistle shout. She looked around and saw that he was up and on his feet, swashing away at the tentacles nearest to him.

Kyria drew her knives and threw Alex her cutlass.

"I thought you said not to hurt the plants," Alex said.

"Well, tha' was before they were trying ta eat us. Chop away!" she responded.

Alex began to attempt to chop at the nearest tentacle, but she quickly figured out that it was useless. As soon as she felled one, it would generate nearly as fast. "I've got to be smarter about this," she muttered to herself as she looked around the camp for solutions. She spotted the frying pan and had an idea.

The flame was still burning in the frying pan and she reached down and grabbed it. She then sliced through the nearest tentacle but before it could reform, she brought the hot metal underside of the pan down on the severed end. It sounded like it was screaming as the tendrils sizzled and popped. Alex cautiously removed the pan, and to her relief, it did not grow back.

It didn't take the plant creature long to realize it was now on the losing side of the battle, and it finally retreated into the underbrush, fading seamlessly into the dense foliage as if it had never been there.

"Ok," Alex began. "Thing one. What was that? Thing two. Where are we?"

Thistle was still nursing a nasty-looking scratch on his flank and replied without looking up. "This forest is old. Older than the Court of Hours, older than the realm of Aquillon, older some say than the gods. There are things here which no man has seen, and no man has named. We should consider ourselves lucky to have only encountered a lesser among them."

Alex pondered his response with silent respect. The forests she had seen on Earth paled compared to this place. On Earth, forests were just a resource for people to use, or destroy or build on, sadly. This was a primal place, a forest that no human had or ever would conquer, and it filled her with all the more respect for it, and fear.

"Hold up. If this place is so old, how did the Hand of Eleven dig her slimy claws into it?" Alex asked.

Kyria shrugged. "Nobody knows for sure. Some o' the old folks used ta say she was once a forest spirit, and she drove herself mad with her hatred o' humans, so she signed her soul away ta the Court. Others say the forest sprang up around where she entered our world. Just old legends; hard ta sort the truth from the folklore."

"And how about where we are? Got any wisdom to offer about that?" Alex asked.

Now that the tide of battle had subsided, Alex looked around and could tell they had moved somehow. This area of Shelhyle looked different. The trees were darker and taller, and the light from the roof of the canopy seemed as distant as the stars it resembled. Now that she had a moment to properly take in her surroundings, she saw that they were at the base of a great fallen tree that formed the superstructure of a vast network of roots. Flowers bloomed here, but only in deep reds and purples that seemed the glow with shadowy light.

Kyria spoke up.

"I'm thinkin' we drifted a spell. I heard tell about it; the forest moves while yer asleep. Forever changin', shiftin' wanderin' so's ta keep them lost what's intruding or looking for the hall where that foul witch keeps her counsel."

"So, we're lost?" Thistle asked.

"Seems that way. Even if we could get some bearing on where we were, as soon as we went ta sleep, the forest would just shift again," Kyria replied.

"So, our plan is to just wander until we find an exit?" Alex interjected.

"Unless you've got a better one," Kyria said, almost sounding hopeful that Alex had figured up some brilliant scheme at the last moment.

"Fresh out of better ideas at the moment. I guess we're moving out." Alex said with a resigned shrug.

They climbed the fallen tree, . Given how old it looked, it was in excellent condition and only gave out once or twice. Alex figured anything that only tried to kill her a few times in Aquillon was behind the curve, but she wasn't complaining.

Once the last of the trio had scampered up the tree, they found a better vantage point of their surroundings. This part of the forest was a different ecosystem than the one they had been traveling. The fallen tree (which thankfully had fallen in the direction they were traveling) offered something of a road, but around it, the jungle was exploding with growth and foliage. A waterfall cascaded over a cliff in the distance, and the water trickled into a small brook that ran into the dense brushes at the floor of the forest. Strange colored birds flew overhead and regarded them with irritation, squawking at them.

"So which way then?" Kyria asked.

"Forward always seems the best plan," Thistle replied with gusto. "Forward and upward I always say!"

Thistle had never said that as far as Alex knew.

"Wait..." Alex said. She looked around for the nearest tree. Her dad had shown her this trick once when they went camping, in case she ever got lost. She looked around for a tree. It didn't take her long. Bingo! Sweet green pay-dirt. Moss covered the tree, but only on one side. "Is Shelhyle in the north or the south of Aquillon?"

"South," Kyria replied, looking puzzled.

"Then we need to go this way. As long as we follow the same direction, we should get out eventually."

She went on to explain that in the south of Earth, moss grew on the south side of trees. The north side was bare. "Not sure if things work the same here, but it's worth a shot."

"Ingenious," Thistle said.

"Tha's a good trick," Kyria said.

"Yup. My dad was a smart guy," Alex said, smiling to herself. It wasn't a sure-fire plan by any means, but Alex figured that moving in one direction might vaguely reduce their chances of getting eaten by...well, everything.

Guided by the green fuzz, they started off in what Alex hoped was a northern bound direction. It took the group several hours of walking to reach the end of the fallen tree. Getting down was a monumental effort (and nearly fatal), but eventually, they reached the forest floor. It had been a long and taxing day full of climbing and near-death by angry plant monsters, but no one wanted to stop. They knew if they went to sleep, they might drift again and lose all the progress they had made. So, they marched on.

It was slower going through the underbrush. Small bushes and tall grass concealed the ground, making footing treacherous. Every five or ten feet they would nearly run smack into a tree trunk. It eventually thinned out into a small path which they continued to follow. They looked like old hunting trails to Alex, though what had maintained them remained a mystery.

They had been walking for a long time and each step was taking its toll. Alex was nearly falling asleep on her feet when she heard a wonderful sound. Water.

"I know we can't waste time, but I'd kill for a bath," Alex said, as her ears soaked in the sound of the rushing water.

"I agree. A bit of refreshment could do us all some good!" Thistle said. Kyria offered no objection or alternative, so they proceeded towards the sound.

The underbrush opened up to reveal a small lake which formed from the runoff of several waterfalls nearby. Alex bent down and put her hand in the water and squealed with excitement. It was ice cold, and in the forest's heat, it was the best thing she had felt all day. She then realized (and was subsequently mortified) that she smelled like a construction worker in July. She thought about it (and smelled about it) and realized that Kyria and Thistle weren't much better.

"All right," she announced, "It's bath time. Ladies first."

Kyria nodded with a big grin and they shooed Thistle away, telling him to stand guard and that they would come to get him when they were decent again. As soon as he had wandered off, they stripped down and jumped in the water. The frigid water was a shock to Alex's nerves, but it felt amazing. She felt the energy coming back to her as the cold water chilled every part of her body. Kyria was swimming around happily and splashing the water at nothing in particular.

As Alex watched her, she saw with a sad familiarity that Kyria was still a kid; a kid who grew up far before she was ready to, just like Alex. She hadn't asked how old Kyria was, but she couldn't have been older than seventeen. Seeing Kyria's goofy smile and watching her paddle around the pool made Alex smile. She wondered sadly if this was how it was all over Aquillon. Kids forced to grow up overnight. The thought of it made her angry inside and further solidified her resolve to do something about it if she could.

A blast of cold water Kyria aimed at her, cut her musing short.

"Why you little..." Alex said, laughing as she returned fire. They continued their battle to a bitter stalemate and begrudgingly agreed to a truce when they realized that Thistle needed to bathe too, and they were pruning.

Getting out of the water, Alex couldn't believe how good she felt. It wasn't quite a good night's sleep, but it was something. Once they re-dressed, they called out to Thistle.

He didn't answer.

"Ah come on," Alex crooned. "We're sorry we hogged the water, don't be a boar!" Alex and Kyria cracked up at her stupid joke, but when Alex didn't even hear an indignant snort, she began worrying.

"Thistle?"

A rustling at the edge of the underbrush brush startled them, but Thistle walked through and they both breathed a sigh of relief. The relief turned to fear though, when they saw his face. It was cut and bruised and one of his eyes was swollen shut. They asked him what had happened, but their answer walked into the clearing.

Standing at the edge of the underbrush, and pointing an arrow at them was a centaur, or what kind of looked like a centaur to Alex, anyway. It differed from the cartoon she had watched growing up though. The creature was all horse from the waist down, with flesh composed of plants and wood, as though someone had carved it from a tree that was still living. Plants on the creature's hide seemed to blossom before Alex's eyes and die in moments. Out of his flank grew a quiver of vicious looking arrows.

From the waist up he was human...sort of. The creature's skin was every color of green imaginable and offered him a perfect camouflage of the forest. His face looked carved and wooden, and his demeanor was an angry snarl, and eyes glowed yellow. From behind him two more tree-centaurs came. They looked no friendlier.

Alex opened her mouth to speak, but she felt an arrow whiz by her ear and she froze and closed her mouth. The arrow had not missed. It was a clear message about unprompted speech.

The lead tree-centaur spoke. His voice was a collection of nature sounds that somehow formed into words.

"You are intruders in our Lady's forest. You will come with us to answer questions for the Lady, and then you will die."

Well, at least they were upfront about it, Alex thought. Not a great forecast of events, but it could be worse. If they wanted information, Alex had a bargaining chip, and she had time.

And after all, all you really need is time to plan a daring escape. Time and an insane amount of good luck. Well, at least Alex had time, anyway.

10

The Hall of Black Boughs

Alex felt a tight pressure as vines sprout from the ground and climb their way up her body, forming a binding around her arms. The centaurs led them forward, one tree-centaur ahead of them and the other two taking up the rear.

As the centaur walked, the forest parted before him, like water receding from the beach as the tide goes out. Alex watched in amazement as plants buried themselves back in the ground and tresses shifted their roots to clear a path. Of all the things that had tried to kill her so far in Aquillon, she decided the tree-centaurs were at least the most interesting. That they were marching her toward her doom was a huge bummer all around since she wanted to like them. They had also beaten up Thistle (who she imagined had put up a valiant fight and resisted telling them anything until they shouted and given themselves up). She hated anyone who hurt her friends, and that included otherwise fascinating tree-centaurs.

They were cutting a path through the forest at an alarmingly rapid rate. The surrounding forest continued to move and shift one scene changing and melting into the next. Their path, however, remained constant. The tree-centaurs seemed relatively distracted so Alex whispered to Thistle.

"What's the plan here?"

"I wish I could be of more help here, but this is uncharted territory. No man or woman has ever seen the Hall of Black Boughs and lived," he said in a whisper.

"Outstanding. Well, there's a first time for everything," she said, "and what exactly are these things?"

"Sylvans; corrupted nature spirits. When madness came on the Lady of the Wood, here servants were soon to follow, as was the forest. That's why nothing here acts as it should."

"Quiet!" The female sylvan said, hissing at Thistle and he stopped talking with a defiant snort.

They proceeded on the untraceable path for most of the day and into what Alex assumed was night and stopped for a short rest. It seemed the sylvans were under orders not to kill them and noticed that their prisoners were stumbling about. Alex sat down on a tree stump and took a deep breath. The sylvan's glowing yellow eyes never left her.

They ate some food from Kyria's pack and drank from a leaf that one of the Sylvans gave them which seemed to produce water endlessly. The water sprouted first as dew drops in the back of the leaf and rolled down into a pool which Alex drank from. Alex stood up feeling rejuvenated, and they began their march again.

She had been all over the United States with her dad, and she saw represented in Shelhyle every ecosystem she knew of and some she didn't. All around her Alex noted the different forests that flashed by her as they traveled. Seattle rainforest melted into Alaskan alpine, into Florida scrubland. The only consistent thing was the level of light; it never changed. Shadows from the dark canopy high above shrouded the world

With little warning, the path ended and before them was a massive opening in the wood. All around the edge of the clearing a translucent field of energy shimmered and danced in the shadows of the canopy, showing different scenes from different forests that comprised Shelhyle. This part of the forest opened up and the night sky above it shone down, bathing the landscape in moonlight. It took Alex's vision a moment to adjust to the almost blindingly bright light after having been in the forest's darkness for so long.

Surveying the scene around the clearing, she saw animals from every climate and forest. Tigers walked calmly alongside chimps, and Kodiak bears sat lazily eating berries while wolves lay sleeping at their feet. All around the clearing sylvans pranced about and attended to various duties. Large lamp-like objects hung from low-lying trees and Alex realized they were clumps of fireflies gathered together, forming one glowing ball that lit up the path.

In the center of the clearing, she saw the hall. It was composed of large, black trees, their trunks woven together into walls and branches extended over the top to create a roof. Red runic writing shimmered across the trunks and two massive sylvans guarded the path into the open hall A soft red glow illuminated the hall and Alex barely made out the silhouette of a throne, but not much more than that. The scene would have been something out of a daydream. It had a surreal quality to it that was threatening and alien.

The sylvans again seemed distracted, so Alex turned back slightly to Kyria. "Ok, plan time. I'm assuming that's a terrible place filled with things we'd rather not meet?"

Kyria nodded.

"Do you still have any of that smokeless fire left?" Alex asked, in the quietest whisper she could manage.

"Aye, I do, an' matches," she whispered back.

"All right, once we make it clear of this creepy zoo, maybe we give our sylvan friends a more practical demonstration on how it works."

"Great plan, except how do we get our supplies back?"

"Leave it to me," Alex said. It was a long shot plan that involved a lot of running and a lot of luck, but she figured it was better than no plan at all.

Sylvans prodded them down the path roughly and Alex noticed all eyes turn towards her. Animals snarled menacingly at them as they passed and the Sylvans who galloped around the clearing sneered at them. As Alex got closer to the animals, she realized why she was uneasy; each animal appeared normal from a distance, but up close the features of different animals blended together in a terrifying way. A bear had crocodile scales on its face, and a wolf had a coat made of writhing serpents. Like the forest in which they lived, they were twisted and out of sync with the natural order of things.

As they approached the hall, Alex gazed up at the black trees. Each was twisting and contorting into the next and Alex realized they were moving. The trunks seemed to shift and coil as she watched them. It appeared the trees were forced together and were in rebellion at the torment they endured. As Alex looked closer, the outline of a face protruded from one trunk in a silent scream and Alex let out a real scream of her own. She felt a hoof kick her in the side, and she silenced herself. The sylvan who kicked her shot her a deadly look.

As she entered the hall, Alex's skin crawled with fear and apprehension. Inside the hall, trees grew in various gnarled shapes and Alex noticed the outlines of people in the bark. She stifled a second scream. The forest had started as a charming, otherworldly curiosity, but it had descended into a nightmare.

Creatures that looked like sylvans but stood on two legs lined the path to the throne. All around them the dark red light emanated from an unknown source. At the end of the hall, on a large throne of twisted black branches, sat the a woman who was equal parts menacing and enchanting.

Alex took a deep breath as she looked at her. She was beautiful; a woman carved of nature itself. Her torso was wood that seemed always to be in motion and blossoming branches formed her limbs that entwined in the shape of hands and feet. Her hair was a flowing river of grass and flowers and every other form of flora. Shining eyes of yellow gleamed out of a calm face that seemed to watch everything and nothing all at once.

There was something else about her though. Like everything in her forest, her beauty hid a corruption that ran deep. Black veins ran the length of her body and bones surfaced here and there in her hair. Beneath her serene face, and deep under her yellow eyes was an unspoken hatred and malice that flowed out from her. Alex realized with horror that the red energy pulsed from the Lady of the Wood, and without being sure how she knew, she knew what it was. The Lady was sick, infected with corruption, and it had spread to every corner of her forest. She was death and rot disguised as beauty.

Alex realized with a start they were almost out of time, and she winked at Kyria. Alex collapsed on the path and summoned her inner drama student. She convulsed and fluttered her eyes. One of the sylvans turned to Kyria.

"What is the matter? Get her up!" it hissed.

"Ya kicked her an' set off an. allergic reaction! She needs her medicine from our pack!" Kyria said, sounding deeply genuine.

Alex almost smiled. The girl was crafty.

"No, just get her up! We cannot keep the Lady waiting," another Sylvan said.

Thistle jumped in this time, catching on to what their plan was. "If you oafs don't let the girl to her medicine, she'll be dead in minutes, and then where will you be? Another twisting soul in these trees

I'd wager. I've never heard of the Lady of the Wood offering second chances."

Perfect Thistle! Ham it up, Alex thought to herself. The sylvans exchanged nervous glances and then threw Kyria the pack. "Be quick thrall, or she will wish she was dead."

Kyria rifled through the pack until she found what she needed. "Ok... got it."

"What is the delay?" the female sylvan asked Kyria, walking towards her. It was all the distance Kyria needed. Turning like lightning, Kyria slammed a jar of jelly into the sylvan's chest followed by the lit match moments later, and the creature exploded in an immolation of blue flame. Alex wasted no time and sprang up running, Kyria and Thistle on her heels.

Alex had nearly made it to the entrance when she saw vines wrap around her feet and pull them out from under her. She landed with a thud on the ground and felt herself being pulled. She kicked and grabbed at anything she could, but soon the vines had lifted her in the air and pulled her and her friends towards the Lady. As they hovered in the air, the Lady spoke.

"Did you think it would be so easy? To defy the will of a god?" Her voice was horrible; it was the chittering of a thousand rodents, the breaking of branches, and the howling of an angry wind through leaves. The vines dropped them on the ground and Alex stood up to face her enemy.

"So, this is the thrall I've heard so much about. I have to say, I expected more. You angered my fellow courtiers, and then you seek asylum in my kingdom? The arrogance of you thralls never ceases." As she spoke, anger seemed to rise and fall in her voice, like a wave breaking on the shore.

"Look, lady," Alex began. She heard that little voice in her head telling her this was a bad idea, but Alex was tired, and in no mood for mincing words. "I didn't see your name written on the woods, and as we say where I come from, it's a free country."

In a microsecond, the Lady lost all pretense of serenity and her features changed to match. Frost erupted from her limbs and her hair turned to grass gripped by snow. Her eyes lost their yellow glow and became red. She rose and as she stepped towards Alex, the ground around where she stepped was consumed with frost and died. The Lady spoke only inches from her face.

"Watch your tongue, wretch, or I will

remove it. I am not as forgiving as that

half-drowned fish woman. You draw breath for only as long as my curiosity goes unsated."

"So, what's my motivation to talk?" Alex asked with a skeptical tone of voice.

"You do not know how to suffer, and I will take my payment from your friends." The Lady held up her hand and Kyria screamed. Alex looked behind her and saw that barbed vines had consumed Kyria, twisting and writhing, crushing her not so slowly.

"Fine. All right!" Alex shouted. "I'll talk, just let her go!"

She felt her battle senses kicking in. The Lady relaxed her hand and Kyria slumped over. Thistle caught her and shot a hate-filled glance at the demon.

"Tell me thrall," the Lady said. "How did you do that parlor trick in Vandlehaven? Show me, and I may keep you alive."

"I don't know. Honestly, it just happened, and I haven't been able to make it happen since," Alex said. It was the truth, but she had a bad feeling that it wasn't the answer the demon was looking for.

"I see the truth in your eyes, thrall. I commend your honesty. I am disappointed. I had hoped for more. Well then, feed them to the maw," the Lady said, waving them away dismissively.

Alex didn't know who or what a maw was, but the look of pale terror that washed over Thistle's face provided her with a reasonably good idea. Besides, nobody was ever fed to anything as a reward, and it was never a good thing. Alex was at least sure that was the same on Earth and Aquillon.

Alex felt herself being pulled roughly towards the back of the hall where she noticed the floor moving, which she figured was a bad sign. As they were pulled closer to the maw by the sylvan guards, she saw that the floor of the hall had untangled itself from the web of gnarled roots and earth. Below the facade the outline of huge teeth and a slimy tongue caught Alex's eye.

Alex motioned with a concerned eye towards the giant mouth in the ground and Thistle gulped audibly.

"Lesser demons that serve the Hand of Six," Thistle yelped. "If you really want to call them that. Their collective mouths feed the Lady of Hunger. We can expect to be slowly digested as we arrive into the greater stomach of their master."

"Good. Now I'll finally have something in common with Boba Fett. And no, no time to explain," Alex said.

As the mouth opened, a horrific stench billowed out. Alex gagged as she saw the remains of a body, or what appeared to be one surface in the ocean of teeth. It looked as though it had been there a very long time. Alex decided that she would not be joining them, but she needed time she didn't have. They stood on the edge of the pit now. Kyria was coming back to her senses and was struggling wildly but to no avail. Alex breathed deep and closed her eyes.

When she opened them, her battle senses had kicked in. She had no idea where they were coming from, but she wasn't complaining. It focused her mind and she could see every tactical element of the situation, as easily as she would read the words on a page. They seemed to have decided Kyria was first to go, but she was struggling against them as much as she could. Time seemed to slow and at that moment, Alex found the opportunity she needed.

One of the Sylvans had wandered too close to the pit and Alex took advantage of the demon's poor choice of footing. Lowering her shoulder, she bull-rushed the sylvan, knocking him off balance, and sending him careening into the pit. Although he was an evil tree-centaur, Alex felt a slight twinge of pity as the mouth crunched down on him. The Lady of the Wood screeched and doubled over for a moment, as if a small part of her was being devoured as well.

Kyria and Thistle wasted no time and had freed themselves from the vines that bound them and fought the Sylvans guarding them. Thistle was head-butting one while Kyria had found a large stick and was beating a sylvan senseless with it. They were doing fairly well when the Lady shouted.

"Enough!"

The branches around the hall shuttered and a large group of armed Sylvans charged in, some wielding bows made of living wood, and others had drawn gleaming swords, quickly surrounding the three of them. The Lady looked at them, threw out her arms, and vines shot out toward them. Alex looked one way at the charging Sylvans and the other at the cyclone of vines and barbs erupting at her. The thought of the impending fate of being chomped and slurped for eternity terrified her, but another part of her was very annoyed at her increasingly bad luck. Most of all, Alex just wished her stupid powers would bother showing up more regularly.

The first sylvan was creeping closer, when Alex's bad luck finally took a turn for the better. From the darkness above the hall, an arrow slammed through the neck of the leading sylvan, who collapsed into a twitching pile of leaves. Alex looked to see where it had come from, and before long she saw a rain of arrows pouring down into the sylvan guards, until finally all that surrounded her were twitching piles of leaves.

Above them, Alex heard a loud noise of hooting and low drumming erupted from the trees. A massive gorilla dropped out of the canopy with a thud, holding a large bow. It stood up and motioned with its free hand and several more dropped. Alex had a hard time distinguishing them from their surroundings as they were decked out in hunters clothing and brown and green camouflage pain.

Alex was taken aback at the bizarre nature of what she was looking at, but given she had almost been thrown into a giant mouth in the ground five minutes ago, she was doing her best to keep it all in perspective. Besides, the enemy of her enemy was a friend, even if that friend was a heavily armed gorilla.

The leader looked around and made several grunts. It stunned the Lady of the Wood for the moment, but she was quickly bouncing back, and the sound of hooves was not far off. Alex looked at the leader.

"Thanks," she said.

"No time for words, human," he replied in a deep, rough voice. She wasn't surprised that he spoke, and oddly enough his voice sounded exactly like what she imagined a gorilla's voice should sound like. "The demons return soon. We go. Come, live. Stay, die. Choice yours," he said.

Compelling options, as usual, Alex noted mentally.

"Going sounds better and better," Alex replied as she looked around. "Yeah, we'll go."

Without further conversation, the leader put his bow away and scooped her up like a duffle bag and threw her over his shoulder. Alex was too surprised to complain, and really, what do you say to an eight-hundred- pound gorilla that just picked you up? Kyria was less resigned to being handled like a sack of potatoes and was punching and kicking, but this just seemed to tickle the gorilla that was carrying her and it was chuckling. Thistle had passed out, overwhelmed from the bravery he had shown earlier. Alex shook her head and sighed.

With a roar that left Alex shivering and feeling tinier and more powerless than usual, the leader slammed the ground with his other fist, and the earth shook. She felt his muscles flex and without warning; it launched them in the air with a powerful jump that sent them sailing upwards towards the canopy. When they neared a branch, the gorilla caught it and they were at once swinging to the top of the canopy. Within seconds Alex, her new gorilla friend, and the others were poised at the top to the hall. They moved far more gracefully than she would have thought possible.

They stood now on the roof of the Hall of Black Boughs and Alex looked around, her

heart sinking at the hopelessness of their predicament. Sylvan warriors and vicious animals surrounded the entire hall. However these gorillas had gotten in, Alex had a bad feeling they weren't getting out the same way. As if their immediate problem wasn't bad enough, she heard a sinister rustling coming from behind them.

She turned in time to see the image of the Lady of the Wood erupt in vines and branches behind them. She smiled the same wicked smile as before, and her eyes watched them intently. Opening her mouth, the horrible tree woman spoke.

"Koga, my pet. Why do you rebel against me? Come home, and all will be as it was."

The lead gorilla bared its teeth at the image.

"Koga no go. Mother sick. Koga fight. Mother sick."

"You always were a disappointment to mother. If you will live as a lawless beast, then die like one!"

Alex saw a look of remorse pass over Koga's face, but resolve replaced it just as quickly. As the Lady finished speaking, her image collapsed and several plant creatures burst from the top of the trees and moved towards the apes. Koga reached out his arms and vines shot towards him from the taller trees to the side of the clearing.

103

He wrapped his arms in them and climbed. He extended his arms downward; the vines followed and the other gorillas climbed as well on the makeshift rope ladder.

Alex looked down and almost passed out from the height, but saw the entire forest floor shifted and moved until it resembles the outline of the Lady's face, which laughed wildly.

"Run, foolish beast. Mother will find you! The human's stink is all over you. Mother is coming and this time I will not be so merciful!"

Alex briefly pondered the relationship between a large, sentient gorilla and a woman made of evil plants, but decided there would likely be a better chance to think on things. For now, she focused on not letting go of Koga.

They took some time, but eventually, they reached the upper canopy. The trees here differed from below. They were brighter and cleaner as if the corruption had not spread up here. The air was cleaner too and above Alex's head was something she desperately missed as soon as she saw it; daylight. It streamed in like a broken window here and there. Her face caught a ray of sun and she almost wanted to cry. She breathed deeply and was almost feeling better.

The apes swung through the trees for a while before arriving at a collection of huts anchored into the thicker branches. Koga stopped on a platform in the center of the huts and let Alex down. Her legs were wobbly, and she took a moment to steady herself. She grabbed for a railing, but realized, almost too late, that there wasn't one. She turned and was face to face with Koga, who was looking deep into her eyes.

"Speak. Koga listens. Then choose what do. Human not thrall. But not ape. Koga decide."

As Alex looked around her, she realized dozens of eyes were watching her from the trees. The tribe of Koga had come to hear her.

11

The Will of Koga

She looked all around, astounded at how many there were, and how silently they had approached. Alex has seen gorillas before, but these were different, and not in a terrible, corrupt way like the rest of Shelhyle had been. There was a kindness to their faces and human intelligence that resonated beneath their eyes. They seemed, at least on the surface, like normal gorillas.

Looking around, Alex could tell which ones were warriors, and which served some other function in the tribe. The warriors wore a mask of solemn indifference, and their eyes were always watching the perimeter, even while in their homes. The others were more curious than cautious and spoke to each other in hushed tones. Koga raised his fist, and a hush fell over them.

Now she could study him, she knew why he was the alpha. Koga was larger than the largest of the hunters by several feet in both directions, and his face was all outward power and authority. No other member of the tribe met his gaze. He was old; deep wrinkled lines of sadness and anger had carved themselves deep under his dark eyes. His eyes were sharp ebony hawks scanning the horizon for threats while scrutinizing

Alex. She had trouble meeting his intense gaze when he turned to speak with her.

"Now human speak. Koga listen." His voice was the rumbling growl of a thunderstorm.

"Hi. I'm Alex," she said profoundly as if it would explain anything. "These are my friends Kyria and Thistle." Kyria eyed her skeptically as if to say, *Really, Winters? That's the best thing you could come up with? We're doomed.* Kyria rolled her eyes at Alex and nodded at Koga, and Thistle bowed deeply.

"Why you walk in forest of night? Humans never come. This place death for your kind. Why now? Why you?" Koga's tone seemed suspicious but not outright hostile.

"We were running from the pride," Alex said.

At the mention of the pride, the apes roared into a frenzy, hooting and bounding their chests angrily. They weren't fans of the demon cats either, so Alex figured that was something in their favor. Koga held up a fist to quiet them. Alex continued.

"We need to get to the Wyld Places, but we don't know how."

"Why humans want go to Wyld Place? Only death there," Koga said, beating his chest to silence the last of the hooting.

Kyria spoke up.

"We're lookin' for the Eastern Watch. That sack o' nae good mystics brought our friend here an' we means ta find out why." She may have spoken with borrowed confidence, but at that moment she was her father's daughter - fiery and sure of herself.

Koga silently considered her words. "We hear whispers. Girl fight Hands. Hands fear her. We know this. This why we save girl and friends."

"And we thank you for that, mighty ape Lord," it was Thistle who spoke this time.

The great gorilla's nostrils flared, and he roared. "Koga not Lord.

Koga lead. Koga, not leader."

"My apologies. I meant only to convey our deepest thanks to you my... friend." Thistle sputtered as he tried to backpedal. "We would ask that you continue to assist us to the borders of your realm," he said.

"We risk much already saving you. Why Koga help more? Why clan help more?"

"Same reason ya saved us. Because if yer enemy is truly the Court, this might be the only good chance at defeating them an' ya know it! If it was worth the risk ta save us, this should be a simple request." Kyria said firmly. Alex looked at her, feeling deeply humbled by the trust she placed in her. It hadn't been long since Kyria had a knife at Alex's throat and now she was vouching for her, maybe even as a friend.

"Strong words, human. Koga must consider. Speak first light."

He waved his hand and the rest of the clan dissipated, muttering to themselves. Alex breathed deeply, relieved they had somewhere to sleep, at least for tonight. She turned to Kyria and Thistle,

"I haven't thanked either of you," she
said with a smile.

Kyria smiled back. "Thank us for what? Savin' yer rump?" she said.

"It's just good to have friends. I know the trust you're placing in me is a lot, and you're risking everything," Alex said.

"M'lady, we risk nothing," Thistle interjected. "While the court rules, we can't have anything. Not joy, not freedom, not a real life. I for one would rather die for something than live for nothing, harrumph!"

"The pig-man is right," Kyria said, "an' if my father believed in ya, so do I. Besides, yer the first real hope we've had in longer than I can remember. My father fought the court an' died, an' his father fought the Court an' died, an' his father before him. I aim ta break the cycle!"

Alex smiled and tears crept into her eyes. Thistle caught Alex and

Kyria (to Kyria's vigorous protesting) up in a bear hug. Alex turned as she heard someone approaching. She saw an older gorilla in robes with a gnarled staff walking towards them.

"Agu speak?" he asked.

"Sure," Alex said.

They walked over to a deserted part of the platform and sat in a circle. Kyria took some rations from her pack , and handed them out. Alex realized she was starving and hadn't eaten since the campfire that morning. Kyria offered some to Agu, but he refused politely.

"Agu see great hope in human girl coming." His voice was old, but not as a gruff as Koga's.

"Well...that makes one of us. I'm just looking for answers." Alex realized it wasn't probably what he wanted to hear, but she also figured trying to lie to a huge gorilla with a stick was a bad idea.

"Agu know these things. Koga must consider. Good of tribe at stake. No time for ideals. If help more, Koga risk much,"

"Well, why help us in the first place, then?" Alex asked.

"When scouts say human girl who hurt two hand come, Koga listen to forest. Forest say great bounty on girl head. Hour court fear great. First time scared since Fall. Scouts say she captured. Koga rescue. If Mother capture girl, girl die. Court win. No good."

"But why not help us more? It seems like we have a mutual enemy in the court," Alex countered.

"Longer you stay more human stink rub on us. Koga magic weaken." Saying this, Agu pointed to the edge of the encampment. It took a moment for Alex's eyes to see it, but a barely detectable field of energy shimmered just beyond the village.

Thistle spoke up. "How is it Koga can do magic, and why does he call the Lady of the Wood mother?"

"Questions two. Answers one. Long year ago. Before first man walk Aquillon. Only four primal gods. Lady one of them. She walk

108

forest many year alone. One day she find young ape. Mother lost. Ape dying. She bring him back home. Make healthy. Teach speak. Teach forest magic. Name Koga. Give long life."

A happy story so far. Alex was just waiting for the 'but'.

"Then one day." Close enough. "Court come. Lady make deal. Koga beg not, but Lady say only way kill humans, save forest. Koga agree at first, but then see what mother become. He run. Find other ape. Teach them. Make like Koga, but no magic. Only Koga magic. Only Koga long life." Agu paused, sighing sadly. "Koga still love mother. Try to save her. He know only when court gone, madness end for mother. She hunt him everywhere. Kill all other apes in forest. Stop Koga from build army. We all that left."

"That's terrible. Do you think someone can save her?" As Alex said this, a deep sadness bit at her chest.

"Agu not know. Agu only follow Koga. Koga know will of forest. Koga know he risk life of tribe if help. But perhaps worth it, if Koga can save mother."

"Thank you for telling us all of this," Alex said.

"Yes, thank you, great sir. Your parlance is invaluable to our crusade." Thistle said.

Agu stared at him in bewilderment.

"My fancy friend means ya been real helpful. I thank ya," Kyria said.

Agu nodded. "Agu believe in you. Even if other tribe not, Agu does. Agu read much of the will of the forest. Agu learn many things. It like Koga always say, knowing things sharpest spear. Agu go now, get rest."

They all waved goodbye and watched Agu disappear into the trees. Alex pondered everything Agu had told them. She hoped Koga would help them, but in the face of risking his tribe, she wasn't so sure. As she looked around, she noticed Thistle was falling asleep, and Kyria's eyes were drooping. She retrieved a blanket out of her pack and made the executive decision to go to sleep. The other two followed suit.

As Alex lay on the wood platform, looking up, she saw a single star glimmering through the canopy. She wondered if anyone was watching all of this, laughing or crying or thinking nothing at all. Despite her friends happily snoring around her, Alex felt alone. Finally, her will to sleep triumphed over her mind's chattering and sleep washed over her like a warm blanket.

It only seemed like moments later that Alex felt Kyria's hand on her shoulder shaking her awake. Alex rolled upright, bleary-eyed, swatting Kyria away like a fly. When her vision cleared ,she saw the expression of concern on her friend's face.

"What's going on?"

"Tha' witch's nasty little buggers seem ta have caught up with us," Kyria said, spitting on a nearby leaf in disgust.

"How?" Alex asked.

"Human stink," said a gorilla nearby who was holding a spear and walking towards the perimeter. He shot them a nasty glance. Agu's support of them was the minority opinion. All around them, angry gorillas stomped past, glaring at the three of them. Nothing quite makes a person feel as small as being in the center of a group of angry gorillas. Alex wanted to tell them it wasn't her fault, but she understood where they were coming from. Just because their leader made a choice didn't mean they were happy about it, especially if it risked their homes and their families.

Alex, Thistle, and Kyria looked around, and each grabbed a spear from a barrel of them nearby and headed to the perimeter of the village. As they walked through, Alex was astounded by how well built the village was. Sturdy platforms and pathways led over it, but she noticed most of the gorillas preferred to jump from branch to branch. It was as if the huts and walkways were part of the trees themselves. They arrived at the perimeter where a large group of warriors had gathered around Koga.

Koga was rallying them for battle.

Alex peered outside the village and noticed a small force had massed. They looked like people made of vines and leaves, and Alex sighed. More evil plants? If Alex ever got home, she would burn her window planter geraniums as a precaution.

Koga walked over to them. "When battle over, humans go. We cannot help. Not worth risk. Already we are discovered."

Alex opened her mouth to reply, but she realized from the look on his face, it wasn't a statement open for debate.

Alex focused on what she could control and focused on the enemy. They had multiplied now and Alex could get a better look at them. Their faces were twisted roots and gnarled vines that formed harsh sneers and scowls. They had no eyes but moved about nimbly by growing limbs out of the canopy itself. Alex could feel the Lady's foul magic swirling through them; they were extensions of her power. She didn't know how she knew, she just knew. There were hundreds now, massing on the border of Koga's spell barrier. Alex look at her friends and they looked nervous too. She felt better about being on the side with large gorilla warriors, but the plant demons still outnumbered them by a large margin.

One of the vine demons opened its mouth, and the Lady of the Wood's shrill voice echoed around the branches.

"I have outmatched you, my pet, beyond hope of victory. Surrender them and I will leave your people in peace."

This caused a great deal of howling and hooting, but Koga silenced them with a pounding on his chest and a massive roar. When he roared, the surrounding air grew still, as if it was afraid to move without permission and further offend the ancient beast.

"Mother lie. Mother always lie. If this is will of the forest, Koga will die here. But Koga will die free. Not slave like these. This is will of Koga." Another roar and the battle had begun.

The apes were frantically swinging on vines that Koga summoned and slashed and pounded the demons with all their might. Koga himself sailed from branch to branch, wielding a massive club, each swing dissolving several demons at a time. He was a master of war, but he could not keep up; they regenerated faster than he was killing them.

The plant demons had invaded the platform and Alex and her friends dispensed them. Despite having never used a spear, it came to Alex as easily as the pirate's scimitar had. She was quick, with lightning in her heels, striking with deadly poise and accuracy, each thrust destroying several evil plants. Kyria had split her spear in half, stabbing with one end while beating with the other. Thistle had abandoned the weapon altogether and was pulling them and throwing them over into the abyss below. His usual battle gusto did not disappoint.

"Haha, fiend! Take that! Die, interloper! Begone you overgrown cabbage!" he howled as he fought.

They formed an effective fighting unit, but their luck was no better. Each time they beat down or eviscerated a plant demon, it would regrow moments later. It was a battle they couldn't win, and the tide was turning.

As Koga roared as the demons overwhelmed one of his warriors, Alex saw them. The lines of energy skirted just on the edge of her vision. *About time*, she thought to herself. So far her powers only seemed to show up when absolutely necessary and they took their sweet time about it. She closed her eyes and breathed deeply, and the world slowed before her.

As she opened her eyes, she saw the world around her had changed. All around her she saw lines of energy snaking about the battlefield.

She focused on one of them and it seemed to look back at her, as if open for suggestion. She looked at a plant demon, the one about to stab Thistle in the back, and pictured it on fire.

Without hesitation, the line of energy responded and wrapped itself around the demon. Before the demon could move further, Alex pictured a roaring flame, and the energy responded, exploding into fire and roasting the screaming plant demon with it.

After it burned up, Alex waited for a moment and when it didn't regenerate, took care of the others. When she had incinerated the last of them, she paused. Everyone was staring at her in amazement. She looked around and just smiled sheepishly, unsure of what to do. All at once, a great cry erupted from the gorillas. Kyria and Thistle joined in too.

Koga swung over to their platform and approached them. For the first time since they met, Alex saw a smile on his face.

"Koga thank. You brought here for reason. Koga know that now. Koga not see mage-fire in many age, but Koga know it."

"Mage-fire?" Alex asked, looking around for an explanation.

"Legends say it was a spell of the most talented magi in ages past," Thistle answered. "And you did it so quickly. How did you do it?"

"Quickly?" Alex pondered for a moment and realized that something about... whatever these powers were, altered her perception of time, "Again, I don't know. It just happened."

"Well, I believe that this means, more than ever, we must get you to the Eastern Watch. They will sort this out," Thistle said.

"Seems only fair since the eegits' brought ya here in the first place," Kyria said with a smile. She turned to Koga. "Ya been walkin' this world for a spell or two. Any idea of how ta get to the Wyld Places?"

Koga paused and thought. The other gorillas went about clearing the debris of burned plants from their village. After a moment on pondering he spoke, "Koga not know. Even Mother not go to Wyld

Places. Too dangerous. But Koga know man who might. Old man, last of kind. Paladin of Seventh Dawn."

Kyria's eyes widened at the name, and Thistle seemed awestruck. "Good sir," he said, "you must be mistaken. They were all wiped out. The last of them died five hundred years ago."

Koga shot him an irritated glance. "Koga know what Koga know. Yes, many paladins killed by court. But one remain."

Kyria spoke up, mostly talking to herself, "Tha' is grand, just grand. He'd be a valuable ally himself, never mind what he could do for us!" She was visibly beaming with happiness.

Alex spoke up. "Anybody care to explain why these paladins are so great?"

Kyria answered, her voice echoing an almost religious reverence. "I've heard tell o' them since I was a grass sprout. Knights they were, o' the old empire, before the Fall. Immortal guardians o' humanity. Just legends now, since nobody remembers a thing before the Fall, but if there was one human breathing tha' knew how ta get ta the Wyld Places in one piece, I'd bet my last imperial marc it would be him."

"Great, so where is this fancy fellow?" Alex realized she was being snippy, but if this guy really was all that and a bag of chips, Alex wondered why they hadn't thought to go looking for him, to begin with.

"Koga last hear of him in Alcrest, in Shattered Hills." As he said it, Alex saw the look of joy and hope vanish from her friends' faces.

Alex sighed. "Let me guess, we know where this is, but it's ridiculously dangerous and we probably won't survive the journey," she asked with an eyebrow raised.

"Tha's about right Alex," Kyria said with a sigh of frustration. "Alcrest is the largest o' the slave-cities in the Shattered Hills; realm o' the Hand o' Seven," as she said his name, her nostrils flared and hatred swept into her face like a crimson tide.

114

"Great. So how do we get in?" Alex asked.

"Surely you can't be serious?" Thistle said. "We can't run headlong into the belly of the beast. There must be some other way."

Koga shook his head grimly. "If is, Koga not know about it."

"If it was easy, it wouldn't be Aquillon," Alex said with a wry smile.

Kyria chuckled and nodded her head. "Seems like there's nothing for it. Towards Alcrest we go."

"Warriors take you to edge of forest nearest border. It will take Mother time to regain strength after so many of her creatures dead. If go soon and quick, can escape before she awakens. Will go by way her demons not know."

"How can we be sure it's the edge? Won't the forest shift?" Alex asked.

"Only bottom of forest shift, part corrupted by mother. Her magic no good up here. Trees not move, only ground beneath them," Koga said.

"I see. Any suggestions about where to go once we leave?"

Koga removed a necklace of beads from around his neck, and handed it to her. "This hide your essence from pride. Still must use safe roads, avoid direct contact, but will help. Cannot tell you how to get into Alcrest, but human city close to here. Felwind. Maybe they know?"

"I've got kin in tha' part o' the world, an' some Guard contacts," Kyria said. "We should be able ta find the help we need."

Koga nodded and turned back to Alex. "Promise Koga one thing. All Koga ask in exchange for help."

Alex nodded. "Anything."

"When find a way defeat court, try save Mother. No kill if not have to. If cannot save, then let Koga end her. I son, my duty." His words echoed with profound sadness and heartbreak.

Alex smiled. At that moment she knew Koga still loved his mother, and despite all the evil she had done and become, he still desperately wanted to save her. Koga was a mighty warrior and a great leader, but beneath it all, he was still just a child who loved his mother.

"I will. You have my word," Alex said.

Koga smiled in return. He motioned for three warriors to come over and he spoke to them privately. All three turned and lowered themselves so that a rider could cling on. They mounted the warriors and waited to leave.

"Goodbye, humans. Live well. Koga hope you succeed. For all of us."

They waved goodbye to Koga. As she did, Alex felt the mighty ape beneath her jump into the branches above and they were sailing away, the village fading into the background. As they left, Alex reflected on many things; the challenges they faced ahead, if this paladin could really help them, and why her powers came and went as they pleased. There seemed to be no order or logic to it. She also held on for dear life, occasionally reminding herself that she was on the back of a gorilla sailing hundreds of feet above the ground.

Of all the things Alex had left back on Earth, Alex missed the peace of mind the most, just knowing where she was and who she was, and where she was going next. All of that was a luxury she couldn't afford here. As they sailed through the forest, the future seemed less and less certain, but Alex looked at her friends, and she took comfort in their presence.

After all, fighting apocalyptic demon armies was best done with friends.

12

The City Between Great Waters

The gorillas stopped at the edge of the forest and dropped them off. The light flooding in from beyond the tree line nearly blinded Alex. It seemed surreal, as if she was returning to reality from a dream. They were let off their respective rides, and Kyria was several shades of green lighter than the leaves nearby. She took a moment in the bushes to "reconnoiter" as Thistle put it. Riding a gorilla was not her preferred mode of transportation.

While Kyria was reliving yesterday's lunch, the lead gorilla took Alex several steps away and pushed aside a plant to reveal a small chest. Alex looked at the chest and back at the gorilla. He pointed at it and grunted. Alex shrugged and opened it with a squeal as she saw a fresh set of clothes and weapons inside. She turned to the gorilla and hugged him, or at least as much of him as her arms fit around. The gorilla rolled his eyes and snorted.

"Not me. Koga gives," he said.

"Well then, give him my thanks, and that hug," Alex replied.

Alex and Thistle equipped their new gear by the time Kyria returned from the bushes. She was grumbling and cursing while staring daggers at the gorilla who carried her. The gorilla was chuckling, trying to contain his laughter. Her mood improved however when she saw the supplies. Kyria claimed a pair of hunting knives, and Thistle grabbed a large mace. This left a long, thin scimitar for Alex. She liked the look of the weapon, and when she picked it up, she liked the feel of it even better. Below all the weapons were several small pouches of tied leaves, in which Alex assumed was food. She took them and put them in Kyria's pack.

Once they had taken the last of the supplies, the chest was slowly consumed by vines until it disappeared below the forest floor. Alex turned to thank the warriors one last time, but they had vanished silently, leaving no evidence they had ever been there. Alex smiled. She didn't know if she would ever see Koga again, but she considered herself fortunate to have met him.

Leaving the forest, a small path led out onto an open plain of rolling hills and abandoned farms. Far in the distance, beyond the edge of the Lowlands, Alex saw the sun glinting off the water. Alex pointed over the horizon to Thistle.

"The sea?" she asked.

"No, better. The Twin Sisters, Lake Telen and Lake Felen. Between them is Felwind, the last free city on the border of the realm of the Hand of Seven. If we're to find a way into Alcrest, we'll find it there."

"An' a decent night's sleep perhaps," Kyria said with a grumble.

"Isn't there a Hand in this area?" Alex asked.

"Not one, that's the beauty," Thistle said. "It's a no-man's-land for them. The Court couldn't decide who should have it, so none of them did. They still keep tabs on the area, but it's as close to a free human city as you'll find in all of Aquillon, west of the Marches anyway."

"Free..." Alex trailed off, thinking about the last time she felt free.

She was forgetting. At least she was free once. This entire world hadn't been free in a thousand years.

The group traveled in the hills and grasslands, avoiding the road, but always keeping it in sight. With the help of Koga's necklace, they seemed to have shaken the pride for now, but Alex had no wish to engage them again. Travelers on were a rare sight; a collection of hearty traders, miserable looking peasants, and the occasional pack of demons, which they hid from.

Alex marveled at the sheer variety of creatures she saw, from blood covered goatmen to demons whose skin reflected everything and who shape-shifted from one form to another. She also spotted a group of Golden Host walking along with some brainwashed cultists in tow. In the midafternoon, a group of creatures in long cloaks and masks passed by them. Wherever the creatures stepped, the ground rotted and died. If any of them had been searching for Alex, they didn't make it obvious. *Maybe the pride were the trackers of the Court,* Alex thought to herself. She wasn't complaining.

As they traveled along, Alex and Kyria got to know each other better.

"So yer an orphan?" Kyria asked Alex late in the afternoon as they meandered through
the rolling hills. It was a blunt and impolite question, but Kyria hadn't struck Alex as the type to mince words.

Alex didn't know why, but she was fine talking about it to Kyria. She had bottled her emotions up and away from foster-parents, counselors and support group meetings, but something about nearly being killed with Kyria more than a few times put her in a more trusting mood.

"Yeah. Lost my mom when I was little. My dad never told me how she died, but he always got sad when he talked about it. Mom was a truck driver, so I'm guessing it had something to do with that." It took Alex a while to explain what a truck was. "After that, it was just my dad and I.Until the fire anyway."

"What was he like?" Kyria asked.

It was a sore subject, but Alex knew losing Rex was still raw in Kyria's mind. Maybe hearing about someone else's dad would help her not think about it.

"He was the best..." she trailed off wistfully. "He raised me to be a hard worker, and fight for things worth fighting for. And he introduced me to the greatest baseball team in the world, the Boston Red Sox!" As she said this, she waved her hat around with pride. She hadn't worn it in a while, but just holding it made her feel better.

"What's a Red Sox?" Kyria asked, sounding bewildered.

Even Thistle, who was eating his plant and daydreaming looked up, intrigued.

Alex's eyes gleamed when she realized she could be the first person to introduce baseball to Aquillon one day. Alex went about explaining the sport to Kyria and Thistle, who were both enraptured by the topic.

"So, then the players may steal the next base, should they prove stealthy enough?"

Thistle asked, transfixed.

"Right, but if they get caught, they're out. So it's a risk, reward thing," Alex said.

"Fascinating! How devilishly fascinating! I should like to come to your world and see this baseball one day!"

"I'd like that, Thistle, I really would."

"Sounds like a holler," Kyria said, kicking a rock from the top of a hill into a nearby hole that looked as though a gopher had dug it. When she did, a large, ugly penguin-looking bird poked its head out and squawked angrily at her. Quicker than lightning, Kyria threw her hunting knife at it, landing squarely in between its eyes.

Kyria picked up the dead bird with a smile and said, "Dinner!"

They stopped for the night in a shallow cave, hidden away from the road. Kyria used what she had to whip up a mean penguin stew and everyone ate it in silence, too hungry to talk between bites. Alex checked on the leaf packages and they still seemed fresh. She suspected some of Koga's magic was at work . The food would be useful down the road. For tonight, greasy prairie-penguin it was.

After dinner, Thistle had rolled into his bedroll and began happily snoring away. Alex volunteered for the first watch and went to sit up at the edge of the cave. Outside the cave, a small depression in the ground formed a divot in the soil, with small hills around it, perfectly sheltering the cave from the road, but still providing a good vantage point. She sat and peered upwards from the mouth of the cave at the stars outside. Alex hadn't seen stars this pretty since she had gone camping with her dad. They had hiked deep into the Appalachians, and the sky was so clear. He called it a big bowl of diamonds, and Alex had looked at it like that ever since.

These stars were far more beautiful . The sky stretched in every direction, and out of the soft blackness of the heavens, hundreds of stars beamed into the night. The soft glow of starlight lit up the plain outside the cave and little prairie dog looking animals wandered around looking for grubs. Alex was thoroughly under the spell of the night sky when she heard Kyria speak behind her.

"Does the sky look tha' way where ya come from?" Kyria asked quietly.

"Not nearly as nice," Alex said with a smile.

"Can I join ya? I can't catch a lick o' sleep. Too worried somethin' is gonna bushwhack us and I'd jus' as soon die on my feet with my boots on."

"Sure, park it," Alex said and patted the spot next to her.

The two sat for a while in silence, just taking in the spectacle of the night sky, when Alex spoke up. "I never thanked you for coming with me. I know you're risking a lot and there were plenty of good chances to leave me twisting in the wind so... thanks."

Kyria shook her head. "Nae thanks needed. Jus' doin' what my father raised me ta do. Fight a good fight, an' tell the truth," She let out a deep sigh. "Truth is, I watched my father fight the good fight his whole life, only ta be cut down jus' like everyone else. What ya did ta those plant beasties back there? Well, I don' know what in Aquillon it was, but that's what we're gonna need if we're gonna win this war. Dad always said that courage makes for half the battle, but I been watching brave men die my whole blazin' life. I think we're gonna have ta fight smarter if we want ta take our place back in this world."

Alex nodded in silence. She enjoyed the comfortable silence for a moment and thought about what Kyria said. She might have been young, but she spoke with wisdom only suffering can teach, in the words of an older woman

"Well, thanks all the same. It's good to have a friend," Alex said.

"Aye, it is," Kyria replied.

Alex and Kyria stayed up for a while, trading questions about Earth and Aquillon. Alex felt her eyelids getting heavy so she and Kyria wandered back in the cave and woke Thistle, who, with some grumbling, took their place. As soon as her head hit the bedroll, she fell deeply asleep and did not wake for anything until the dazzling sunlight of morning flooded the cave hours later.

Several days of traveling brought them to the end of the Lowlands. Alex and her friends stood on the crest of a hill, close to the road. Below them, a massive valley spread out between two of the biggest lakes Alex had ever seen. The mammoth bodies of water glinted and glimmered in the sunlight. Little black dots of fishing boats moved about the lake and at the edge of the valley, on a thin patch of land between the two lakes, stood Felwind. As they traveled closer the details of the city came into full view.

A great stone wall surrounded the city of Felwind on all sides. The walls looked old but sturdy; time had done little to wear them away. Everything else outside the walls was new and hastily assembled. Once they neared the gates, a teaming ocean of merchants and hawkers greeted them and spent a long while trying to sell them a variety of goods. The merchants had set up shops in tents and rickety wooden shacks outside the city, and it surprised Alex to see so many goods for sale. Felwind seemed to be the only city in Aquillon not in a state of destitute poverty.

As they walked into the city, Kyria spoke up. "All right. Hopefully, my Guard contact is still around these parts... assumin' he 'asn't pickled his liver yet."

Reassuring, Alex thought.

Small children ran between stalls, grabbing what they could before the merchants could see them. Kyria moved quickly between them, waving their goods and offers away. She was looking for someone or something. After a moment, she walked to an old man who sat on a barrel eating a large pickle. Kyria kicked him.

"Whoosunit," he said, stammering.

As soon as she got within five feet of him, Alex gagged at the stench wafting up from

him. Part booze, part sewer, part body odor and part... lavender?

"Wake up Horace, ya ol' drunk," Kyria said in a voice that hid her amusement poorly. Horace looked up at her, and from his facial expression, seemed a little unsure of what he was looking at.

"Are you a fish?" As he spoke, an equally stomach-churning smell drifted towards Alex. She tried her best to hold down breakfast.

"Oh, gods," Kyria winced and rubbed her temples. "We need ta get him ta some water." Kyria looked around and pointed towards a small barrel of water. Alex and Thistle assisted dragging Horace over to the barrel and plopping him down in the mud. Lifting the barrel, the three of them dumped the contents onto Horace, who shot up with a shriek of a terrified-four-year-old girl.

"I'll have at you!" he said while trying to swing at Thistle.

"Sit down before ya fall down ol' man," Kyria yelled. She grabbed him by his collar and pulled him over to the barrel of pickles he had been sitting on. "It's Kyria. Rex's girl." She spoke carefully and slowly, but despite this, it seemed like Horace only picked up about half of it.

Horace squinted for a moment from behind ratty black bangs that obscured his vision. He had a sunburned face and his teeth were yellow, somewhere between a lemon and mustard. After another moment, a large toothy grin engulfed his face and his sprang up and grabbed Kyria in a huge bear-hug. She squirmed and tried to punch him, but there was no avoiding or escaping the hug.

"Kyria, my girl! It's been too long. Tell me, how's your father?"

A pang of sadness hit Alex in the gut. From his expression, she realized the news of Rex's death hadn't traveled far. Kyria held it together and answered.

"We 'ave a lot ta discuss, but no' here. Can ya take us ta the safe house?"

"Of course. We shouldn't stay out here anyway," he said, eyeing the market with suspicion. "Felwind isn't as friendly a town as it used to be."

Alex and Thistle followed Kyria and Horace into the city. For the first time since arriving in Aquillon, Alex was somewhere alive, not just existing, but truly alive. The city buzzed with life and Alex smiled at the sound of people talking and socializing. Crowded cobblestone streets and homes pushed too closely together filled the city. Humans from all walks of life moved about. As she walked, Alex took in the city's noise and smiled. It had been too long since she had been around humans talking and just, being human.

As they walked down the street, she saw two figures coming towards them. They owore flowing crimson and orange robes with masks that obscured their faces in the likeness of foxes. It painted a sneer onto their features. As soon as Kyria and Horace saw them they ducked down a side street and Alex and Thistle followed.

"Demons?" Alex asked.

"Nae. Worse." Kyria responded. "Members o' the Fox Guild. Humans who made a fortune tradin' with the court. Worse than demons, traitors ta their own kind. Foxes deal in slaves, weapons, an' anythin' that will turn a profit. They'd sell us ta the Court in a heartbeat."

"That's despicable," said Alex. She hadn't considered that humans might work with the court. It made grim sense. There were always ways to make money in a desperate situation if you didn't find yourself burdened with an overactive moral compass.

After their close call with the foxes, they steered clear of main streets until they arrived at an ordinary-looking house. Kyria knocked on the door and a slat opened. A narrow pair of eyes peered at her and a harsh voice croaked.

"We're not buying meat today!"

"Good news then! I'm sellin' vegetables!" Kyria responded to the unknown voice.

"What kind?"

"All kinds. Perfect for stew."

"Come in and share a bowl then."

Alex had seen enough spy movies to know a code when she heard one. She also hoped they had stew. Gopher-bird can only get a stomach so far.

The door opened slowly but the eyes never left them. The eyes belonged to a stout little man in dark clothes who looked at them suspiciously. He held a crossbow out.

"What gives, Ralph? We spoke the code." Horace said.

"She," he pointed his crossbow at Kyria, "spoke it. You are drunk, as usual, and I don't know who these people are," His voice was a gruff accusation.

"They're friends o' the Guard. Jus' let us in already. I'm Rex's little girl. Would I lie ta ya?"

Ralph's nose ruffled a little. "I suppose not. We've been on high alert since the fall of the stone-moot. We take extra precautions. My condolences about your father."

Horace spoke up, "Rex died? Why doesn't anyone tell me anything?"

Ralph rolled his eyes in disgust. "If you could occasionally find your way out of the bottom of a bottle and stumble into the safe house, we would be able to catch you up on things," he said. "Come inside. You're safe, for now." He aimed the last two words at Alex and Thistle.

They walked into the darkness and down a long descending path of stairs. On the surrounding walls were old portraits of regal knights in blazing red armor, charging on mighty warhorses. Candles burned around them. Alex assumed these were the heroes of the Old Guard.

Kyria saw Alex looking at them intently and explained. "The founding praetorians o' the

ten legions of the old empire. They brought us to order and law from chaos, an' saved the empire a hundred times over, or so the legends tell." Alex could hear the wonder and reverence in Kyria's voice, like a kid talking about her favorite superheroes.

"I guess everybody's got, heroes. At least yours were probably real. They seem incredible, or at least they paid their portrait artists well," Alex said with a chuckle.

Kyria shot her a nasty look and Alex made a mental note to tell any more praetorian jokes. Kyria composed herself and continued speaking.

"Their strength gives us strength, even now, a thousand years after the court cut them down. Every man, woman, an' child o' the Guard lives our lives in their image."

At the bottom of the staircase, a large space opened. They were beneath the city now, at least several stories deep. The safe house looked similar to the stone-moot, only more modern. Wooden buildings about a story high lined the cavern and lanterns hung out of windows. People bustled about a central square, but they stopped when they saw the party of people descending. Above them, a dark opening stretched up into the darkness and the noise of the city bustling about echoed into the cavern below.

Word of their arrival seemed to have preceded them. As Kyria walked into the square a silence passed over the crowd. They all crossed one arm over their chest and bowed towards her. Kyria did the same and Alex saw tears welling in her eyes. Alex grabbed her shoulder and squeezed reassuringly, and Kyria smiled back at her. From out of the crowd, an older-looking woman in dark clothes approached them.

The woman's hair was gray and pulled back into a tight bun. Her face was sharp and worn with years of worry and strife but they had not softened her eyes at all; they were gray falcons on a clear day, surveying the area relentlessly. She smiled at Kyria and caught her up in a hug which Kyria returned. Her sharp gray eyes never left Alex and Thistle.

"My dear, I am so sorry about Rex. We feared all was lost when we were told about the pride breaching the safe house, but your return to us is a greater gift than we could have hoped for." The woman spoke in a soft, measured tone as if assessing the strategic value of each word before she spoke it.

"Good ta see ya too," Kyria said. "It's been a long, strange trip, and we're no' nearly done. We need yer help."

"For you dear, anything," she said, smiling, "but we will need to learn who your friends are first. After the stone-moot fell, we've been taking great precautions." Her voice had lost all of its warmth and she was staring at Alex with lethal intent.

"They're good folk. I wouldn't 'ave made it ta ya if not for them. She's the girl from Vandlehelm, and he's an honorable knight in her service."

All at once, the woman's demeanor changed, and she transfixed Alex with her piercing gaze. "So you're the one that has the Court all in a tizzy. It's a pleasure to meet you! I'm Salarana Helton, but everybody just calls me Sal."

Alex clasped arms with her.

They followed Sal back to her office, or what looked like an office, and took seats. Sal poured them a cup of hot tea from a nearby kettle and Alex sipped it happily. It warmed Alex and helped put her mind at ease.

"So, what can the Old Guard do for you all?" Sal asked.

"We're lookin' for a Paladin o' the Seventh Dawn. We heard a rumor tha' one might still live in Alcrest," Kyria said.

Sal smirked. "You'd save yourselves a lot of trouble by just buying a storybook of the old legends because that's the only place you'll find one. Paladin in Alcrest? Bah! Pure fiction! If there was one alive, we would have found them by now. We have spies in Alcrest and they've reported nothing like that."

Alex spoke up. "Our source is reliable. I'd bet my life on it."

"Well, that's all well and good, but I'm not willing to bet mine or any of my fighters. Kyria, you buy this hogwash?" Sal asked.

"I wish I didn't, but I do. I trust the source too, an' we need ta get into Alcrest."

Sal chewed on their words for several moments before responding.

"How about you, pig-man? What's your story?"

"Ran afoul of a Hand. He made me this way, and I plan on serving him his comeuppance personally. And for what it's worth, I believe it too. Besides, where the Lady Winters goes, Sir Thistle goes," he announced gallantly.

Alex grunted and rolled her eyes at him. Kyria continued, "We don' need soldiers, we wouldn't ask. I know resources are thin right now. We jus' need a way into Alcrest. The Court has bounties on our heads, so stealth would be preferable. I doubt we'd be able ta walk in with our heads remaining this pretty. Well…" she glanced at Thistle, who snorted indignantly.

Sal paused a moment and then produced a pipe, filled it with tobacco, and struck a match. Kyria looked at her with an upturned eyebrow.

"Ish my tinkin' pipe," Sal said with a mouth full of pipe, responding to Kyria's unspoken question. Sal continued to puff away on her thinking pipe and finally responded again. "Aye, there may be a way," she said, removing the pipe from her mouth, "but it'd be near certain suicide and I'd not be doing Rex one blasted favor by sending his little girl off on a fool's errand."

"Well, it's a good thing he didn't raise a daughter who couldn't handle a tall order," Alex responded with a smile. "He died so we could get out. He gave his life because he believed that I'm the key to ending this war. I need to journey to the Wyld Places, and only a paladin can help. Please, Sal, I know we're young but, Kyria wouldn't ask if I wasn't sure. You know that."

She paused for a moment longer before continuing. "Rex really believed in this?" she asked, redirecting the question to Kyria.

"Aye, He did. An' so do I," she said.

"Well, your daddy wasn't a fool, nor was he given to pointless acts of heroism. He enjoyed living too much. I'll assume the same is true of you." Sal sighed and raised an eyebrow as if finally giving in to the foolishness with muted resignation. "Only way you're gonna sneak into Alcrest is in disguise, but it must be one they can't remove, at least not physically."

"And that means what?" Alex asked, a tone of concern in her voice.

"Calm down, it wears off, usually. You happy bunch will pay old Maggie a visit."

"Oh, nae!" Kyria said, "I 'aven't been back there since I was a wee sprout, an' I got no plans on puttin' my hide back in tha' swindler's claws!"

"Wait, a minute? Who is old Maggie?" Alex asked.

"Vile witch that lives out on the lake. Sells potions and other things to them that have the patience to deal with her," Sal replied.

Thistle shifted around uncomfortably. "I've heard tell of witches out in the wilds of Aquillon. Unsavory characters, the lot of them. Best we steer clear of her."

"What are you afraid of, that she'll turn you all pig?" Sal asked him with a smirk on her face.

"Yes," replied Thistle indignantly as he munched on a patch of his plants.

"Look, Maggie aint' half as bad as she used to be, and if you want to get into Alcrest alive, she's the only option I can think of," Sal said.

Kyria and Thistle seemed less than thrilled and were about to launch a fresh set of protests, when Alex spoke up, ending the discussion.

"We'll see her. How do we get there?"

"Well now that," Sal said, chuckling, "will take some doing."

Alex sighed. *Why wasn't the potion witch ever just next door, preferably next to a bakery?*

13

Old Maggie's Potion and Discount Rabbit Emporium

Some doing, as Sal put it, involved a boat ride into the center of the lake, kidnapping and an old shoe.

They spent the night in the Guard safe house, and Alex was glad for it. She felt a sense of peace knowing, for the moment, that the pride didn't know where they were.

That night the Guard threw them a welcome party. With the gravity of everything going on, Alex wasn't in a partying mood. The people seemed like they needed a chance to blow off steam and relax, and she would not get in the way of that. The soldiers brought large kegs of beer out and a spit-roasting pig (which seemed a touch insensitive to Thistle, but he seemed ok with it). The soldiers produced a small band's worth of instruments, and in no time at all, the party was roaring and Alex was smiling as she sipped some water and helped herself to some pork.

Alex smiled as she watched the guardsman and their families cut loose. It was good to relax, even if it was only for an evening. Kyria whirled on the dance floor and knocked back several drinks quickly.

Alex idly wondered if there was a drinking age in Aquillon, but if there was, she knew nobody would object to Kyria breaking it. The girl had earned a few drinks.

"A dance m'lady?"

Alex looked up and realized Thistle was standing over her with his hand extended out in a very dashing and chivalrous manner.

"No way, I don't dance," she said. Before she could protest further, however, he had scooped her up and off they whirled around the makeshift dance floor. She remembered awkward dances in middle school, but this was somehow better, despite her partner being a pigman. As they careened across the dance floor, she grinned wider and wider until finally, she was laughing uncontrollably. It felt good to have fun, and to be somewhere other than the center of some epic war with demon lords and noble heroes.

After a while of twirling and dancing, she sat down, feeling dizzy and uncoordinated. Her sides hurt from laughter, and her head was still spinning, but she hadn't stopped smiling. Thistle was a good dancer, despite being half pig and middle-aged. He sat down next to her.

"You are quite the dervish, Ms. Winters. Thank you for indulging an old knight. That took me back to my younger, better days," Thistle said with a grin.

Alex smiled back at him. "Where did you learn to dance like that anyway, Sir Fancy-Feet?"

"I wasn't always an overweight pigman or a knight for that matter, but that's a longer story than we have time for.".

Alex shrugged. "It doesn't look like we need to be anywhere for a while ."

"A long time ago there was a boy who lived by the sea. He kept to his farming and his family. He flirted with girls, he danced, he loved. Until a shadow came over that land and it took everything from him.

He protected those he loved, but he ran. When the smoke cleared, and he counted the bodies, he was empty. He had nothing and no one to blame but his own cowardice. So he set out to make it right. He set out to make a difference."

"Well?"

Thistle looked like he snapped out a dream as he spoke. "Well, what?"

"Did he?" Alex asked.

"I'll let you know," he said with a wry smile.

Alex nodded and punched his shoulder playfully. "Tell me something else. Do you really think we have a shot or are you following me out of some misguided sense of guilt?"

"Where there are people like you who stand up and say enough, there will always be, as you say, a shot."

"I hope so. It'd be a shame to come this far for nothing," Alex said with a chuckle.

"While you draw breath, my dear, we've got a shot. I know that as much as I have ever known anything," Thistle said calmly.

"Thanks, I wish I was as confident as you."

They sat in silence for a while. His confidence honored her, but it also made her nervous. She had gotten her powers to work twice, but there had been no method behind the madness. They showed up when they wanted to and didn't when they didn't. If these magi were able to explain that alone, it would be worth the trip.

She slept uneasily that night. Sal shook her awake in the morning, but it seemed to Alex like she had only slept a few hours. Thistle was already up and getting ready, and Kyria looked like she had hardly slept. The Guard was kind enough to equip them with fresh supplies before they left, and Alex figured it was some kind of parting gift. She doubted she would be back in the safe house, or Felwind, any time soon.

Outside the safe house, the weather was stunning. There was a light breeze and not a single cloud in the sky. Alex's dad used to call it God's weather because he said he knew God had nothing to do with typical Boston weather. They walked down to the eastern edge of town and the crowded buildings and the bustling city opened up into a teeming wharf of fisherman's ships, and small merchant vessels. From the top of the hill leading down into the wharf, Alex could see more of the lake. Felwind nestled itself on a thin strip of land between the two massive lakes. On the western side of town, an equally busy wharf buzzed with life and commotion.

A group of guardsmen, accompanied by Horace (who wasn't even remotely sober - a fact Alex hoped had something to do with an elaborate cover identity) shadowed them as they walked down to the wharf. Alex saw no foxes, but Felwind had its fair share of shady looking characters. Alex made a point of not throat-punching every slimeball who catcalled her as they walked.

By the time they had reached the wharf, merchants had offered Alex seventeen different things (which she almost bought), including a bizarre multi-headed, purple cat that the merchant swore would bring her seven years of good luck. They walked past a dozen houses out of which multiple families were living. It reminded Alex of the tenement housing she had heard of in the 1900s New York. The families seemed crammed into the buildings, which were fairly grimy, but everyone seemed happy enough.

At the wharf, the Guard departed, and Horace said his goodbyes and wandered into an alley where he slipped and fell into a pile of old fish. He did not move from the spot.

"So, I'm assuming you know how to get to this Old Maggie?" Alex asked.

Kyria mumbled something inaudible and balled her fists.

"Speak up, dear. The rest of the class can't hear you," Alex chided.

She grumbled for a moment. "Yes. Sal told me, an' it hasn't changed, unfortunately. We need ta get a boat."

They took a while, but they eventually found a bored looking man sitting by his boat. He didn't seem inviting or all that reputable, but there seemed to be a lack of other boats potentially for hire.

Kyria put on her cheesiest smile. "Hey sailor!"

Alex rolled her eyes. She had a lot to learn about flirting.

"Doesn't look like yer boat's getting much use today. How about ya give me and my friends a ride out onto tha' lake?"

He looked her over and rolled his eyes, immune to her wiles. "Pleasure cruise, huh? Five marcs."

Kyria's indignant expression told Alex that a five marc price was highway robbery, or in this case, waterway robbery. Kyria was about to say something Alex suspected would prevent them from using the man's boat, so she cut her off at the pass.

"Well, that's a fair price, friend, but we have the location on some imperial gold marcs that sunk on a trader ship out on the lake. Take us out and we'll split the profits fifty-fifty. Just think, you'll be filthy rich this time tomorrow!"

He raised his eyebrow for a moment as he considered the offer but shook his head.

"No deal. I don't trust treasure maps or any such hokum."

"We'll throw in our trusty man-slave? He's part pig so you can feed him acorns and beat him when he gets cross," Alex retorted.

Kyria almost burst in giggles but held it together. Thistle, meanwhile, had a foul grimace on his face but played along.

"Whatever the ladyship wishes. I live to serve," Thistle said with as much gusto as he was able to manage.

The fisherman paused for a moment and then nodded. "Could use me a good man-slave to scale the fish and haul the guts out. Deal. The Guppy and her cap'n are yours for the afternoon!"

After a while of rigging and tying off ropes, the ship was ready. A breeze rushed through the docks and the smell of fish wafted about in the afternoon sun. It reminded Alex of Boston Harbor, although she hadn't missed the fishy smell. Sunlight glimmered off the water and reflected from the docks onto the houses nearby. Painted in a kaleidoscope of cheerful colors, the houses' color shimmered along the waves of the lake. Despite everything, these people still expressed themselves. Then she noticed something she wished she hadn't. Three figures in flowing orange robes and fox masks were rapidly making their way towards the docks with a purpose.

"Guys, I think we should leave soon, Alex said. "Now would be good, in fact. Now is looking better and better!" As Alex said this, she motioned with her eyes toward the high street where the foxes were coming down from.

Kyria turned to the captain. "Are we almost ready?" She tried to hide the panic in her voice.

"Almost, just need to rig this safety net. Wouldn't want such fine, fancy ladies getting thrown overboard by a squall."

Alex looked around at the clear blue sky. *Right. Squall.*

"We're not worried about it! Really, we'll be fine!" Alex sounded more urgent than she wanted to, but the foxes were closing fast.

"Well, all right, if you insist. Climb aboard," he said with a shrug.

They climbed aboard the boat and the captain cast off. As the sail dropped, and a breeze caught it, Alex looked back at the dock. The foxes were speaking with several fishermen who were pointing in their direction. Someone had sold them out. This didn't really surprise Alex. Just because Felwind was free didn't mean it was free of desperate people who would turn them in. The foxes walked calmly to the edge of the dock and she saw that one, a tall man, was smiling at her and she saw him mouth words, but she couldn't hear him. They turned, seeming to have lost interest for now, and returned whence they had come.

They took the better part of an hour to reach the center of the lake. Once they arrived near the center of the lake, they stopped at Kyria's request. She told the captain she wanted to take the sun in to warm her delicate complexion. She then made a gagging face to Alex.

Waiting until weighing the anchor distracted him, Kyria smacked him with the pommel of her hunting knife. He keeled over, but Kyria caught him before he fell overboard.

"Kyria. Why exactly did you just knock our captain out?" Alex asked, trying to remain calm.

"Alex, help, this eegit' weighs more than I thought!"

She scrambled over to help her.

"He tipped the foxes off about us. He was jus' waitin' till they came back ta ambush us. I figured I'd strike while the anvil is hot. That's the expression ya told me, aye?" Kyria said cheerfully.

"So," Alex said, "what's our plan for getting back to shore? Also, in the future, can we have a policy of bludgeoning civilians after someone has informed the group? I really feel like it will help make the body hauling more efficient." She rolled her eyes, and they lugged the captain towards the door leading to the lower decks.

Kyria shrugged as they, with Thistle's help, threw the captain down below. Kyria locked the door to the lower quarters and returned. Before she did, she tossed a single gold coin in the door after him.

"So about getting back to shore? I'm a little rusty at captaining small ships," Alex said.

"If this goes the way we want it ta, we won' need ta worry about it," Kyria said.

"And if it doesn't?"

"Well then, a lack o' a captain will be the least of our worries."

"Ladies," Thistle interjected.

They turned but before he could say anything. They saw the reason he was getting their attention. A large ship, moving quickly on the wind was coming their way. Three fox guild members stood on the prow, smiling.

"Ok, here goes. If anybody's listenin'," Kyria looked towards the sky, "please let this work." She tossed another gold coin in the center of the lake, and then inexplicably threw a boot which she had recovered from the captain, in after it.

The foxes were closing in now as their small vessel raced over the clear waters of the lake.

"Any time Kyria!" Alex said with a tone of increasing urgency.

"I did what I was supposed ta, now if tha' no account, low life, skull-duggin..."

Before Kyria could finish whatever string of colorful adjectives might have followed, a low hissing sound echoed around the lake. Alex looked at the area from where it had come and saw a line shimmering in the air, like a mirage. Before long, the image of an island appeared. By the time it had fully materialized, the foxes and their vessel were within striking distance, and

Alex felt a thud as two star shaped blades on the end of long chains dug their way into the ship. With a great tug, the foxes pulled themselves forward in the air, landing gracefully on the deck. Thistle had already drawn his mace, but Kyria shook her head,

"Time ta go!" She pulled him by the scruff of his neck backwards and then jumped overboard. Kyria was a scrappy fighter, so if she wasn't staying to fight these Fox Guild soldiers, neither was Alex. She followed suit and leaped off the boat towards the island, and Thistle soon followed. As she passed through the shimmering barriers, the details of the island took shape, and the first thing Alex saw was Kyria arguing heatedly with a beautiful brown-haired woman in a long, shimmering green dress.

"Listen here, ya half-baked hag," Kyria said.

"Well, I never! The nerve!" the woman yelled back.

"If ya don't close this rift, there won't be nobody ta bargain with anyway," Kyria said, pointing frantically at the rapidly approaching Foxes.

The woman's eyes flared, and she threw her hands up. Just as the fighter leaped toward the island, the barrier faded and Alex saw them hit the water, cursing. Outside the barrier, the image shifted. A great sea now surrounded them, Felwind, and the foxes were nowhere in sight.

Alex stood up slowly, getting her bearings. The island was larger than it had first appeared, but it was still small enough to walk around inside an hour. A sandy beach ran the length of the island, but as she looked further inland, tall grass swayed in the ocean breeze. Large stones jutted out here and there and palm trees rocked back and forth. A small thatch hut and campsite were barely visible in the distance, and a tiny pool nearby gushed blue water. It seemed like something out of a postcard, only missing a hula dancer and beach chairs. Everything seemed normal, except the rabbits.

All over the island, hundreds of rabbits hopped about lazily, grazing on grass and staring vacantly into the distance. Once in a while, one would hop into the water, roll around, and then hop back out. They seemed as cute and fluffy as earth rabbits, but knowing Aquillon, Alex was sure they had razor fangs and spit acid.

Kyria and the woman had concluded their argument like adults; they were both several hundred feet from one another, arms crossed and staring holes into the ground in the opposite direction. Alex sighed. She approached the woman. Thistle was talking Kyria down with some success.

"Hello there," Alex said, smiling.

The woman turned coldly and nodded at her.

"Nice rabbits you have here."

She seemed to perk up at the compliment. She cocked her head and said, "you really think so? No one is ever really impressed with them. You're the first one in a long time to even mention my poor darlings." She lingered on the word 'poor' a little too long, like a rich woman speaking about a prized poodle.

"Yes, they're quite something," Alex said, trying to create a rapport with her. She hoped it was working because there was only so much you can say about rabbits.

"Aren't they though…" Her voice, which was sickeningly sweet, trailed off wistfully. "Oscar here is getting superb at counting!" She picked up a very fat, black rabbit and set it down near several piles of stones. "Show mummy three, Oscar!" She cooed and waited. The rabbit sat idly staring at Alex for a while before pooping several pellets and hopping off into a bush. "Well, he gets performance anxiety," she said, with a sigh.

"That makes perfect sense," Alex said, nodding her

"So right it does my dear! So, what can I do for you?"

"Well, we're looking for Old Maggie…"

"People still call me that?" she asked, sighing deeply.

Alex stepped back and looked at her. "Old" Maggie didn't appear a day over thirty. Long, silky, brown hair cascaded down petite shoulders. Her skin was smooth and well taken care of, with perfectly manicured nails. Her eyes were curious emeralds, gleaming in every direction, and her lips had a coy smile that never seemed to match her eyes. Her smile was inviting enough, but her eyes revealed an agenda of their own.

"Well, that is what *some* people call you, but I see the name hardly does you justice!" Alex smiled at her as they spoke.

In the distance, Kyria sat on a rock, shooing off rabbits as she ate

OLD MAGGIE'S POTION AND DISCOUNT RABBIT EMPORIUM

a piece of cured meat. Thistle sat idly by munching his plants. They kept their distance, leaving the negotiating for Alex. The compliment had somewhat unruffled Maggie's feathers, but she still seemed to pout.

"Well, I'm glad there's one civilized soul left in that realm of roughians! There's a reason I rarely bring my island into their realm. My poor babies can't handle the stress, their fur falls out, they stop eating..."

Alex looked around. Most of the rabbits could stand to stop eating for a while. Several were so fat they had ceased any attempt at hopping. She took a moment to process what Maggie said.

"Wait. You mean we're not in Aquillon?" Alex asked.

Maggie giggled. "No, my dear. Far outside it! You could swim for a thousand years in any direction and you'd never find anything except this island."

"A spell?" Alex asked.

"No, it's just this place. It's just a step removed from the dance of the rest of the world. I found it years ago, and whenever I want it to, it jumps back to Aquillon. I can't leave it..." as she said this, tears welled up in her eyes. "But, why would you want to?" She asked this to no one in particular.

Alex looked around at the sand, the rabbits and the rocks. *An eternity on a rabbit filled tropical island? Who could say no to that?* Alex thought to herself.

"I fear we've gotten terribly off topic. What can I do for you?" Maggie asked, turning back to her.

"We need disguises. Ones no one could remove. I'm told you're a potion maker of great skill?"

"I am! My main job is being a mother to my sweet angels, but a girl must have hobbies. I can make the potion you require. But I won't." As she spoke, she made a sour face at Kyria.

"Look, I know there's some bad blood between you and the Guard, but this is important!" Alex implored.

"That's what they all say! That's what those Old Guard thugs said when they came here for help! Then they ruined my reputation and worse, they insulted my rabbits! Called them mangy and flea-bitten," Maggie said. Her voice was an angry growl.

"Isn't there any way we could convince you to assist us?"

Maggie paused and pouted her lips, thinking. Then she smiled and Alex had a feeling Kyria would not like her price.

"I will help on two conditions. One: that one (she waggled an angry finger at Kyria) will apologize to myself and my rabbits. Two: The Guard will agree to a binding adoption of no less than twenty rabbits, for two marcs each. Not for food, only for companionship."

Alex looked puzzled. "I thought you loved your babies?"

"Oh, my dear, I do! But the trouble is, I get so few customers and the rabbits will, well, be rabbits, and I end up with so many offspring. It would be good to have a little coin to spruce up the place. Besides, this is Maggie's Potions and Discount Rabbits after all, and if I sell no rabbits, how will I advertise? It's just good business all around."

Alex sighed. While getting the Guard to adopt twenty bouncing, furry bundles of joy might not have been too hard, getting Kyria to apologize was another matter. Alex looked over to where she was sitting, hoping her mood had improved. She was still sitting on the rock, sharpening her hunting knives. A rabbit made the poor choice of hopping in front of her and she gave it a glare so terrifying if dropped several pellets, squeaked, and scurried away. Alex took this as a bad sign but made her way over all the same. *This should be fun,* she thought.

Kyria saw her and grunted.

"How go negotiations with tha' guttersnipe?"

Yup. She was in an apologizing mood all right.

"Fine. We may have reached a deal."

Kyria cocked an eyebrow.

"The Guard just has to "adopt" twenty rabbits for two marcs each, and," Alex said. She dropped her voice before continuing, "You have to apologize," Alex's voice dropped off quietly at the end, hoping Kyria hadn't heard it and would just agree.

"What? Of all the arrogant, vile, low-life…"

She had.

"unreasonable, nae good…"

Alex cut her off. "Look, I get that ya'll have bad blood, but couldn't you just put it aside for this? You've risked your life for this mission dozens of times already; what's an apology? Besides, what did she do to you people? She seems harmless."

As soon as she had asked, Alex regretted it. A storm cloud was brewing on Kyria's face.

"Oh, she…" She took a moment to gain the composure to tell the story. "We used ta deal with her for potions. Healing potions an' invisibility vials an' whatnot. Everything was fine an' dandy until one day, a guardsman is here, business as usual. One o' these stupid, nae good, rotten, flea-bitten piles o' no account tomfoolery (Alex was getting impressed with Kyria's ability to string colorful adjectives together) bit him in the leg for no reason. So, he curses at it, calls it some names, an' moves on. Didn't even kick the thing! Nae problem."

Kyria took a breath and continued.

"Well, that one," she waggled an equally angry finger at Maggie "hears him and decides ta get back at him by swapping the healing potions out for digestive aid potions. And ya don' want ta know what the invisibility potions did.

Alex did but there wasn't time to ask.

"So after the debacle, we stopped buying there an' made sure others did too! And it's a matter o' honor Alex. We aren't in the wrong, so

I'm no' apologizin'."

Alex sighed.

"Look, that all sounds about right, given my interactions with her, but sometimes in life, we have to be the adult when the other person won't. We need her help and if the worst that comes out of it is you saying an apology you don't mean, and the Guard having to adopt some stupid rabbits, I think it's worth it," she said with a grin.

Kyria mulled it over for a while and finally nodded and grumbled. "Yer a wise one, Alex Winters. Fine, I'll do it. Can we at least eat some o' the stupid beasts?"

Alex shook her head.

"Gah!" Kyria threw her hand up in the air. "Let's just get this over with."

They walked over to Maggie who was idly picking rabbits up and attempting to arrange them in a straight line. It wasn't working at all, as they kept hopping away from her, but that wasn't stopping her from trying.

"All right, Maggie, we've agreed to your terms," Alex said.

She turned around and eyed Kyria suspiciously. "All of them?" she asked, emphasizing all.

Kyria grumbled. "Aye, all o' them'"

A wide, cat-like grin rolled across Maggie's face and she stood, folding her arms and waited.

"I, we, the Old Guard, apologize for any trouble we may 'ave caused." She tried to end her apology there, but Maggie gestured for her to go on. "An' any reputations, human or rabbit, that we may 'ave sullied, an' we will no' do so again, even if one o' them wee babies bite us," Kyria finished, looking as if she had just eaten something unpleasant.

Maggie paused for a moment, considering the merit of the apology. She smiled again and said, "apology accepted! Now we can do business! So, you need three potions of hidden face. That we can do."

She looked over to where Thistle was building a sand-castle. "Better have two for him." She whistled, and a gargantuan rabbit waddled over. She cooed at him and then rubbed his throat. The rabbit hacked for a moment and then regurgitated four small vials of orange liquid. Alex looked horrified, but Kyria seemed to have seen this trick before. Maggie cleaned them off with her dress and handed them to Alex, who promptly stored them in her pack.

"Now they'll work for only a week, so whatever business you need your face hidden for, make sure it's handled by then."

They nodded.

"Do we need to deliver the rabbits for you?" Alex asked.

"No dear, I'll make sure they get where they're going. Speaking of..." She extended her arm and the wall of shimmering energy appeared again, the image of the lake coming back into focus. This time they were on the eastern shore, far from Felwind, and the foxes.

A small path of stone rose from the water. Alex packed up to leave the island. As she did, she turned to Maggie.

"Can I ask you a question?"

Maggie nodded.

"Why the boot? I get the coin, but why the boots?" There was a lot going on, but Alex had to know.

"Oh, I learned long ago that people with one shoe are more honest in business transactions," Maggie replied sagely like she had read it in *Forbes*. "I made an exception for you," she said with a wink.

Alex pondered the odd response and turned back, but the island had already vanished. They crossed the stones, which vanished as they reached the shore of the lake and collected their belongings to make ready for the trip.

Kyria sighed. "I almost feel bad for her, trapped out there for all eternity."

Alex looked at her with a raised eyebrow.

"A long time ago she took a boat, an' wandered out there with two o' her pet rabbits. Just some farm girl who stumbled on ta the wrong patch o' ground. It trapped her from tha' point on, an' she was cursed ta watch the world turn, an' all o' her friends die. That's why they call her Old Maggie. She'll be there long after we're gone."

"And the island?" Alex asked.

"Who knows? There's magic in Aquillon that's older than humans by a spell or two. Like the stone-moots. Things leftover from a time long since gone."

"We are but glittering fireflies in the cosmos of eternity. Beautiful for but a moment, but finite to the last." Thistle said.

Alex and Kyria both looked at him, a look of surprise on their faces.

"What? My brain isn't all bacon yet."

The three burst into laughter.

Collecting themselves, they struck out on the next leg of their journey. As they put Felwind behind them, Alex thought about Maggie. Such a lonely life, and all because she wandered onto the wrong patch of earth. Just in the wrong place at the wrong time, trapped by forces beyond her control. Alex could relate. Still, she had to smile picturing Sal standing next to a crate of rabbits. Maggie may have been crazy, Alex thought, but she sure knew how to settle a score.

14

Alcrest, City of Chains

Within days they had left the lowlands entirely and entered a region Thistle called the Shattered Hills. The atmosphere changed almost instantly.

The lowlands were bleak, but still beautiful in their own way, and humans seemed to have carved out simple existences. Not here. The Lord of Long Shadows' domain was cold and unforgiving. Nothing grew, outside of sparse grass and sickly trees. Where hills had once sloped gracefully, hollowed out pits scarred by mining and charred by flames remained, like shallow graves of the natural world.

The demons had decimated the natural world, but it wasn't the only thing that had been destroyed. Chains with skeletal remains littered the landscape. The only remnants of the slaves or their masters were massive stone statues depicting an upright lion in armor, wielding the crescent axes Alex had seen the Pride carrying. It felt to Alex as if the statues themselves radiated a singular message: *Your lives are not your own. You belong to me.*

"It chills the blood to return to these lands," Thistle remarked quietly.

"You've been here?" Alex asked.

"As a boy, I passed through these lands. I have never forgotten the horrors I saw here. Only by the grace of the gods and a little dumb luck I avoided capture," he said, his voice without levity or joy.

The deeper they passed into the Shattered Hills the worse things got. Alex saw no trace of life, and everywhere the remains of hills and mountains haunted the landscape, forlorn ghosts of the land that once had been.

The group passed yet another quarry littered with the remains of more workers. Alex tried not to let her gaze linger, but the remnants of human suffering surrounded her. Sadness weighed down over the land like thick smoke, pressing on her chest, making it hard to breathe. As they traveled, the statues continued too, in all sizes, but always the same. The Lord of Long Shadows watched over every inch of his domain.

"Why do all of this?" Alex eventually had the stomach to ask. "What did he hope to gain?"

Kyria spat in disgust and replied. "Power. Just a vulgar display o' power. Thousands died breakin' rocks so the world would know that even the mountains bow before the Hand of Seven. The vice he treasures is slavery an' oppression, so he grew stronger with every mountain they broke. You'll see." She pointed farther up the road.

As they rounded the bend of a large rock outcropping, Alex gasped. It looked like a large range of mountains had once stood here, but great piles of broken stone were all that remained. Great heaps of broken stones lay everywhere, shattered pieces of stone piled in hills the size of large houses. Even from a distance, she was able to see the small white dots of skeletons littering the landscape. In the center of the hills stood the city of Alcrest.

The city was a visual metaphor of the demon lord's power. A series of circular stone walls surrounded the city, and from their vantage point, Alex saw that smaller stone ring walls divided the city into different levels. Each ring wall was smaller than the one before it, and higher making the city look like a massive demonic wedding cake. Between each of the great stone rings were large buildings and even from this distance, Alex made out the vague outlines of people moving. Each wall had massive carvings of the demon army's victory over the humans and their subsequent enslavement. Below the carvings, a long series of chains ran in and out of the walls. Each link of the chain was the size of a large truck and must have been heavy, but each was held tightly against the walls. She couldn't see any way in or out of the city.

Alex turned to Kyria and Thistle to devise a plan but stopped when she saw the look of terror on their faces. They had been in scary places before, but this was different. Fear radiated from them and the hairs on the back of Thistle's head stood up. It took Alex a minute to collect herself, and every second she stood in the city's shadow made her want to turn tail and abandon the mission.

"So how are we getting in there? Even with disguises? There's no gate." Alex asked.

Kyria held up a finger and pointed. A horn in the distance shattered the silence and Alex turned.

A group of pride was returning to the city, with captives in tow. Alex could barely make out details, but they seemed to be men and women in a long line of chains. Two lions walked before them, and behind them, and another one drove them forward with the crack of a whip. As they waited before the stone wall, a grinding sound echoed across the plateau.

Alex watched as the chains surrounding the city moved. Slowly at first, and then quicker, picking up speed and finally sliding fluidly in a groove on the wall. As they moved, the walls of the city moved, pulling slowly until they revealed a large entryway, hidden within a layer of the wall. Alex watched the city moving, like a great gear churning in circles. Each wall of the city had an entryway that remained inaccessible, except by moving the wall to the correct orientation. The party of slaves and lions walked in and the great grinding began again, sealing the city once more. It was the perfect defense. Nothing could enter or leave. There was only one way in.

"All right," she said to them, hoping to get back on track. "We're gonna get captured!"

"Excuse me?" Kyria said with a tone of indignation, temporarily returning to her feisty self. "Absolutely no'! There has ta be some other way. Those filthy cats are no' puttin' their paws on me!"

"Ok. Then you tell me how we're getting past the big scary walls. I'll wait," Alex said.

"Well, we could... nae tha' wouldn't... we might be able ta... no tha's no good either." A couple of minutes of her sputtering yielded no useful plans, and she growled at Alex, who figured that was Kyria's way of agreeing to Alex's plan.

Alex retrieved Maggie's potions from her pack and handed one to each of them. The orange fluid sloshed lazily back and forth in the vial and had the appearance of half-melted frozen orange juice concentrate. If only it smelled that way. They opened the vials and a putrid stench erupted all around them. Alex nearly fell over coughing and wheezing, and Kyria found a nearby rock where she promptly deposited her lunch. Thistle stayed still and turned a shade of green.

Once they recovered from the vile odor, they looked down at the vials with disgust and hopelessness. Counting backward from three, they downed the vials and did everything in their power to keep from expelling the foul tasting liquid onto the nearest rock. The knowledge that it would be impossible to get more of the stuff was the only thing that kept Alex from vomiting it back up. With a final, labored gulp she downed it and sat down uneasily.

It took several minutes for any of them to form words. Kyria was the first one to speak.

"If this doesn't work, I'm gonna kill, tha' witch an' make enough rabbit stew ta feed Felwind for a week," she said, shaking with anger. Or nausea. It was hard to tell.

Alex turned because even though she somehow knew it was Kyria, her voice had changed. The potion had replaced the sweet, clear sound of the young girl's voice with a scratchy old crone's. It reminded Alex of some morning customers in the diner, whose breakfast for forty years had been coffee and cigarettes. When Kyria stood up, her outward appearance had vanished, replaced by a haggard looking old woman.

Kyria didn't appear a day over sixty-five, but she wasn't a day under it either. Hair that had been a firestorm of auburns and deep reds was now gray as the rock behind it and tumbled down over a weather-worn face that looked like leather nobody wanted to use for boots. The rest of her features had not stood the test of time any better.

"You look good," Alex said gleefully. Her voice was just as hoarse and much deeper. She yelped and grabbed her throat. As soon as old woman Kyria looked at her, she nearly collapsed from laughter.

"This is bad, isn't it?" Alex asked nervously in a voice that sounded like Burt Reynolds.

"No' bad at all, my darlin'," Kyria said before falling into another bout hysterical cackling.

Alex drew her scimitar and angled it to see her reflection in the dying sunlight of the late afternoon. She dropped it with a soft scream. Alex was a balding man in his mid-sixties, complete with wrinkles, nose hair, skin blemishes and crow's feet. She sat back down on the rock nearest to her, silently cursing Maggie.

Alex and Kyria both turned towards each other, realizing they hadn't checked on Thistle. He wandered from behind a nearby rock. The contents of the vial had reduced the valiant pig-knight to a small black-haired boy who smiled sheepishly at them. "Greetings mother and father!" It was several more minutes before any of them had recovered from laughter enough to form a plan.

The afternoon turned to dusk, and the sun receded into the east, revealing the stars, which seemed to be the only beautiful thing in this part of Aquillon. The group made camp at the base of a hill, near the city. They set a fire and made a loud production of dinner, banging pots and belching loudly (which seemed especially easy for Alex). It didn't take long for them to see eyes watching them in the dark. The leader of the squadron of lions strode out of the darkness confidently.

"Thrall scum on these lands? And free of chains? This will not do," the leader growled at them in guttural tones.

"What?" Alex asked while craning an ear towards him.

"I said human scum on these..."

"What? Kitty, if you're speaking, you've gotta speak up. My ears ain't what they used to be. sonny!"

"Insolent wretch!" The lion raised his ax when Thistle piped up in a squeaky voice.

"Please sir, my father is old, but he's a good craftsman! He's useful! He makes fine statues! We know how much the Lord values good statues. Take us as slaves and we will adorn the palace of the Lord whose shadow covers all."

The lion paused, his green eyes gleaming in the firelight. "Humans lie, and you would say anything to spare yourselves from death. Prove that what you say is true!"

The lion lowered his ax and pointed to a stone which had fallen from a nearby hill. Thistle glanced nervously at Alex who hobbled to her feet and ambled over to the rock. She spotted Kyria gripping her knives beneath a blanket but she put a hand on her shoulder and squeezed. She walked over to the stone.

"I need my tools. Cannot create without them." she said, desperately trying to stall for time. Alex looked down into Kyria's bag and miraculously, a pair of tools materialized, as if responding to her need. Alex silently thanked her powers and grabbed them, returning to the rock. She held them near the surface and her hands flew to work by themselves. If her powers were acting up, it was the most bizarre and oddly specific display of power she possessed, she thought to herself as she began carving... whatever she was carving.

It took several minutes, and she barely followed her hands as they flew around the stone,

but eventually, the outlines of a lion's angry face formed and she turned to the demon. "Tah-dah," she said in her most impressed voice.

Even he seemed impressed, but quickly muted his face and grumbled, "You may yet hold some promise and serve some use in my master's hall. Come thralls, your lives are not your own anymore."

After being slapped in rough, iron chains, they followed the warriors to the entrance of the city which was still quite a hike. By the time they reached the walls, the first wisps of morning light danced on the hills in the distance. Alex stood and lifted her neck upwards to take in the walls. The potion had done an annoyingly good job of mimicking old age; her neck and back were killing her, and she had to pee badly.

From the hill last night, she had not fully taken in the scale of the walls. They stood dizzyingly high, and Alex felt herself getting a sense of vertigo as she looked up at them. She had been on a trip with her dad once to Kennedy Space Center, and it reminded her of the towering Vehicle Assembly Building. As they neared the spot where the demons had taken the prisoners into the city, the lead warrior reached into his pouch and produced a small token. It glinted in the sunlight and he held it up to make it catch the sun. Once it did, the token glowed, and the lion tossed it up into the air, and it shimmered into nothing like a mirage. Soon after the horn blasted, the token reappeared in the air, where the lion caught it.

Alex felt her knees shake as the earth rumbled. Dread filled her chest as the chains, each link as large as a work truck, ground forward across the wall. A deep rumbling consumed the earth and all around them dust danced in the wind as the massive wall moved forward on its circular track. Alex studied it. She couldn't tell how far underground the wall extended, but she couldn't see any mechanism that moved it. Once the gap in the wall became visible, she saw the mechanism: slaves, thousands of slaves.

Between each of the walls, huge teams of slaves, mostly men, pulled on ropes that fed into underground chambers that Alex guessed connected to the chains that moved the walls. They looked exhausted, and several of them collapsed until the sound of cracking whips compelled them to return to their duties. The lions hustled her along past the legions of slaves and into the inner ring of the city, her friends in tow.

Alex, Kyria and Thistle exchanged horrified glances. They entered now into a large slum. Shanty houses and mud huts stood everywhere to house the massive population of slaves, which teemed all around them. Thousands of them moved in every direction, all with purpose and speed. They each wore a similar outfit: simple cloth robes, with bare feet. The slaves' eyes stayed down-turned, careful not to catch the eye of a master. Lions moved about on platforms above them and through the crowd. There wasn't an inch of the square that went unwatched. All around the town, which extended in each direction of the circle, masters watched slaves and slaves moved like schools of salmon trying to swim upstream.

As far as Alex could tell, there were two classes of lions. Warriors moved about and watched the workers, but there was another class. These lions were more like civilians, attending to a variety of administrative tasks such as filing scrolls and reviewing what appeared to be inventory sheets for the slave population. Their captors led them up to one of the civilian lions and left by themselves. The warriors seemed unconcerned by the prospect of them escaping, but Alex couldn't blame them. Even if the walls hadn't closed, there were hundreds of demons in all directions. The lion ahead of them cleared his throat and Alex looked at him.

He was fat. Very fat. It caught Alex off guard in fact and she almost laughed, but he didn't appear to be in the mood for a chuckle.

"New thralls? Artisans by the look of you, since you seem fit for nothing else." He even spoke differently than the warriors. His voice was less harsh, and he looked bored as if he was looking at sheep. Alex imagined that was how he viewed people. He sat on a large stack of pillows under a cabana and two young women slaves fanned him. Alex rolled her eyes and couldn't help but picture Jabba the Hutt. Aside from the vaguely lion-like features, the resemblance was uncanny.

"Aye! Stonemasons, very skilled!" Kyria said with enthusiasm.

"Calm yourself, thrall. No need to prove yourself, I'm not going to kill you. If anyone would have, it would have been that brute squad." He rolled his eyes. There seemed to be no love lost between the different classes of pride. "So then, you are to report to thrall-housing section three. Your official duties will begin tomorrow. Report to the building behind me for branding."

Alex glanced over and Kyria's eyes had widened. She looked at a nearby slave and saw a large brand, burned into his forearm. Alex replied quickly,

"But, we are so old! We wouldn't want to trouble the brander since I doubt we'll live long! Why not skip the branding, and we promise we'll be dead within a month?" She promised with sincerity.

The lion rolled it around in his brain before replying. "Normally I would punish a thrall who dared to propose anything to me, but it is close to lunch, and I suppose you appear sickly enough. We must brand the boy though. No way around that."

Alex grabbed his wrist and focused her mind on the image of the brand and prayed a little before holding his wrist up. "But my liege, he is! They brought here him last year, but he managed to slip out of the city when the walls opened for hunting parties. We adopted him on the road." Alex paused and hoped her trick had worked. The lion stared at Thistle's wrist and squinted.

"It's faded, but I suppose it's up to regulation. No need to make the brander go through the trouble of redoing his work. All right, report to housing complex three. It's that way up the road. Someone will take your bags to your lodging once we have searched them."

"Don't you need our names?" Alex asked.

"Thralls don't have names, and neither do you anymore," he said.

Alex nodded and turned, redirecting Kyria who looked only seconds away from an explosion of words that would have ended with lethal consequences. "Come, dear, our new home awaits," she said as she tugged Kyria's sleeve and motioned away with her eyes.

They walked in silence for a while, but the city buzzed with noise. Chattering of slave children, who hung from rooftops and awnings, mixed with the conversations of adult slaves who mingled in the streets and lingered inside of doorways just out of the midday heat. The sun beat down on cobblestone streets and everything seemed to sag in the sweltering heat. They walked through the streets, following the curved path until Alex saw three white claw marks etched into the wall. The road fed out into several small cul du sacs where large tenement buildings sat, indistinguishable from the ones they had passed. As the group came to a stop, a spindly looking man approached them.

"Welcome friends! May the Lord's claws pass over you." He had the manic voice of a slave long since separated from any thought of rebellion or escape. It was the voice of the obedient.

Alex nodded and repeated the greeting.

"We're here from the main gate," she said, "new arrivals for work."

"And we are glad to have you, it is so rare we find an artisan! Perhaps if you do well, we'll get double rations! Praise be to the Lord's mercy."

Alex looked over at Kyria and Thistle with a raised eyebrow. They shrugged.

"So, you like the Hand of Seven I take it?" she asked.

"And why wouldn't I? His mercy flows from above." He gesticulated wildly upwards towards the palace on the top-most layer of the city. "We would lose humanity to chaos and disorder without his wisdom and guidance. We need them to show us how to be of use in his great plan." As he spoke, Alex watched his facial expression soften. The man really believed what he was saying.

He really drank the Kool-aid, Alex thought.

She decided not to ask him any more questions. The sooner they could go about finding this paladin, the faster they could get out of the city and on their way to the Wyld Places.

The fanatical slave led them to a small room within a nearby tenement. The dwelling was roughly the size of Alex's living room in the trailer back home. Patches of hay served as beds, and a single candle stood in a carved alcove within the wall. There was a hole in the ground and a wooden bucket, near the back. Alex shuddered. A small opening in the wall next to the street with a flapping cloth cutout was all that served as a window. Alex never thought she would say it, but she had been in nicer motel rooms.

The group got settled and looked through their bags. There was no sign of their weapons, but the guards left everything else alone. It seemed surprising, but Alex imagined they did it to keep the new slaves content. Koga's rations were still there and Alex still had Koga's charm that would hide them once they escaped. They opened one of the leafy ration packages for lunch. Inside was a rice and fruit mixture, still fresh as though it had not aged at all. The food tasted unusually delicious. As Alex ate, she felt her energy and, to a lesser degree, her spirit, lift. The others seemed in a better mood.

That night, after the taskmasters had gone through to make sure everyone's lights were out, they started planning for the day to come, careful never to make too much noise.

"So, what now? This was yer plan," Kyria said, still sounding sour about being captured, even if on purpose.

"We need to find this Paladin," Alex said. "After our run-in with that slave who seems to be president of the demon lion fan club this afternoon, I'm thinking we shouldn't trust anybody."

"That is mostly true. I know the Guard has spies tha' 'ave lived in this city for years. I can find them an' see what they know," Kyria offered.

"All right, well we will have to hurry because we've used a day of our potion already and I saw wanted posters for us on the way. They've got our image pretty well captured. Thistle, you'll wander around tomorrow and gather up info while I'm working, and Kyria is looking for her Guard contacts. Maybe you can overhear a thing or two?"

"My ears are at your service."

"For now, let's just get some sleep," Alex said, which concluded their planning. No one argued with her and soon they were trying to sleep. Thistle fell asleep at once, as per usual, and even Kyria drifted off before long. Alex took longer. The sounds of whips in the distance and the occasional scream accompanying them kept her awake for hours. Eventually, however, she drifted into a dark and dreamless rest.

The morning came swiftly, and with little rest. Alex awoke to the sound of the taskmasters' voices echoing through the streets,

"Thralls up! Get to work! Report to your duties!" The loud proclamation echoed through the streets.

There was moving across the tenement square as people got up and shuffled about. A slow stream of exhausted slaves drudged their way back from the overnight shift, met by slaves leaving for the morning shift. Alex was ready to begin her day, but her old man back wasn't. She moved as quickly as she could but was barely ready when a taskmaster passed by the window and glared at her menacingly. Kyria was up and leaving to go look for her Guard contact and Thistle was still sleeping. Alex figured they didn't care much about what the little kids were doing so she let him sleep.

As Alex walked out into the streets, the noise and squalor of the slave quarter surrounded her. People bustled back and forth, carrying large pallets of goods and baskets of food. There was a long line nearby for stale bread and grimy water, but Alex wasn't hungry; Koga's rations from the night before had filled her up and were holding her over well, which was surprising given how little they were. She inquired with several passing slaves where stonemasons should go and they pointed upwards. There wasn't any skilled labor in the slave quarter and most of the other artisans seemed to head into the inner city with their tools.

Alex went back to the center of the ring where the overseer had spoken to them the day before. He was back on his pile of pillows, filing through papers and records, but he paid her no mind. She doubted he even knew who she was anymore. As Alex looked around the square, she saw a group of craftsmen gathered before a large blank section of the inner wall. A taskmaster tossed a coin in the air and the great grinding consumed the other noises of the square. This time it was the inner wall that rotated. It shifted slowly until finally, the inner city was visible, above a small ramp of stairs between the walls. Alex hurried over and shuffled into the crowd as they entered the gap.

This gap had far more guards than the last. Three massive lions in war-gear, wielding axes, stood silently in perfect formation on the other side of the wall, at the top of the stairs. They glared at the slaves who passed by and a few snarled, apparently just for the pleasure of frightening unarmed people. High school bullies would have loved the Hand of Seven and his cronies.

As they passed into the inner circle, the scenery changed almost immediately. Gone were the slums, wooden shacks, muddy streets and despondent slaves. Here instead, were brilliant alabaster homes and gleaming streets. The pride was everywhere, with squadrons of soldiers marching through the streets. Overseers sat on platforms and walked in and out of houses and buildings. It was odd to see demons going about everyday business, but they all seemed to have a purpose. Humans were scarce, only present where needed, sweeping streets and attending to masters. Small parks of manicured nature looked fresh and inviting, full of exotic looking animals and birds. Lions lounged in them on long chairs and piles of pillows, fanned by slaves behind them.

Even the air on this tier of the city was better. Air vents built into the wall pulled in air and pumped out sweet fragrances that danced in the breeze. Had it not been for hundreds of demon lions in every direction, it would have been a nice place to live.

The craftsmen dispersed to various buildings and Alex continued to wander on until she found the stonemasons' building. Dust hung thick in the air and she pulled a piece of cloth from a nearby workbench to cover her mouth. Inside, humans bustled between studios where the sound of chiseling and chipping buzzed. An older gentleman stood at the end of the hallway that connected all the studios. He saw Alex and approached her.

"Good. You're here. The last stonemason took a month to replace, so it is fortunate that they captured you when they did. We're behind on quota and I don't want to get flogged again. Your studio is there. You're working on busts. Get to it." He turned without saying anything else and she wandered down to the studio where slaves were working on busts.

Inside the studio men and women chiseled and chipped away at blocks of white stone. Some were further along than others, but they were all carving lions or humans. The busts of the lions looked solemn and dominant. They were not the same though. Apparently, different overseers and taskmasters had commissioned them. The human busts were of slaves in various stages of agony, which apparently passed for art in the demon world. There was an unoccupied block at the end of the row. Alex made her way to her station and started to work.

With no one watching, and with no imminent danger her powers seemed to have no interest in assisting her. She tried for an hour and only seemed to mangle the stone, which looked more and more like a rotten potato. Thankfully, none of her fellow sculptors were paying any attention to what she was doing. They seemed singularly focused on their own tasks.

After several exhausting hours, and her potato looking somehow worse, the head craftsman relieved them for a lunch break. They ate bread and drank water in silence. Alex was hoping there would be some conversation for her to soak up or information to glean, but there was just silence and dusty, stale bread.

By the end of the day Alex had learned nothing, carved nothing, and her arms burned from the repetitive motion. That evening she trudged home, looking as exhausted and miserable as the surrounding slaves.

Returning to the slave housing put the horrible conditions into a renewed perspective. Once she left the shiny houses of the pride, the gloomy, horrible world of the humans came rushing back in vivid detail. The smells were worse, the air fouler, and there was a dirt taste she couldn't get out of her mouth no matter what she did. Still, after a day of hard labor, her straw bed felt good. Way better than a straw bed should have felt.

An hour later Kyria wandered in, looking defeated.

"How was your day, honey?" Alex asked with a cheesy smile.

"Well, I've learned a hundred places where my Guard contact isn't, an' I've learned five great ways ta cook a rat. That's how my day was," she said miserably.

"I made a stone potato," Alex said with equal enthusiasm.

A little while before the guards outside called the curfew Thistle wandered in, covered head to toe in mud. The girls looked at each other and then at him.

"Thistle what the…" Alex began.

"Don't ask," he said.

Kyria pressed him again. "No but seriously, what happened?"

"Don't. Want. To. Talk. About. It." Thistle said.

They didn't push the issue further.

Alex hoped their luck would turn favorable in the next few days.

It didn't.

If anything, it got worse. Alex found out the supervising overseer for the stonemasons was doing an inspection of their work the next day. She had created two smaller potatoes, and that was about it. Kyria could not leave the washing well where she had only learned gossip (not even good gossip), and Thistle's only major accomplishment had been narrowly avoiding death several times.

Alex reported early to the stonemason shop. She hoped if she put extra effort in, she might make something recognizable out of her potato. Nobody was inside and she slipped into the studio and walked up to her potato. As she raised her chisel, she heard someone clearing their throat.

"Who are you?"

She whirled around and saw the master stonemason staring at her in the pre-dawn gloom.

"I'm..." she realized she didn't have a cover name. "David... Bowie."

Seriously, she thought to herself, *that was the best thing you came up with?* There wasn't much chance they knew who that was but still.

"No, you're not."

Maybe David Bowie really was the goblin king and had made a stopover on Aquillon once.

"Yes I am, I'm David Bowie." Alex was having a hard time saying it with a straight face.

"Well, you may be David so and so, but you are not a highly skilled stonemason, as my superior told me. So either they are stupid, which is unlikely, or you are a great liar. Tell me, which is more plausible?"

"Stupid lions?" Alex said it with what she was sure was a thoroughly unconvincing smile.

"Enough with the games. Who are you, girl?"

Alex looked down at her non-female anatomy and gave him a perplexed look. "I'm not a..."

"I'm old enough and clever enough to know a hidden face charm when I see one. Besides, you hold your tools the same way as the other women. Only they aren't terrible at it." His voice was a sharp blade, dripping with the truth.

She wanted to argue but her stone potato was more than proved he was right.

"Seriously, did you put any thought into this plan? You're lucky those loathsome cats are as stupid as they are vicious. Last chance. Tell me why you've snuck into this cesspool of a city or I'll turn you in," he said harshly.

"Won't you just do that if I tell you?"

"I could. Or maybe I'd have reason to help someone brave enough, or stupid enough to sneak into Alcrest. Either way, I'm done wasting time. Speak or I call the alarm."

She sighed. Looking at her plan now, it seemed fairly stupid. She could probably take him out before he could call the guard but that would eventually end badly. Besides, he had called her bluff, and she was out of options.

She told her story (she left out the parts that seemed less than believable). When she finished the old man stared at her in silence. Then he burst into laughter. He went on for a while but finally spoke between guffaws.

"You... what... how... Sal sanctioned... why would anyone..." he stammered between bouts of laughter. "Oh my, well...now I know you're telling the truth. Nobody would make up a story that absurd. Well, for now, let's get this cleaned up," he said pointing at her sculpture. He walked over and chiseled away gracefully, a master at his craft. Soon the face of a menacing lion emerged, and he worked every detail into its face. He looked over the work one last time and turned to her.

"Now that that's taken care of, we can maintain your cover. My name is Calvert Killburn, I'm Kyria's uncle. Old Guard, deep cover. I'd be who you are looking for, though how in Aquillon you found me, I'll never know with a plan like that. I'm shocked you're still alive. You must be the luckiest girl in Aquillon," he said with a final chuckle.

"Yup," Alex said, sighing, "that's me. Mrs. Lucky. Kyria never mentioned an uncle?"

"She wouldn't have. I left on this mission twenty years ago. My brother was still a scrappy youngster with his first command in the Guard. How is he anyway?"

Alex was getting sick being the bearer of bad news.

"Oh, you don't... you wouldn't I guess. He died in a pride attack."

"I see," There was a moment of silence and Calvert look like a tidal wave about to crash, but he collected himself and continued. "Well, it's a shame, but he isn't the first relative I've lost to the Court, and he won't be the last. Losing folk is just a way of life for us. Anyway, just go home for today. I'll say you got sick. I can meet you and Kyria and this pig-knight tonight, after curfew. They gave me your housing unit with the rest of your paperwork."

Alex nodded. She wanted to say more, do more, but she knew she couldn't. He was right, and they had used up their time. She heard the din of slaves shuffling outside. She left quickly, taking back roads down to the gate. At the gate a warrior questioned her, and she told him she was ill and was taking her illness back to the slums. He didn't seem interested in detaining her, perhaps out of fear of her cough and sneezing, or just laziness. She made her way through the gap and back to the slums.

Alex spent what remained of the day exploring the slave quarters. Once the shifts had changed, it was relatively quiet. Most of the labor slaves slept through the day. Given the back-breaking work she had seen them doing, she didn't blame them. The slums went on and on, and she took most of the afternoon to make her way all the way around the city. By the time the sun was sinking in the east (another quirk of Aquillon that she hadn't adjusted to), walking had exhausted her legs and she made her way back to the hut where Kyria was waiting.

"Please tell me yer day was more productive than mine?" Kyria said, almost pleading.

Kyria seemed thoroughly drained, and not just from her haggard outward appearance. It had been days with no luck finding anything, and the shadows of hopelessness were creeping into all their brains. Wanted posters Alex had seen around town with startlingly accurate pictures of their faces (to be fair Thistle's wasn't hard to capture) were active reminders that as soon as Maggie's potion wore out, they would be dead, quickly. Alex finally felt confident she had good news to deliver.

"I found the Guard contact, and I learned I am awful at sculpting, so that's two things,"

Alex said, as cheerfully as she could manage.

Kyria perked up at once. "Really? Ya found him?"

"Yes, she found me. I heard ole' Rex finally had that daughter he wanted. You've got your father's eyes, girl." Calvert stood in the hut's doorway and flashed a smile at Kyria. She turned.

"How would ya know anythin' about me?" Her voice was bitter and cold, like the icy wind that howled through the moonlit streets behind them.

"I should know. I grew up with the oaf. He never mentioned me? I'm Calvert," he said.

"Nae. He didn't. He told me he had a brother, but he died a long time ago," Kyria said. Her voice spoke distant, to a stranger, not to kin.

"I guess that makes some sense. We didn't part on the best terms. He never wanted me to go on this mission. Truth be told, neither did I. But here we are I suppose. The gods have a funny idea of chance," Calvert said with a wry chuckle.

They regarded each other in silence for a moment longer. Kyria relaxed her arms and moved closer to him.

Alex heard the taskmasters outside talking in hushed tones and she knew the guards would call soon curfew.

"I don't mean to be insensitive, but you need to be scarce," Alex said.

Kyria nodded in agreement.

"You're right. I'll be back in a few hours. I'll answer all of your questions then." He and Kyria shared an awkward goodbye and she and Alex settled in for the night. A short while later, Thistle wandered in and looked around at them with a puzzled expression.

"Such a pall seems to have fallen over you. What did I miss?"

"A lot, actually," Alex said, with a coy smile. She filled him in on the

166

day's events until the guards swept by the tenement.

"Lights out! All thralls silent! Night shift up!"

\#

An hour after the night shift left, they heard a knock on the door.

"Who is it?" Kyria asked.

"David Bowie."

"Let him in," Alex mumbled with a smirk. Thistle and Kyria exchanged puzzled glances but decided not to inquire.

"All right," he said in a hushed half whisper, "now we can really talk, what can the Old Guard of Alcrest do for you?"

"We're looking for a Paladin of the Seventh Dawn. We were hoping you could help us find one? We heard a rumor that one lived here," Alex said.

"You heard right. We kept hearing rumors from our informants of a heavily armed resistance fighter than was killing guards in the upper ring of the city. We tried to contact him, but we never found him until last week."

"Well, that's great news! Capital!" Thistle piped from the back of the room. They all hushed him and Calvert spoke again.

Calver frowned. "Not really," he said.

Alex sighed and rubbed her forehead. "Why not?"

"He's being executed in the morning in the Colosseum at the top of the city."

Two steps forward. Five hundred feet back. Alex sighed. She was Mrs. Lucky all right.

15

The Last Paladin

"How in the blazin' abyss does tha' help us?" Kyria snapped in a voice so loud, Alex almost forcefully covered her mouth. Calvert shot her an annoyed glance. "Look, you're lucky we found him at all. Stupid as they may be, the cats are fairly secretive, and information is a rare commodity. Besides, we're not too late."

Alex gave him an annoyed glare. "If he's in an arena being executed tomorrow at the top of the city where no human can go, how exactly are we not too late?"

"Because, the Old Guard hasn't spent twenty years here making lion sculptures," he replied, rolling his eyes. "We've been mapping the city, and we know how to get just about anywhere."

"Then why don' ya just get out? An' why not send this information ta the rest o' the Guard? Didn't occur ta ya that some people might 'ave missed ya back home?" Kyria asked, a hint of hurt in her voice.

"Look, kid, our mission is not finished. We've been finding vulnerabilities in the city's defenses to prepare for a full-scale invasion. Never leave a job half done. You either finish gutting the fish, or you throw it back in the water, as your old man would say. As for why we didn't inform anyone, we stopped sending messengers out years ago. It always turned into a suicide mission so we focused on using our soldiers internally."

Kyria said nothing. Thistle spoke up, "so what then is our brilliant plan sir, if you don't mind me asking?"

"The sewers, my good fellow," Calvert replied.

"There are sewers here? I've been all over these streets and I haven't seen them." Thistle sounded skeptical.

"Well, you've got to know where to search. They aren't in use. A thousand years ago, when the Hand of Seven conquered this city, they built a massive system of sewers that connected every level. The demons never finished them, but if you're clever and don't mind the dark you can get around just fine," Calvert said.

"Why aren't they under guard, or better yet why haven't they been closed? Alex asked. "Seems an obvious security risk."

"Let's just say we have an arrangement with the guards on this level. I can get you in and take you to where this paladin is being held. I normally wouldn't put my neck this far out, but if you're friends of kin, I don't mind."

Thistle grunted, seeming unsatisfied, but didn't press the issue further.

"We will have to leave quickly if we're going to make it by sunup. My sources tell me he's a dead man as soon as the sun hits him," Calvert said.

"All right, we're in, but how do we get out without being seen?" Kyria asked.

"I know a path that avoids most of the guard rotations in this part of town. Should get us close enough to the sewers," Calvert replied.

"Seems like we finally 'ave a break in our foul luck!" Kyria said, sounding hopeful.

Alex was less sure. She heard the reservation in Thistle's voice, but there wasn't much she could do about it at the moment. This was their only lead and time was running out. The Killburns were good people if Rex and Kyria were any indicators, and it stood to reason that Calvert was from the same stock, Alex assured herself.

They collected their belongings and followed Calvert into the dark streets. Cold winds swept through the alleyways like angry wraiths and Alex shivered. Taskmasters patrolled in regular intervals but the torches from their shadows made avoiding them simple enough. They were also not the quietest of creatures. Alex supposed that after millennia of being at the top of the food chain, they didn't need to be.

After an hour of tiptoeing through the deserted streets, they arrived at the sewer entrance. Along the way, a few curious slaves had poked their heads out of huts but ducked them back as quickly. Alex figured the slaves probably saw them as trouble or runaways and associating with either would be lethal. As Calvert had told them, two particularly menacing lions guarded the entrance to the sewers.

Calvert cupped his hands and whistled a sharp note into the night air. Alex was about to deck him when he pointed with a sly smile on his face. The guards exchanged words and departed slowly, leaving the sewer entrance unguarded.

"Never let it be said that the Old Guard is without its supply of wiles. We're not all without some level of subterfuge and clever tricks."

"Fair enough. Let's just get inside before your head gets too big to fit through the grate," Alex replied with a smile.

They walked through the streets towards the grate. It was massive, wrought of iron, a quarter of the height of the wall behind it. It would have been impossible to open, but the bars were large enough to slip through. Alex was five feet from the grate when a savage snarl from behind them caught them all by surprise. She turned to see a large lion baring his teeth at them, with an ax brandished at their throats. The others stopped.

"Thrall scum. Thought you'd slip by, did you? Well, I've got bad ne..." He never got to finish his sentence. A long dagger flew from Calvert's hand into his throat, and he fell, dissolving into black ooze.

Alex breathed a sigh of relief that Calvert's reflexes had been quicker than the guards. She was also silently thankful for the pride's poor habit of villainous monologuing. Now they had a way in, Alex felt as close to hopeful as she allowed herself to be. Even Thistle looked relieved. Alex was glad they would leave soon. The potion had worn off Thistle faster, and he had grown a foot and some of his neck furs were bristling through. Alex was just hoping everyone assumed it was puberty.

The group snuck through the gate and into the sewers. Moments after, the two guards returned from wherever they had gone and resumed looking menacing and fierce.

It took Alex's eyes several minutes to adjust to the darkness, but eventually, the shape of the sewer tunnels materialized before her. Massive pipe ways led in every direction, and putrid water sat in stagnant pools in the canals. As they walked, the remains of a slave would wash up every so often and Alex shuddered, trying not to think about how they got down here, or how they met their end. Following Calvert's lead, the group ventured down the passageway and took the first right that presented itself.

Alex gazed silently at the intricacy of the stone craft in the tunnels. These tunnels were a modern marvel in a medieval world, extending in each direction for untold distances. Cogs and wheels extended from the walls, caked in dust. At each of the intersections of tunnels was a pulley station which seemed like it would have raised and lowered water levels. Well, they would have if it hadn't been a thousand years old, anyway.

"So, they really never used this place?" Alex asked Calvert as they walked.

"Not once. Like the shattered mountains. The Lord of Long Shadows just made the slaves build these and never used them to remind humans that he would disregard and ignore their work. They are pawns. Meant only to be used and discarded."

"That's...terrible, and stupid," Alex said, shaking her head.

"Especially for the ones that died down here, or who lost relatives," Calvert said.

They proceeded on in silence for a while deeper into the sewers. The network of canals and levees was dizzyingly large, but Calvert seemed to know his way around well enough. After an eternity of twists and turns Calvert stopped and looked left and right, contemplating each direction. He turned left, and the passageway opened up after a hundred feet into a winding set of stairs. Near the top, they stepped off the staircase which continued up into the darkness. They stood at the edge of a new passageway.

This one was different. While it shared the architectural structure of the ones below in the lower city, there were unsettling details that distinguish it from the ones below. Here and there dark red smears painted the walls and the water in the canals on this level wasn't stagnant, nor was is murky. It was thick and red.

"Where are we?" Alex asked, desperately hoping that these canals backed up to a dye factory or a cranberry market.

"The blood canals," Calvert replied.

Definitely not the name of a cranberry market, Alex thought to herself.

"They drain the blood from slain gladiators down into the sewers on this level. That's our way in, we'll get into the fighting pits where the combatants wait before a battle and free your friend."

"And then get right back out through the sewers," Kyria said, finishing Calvert's sentence.

"Good plan," Alex said.

As she spoke, she heard her own voice for the first time in days.

Looking at her hands she realized the potion was wearing off. As they walked, she noticed a spring in her step and her joints ached less. By the time they reached the end of the passageway Alex felt her long, blond hair on her shoulders, and felt like herself again. As she turned around, she saw that Kyria was back to normal, and Thistle's large boar head bobbed up and down at the rear of the party. They stopped just shy of a small door built into a solid metal wall that closed off the rest of the tunnel.

Calvert looked at Kyria and smiled. "There's the niece I heard about! You're looking better. And just in time too. The fighting pits are through this door, hurry, we might be too late already!"

Kyria offered him a firm handshake and walked through the door as he opened it. Calvert held it open for Alex and Thistle, and they followed. As soon as they did Alex heard the door slam. Alex whirled around as the sound of a lock clicked into place. A horizontal door slot opened and Calvert's wicked eyes laughed at them.

Kyria spoke, her voice wavering at first.

"I don' understand uncle...why?"

"Well, I'm not your uncle, so it's really nothing personal if it makes you feel better."

Kyria's sadness had blossomed into fiery anger.

"What? Where is he then? What did ya do ta him?"

"You should have listened to your dear ole' dad. His brother died years ago, at my hands. I just adopted his identity and came here. It wasn't even hard to get the Guard to buy my story. I've made quite a living for myself off selling them to the master. I had actually just run out, and I wasn't sure what to do, but then you stumbled into my path. How fortunate!"

Alex felt a fire in her gut. "You murdering coward. I'll kill you. No matter what else happens, I'll kill you," she said, the words seething out of her mouth.

"No' if I beat ya ta it," Kyria said in a voice that wasn't hers. It belonged to a rage-filled firestorm about to explode.

"Look, you're the idiots who fell for a story that was too good to be true. Think about it. You didn't think it odd that the Guard contact you had been looking for was in the exact spot where you ended up? Did you think this was some cliché story where everything lines up and the hero always come out on top? Seriously, girl, I don't know where you come from, but you aren't too clever." Calvert laughed a deep laugh, full of malice.

"To be fair, I didn't lie about everything. Your paladin is right out there. He won't be of any use to you, because you'll be dead, but there you have it. Well, I'm off to see you die, and you're off to well, you get the idea anyway. Ta."

With that, he smiled and shut the slot. Kyria pounded on the door, screaming with all of her fury. Alex pulled her back. Thistle came to them and pointed ominously to the end of the corridor where light flooded in. The canal and the corridor ended, opening up into a large circular space where daylight radiated in. Even from where they stood, they could hear the roar of the crowd. Alex had a sick feeling, and she knew where they were even before she looked farther.

The arena.

She sighed. "Well, nowhere to go but forward I guess."

Alex walked out into the blinding light. Daylight had just begun to shine and Alex realized they had spent at least three or four hours in the sewers. As vision returned to them, Alex looked around and realized demons filled the stadium. They all roared with bloodlust, but she realized that they focus was on her or her friends. The crowd's focus was on the middle of the arena.

In the center of the sand, a large pole protruded from the ground with a man tied to it. His breathing was labored, and red lash marks covered most of his young, muscular body. The lash of the whip had torn his shirt to tatters by the whip. Shaggy black hair swayed in the afternoon breeze, but Alex couldn't make out anything else from the distance she was at.

The paladin's youthful appearance surprised Alex. She thought a thousand-year-old man would have looked older, but she figured she had lots of time for questions if she could figure out how to avoid being publicly and gleefully murdered by angry lion demons.

Alex moved forward into the arena. They couldn't get back in the sewers and fighting in the shallow gullet with your back against a wall wasn't an especially good way to go about surviving. The sunlight in the arena was blinding but Alex took some pleasure in the fresh air. If she was dying today, at least she'd do it under an open sky, and in pleasant weather. She prided herself in finding silver linings. As they reached the center of the arena an inordinately fat lion addressed the crowd from the center of the stands. He spoke from a raised dais covered with large tapestries, and a small swarm of slave girls attended him.

"Well, now we can begin!" the lion said, projecting his voice over the arena. His voice carried the same snobby accent of the lion Alex had spoken within the slave quarters; aristocratic and malicious. "Welcome, enemies of the state, to your public execution!" He said everything with flair and gusto, like a soccer announcer shouting "goal." "I, Master of Games, have prepared a visual treat for you all today. Our patron, and Lord on High," he pointed to an empty throne next to him, "sadly could not be in attendance. We carry on! For your delectation and delight, four enemies of the state most righteous stand before! They stand accused of desecrating a member of the Court of Hours!"

At this, the crowd howled and roared scornfully and several threw rotten fruit and vegetables at Alex and her friends. Fortunately, their aim was poor, and the distance was far. Alex wondered vaguely why there was always a surplus of rotten fruit.

"Without further ado, let us get on with the games! Let us see what these vile miscreants make of our first offering!"

The Master of Games sat down with an evil smile on his face and Alex heard gates opening with a grinding metal sound that made her stomach drop. She ran up to the man, with Thistle and Kyria following up behind her. Up close she got a better look at him. The paladin's hair blew listlessly in the wind over dusky brown eyes that looked old, like eyes that had seen too much and suffered a great deal. He appeared emaciated and his wounds oozed blood. His breath was short, and he looked like he was hanging on by a very thin thread.

Kyria looked at him. "Hey, listen buddy, we're here ta rescue ya. We went through quite a spell ta do it and it doesn't look like it's getting much easier so I need ya not ta die on us, all right?" She gently punched him in the arm.

The paladin smiled weakly at her and mumbled, "daring rescue? I suppose I'm game."

Alex looked at her friends. "All right, guys, anybody got a brilliant plan? Because in case anybody was saving a great plan for a rainy day now would definitely be the..."

A deep growl echoing from a dark alcove at the other end of the arena interrupted her. Out of the shadows, a massive tiger skulked slowly into the sunlight. It was twice the size of a normal tiger, with two sets of emerald eyes that gleamed with hunger, and a mouth of serrated fanged death. It took its time walking towards them, feeling no pressure of urgency in the face of lesser prey. Death walked in the beast's shadow, and even the surrounding wind slowed in deference to the creature.

"...time," Alex finished her sentence with a stutter, fear clinging to her voice, and terror filling the spaces between her words.

The paladin spoke weakly. "Just get my hands free and I can help."

Alex looked through their packs and unless Koga's rice patties could incapacitate the evil tiger, she had a rope, the charm which hid her essence, and more rope. Nothing to cut the paladin's binding with, but she had a rope, though. A clever girl could do a lot with that, and her brain was already pacing.

"Just buy me some time guys, I have a plan," she said to her friends. They gave her a look that said, "sure, Alex, we'll play with the demon kitty. Simple. Easy. No problem."

The tiger came within striking distance and paced in circles around them. It wasn't the least bit concerned with them but seemed to work out in its head which one looked the tastiest to eat. Kyria tore a strip of her pants and fashioned it into a sling and found stones to use as missiles. The tiger seemed intent on striking at the paladin but Kyria let a stone fly which smacked into its temple with a sharp thud. It roared in pain and charged in her direction.

"That's nae good," she muttered as she rolled out of the way. "All right, we 'ave successfully annoyed the giant tiger o' death. Alex, be a deary an' work quickly!"

Alex grunted and waved her off as she continued to work with her rope. She wanted to make the one year she spent in wilderness scouts count for something (although this wasn't really the scenario she had been preparing for when she earned her rope badge). She continued her knotting and looked up to gauge the thickness of the poll. It looked like it should be thin enough but still had some weight to it.

Meanwhile, Thistle had diverted the tiger's attention by squealing and running amok like a madman. The crowd roared with laughter, and Thistle smiled that they weren't paying any attention to Alex. Still, he was getting winded from the chase. At the moment before the tiger lunged for a lethal strike, Kyria placed a well-aimed shot at one of its four eyes and brought it down momentarily. She jumped up and down in triumph but realized almost too late, the monster was rising again, this time with twice as much purpose and ferocity. It wasn't a fan of its food playing back with it.

"Um, Alex, tha' tiger looks like it's done playin' around. Please tell me yer ready? Or at least willing ta commit my last will an' testament ta memory?" Kyria shouted at her in a desperate voice.

"Almost...can you buy me five more minutes?"

"How's thirty seconds sound?"

"It'll do I guess," Alex said with a resigned sigh.

Alex worked as fast as she could manage, and put her rope tying skills to the test. Soon enough had a constrictor knot fastened around the bottom end of the poll. She then walked about ten feet out, leading the rope behind her and fashioned a fixed snare like the one her dad had shown her how to make on their hunting trips. The prey was considerably large, but the concept was solid. She looked up at the paladin who was hanging suspended above her, watching her intently. Kyria was screaming obscenities as she ducked and dodged the tiger's strikes. Alex wasn't sure how many of them Kyria had aimed at her and how many were at the tiger.

"So, how are you feeling up there?" Alex asked in as jovial a tone as she could manage.

"No real complaints, milady," he said back to her. She couldn't tell if it was excellent sarcasm, or the heat had made him delirious.

"So, I've got a plan, but I don't know if you're gonna like it," Alex said to him. She explained her plan, and he nodded as if it seemed simple enough. Now she just had to pray the rope would hold. Koga and his hunters made it, so she was relatively sure it wasn't just any old rope. *Only one way to find out,* she thought grimly to herself.

"Hey! Big furry idiot!" Alex launched a nearby pebble with a well-placed throw and it knocked into the side of the beast. At first it worried her that the tiger hadn't noticed, but it turned and she regretted that it had. She stood her ground as a thousand pounds of fury and hatred charged at her, snarling and snapping. At the last moment Alex ran behind the pole and waited.

Just as the tiger's front paw entered her noose, Alex jumped back and yanked on the chord. The noose closed, but the tiger didn't seem to notice, at least until it was on the other side of the poll, charging at Alex. As the lead ran out, the rope pulled the tiger backward with a lurch and it yelped. It struggled and slashed with its paw but the more it did, the tighter the noose drew around its paw. The paladin pulled himself on top of the poll, pushed on by what looked to be a seventh wind and an extreme desire to avoid death by angry tiger.

Alex watched as the beast struggled and the rope held. As the tiger roared in frustration and pulled harder towards her, Alex's constructor knot tightened around the base of the pole and it splintered. When it had become weak enough, Alex whistled, and the paladin leaned over the top, using his body weight to push the poll down on the tiger who slumped under the weight. Alex wasn't sure if it was dead or not, but for now, it wasn't trying to eat her and that was good enough.

Alex walked over to her friends as the crowd erupted with outrage, building into an angry crescendo. Apparently, refusing to be eaten alive was considered being a bad sport, and entirely in poor taste. "All right, so how do we go about getting our friend out?" Alex asked them.

The group looked over at the paladin who landed on top of the pole and beast, but his bonds remained secure. He smiled a toothy grin at them. "Excellent plan, now if you could find something to cut these bonds, I'd just as soon not spend any time snuggling with this delightful creature!"

Alex cursed and then looked around when she saw a shimmer in the sand and concentrated on it.

Her friends gave her a concerned glance and moved back a little unsure of what she was planning. Alex focused her mind on what she needed and felt the surrounding sand heating until it was red hot. A hush fell over the crowd and they shifted nervously. In a flash of fire, the sand ignited and changed its form, becoming glass in the shape of swords. When the swords had fully materialized and stopped steaming, Alex picked one up. Kryia and Thistle followed. They were delicate blades but had a vicious appearance. Alex doubted they would hold up to a real sword, but they would do for now. She was grateful her powers decided to make an appearance.

The crowd had turned ugly and now howled and hissed in outrage, cursing them and calling them all manner of vile names. They were mostly overseers with a few warriors among them, and none seemed tempted to enter the arena. The Master of Games' voice boomed from the pulpit,

"Calm yourselves! This is all part of the show! Our divine master knew that a display of such simple carnage would not sate you! Better to watch these vile interlopers die armed, and at the hands of worthy challengers! Enter, Twins of Death and Fury, Eaters of Men and Reapers of Souls! We're just getting started, my people! On with the main event!"

Alex was fairly sure he was covering up for an unexpected plot twist, but his bluff worked. The crowd's outrage had turned to amusement and mockery. Whoever these twins were, they were going to make the tiger seem like a warm-up scrimmage. Alex focused on her main priority.

Alex walked over to the unconscious, possibly dead tiger and noticed subtle breathing. So, not dead then, she noted. Avoiding it carefully she went over to the paladin and cut his bindings when she noticed something.

Suspended by the rope, the lions had bound the paladin's hands separately with a sash of fine silk. The silk glowed with blue runes. He was in no condition to answer a question about them and she didn't have time to ask anyway. The sound of grinding gates rumbled from the other side of the arena, and Alex could make out two massive silhouettes striding calmly out of the shadows. She figured the runes would not cut and slice away at the regular rope. When she finished cutting the rope, she helped the paladin up and away from the sleeping tiger. By the time she returned to her friends the two silhouettes had taken shape in the area's sunlight.

The twins were lions; gargantuan warriors, even bigger than the pride Alex had seen in the city or elsewhere. Each stride was powerful and muscles rippled beneath arms and massive paws.. The lions wore full suits of armor and each wielded a crescent moon shaped ax, which glinted, shining death in the mid-afternoon sun.

"Ok paladin man, we got you loose, so, please tell us you've got a very nifty trick hidden somewhere," Alex said desperately.

"I need..." he struggled to speak, "time. Stall them." His voice sounded depleted and broken.

Alex looked down at her glass sword, which seemed about as useful as a toothpick, then she looked over at the half-dead man who supposedly knew the way to the most dangerous place in Aquillon, and then at the towering gladiators who smiled with teeth bared at their competitors (victims). Hopeless didn't even describe it.

Still, they had come this far and Alex had to believe they could buy him time. She had to believe it, because to doubt was to delay, and to delay was to die. And Alex decided she didn't want to die at the matinee show of "Alex Winters Dies at the Hands of Evil Psychotic Cats". She'd escaped evil pirates, a woman made of eels, malevolent trees, centaurs, vine-people, and Thistle's snoring. She'd survive this.

"Ok, we can do that. Come on, guys." Alex motioned them into a huddle. The gladiator twins were taking their sweet time coming to the group, clearly not finding them any more threatening than the tiger had.

"We need to buy this guy time, and then, well I'm not sure, but let's get him time. Kyria, you're faster than me or Thistle, so you take one and we'll take one."

They nodded and glanced over at the gladiators nervously. They looked over at the paladin. He looked more composed. He was on his knees with a pensive look on his face, with both arms extended outwards, grasping at some invisible force. Alex figured they would let the man be, but she tossed him the last of Koga's rations from the pack. He ate them and thanked her, then returned to his meditation, looking far better.

They broke off as the gladiators entered the center of the arena. Kyria wandered over towards hers, keeping her distance just outside a long swing of his ax. Thistle and Alex circled the lion they engaged, waiting for him to make the first move. With a huge downward swing, the gladiator brought his ax down only feet from where Alex stood. She jumped backward, and the lion moved towards her, moving carefully to keep Thistle in his line of sight.

As Alex's heart calmed down from the thundering strike, she abandoned any plans of swordplay. Her opponent was far too strong to parry or deflect. Avoidance was the only plan with positive survival prospects. She looked around for any tools that might help since her sword would not hold up to a direct attack.

Across the arena, the crowd roared as Kyria nicked a small cut her foe's side, only for the lion to kick her backward fifteen feet. Alex looked over and winced, but she refocused on the lion ahead of her just in time to duck underneath a nearly fatal swing. She cursed herself for being distracted and tried to refocus.

When Alex was little, her dad had not only taught her to fight, but also how to fight smart. His words echoed in her head as she studied her enemy. "Don't fight on their terms, Alex, fight on yours. Use everything you have. Out-think them, and you've already won. The smarter fighter will always walk out on top."

Think, Alex, Think. What can I use? Thistle bought her some time by engaging the lion, ducking and dodging fierce strikes with a grace Alex didn't think he had. She looked around the arena and had an idea. It seemed crazy, but then again, when fighting demon lion gladiators using glass swords, Alex figured some out of the box thinking wasn't the worst idea. She saw the tiger who had either passed out or gone to sleep, and she smiled. She whistled sharply at Thistle and he looked where she was looking. He gave her a thumbs up without being decapitated.

They slowly moved back towards the pole and Alex sliced a small chunk out of the gladiator's leg. He roared, striking twice as viciously in her direction. She positioned herself between the gladiator and what she hoped was a fully recuperated tiger and made an obscene gesture toward the lion. With a final roar, he swung at her and she sprang out of the way. His ax buried itself into the pole, severing the noose holding the tiger to the cracked pole and part of the creature's tail. It awakened in a foul mood and sprung fast as lightning on the gladiator.

Alex ducked to the side and high-fived Thistle. They looked over to Kyria, and the rush of victory died in them. She was bleeding, and cornered against the wall, holding the shattered remnants of her sword.

The gladiator ignored their attempts to distract him, and even the dying screams of his twin did little to stop his bloodlust. He lashed out again and again, each strike growing stronger. Kyria dodged them, but she was tiring, and he came closer to killing her with each strike. He only had to hit her once.

Alex and Thistle sprinted across the arena, but they knew as Alex ran, they wouldn't make it in time. Alex stopped to look at the paladin, who was still on his knees holding out his hands. His strength seemed restored, but he sat motionless.

"All right, paladin man, any day now," Alex yelled at him. Her voice was desperate and angry.

After a moment he turned his head and looked upwards towards the sky. A sharp whistling sound came over the roar of the crowd and a small glinting object flew over their heads at dizzying speed. It slammed through the silk bonds, which floated to the ground, and into his hands and he stood up. The object, a gleaming sword, was finer than any Alex had seen anywhere in Aquillon. It was long, nearly three feet, and wide. A broad hilt and a long handle led up to a vicious-looking steel blade, etched with runes and markings along the length of the blade. It looked heavy, but the paladin swung it with ease, as one would swing a hunting knife. In a low voice, which only Alex could hear, he said, "my turn."

As soon as the sword was in his hand he seemed filled with new energy and ran at inhuman speed towards the gladiator. Even if the gladiator had been paying attention, he wouldn't have been able to react. Leaping into the air, he brought the sword down on the head of the lion. It cut through him as easily as it would have cut through paper and the paladin brought the sword all the way to the ground, completing the killing blow.

It took the audience a moment to take in what happened. They sat in stunned silence, seemingly unable to comprehend that thralls could have brought down their champions. The paladin looked at them, venom in his eyes, and hatred in his voice. "I'll give you more warning than the humans you cut down every day; I'm coming for any demon left in the stands in thirty seconds, and you won't be walking away from it!"

The paladin's words went off like a bomb in the stands. Lions were tripping over themselves to run out of the stands and out of the coliseum. Even the warriors, seeing the fate of their great champions, dropped their weapons and ran. Once the arena was empty, the paladin helped Kyria to her feet. She seemed star-struck at first but regained her balance and smiled sheepishly at him. "Thanks, I guess. I pretty much had it handled, but killing him might 'ave been a bit tiring. Thanks for saving me the effort," she said with a shrug and rejoined Alex and Thistle.

They regrouped, and the paladin joined them. By now most of the crowd had vacated the stadium, including the Master of Games. For whatever other traits they possessed, the overseers seemed to have no courage. Alex supposed they were the brains to the brawn of the warriors.

"We need to get out of here. The overseers are fearful but the city guard will be here soon in numbers even I can't deal with." Now that he had recovered, the paladin's voice was smooth and rich.

"Got any idea where to go? The fluffy idiots sealed the way we came," Alex motioned backwards towards the walled-off alcove.

The paladin wrinkled his nose. "Well, not the entire way."

Alex realized what he meant and her stomach did a somersault. A small metal grate in the ground at the end of a stone canal led into the blood soup river they had walked by earlier.

Alex wanted to protest and find a better way but she looked around and there just wasn't one. The walls of the arena were fifteen feet high or higher and they were sheer, save for chilling scratch marks where slaves had met their end to cruel fates.

Kyria looked equally unhappy, but Alex cut her off. "He's right. Into the blood soup, we go."

By the time they reached the canal, they heard the marching of warriors echoing off the deserted stone steps of the coliseum. With each passing moment, the urgency grew thicker in the air, but it didn't make the smell around the canal any better.

"Well, nothing for it now. Bottoms up!" Thistle said, trying to put a positive spin on his words, but even he couldn't summon much enthusiasm. The gagging sounds he made when he splashed down in the putrid red water didn't help either. The pride had made their way into the coliseum and jumped down into the arena, and it was the final push Alex needed. She held her breath and jumped.

It was warm. Disgustingly warm, and the smell was worse than anything she had ever smelled, and she'd been in a dish room when the dishwasher backed up and spit out food sludge. She felt bones and remnants of the arena's victims as she swam and almost threw up several times before she found a ladder and pulled herself up. Her friends and the paladin were drying off and trying not the empty their stomachs.

Kyria was the first to speak. "So, now tha' our daring rescue is over, we need yer help," she said to the paladin but a massive slamming noise against the door behind them interrupted her. The sound of what Alex assumed was a battering ram rumbled in the sewers and they looked up to where the door was. It held, for now, but cracks in the door meant angry lions would spill through soon.

"Well," Alex pointed out, "maybe now isn't the best time. Was anybody paying attention when that scumbag was leading us through here?"

Kyria and Thistle shook their heads.

"I can guide you. I know these sewers well, and I do owe you a great debt," the paladin offered.

"All right, well, we follow you, Sir…" Kyria trailed off. Alex realized they didn't know his name.

"Ahrun Valheim, last of the Paladins of the Seventh Dawn ," he replied. "I have a hideout in the lower city with supplies. We can lie low there."

"All right, Ahrun o' the long name, I'm Kyria o' the doesn't want ta die at the hand o' angry cats. Lead the way."

The group followed Ahrun's lead, and Alex, Kyria, and Thistle made their way back into the sewers. The sound of the door exploding rocked the tunnel, and the group moved faster even though they had no energy left. Ahrun paused momentarily at each intersection before moving on, as if consulting an invisible map. As she ran, Alex heard the stomping and growling growing closer. Ahrun turned down a corridor, and she followed, but the corridor ended abruptly. Ahrun turned and was about to speak, but Alex focused on the group of Pride warriors, at least twenty deep that blocked the entrance.

The lions' leader spoke with a vain sneer. "It was a valiant effort, thralls, but the rats will feast on your corpses tonight."

Alex felt panic growing in her chest and hyperventilated. The darkness and the walls seemed twice as oppressive and she couldn't see over the wall of menacing emerald cat eyes. She closed her eyes and when she opened them, to her surprise, she saw waving lines of energy near the top of the ceiling, where the lions waited.

"Guys, step back," she said to her friends and then turned to the demons.

"Well come get us then, moronic cat!" Alex yelled at them.

It was easy to bait a reaction out of the warriors and they sprung forward. Alex reached out with her mind and sent a pulse of energy to the stones in the ceiling. The ceiling shuddered, and then collapsed on top of the lions. As the last stone fell, sealing the entrance, the light died, bathing Alex and her friends in a void of darkness.

16

A Light in the Darkness

At first, there was only the sound of shallow breathing and the trickle of water in the canal next to them. Alex wondered if she was alive or dead, but she figured if she was thinking about it that was probably a good sign.

"All right, anybody dead?" Alex asked in a raspy voice clogged with dust.

There was a general collection of grunting and groaning as the group recovered, and Alex was fairly sure she heard everybody. Feeling around, she found her way to her feet but didn't want to move farther, with the sound of the canal next to her. If there was anything that could make falling into a river of sewage and human remains worse, it was doing it in the pitch-black darkness. Alex heard the others standing, but they followed her example of not moving.

"Anybody think ta pack a torch?" Kyria asked.

"I'm afraid not," Thistle responded.

"No torch here," Ahrun sounded off.

"Fresh out," Alex said.

"Well, I for one don' want ta fall headfirst into the blood river again.

Anybody 'ave any bright ideas?" Kyria asked.

Alex wanted to laugh at what was clearly an unintentional, but still hilarious pun, but being trapped in a pitch-black sewer in the middle of a demon-infested city was a bit of a mood killer.

Alex pondered the problem and didn't have any solutions, so she concentrated instead on the image of light, hoping her powers might reappear. Erratic and unpredictable as they were, they seemed to make more regular appearances of late.

Alex felt something. It started as a glimmer in her palm, but slowly the darkness gave way to a dim gloom that partially lit the area. Alex held out her hand and in it she found a small tongue of flames dancing happily. It continued to grow until it was the size of a torch flame.

The others slowly realized where the flame was coming from and looked at her in awe.

"I know I've witnessed them a time or two, but your abilities continue to confound and astound m'lady," Thistle said, a rarefied reverence in his voice.

"How is this accomplished?" Ahrun asked. "You can't be..."

The light was better now and Alex looked to him. There was a religious look on his face as though he was witnessing something altogether rare.

"How long have you been able to do these things?"

Kyria answered cheerfully. "Well, my valiant friend, we were coming ta see you about tha'. Our dear Alex is a bonafide curiosity an' we want ta take her ta see the only people who might be able to explain it, the..."

"Eastern Watch," he said, finishing her sentence.

"Aye," Kyria said, looking at him with an upturned eyebrow.

Ahrun seemed like he had more to say, but he declined to comment further.

The collapse of the roof had struck a large hole in the wall behind them and it shocked Alex that the cave-in hadn't crushed them. Not being crushed by rocks was always a huge plus in her book. Rocks lay crushed around them, forming an almost perfect halo. Alex decided not to question good luck when it came by any more than she questioned her abilities.

Ahrun, seeming much more revitalized, took the lead, and they climbed through the hole which led to an older, dustier part of the sewer system. They navigated for a while until they found a long spiraling set of stairs which led down into a void of night and shadows. It was unsettling to look at, but Alex continued down anyway, on the general assumption that down was good and up was bad.

As they descended, Alex's flame threw its pale light across the wall and a dazzling array of carved figures emerged. Scenes of knights charging forward into battle, and humans conquering their enemies. The scenes seemed out of place somehow, like images of alternative history, or at least one before the Fall.

"What is this place?" Alex asked to no one in particular.

"Alcrest was not always the stronghold of the Hand of Seven," Ahrun said. "My order believes it began as a city of the empire, a thousand years ago, but the demons took it during the Fall before the empire could complete construction. The Lord of Long Shadows ordered these chambers sealed, on the pretext of constructing sewers, lest humans discover their past."

"How do you know this?" Alex asked.

"I am the last of my order. We passed our memory down from paladin to paladin, and we serve as the living memory of Aquillon. While even we do not remember what happened before the Fall, we exist as a record of what happened during, and after the Fall."

"So that would make you…" Alex said aloud, wondering more to herself than anything.

"Ancient," Ahrun said with a chuckle.

190

"Ya' don' look it," Kyria said brusquely. "No' a day over fifty by my reckonin'." She grinned at him and Thistle shook his head with a disapproving snort.

"If I may ask an indelicate question, what happens if you die?" Thistle asked.

"I am immortal, but not invincible. I can fall to the sword as easily as any man. Then all the memories of my brothers and sisters die with me," he said in a solemn voice.

Alex looked at him. Ahrun seemed so young, but there was a sadness in his eyes she understood now. It was an incredible burden to carry. She wondered how it hadn't crushed him by now.

They were at the bottom now and Alex finally recognized her surroundings. Ahrun seemed to know where he was going more, and it didn't take them long to find a grate that led back into the slave quarters.

As they approached the grate, Alex mimicked the whistle Calvert had made, and the guards retreated long enough for them to sneak by. Alex realized they had spent most of the remaining day in the sewers. Overhead the stars shone down brightly, illuminating the huts and tenements of the slave quarters. There were other, less friendly, light sources, however. Torchlight flickered off stone walls and down alleyways and Alex knew that humans weren't holding them. The pride had dispatched search parties all over the city.

The group clung to the shadows and backstreets as they skirted their way through the lower ring, following Ahrun's lead. As they snuck through the streets, they saw the guards harassing slaves and hauling families out of bed to search houses. One family shivered in the cold while the father was whipped. Ahrun put his hands on his blade.

"Not now. I know it's terrible, no' bein' able to help them, but we can no' help them if we're dead," Kyria said, squeezing his hand as she spoke.

He didn't seem happy, but he relented and they continued.

After several close calls, they arrived at a nondescript hut on the other side of town. Alex didn't wait for an invitation and jumped in, narrowly avoiding a patrol of torch-wielding taskmasters. Alex held her breath as one put his snout through the window flap and sniffed. The lion paused and there was electricity in the air as the seconds rolled by, and Alex waited to see what he would do. Satisfied that the hut smelled of a normal level of human filth, he moved on without further investigation and Alex breathed a sigh of relief.

Ahrun moved a rug from the center of the room and dust filled the air as the ancient threads fell aside. Underneath was an equally ancient door which led by a ladder down into a cellar. Ahrun went first and Alex and Kyria followed. Thistle closed the door on his way in.

At the bottom of the ladder, was a cozy space, like the medieval version of a bomb shelter. Small cubes which produced a dim light illuminated it, just enough to see each other. Alex took a seat and Ahrun spoke.

"Well, now we're out of immediate danger anyway, we can speak freely. Why did you come to this place, and what is it you think I can do for you?" he asked, directing his question at Alex.

Alex explained her story from the beginning. It sounded bizarre, but Ahrun took it in stride, his expression remaining quiet and pensive. When she had finished, he replied.

"I know Koga, and he was wise to send you, but I cannot help," Ahrun said.

All three of them responded at once. "Why not?"

"We saved your life," Alex said indignantly.

"I do not discount your actions, and I thank you for them, but I have a duty to these people. As long as I strike at these demons from the shadows for their cruelty, they stay their hand for fear of what may happen if their abuse grows too flagrant," Ahrun said.

"But for how long?" Alex asked. "How long until you're captured again, or let's say you can keep this up forever, what then? Isn't working to free every person in every city worth leaving them for now? People elsewhere may not be slaves but they aren't free either."

Ahrun sighed. "And in the meantime? How long before these poor waifs taste this freedom? I have been alive for many years, and once I might have agreed with you. But now, I content myself to improve the world that is, not dream of a better one."

Alex hadn't thought of a response but Kyria had. She shook with anger, and her voice was low and venomous. "Then yer a coward," she said, throwing each word at him like a well-placed arrow.

"What did you say?" Ahrun's voice dripped with anger to match hers.

"Ya heard me. Yer a coward. Ya hide behind these walls an' tell yerself tha' the world is a better place because ya do but yer just lyin' ta yerself." Kyria's face was a stone mask as she spoke.

In a flash of anger, Ahrun was in Kyria's face but she didn't back down or blink. His hand was on his sword.

"You are a fool, girl, and it is only for your rescue of me I stay my hand. You know nothing of me or my struggles! I cared for this world and fought for it when you were but a crying welp. You speak words you do not, and can not comprehend." Every word he spoke crackled with the heat of anger.

"I know my father, Rex Killburn, died so this world would be free o' the Court an' their filth! Ya can help make tha' mean something, or ya can just sit here and hide," Kyria said, spitting her words back at him.

Kyria and Ahrun snarled at each other for several moments before Alex spoke up, hoping to broker some peace. She imagined if they went at it, she would lose at least an arm in the crossfire.

"What she means is that we have a responsibility to help as many people as possible, and sometimes that means ignoring the needs of one or two people."

Ahrun looked at her and seemed to relent, some anger fading from his face. He sat down and rubbed his eyes for a moment before responding in a calmer voice.

"What you say makes a great deal of sense," he said, "but if I leave to help you on this quest, you will promise me something. I will have your word or I will not move one foot from this city."

"Anything," Alex said.

"If I help you, and we leave this place, promise me we will return and liberate these people. I will not abandon them to the whims of the greater good," Ahrun said firmly.

"I've seen the conditions here, and no one deserves this. We will return. You have my word," Alex promised him and offered her hand. He clasped her hand and shook it firmly before continuing.

"Then we will go. First, we need to get to the village of Damonfall. It lies on the coast of the Heart of Storms, just beyond the Wastes."

Thistle spoke up, "you must be mad. No man has crossed the Wastes in five centuries. It is pure lunacy to suggest."

Kyria had somewhat de-escalated and said, "aye, let's jus' saunter across the Wastes! It'll be a lark!"

"It is the only place we can go where the pride will not pursue us. They will have to go around," Ahrun said.

"Koga's charm hides our essence from them. I'd jus' as soon take my chances just about anywhere else. I'm with Thistle," Kyria said.

"After your stay here, no charm will keep the pride from tracking you. And they know my scent extremely well, having hunted me for years. I'm afraid the Wastes are the only way to shake them for good," Ahrun said, trying to contain the irritation in his voice.

Alex spoke up. "Wait a minute, where and what are the Wastes?

They don't sound nice. Are they nice?"

"Decidedly not!" Thistle said. "The Wastes are the remains of the Elmhurst Farming Basin, but now the realm of the Hand of Ten, Lord of Plagues. The whole place is a festering cauldron of disease and rot. Few humans live there, save for a few miserable wretches who never made it out before the veil of contagion settled a thousand years ago. Mirefolk, they're called, and if we want to survive the journey through the Lord of Plagues' lands, we will need their help."

"Why isn't there ever a nice, easy way to travel?" Alex muttered under her breath.

Kyria shook her head. "We should take our chances elsewhere. We'd 'ave better odds o' survivin' a fight with ten o' them gladiator cats than going into the Wastes."

Alex considered for a moment before speaking. "Do you really think this is the only way?"

"I do not suggest it lightly, but if we have any chance of making it to Damonfall, the Wastes are the best road," Ahrun said.

"Then we go to the Wastes," Alex said.

Kyria looked like she wanted to argue further but Alex pleaded with her silently to drop it.

"Then we have decided, and we leave in the morning. I know an old way out of the city," Ahrun said.

"Well, assumin' we survive this daft plan o' yers, where do we go next?" Kyria asked skeptically.

"Getting to the Wyld Places is a simple boat trip from Damonfall. There are many true things about the Wyld Places, but them being impossible to get to isn't one. I know a captain in Damonfall who will make the journey. Once we arrive in the Wyld Places we will need to find a waystone," Ahrun said.

The group looked at him blankly.

"Right, you wouldn't... When the magi fled after the Fall, they hid their Sanctum with arcane magic that has now lost to the ages. If you are to speak to them, we will need to find a waystone, which can transport us there. My order was on the trail of one deep in the jungle, but only a magus may use it."

"So that leaves us…" Alex interjected.

"In a fine position, since we have a magus," Ahrun said calmly and pointed at her.

"What, no." Alex's head was spinning. "I can't be. I'm not from this world. My dad was from Boston, and my mom was from Queens, New York."

"Alex Winters, I have no other explanation but if the Eastern Watch brought you here, and you have the powers I have witnessed, you are a magus, and a powerful one. Normally children of magi are born with innate abilities, and everything I have witnessed matches records we have of those abilities. Your powers manifest in random and unpredictable ways, do they not?"

Alex nodded.

"And since they manifested you have found yourself with knowledge you wouldn't otherwise possess?"

Alex thought about her bizarre skill with many weapons and nodded.

"And these powers only seem to manifest when you desperately need them?"

Alex nodded again.

"Then the evidence speaks for itself," Ahrun said with a tone of finality.

Alex realized she had been pacing but sat down to avoid falling. It made no sense. Her mom and dad were human, and she was human. She went to her mom's funeral. She remembered her dad dying. And never, not once in twenty years had anything unusual happened to her before all this. Still, she couldn't deny that it made sense in some twisted way.

"Ok, let's say I was a magus. How could they help me?" Alex asked.

"I know little about their order. The Court of Hours sealed my memory from before the Fall, as they did everyone's, and I only remember them leaving. But if they can help you develop your abilities, you could be the key to turning the tides against the court. Legend speaks of the Order's powers being formidable, some say even more so than the Court. Why they fled Aquillon is a mystery, but even one magus on our side would be a victory."

"All right, then I guess we better get started," Alex said, projecting manufactured confidence. She was overwhelmed. She knew something had been going on, but now it had a name, it seemed more real. A power she had never asked for, and a duty to use it that felt like the weight of the world and more. She was starting to understand Peter Parker's struggle.

Alex's friends surrounded her and smiled reassuringly. It seemed like an impossible task, getting to the other side of the world, but as with most things, she was happy not to have to do it alone.

They waited until the sun had risen and the streets buzzed with the sound of slaves moving about. From the sounds of the street, the presence of the guards was still higher than normal, but less than the night before. Ahrun equipped each of them with proper weapons, fresh traveling clothes and supplies. If they could get out of the city alive, Alex thought they'd be in good shape. She was mostly just grateful not to be wearing blood soaked clothing.

When it was around midday when they snuck back into the streets and followed Ahrun to the edge of the ring where he pointed with a wry smile to a small crack in the wall. It was almost unnoticeable to the untrained eye, and it led down to a small opening in the wall. They walked over to it and Alex looked through. It would be a tight squeeze (especially for Thistle) but they'd make it. Ahrun moved through first, and the others followed, with Alex bringing up the rear. She turned to take one last look and saw a child staring at her in confusion. She smiled sadly at him and waved but realized too late that not every human played for the same side.

"Massar! Massar!" the child screamed, and Alex heard the tromping of heavy paws and the clink of chain mail. She couldn't be mad at the child. His family would probably eat well tonight. Alex turned and worked her way through the opening.

"Guys, time to run! Quickly!" She yelled back at them.

"Really, Alex? Ya had ta go an' ruin a perfectly nice day?" Kyria yelled back at her.

"Run now, yell at me later!"

The group ran over the plain. It was wide-open and didn't provide much in the way of natural cover. Alex looked around for anywhere they could take cover. On this side of the city, a wide-open field was before them, and a series of foothills, broken like the others protruded in the distance. They weren't far but from the sounds of growling and weapons clinking behind them; they didn't have long. They all ran towards the hills.

"We need to make those hills! We can bottleneck them there. The Lord won't send an army after us, too much chaos in the city right now. Just scouts and trackers most likely. We can deal with them in the hills and that will buy us time," Ahrun yelled as they ran.

It seemed like a sensible plan, so Alex picked up the pace with Thistle and Kyria in tow, only turning back when they had passed into the first broken hillside. Sure enough, five lions had left the city, at a running pace. The lions dressed for travel, not battle, but they still looked lethal enough.

Kyria set the ambush, telling each of them where to hide. She placed Alex behind a large boulder, and she told Ahrun to hide atop an outcropping of rocks. She hid Thistle away in a hole below eye level, and she sat, holding the short swords Ahrun had given her, as bait. Alex didn't like it, but they needed to bait the pride scouts in somehow.

Alex waited. All she could hear was the wind and her breath, and the sound of approaching paws. Alex poked her head out and saw Kyria, sitting quietly on a rock. The Pride stopped just short of her.

"You are a fool, to wait for us. I would offer to bring you back alive, but I know you will not accept that. You will die and we will leave you to rot, unburied and forgotten. Just another worthless thrall," the leader said, snarling at her.

"For demons who rule the world, ya aren't too smart, an' gods alive yer long-winded. Please, just kill me before ya belt another speech," Kyria said, sounding bored.

"You'll suffer for that, insolent wretch!"

"Oh, well then I guess I'll really suffer for this!" As she spoke she threw a sword directly at the temple of the first lion. It caught him off guard but he moved, so it ripped open his cheek. He roared, doubled over in pain and howled orders.

"Rip her to pieces!"

As they charged towards her, she whistled and the group attacked from their hiding spots. Ahrun brought his sword down and decapitate one. It dissolved, and the ooze evaporated into the earth with a hiss. The rest fought back. These lions attacked differently than the gladiators as if someone had trained them in a different school of warfare. Their strikes were more like vipers, striking forward strategically and recoiling backward before the enemy could reciprocate.

Alex was engaged with one and it nearly skewered her several times. She tried to attack it, but its defensive stance was perfect. Alex wasn't above fighting dirty and kicked a pile of dirt up into the scout's face. The demon hissed and reeled backward, allowing Alex a chance to retaliate. Her battle reflex had kicked in and adrenaline pumped through her system. Rolling forward, she brought her sword up in a cutting motion and it caught the lion in the abdomen. The scout crumpled over and dissolved. As it did, Alex realized the lions had no form underneath their outward appearance. There was no bone or muscle, no organs or internal squishy bits. The entire form of the creature dissolved into the black ooze. These demons were something else, manifesting as lions.

Alex looked around and saw that they had won. Kyria and Thistle were dispatching the last demon and once they had, the group breathed.

"We've bought ourselves some time," Thistle said, "but they will send more. We need a plan."

"Well," Alex said, "Koga's charm might still do us some good, but they can still track us the old-fashioned way. We need to be gone, and quick. You know the way Ahrun?"

He nodded.

"Then it's off to the Wastes," Alex said, sounding as optimistic as she could.

No one argued, and they struck out on their journey. Turning east they kept a military pace. The farther they journeyed from Alcrest the healthier the earth seemed until finally Alex spotted a patch of green grass and she almost sobbed. It had been less than a week since they had entered the shattered hills, and despite her promise to Ahrun, she never wanted to come back. As the earth recovered so did Alex, and by the time they reached the edge of the region, she was feeling entirely better. The air was cleaner, and she even saw small rivers and creeks here and there and the world seemed almost normal.

Still, as they traveled, she couldn't shake the things she saw in Alcrest, the horrors, and brutality of the conditions and the inhumane treatment of the slaves. Some nights she woke up almost screaming into the silent night with dreams of slaves under lash and lions laughing as she died in the arena. Kyria had been quiet, and even Thistle's normal jovial banter was sparse. Alex wondered how Ahrun had possibly kept going, after all, that time, knowing what he knew.

As they traveled, Ahrun and Kyria did their best to mend fences. Kyria gave her best attempt at an apology (it wasn't great but Alex supposed the thought would count enough). Ahrun accepted graciously and apologized for being so pig-headed. Then he profusely apologized to Thistle who acted gravely insulted.

The land they traveled in was a no-man's-land but it was fairly pretty, all things considered. They passed through a small village and Alex could bathe and have a hot meal at an inn which restored her spirits. That night the group gathered around a table and breathed easier.

"The look on that lion's face was priceless!" Alex said, laughing as she remembered luring the gladiator into the not-so-dead tiger. They all shared a chuckle, even Ahrun.

Alex turned to him. "So, you remember everything that every paladin ever learned?"

Ahrun nodded.

"How do you keep that all organized? I can barely remember what I did yesterday!" Alex said with genuine amazement.

"I suppose I look at it like good record keeping. I just compartmentalize the information. It helps to focus on tasks at hand, it keeps the ghosts quiet."

There was a silence at the table.

"Well, nobody can ever accuse you o' being morbid, nope, no' at all," Kyria said with a smirk.

"My apologies. It is the nature of historians to be grim, but I have not lost all hope. There is always light, no matter how long the night lasts," Ahrun said.

THE LORD OF LONG SHADOWS

"Aye, and it is the nature o' Kilburn's ta love dancing, so I want a dance. From you!" Kyria said, pointing with a sly smile at Ahrun.

"I don't know if that's the best idea," he said bashfully.

She giggled. "Oh, yer adorable, acting like I was asking. I'm no' dancing with Thistle. He steps on my toes, so yer up. Come on," she said, pulling him by the hand to a dance floor in the center of the tables. Some musicians assembled behind them and played a lively tune. Alex looked at Thistle and they smiled as they watched Kyria dance across the floor, mostly taking Ahrun along for the ride. He may have been immortal, but he had spent none of those years dancing.

"How about it, Thistle? I don't seem to remember you stepping on any toes of mine in Felwind," Alex said with a smile.

"M'lady, I would not turn down a moment of revelry in this bleak time. We go!"

Alex and Thistle danced their way onto the floor and in no time the four of them were laughing and reeling away. For the briefest of times, there was no Court of Hours, no demons and the world was a brighter place. It was just Alex and her three friends enjoying an evening in a tavern, safe from the biting cold of the night.

The next morning they set out. Each day they traveled, the greenery became more and more yellow, and even though they were away from it, Alex felt the Wastes before she saw them.

It had been a week since they left Alcrest, and they stood now on a hill overlooking the beginning of the Wastes. As the ground grew closer to them, it grew more and more sickly. Yellow grass and patches of rotting trees and dead bushes formed the outskirts. The Wastes were black and stood in such stark contrast to the surrounding land that there was a tangible border line skirting across the horizon, and everything beyond it was dead.

They had escaped the city of chains, and now they just had to get through the death swamp of rotting plague and enter a sea of never-ending storms.

Alex was starting to miss Shelhyle. At least the things that tried to kill you there were pretty.

17

A Land of Rot and Ills

Nowhere Alex had been, on Earth or Aquillon could have prepared her for the Wastes.

They were a vast swamp. The grass was dead and pools of yellow water bubbled and steamed. Trees grew but horrible rotting sores infected them. Alex watched a two-headed rabbit hobble along and fall into a pool of water, where it hissed, dissolving . It was an endless wasteland worthy of its name, and across it, Alex could spot lightning on the sea and a massive storm brewing.

The air hung thick with smoke and smells she couldn't identify. Everything was diseased and unnatural like it had been poisoned and experimented on and not allowed to die. The Shattered Hills had been horrible but seemed a paradise compared to the Wastes.

It got worse the deeper they went in. By the end of the day when they made camp, Alex could no longer see anything past about two hundred feet ahead of her, because yellow smoke that smelled of sulfur choked the air and made her nose burn. Absent healthy soil, life had made due with mutations. New forms of life grew everywhere, but they were horrible to look at, like zombie plants. Roots jutted out of the ground and trees grew sideways, with twisted trunks blotted with purple spots and sores that oozed black puss. They slept in the dark that night because Kyria was certain a fire would ignite the air.

Ahrun seemed to know his way through, however, and that was some comfort. He led the way, and they followed. By the second day, they had constructed makeshift masks, because the air had become unbreathable. Even with a rudimentary filter, breathing was still difficult, but they made due. As they traveled, Alex asked Ahrun about the Mirefolk,

"How do people live out here? I can't imagine a place more hostile to human life."

"People are like these plants. Resilience is in the blood of Aquillon, and these people are champions of that if ever there were any. The Court of Hours oppresses all of humanity with their tyranny, but their struggle is more tangible."

"But how do they raise crops, livestock?" Alex asked, flabbergasted.

"They have made use of what few resources they have. Where you see a twisted toadstool, they might have a stew. Where you see a field of sickly grass, they have food for what livestock will grow in these conditions."

"What created all of this disease and rot?" she asked.

Kyria spoke up. "Like all the ills in our world, it traces back ta the miserable Court. These are the lands o' the Lord o' Plagues. He's a madman, convinced he can improve humanity an' life itself by afflictin' it with all manner o' unholy plagues an' seeing what survives."

"Forced evolution," Alex said to herself. She looked around and took in the effects of profane science. It was a horror to behold, but she was awestruck by the tenacity of life in this region. Thistle tugged her to one side, which snapped her out of her musings. "What the..." she said, shooting him an annoyed glance.

Thistle pointed at the ground she was about to step on. It looked normal but below the plants near what looked like solid ground; she saw it ripple.

"The ground is not as firm as it would appear m'lady. Such pitfalls abound throughout these lands. Step only on what soil you can tell is firm."

She shook herself back into the moment, adrenaline pumping. *Pay attention Alex, or you'll wind up like that rabbit.*

They proceeded along through the swamp for days. Even Ahrun's sense of direction seemed warped. They spent an entire day going in circles before they realized it. Eventually, Alex found an old path that seemed to lead in one direction consistently. As they traveled, they passed through and by the remnants of villages the miasmic swamp had absorbed. Buildings lurched out of the marsh like ruins in a desert jutting just above the sand. There were no villagers though.

Once night had fallen, they made camp in one of the abandoned villages. It was creepy, but attempting to travel the Wastes by night would be fatal. It was hard enough to maintain their footing in the daylight, what little came through the dense canopy of yellow smog, anyway.

They sheltered inside a reasonably intact home and made a fire in the fireplace. Someone had smashed the windows out and the empty frames looked out into the dark swamp, and eerie sounds echoed through the space where the windows used to be. The swamp at night was far more unsettling than during the day. Alex felt transported to some alien world, and she was just waiting for something to rear its head from the shadows. It might have been a trick of the light, but Alex could have sworn she saw shadows moving out in the darkness, just beyond where the light would reach.

The group took turns at the watch and it was Alex's turn to sleep. She went to wake Kyria up, but she grew sleepier and sleepier. A blanket of yellow mist floated into the room and blanketed them all.

She felt herself slipping away until finally, darkness took her.

After an unknown amount of time, Alex awakened, with a thud and a lump on her head as if it had hit a rock. She woke with a start, but still felt woozy, like trying to fight off a sleeping pill. Alex figured the sky hadn't repositioned itself overnight, she realized she was being dragged by one leg through the swamp. As she looked around she saw the unconscious figures of her friends being dragged next to her. Her heart began to thunder and she looked around desperately to assess how bad the situation was. Glancing ahead of her, she saw what was pulling her and did her best not to scream.

Alex had seen a lot of zombie movies. She would even consider herself a zombie movie buff. She had been on a zombie run and gone to a zombie-themed horror park near her town one Halloween. Given all of this, she really thought she would have been better equipped to deal with actual zombies.

They were far more gruesome in real life. The zombie had once been human, or at least that's what Alex assumed based on its general anatomy. From every inch of its body, sores and boils grew in clusters and bits of yellow rotting flesh hung off of open bones and black, necrotic muscle. Its eyes had decayed long ago, and it had patches of flesh sewn over them. The creature's disconnected jaw hung listlessly, waggling back and forth as it moved. It groaned as it carried her. The other zombies around her didn't seem in much better shape.

As she was dragged along she grabbed small pebbles and flung them at her friends, while also trying to play dead. She wasn't sure why the zombies weren't eating them but she didn't feel inclined to ask. Her first throw hit Thistle but didn't wake him. The second hit the leg of one zombie. It paused, causing the others to pause. It looked around vacantly (what the zombies expected to see was anyone's guess). She decided not to try again and let the pebbles go.

Playing dead wasn't nearly as fun as Alex thought it would be. To be fair, she hadn't expected it to be fun at all, but she really didn't want to get eaten and her friends weren't showing signs of life. These zombies were clearly taking them somewhere, so for the moment, they were ok. She imagined something less than pleasant was at the end of the zombies' journey, but she could only really handle one crisis at a time.

Every so often she lifted her head, but the scenery was mostly unchanged. Rotted plants, strange mutated animals (including a crocodile with the body of a snake), and trees. The trees grew in clusters and in all directions, their anatomy seeming to defy the laws of gravity. One had taken on the aspects of a venus fly trap and greedily gulped down a nearby yellow frog.

After some time, the group stopped, and Alex poked her head up to see that the pack of zombies which carried them was gathering with other equally disgusting zombies. Alex cursed silently. They had lost the advantage of numbers and these creatures seemed to be strong. In front of the horde was a cart filled with all manner of animals, reptiles and the bodies of other humans. None were moving, but they had not rotted yet either. Alex figured whatever knocked out her friends had hit those creatures as well. She started thinking desperately of an escape plan because she did not want to find out where that cart was heading. Alex figured if a zombie had you and was planning on eating you, that was bad. If a zombie was fetching you for someone else, that was much, much worse.

Behind them, abandoned windmills and more buildings loomed against the sky, which was lightening with the approach of dawn. Alex looked, and the zombies appeared to be waiting for someone. As the light increased, the fog gathered again, as it had in the village where they had camped. This time however it didn't pass over them. The others were still out cold and Alex was running out of time. The fog gathered over a crumpled body near the cart. Alex watched as the fog receded into the body and it stood. The body wasn't human, but it looked like it had been several humans. Arms and legs and several heads stitched haphazardly together, formed a horrible figure, nauseating to look at. As the last of the fog entered the corpse, it spoke with a voice of hissing steam.

"That thrall is special, put it aside. Rest can go on the cart that is bound for the halls," the creature ordered.

The zombies shuffled again, and one leaned down to scoop Kyria up and put her in the cart. *Ok Alex, final plan time. Any powers?* She looked around expectantly, but she saw nothing and felt nothing. Of course. Why would her powers show up? It wasn't like there were zombies loading her unconscious friends onto carts bound for God knows where. She grumbled to herself, irritated. As she continued to think of insane rescue plan ideas, she realized she had nothing. Well, she had one plan, but it was so bad it wasn't even really a plan. Still, the zombies had almost loaded Ahrun onto the cart and something always beat nothing.

She summoned all the strength she could muster and rolled up onto her feet, drawing her sword (which the creatures hadn't bothered to relieve her of) and she swung it clean through the abdomen of the nearest zombie, cleaving it in half. It fell over and began to moan and snarl. It was an excellent diversion and now all the zombies were staring at her. They shuffled towards her at alarming speeds, and Alex realized that the entire second half of her plan was just to run. So she ran. Hard.

Turning, she ran into the village as the zombies picked up speed. The noises they were making made it easy enough to tell where they were but there were so many it wasn't useful information. She continued to run deeper into the swamp, being careful to avoid the rippling ground (several of the zombies were not so careful and fell in). These were, however, drops in a much larger zombie-filled bucket as she was now being pursued by dozens. She ran in a circular pattern to avoid losing track of the cart but she was tiring quickly and the zombies were showing no signs of slowing.

She ran five circles around the village before doubling back and checking in on her friends to make sure the zombies hadn't removed or eaten them. They still lay on the cart, although just as useless and unconscious as before. As Alex ran out to begin her sixth lap, she felt her foot catch on a root and face-planted in the mud. She cursed and got up but it was too late. Her blunder had given the horde time to come in from their circular chase pattern and she was quickly surrounded. Alex desperately looked around in the village for an escape route. If she could just buy a little more time, maybe her friends would wake up, but it was hopeless. Everywhere she looked zombies ambled inward, surrounding her and the cart. As they moved closer in and sealed the surrounding circle, she cursed and held up her sword, hoping to kill as many as she could before they could overwhelm her.

As they charged, however, a massive heat wave blasted Alex, and she nearly collapsed. Fire lit up the fog (and thankfully didn't ignite the air) as streams of molten flame consumed the horde. They murmured as they burned and fell to their knees, burning away into a pile of crispy zombie bits. Alex gagged at the odor, but all the same, she was thrilled that something was putting on a huge zombie-que.

The heat, or possibly the rancid stink, reawakened the other three who woozily stood up off the cart and looked around in utter confusion. Two of the other bodies on the cart stirred and got up and were not zombies much to Alex's relief. As the smoke cleared, dark figures in masks and hoods approached, holding what Alex could only surmise was the Aquillonian equivalent of a flamethrower. A long handle connected two glass jars of green liquid to tubes that ran the length of the device down to twin flames that burned on the ends of wicks. It was rudimentary but Alex saw how it worked. The figures moved in and removed their masks.

Alex really hoped her face didn't appear as repulsed as she was. Behind the mask, a rotted face looked back at her. It was diseased, much like the zombies, though with far more human features. A thin film covered his eyes and she could see his jaw exposed from where the skin had rotted away. Boils oozed on his cheeks and it was hard to tell what smelled worse, him or the zombie-que.

"Strangers," he began. His accent was thick and sounded like a mix of Welsh and Russian. "You have wandered far into death's grip. What business do you have in this land? Your presence unsettles the dead more than usual." His question sounded almost like an accusation.

"Well," Alex said, "We're just passing through. We need to get to Damonfall and needed to cut through to avoid some unpleasantness that's been chasing us."

"You're no friend of the Court, but that doesn't make you a friend of the Mirefolk. We risked much to help you, and if not for our own, we wouldn't have wasted the fuel."

"Fair enough. We don't need a lot. Just directions through the Wastes."

"We shall consider. For now, come with us. These dead will be a paltry few compared to the hordes the Lord of Plagues will send from the halls when he finds out we interrupted his shipment."

"Don't have to tell us twice. Lead the way," Alex said.

They followed the Mirefolk for most of the day and finally came to rest in an old town. Alex and the group followed the Mirefolk into a small building where the leader tugged a chord and the wall opened up to reveal a hidden series of rooms. The Mirefolk gave them beds and Alex quickly drifted off to sleep.

Thankfully, the night brought no dreams. In the morning they proceeded deeper into the Wastes. As they traveled, the rot and disease got worse. The Mirefolk gave them masks which blocked a small amount of the contagion hanging in the air but it was still thick and difficult to breathe. Throughout the Wastes the Mirefolk had hidden warehouses and hiding places in the ruins of once thriving towns. They called them safe holds. Alex spoke at length with the leader as they traveled.

"When the Lord of Plagues descended on the Elmhurst Basin a thousand years ago, he unleashed the yellow smoke, which we call contagion, into the air. It extended in every direction and polluted everything it touched. Some farmers succumbed, becoming rotfiends, but others gave themselves to it by choice, becoming Plague Hosts, like the one you saw in the village," he said.

"Why do all of this?" Alex asked him as they traveled.

"Gods only know. He is a madman, obsessed with the idea that life is imperfect, and he could only perfect it by infection. Those who died were the lucky ones. Every rotfiend still has a soul. Their minds are still there, bound forever to the will of the Hand of Ten, as the contagion in their blood compels them to. We look at immolation as a sacred duty, freeing our brothers and sisters from this waking nightmare."

"But how did you survive?"

"We did not survive. The people we once were are dead. We merely endured the contagion. It warped our bodies but not our minds. We can still make our own choices."

"Well, what can I do? How can I help?" Alex asked. "I'm on my way somewhere important but I swear I'll come back and help."

"As with every Lord, his power lies in his base of operations, the Contagion Halls. There, the Immortal Engine pours contagion into the air. No humans, not even we, could approach it. There is naught that can be done. If you wish to help us, bring the Court down elsewhere."

"Well, that's the idea," she said.

He paused abruptly in front of a tall tree on an island in the middle of a pond. The pond hissed; bubbling yellow and rotting corpses of animals floating on the surface. This tree was strangely free of contagion and seemed relatively normal. The leader of the Mirefolk whistled sharply, and the sound carried across the pond. The leaves of the tree rustled, and the tree rotated counterclockwise into the ground. As it did, a path of pond water drained into hidden pipes revealing a pathway to a staircase leading below the water. The leader turned to Alex and gestured forward.

Following the Mirefolk's led, Alex and her friends cautiously walked through the path and down into the stairs. The stairs lead down to a small opening between tunnels that ran in every direction.

The leader spoke again. "Welcome to Safe Haven. For five hundred years the Mirefolk have called it home. You are no friend of the Court, I know that now. I cannot lead you across the wastes, but no man could. These tunnels will take you through the heart of the contagion and to the other side of the Wastes. I don't know how you plan to hurt the Court, but I pray for you to succeed."

The Mirefolk came down with them and ran to greet their families. Despite their warped and twisted outward appearance, Alex saw a strong community full of love and friendship. Children ran along the tunnels playing, and men and women walked free here. The Court had changed them but had not broken them, and it made Alex smile. Alex marveled at it all. A city of underground tunnels running the length and breadth of the Wastes. Thistle was right. The Mirefolk were by far the most resilient people Alex had met in Aquillon, and she was glad to have met them.

As they walked through the tunnels, Alex felt some sense of calm. Her friends seemed more at ease. Before long they were chatting like normal and sharing stories.

"So, these cars in Ah-mere-ika," Ahrun asked, "they go how fast?"

"Some of them can travel a hundred and twenty miles in one hour, sometimes faster."

"That is wondrous to be sure. So your people travel often then?"

"Americans? Not as much as one might think. Some travel, but some stay in the towns they grew up in their whole lives."

"But with this car invention, why would they not see the world? It seems such a waste," Ahrun said with a puzzled expression on his face.

Alex sighed. It was refreshing to hear that at least he was as naïve about America as she probably sounded about Aquillon. didn't have the heart to tell him that some people used their cars to check the mail.

The conversation shifted eventually back to present events. "So this captain," Kyria asked, "he can get us ta the Wyld Places?"

"He can.," Ahrun said. "To convince him will be another matter. The Heart of Storms is dangerous. It is rare for a ship to enter and return safely."

"So, when you called it a simple boat tip, you were..." Thistle asked, trailing off.

"I may have downplayed the risk somewhat, but what I said is true. We can make the journey," Ahrun said with confidence.

Alex spoke. "Can I ask a stupid question?"

They looked at her and waited.

"Why is it called the Heart of Storms? I'm really hoping that's like a metaphorical name, or it's like Iceland is green and Greenland is icy?"

They gave her puzzled looks, and she realized why. She'd explain later.

"No," Thistle began, "it is very much real. Inside it, tempests rage eternal and massive waves churn in the cauldron of storms. Lightning strikes are so common, the air has a constant charge."

"So, the least hospitable part of Aquillon yet? Perfect. Sounds great!" Alex said with a nervous chuckle.

"On the bright side," Kyria said, "I've never seen the ocean!" Alex laughed and momentarily forgot that they were traveling through the death swamp to the ocean of doom.

They spent the next several days traveling through Safe Haven. Alex was completely astonished at how extensive the tunnels were. Here and there the tunnel would lead down into a cave filled with dwellings. There must have been several thousand Mirefolk down in the tunnels. Families went about their daily lives and parties of scouts, hunters and immolators went up into the Wastes from hidden entrances. They rested in small alcoves with beds each night.

On the fourth day, they reached the end of Safe Haven. The tunnel ended and a set of stairs led up to the Wastes. Alex spoke to a guard who stood by.

"Please tell your leader we are grateful for the safe passage," she said.

He nodded and made his way down the tunnel to a tube that jutted out of the wall. He scratched something onto paper and put it into the tube which sucked it into the wall and back down the way they had come. Alex smiled at the ingenuity of the Mirefolk. For people without electricity, the internet and other modern inventions, they were, in some ways, more equipped to handle their circumstances than people from Earth. Alex had to admire the irony. The Lord of Plagues' experiment had worked. He had forced the people to evolve, and they had. Simple farmers had become scientists, inventors, architects and engineers. Alex took one last look at Safe Haven and climbed the stairs back into the sunlit world once again.

18

Into the Heart of Storms

Alex and her friends left Safe Haven near the eastern edge of the Wastes. The contagion had spread here, but the distance from the Lord of Plagues limited its effects. By noon, they had cleared it all together, and the Wastes were a distant memory receding on the western horizon.

As Alex looked around, she smiled at how genuinely pleasant the area was. They had entered a coastal region and after days of sulfur and rot, Alex couldn't get enough of the salt sea air.

"So does this place have a clever name?" Alex asked Thistle.

"Actually, I don't know that it does," he responded.

"Well, then I dub it, New Cocoa Beach!" she said with gusto.

"Coco Beech?" Kyria repeated.

"It was my favorite beach as a kid. My dad and I moved around a lot, but we spent some time in this place called Florida and that was my favorite beach there. This place reminds me of it. Well, minus the tourists and seagulls," Alex said with a chuckle.

"What in tha' blazes is a toorist? Or a seagull?" Kyria asked, looking baffled.

"Trust me," Alex said with a grin, "you're better off not knowing."

As they walked, Alex took in the unpolluted nature all around her, especially since none of it was trying to eat, murder, or maim her. Life here grew without contamination or restraint. Tall palms swayed in the salty breeze and low-lying vegetation dotted rocky coasts and gray beaches. The water here shimmered a perfect azure and schools of fish and small sharks chased each other through brightly colored coral. It was by far the most pleasant region of Aquillon Alex had encountered. Even here though, danger loomed just beyond the horizon.

Just glancing at the sea to the east Alex understood its ominous name. Gray storm clouds started a mile out and the farther she peered into the distance, the worse the storm got. Snapdragons made of lightning danced in the wind and lit up the shadows beyond the horizons and the monstrous black clouds, like a theater of primal forces uninterpretable. Even from the shore, Alex could see massive waves rising and falling; monsters from the depths of a mysterious sea.

Alex gulped audibly and pointed towards the east. "So, we need to go there? In a boat? On the water?"

"I'm afraid so m'lady," Thistle said in a grim voice. "Chin up though, I was once a sailing lad and I know my way around a ship. We've nothing to fear with me on board." He held his mace upward in a heroic pose.

"Our hero, Thistle, mighty Knight o' the Realm!" Kyria said with a modest curtsy.

Even Ahrun played along. "We are but humble witnesses to the path of his glory," he said, bowing even deeper.

"Well I do declare," Alex said, affecting her best southern-belle accent, "I feel mighty secure traveling with such a dignified and bonafide hero." She finished her speech with her own curtsy, lowest of all.

Thistle seemed somewhat mottled, but he was a good sport. "Fear not, worthy peasants! I shall protect you all!"

Alex burst into laughter with her friends as they proceeded along the coastline. It was good to laugh. She didn't imagine there would be much laughter in the weeks ahead, assuming they survived the crossing, so she did her best to appreciate how it felt for the moment.

Every so often a flash of lightning far out beyond the horizon would illuminate what Alex swore was a coastline. She shivered. She didn't know what scared her more - the sea or the destination. Despite the moment of fun, her companions seemed restless and unnerved.

"Tell me about the Wyld Places," she said to Thistle. "I've been living moment to moment since the day I got here, so I guess they never seemed real. They seemed like some far off place, or a dream almost."

"As they do to us all m'lady. No one knows much about them. No one knows why the empire never explored it. Too dangerous I suppose. There are legends I've heard but like most legends, I imagine you'd have to sift through them to find the truth."

"How long until we reach Damonfall?" Alex asked Ahrun.

"A day. Maybe less if our pace stays good," he said.

"Well then, we have time for you to tell us those. Nobody will play me in rock, paper, scissors anymore," Alex said.

Kyria rolled her eyes. "Because ya cheat," she muttered as she kicked a stone into the ocean.

Alex let it go. As talented as Kyria was, she was inexplicably bad at the game, and since learning it had only won twice out of a hundred games (even Thistle was better at it than her). Her conclusion, which she had repeated to anyone who would listen, was that they were both liars and cheats.

Thistle nodded and spoke. "We know nothing about the Wyld

Places or the time before the Fall, but legends have surrounded them for an eternity. The legends say it is a peninsula where order and man have no presence. Even the Court holds no sway. Giant beasts, primordial and old as the world lumber through ancient forests that make Shelhyle look like a shrubbery garden. Deep in the earth, ancient terrors lurk in dark caverns, their machinations not known to man. The only civilized presence is the Eastern Watch, who keep to their Sanctum, deep within the Jungles, hidden to all but their own order. They even say that in a cave at the end of Aquillon, the last dragon watches idly as time and tide pull away from the world."

Thistle spoke with the rich and textured voice of a narrator, and Alex let his words wash over her as they walked, her mind running wild.

Kyria spoke. "The guard pays smugglers every so often ta cross the Heart of Storms an' look for the Eastern Watch. None ever came back. We even took ta offering a standin' bounty on any information o' the Eastern Watch o' ten thousand imperial marcs, and it has remained unclaimed for a hundred years. Which is good, because, between me, an' the ocean over there, we don' 'ave the coin." Kyria said, chuckling at herself.

Alex looked at Ahrun. "So, if this bounty has been out there for so long, why didn't your captain take it?"

"I said he could get us to the Wyld Places, I didn't say he'd been. I know his ship and his skill, but it will be perilous all the same. He's not so foolhardy to risk the journey for the coin," Ahrun said.

"So, what's our plan for convincing him?" Alex asked.

"Good old-fashioned charm and diplomacy my dear," Ahrun said with a smile. "And if that fails, he owes me more than a few favors."

Alex continued. "So, if no one ever returns, and it's a jungle of beasts that make the Court too nervous to go there, and it's across a sea of hurricanes and lightning, how are we supposed to survive?" Alex asked with a nervous chuckle.

"Have some confidence," Ahrun said. "We have the first magus in a thousand years with us, a noble swinely knight, the scrappy daughter of the freedom fighters, and a Paladin of the Seventh Dawn! If there is a more equipped group of people to face the challenges before us, I would be hard pressed to find them. Besides, we're plucky and likable. In my experience, the gods favor the plucky and likable."

Alex laughed, "Well, I guess you're confident enough for the both of us. All right, we'll be fine. You've convinced me!"

Alex spent the rest of the afternoon making small talk about various topics. As the group worked their way up the coastline they mostly talked about Alex's world. It made her feel better to talk about it and it seemed to distract the others. The most mundane topics thoroughly fascinated them, and it was a good way to pass the time. As much as Alex wanted to learn more about Aquillon, it seemed every time they brought it up the conversation turned dark, and there would be dark times ahead. No need to bring them on prematurely, Alex figured.

By the time they had each decided which of the various TV shows Alex told them about was their favorite, Alex realized the terrain had changed. As they walked, the elevation on their left increased, until the beach and the land parted ways. It kept increasing, and perched high on a cliff over the ocean, Alex saw the village of Damonfall.

Sturdy looking stone buildings skirted the cliff line and a sheer stone path hugged the cliff side, leading down to a series of docks where small boats harbored. A long series of bridges allowed safe passage over the natural gaps in the path and from a distance, Alex could see people moving up and down the path. Alex saw most of the boats moored to the dock, and the captains were retreating quickly up the cliff to the village. It didn't take her long to figure out why; on the horizon, a dark monster of a storm was approaching fast.

The wind picked up around them and they quickened their pace up the path towards the village. After a while, Ahrun found the road that led up to the village. The group left the beachside, and they made their way on the road up to the village. It didn't look like a storm anybody would want to camp through or be caught it.

By the time they reached the top of the cliff, the climb had exhausted Alex, but she was glad to be back in civilization (well, close enough to civilization anyway). The wind howled around her and she could feel drops of rain on her skin. Ahrun pointed to an old building near the stone path down to the docks. It looked less firm than others, but the captains were all streaming into it. Alex figured the fact that the tavern reeked like liquor might have had something to do with it. She sighed, not looking forward to dealing with a seedy pub, but the storm was fast approaching and drunk idiots were preferable to standing around a raging gale.

The inside of the building was a large parade of seafaring clichés from sailors singing songs together, to an accordion player on a stool to a man with a peg-leg surrounded by others enraptured in a story about a fish he had been chasing. Alex laughed but figured all clichés had some basis in reality. The inside of the tavern smelled of brine and liquor and was damp. Dusky lanterns cast a haunting yellow light over the place against the silky darkness quickly enveloping Damonfall outside.

Alex settled into a corner stall near the back with Thistle and Kyria and Ahrun got up to order food and find his smuggler. Despite the privacy and the roaring fire next to them, Alex couldn't get comfortable. She felt eyes and ears on her and couldn't shake the feeling of being watched. She tried to take her mind off the paranoia and focused on her friends.

Kyria seemed worn out, but in good spirits. She and Thistle were playing an Aquillonian game called knock knock, which Alex figured had been invented by bored soldiers with no attachment to their limbs. Kyria and Thistle locked eyes with each other and extended their hands with fingers spread wide on the table. With no warning, each brought a dagger down hard into the wood between their fingers, missing by only a centimeter. The object didn't seem to have anything to do with hitting or missing, rather which person flinched or made a facial expression. They asked if Alex wanted to play,

Alex wrinkled her nose. "I politely decline your insane offer. I like my fingers right where they are."

"Suit yourself," Thistle said.

While there was no amount of alcohol that could have convinced her to play, it was morbidly entertaining to watch. After a while, Ahrun wandered back with four plates of fish and boiled potatoes and some drinks. The fish looked good, although the fish's eyes watching Alex eat it made it somewhat less appealing. Still, she was more hungry than creeped out, so she gulped down giant bites of fish and potatoes. The drink was dark and smelled like saltwater, so Alex avoided it, opting for water instead. The water still had a salty flavor, but she really didn't want to start her cruise into the sea of death lightning and doom waves with a hangover from sailor grog.

"Any luck finding your smuggler?" Alex asked Ahrun while Thistle lost his fifth game and a small pile of coins to Kyria's steely nerves.

Ahrun nodded. "I met him. He'll speak with us, but he wants more privacy. We just need to wait until some patrons thin out. He knows we're wanted and doesn't want people knowing our association."

Alex couldn't blame him. She imagined nothing pleasant would happen to anyone who aided them. As the evening wore away, sailors and captains left the tavern until only a few remained and they were so drunk, Alex figured they wouldn't understand anything even if they heard it. A figure at the bar slid a coin to the bartender who got up and locked the entrance to the tavern with a massive iron crossbar. The figure turned and walked up to them. Alex jumped up with her weapon drawn; Kyria and Thistle weren't far behind. Under the figure's dark cloak, the cold inhuman eyes of a muradae regarded them.

"Ahrun I swear if you've sold us down tha' river, I'll split ya in half!" Kyria was trying not to shout but her anger got the better of her. Fortunately, the storm outside muffled her outrage from prying ears.

"Calm yourself, girl, I am not what you think," the muradae said. His voice was cold and amphibian, but not hostile.

"Ahrun, explain this. Now," Alex said, trying to keep the snarling wolves of anger and panic at bay in her mind.

"This is Captain Sullas, my smuggler contact," Ahrun said calmly.

"You're working with the Court!" Thistle roared.

"Nothing of the kind, my friend. Sullas defected from the Court three hundred years ago and I helped him escape. He grew tired of the atrocities he and his kind committed on humanity and rebelled. I helped hide him and masked his essence. Even the Lady of the Deep doesn't know about him."

As they spoke, the eel creature watched the scene play out calmly. Sullas waited patiently, his hand on a blade.

"But I thought all lesser demons were part of the Hand they served, composed of its essence?" Alex asked in a skeptical voice.

"I am of the mother, but I am not the mother. When Ahrun sealed my essence, he hid me from her sight, but not her from mine. I still sense my brethren, but I am kept from their sight," Sulas said.

"In all the years since the Fall, he is the only one of his kind. The only demon to rebel from his master in a thousand years. I have relied on his insight time and time again, and he has saved more humans than you know," Ahrun said patiently.

"It doesn't make up for the blood on his hands," Kyria said, snarling.

"One act cannot atone a lifetime of evil ones, but he is trying. I owe him my life a dozen times or more," Ahrun said, raising his arm in a plea for them to lower their weapons.

Alex lowered hers, but after Alcrest, she couldn't bring herself to trust the creature so easily, especially considering what he was. Kyria hadn't budged, and Thistle only lowered his weapon halfway.

"I wanted to tell you all before, but you would never have agreed to meet him had you known what he was," Ahrun said.

"You've got tha' marked right!" Kyria said, rage trembling in her voice.

"Girl, you can hate me. I will not try to sway your mind on that. But if you want to cross the Heart of Storms, no other captain will tender you across that graveyard of ships. Were it not for the fact that I am deeply," he said it with a glare at Ahrun, "in your friend's debt, I wouldn't even consider it."

Thistle slowly put away his weapon, and Alex did the same. Kyria was slower and lowered hers but refused to put it away entirely. Sullas sat down as did Ahrun. Alex and Thistle followed, and Kyria leaned against a wall.

"If we have ta make a deal with this demon so be it, but I won't be a part o' yer pact with tha' devil. Do what ya must, I will be over here, waitin' for it ta betray ya," she said, pointing a hunting knife at Sullas.

As Kyria walked away, Sullas watched her and spoke. "I cannot hold it against her. Hatred is all her people will know of me, and for good reason. I will not try to take her hate from her," he turned to Alex. "You are a magus?" he asked and his eyes shifted suspiciously. It was hard to read the face of an eel, but he seemed like he was analyzing her, and trying to figure her out.

"So I'm told," she said with a shrug.

"I hope for your sake Ahrun, you are right, and it is worth the danger of the crossing. We will need to leave as soon as the storm passes.

The Court has ears everywhere and I sense they will be here soon. It enraged the Lord of Long Shadows when you escaped Alcrest. Even the muradae in the Drowned Halls heard of his wrath and feared it. He has raised the bounty on you even higher and offered a great position in his Court to whichever Lord brings you to him," Sullas said with a grimly factual voice.

"Well, nothing like a bounty to make a girl feel loved," Alex said, shrugging. She had become strangely nonchalant about the idea of demons chasing her.

Sullas continued, "You have made the Court experience something they have never known before. Fear. I sense it in the rippling thoughts of my mother. The Lady of Deep Waters fears you and what you may bring. They sense the hand of fate behind you, and they know fear."

"Well, that's something I guess. So, we leave in the morning?" Alex asked.

"We cannot wait that long. I sense a stirring of shadows in my mind. I hear the muradae speak of hunting parties. We leave when this storm passes, but we may already be too late. Get some sleep. I have paid the innkeeper to close for the night. Ahrun will keep watch and lead you down to the docks when the winds calm down. I will make my way down now and make ready the ship," Sullas said,

"All right. Well, I guess we could all use sleep. We'll see you then," Alex said.

Sullas stood and nodded. He clasped arms with Ahrun and they shared words privately. Sullas opened the door and walked into the torrential downpour, and Ahrun closed the door behind him. Moments before Ahrun shut the door of the bar, one drunk stumbled up and wandered out into the night. Alex exchanged concerned glances with Ahrun and Kyria but the drunk relieved her concerns when he fell back down into a nearby pile of horse manure and did not move for several minutes.

"I don't like it. Working with tha' fishy-eyed son o' a…" Kyria said under her breath.

"You have made your displeasure plain, but we are without option. Either you trust that my friend will do as he says, or you find a captain! Or swim!" Ahrun said with the edge of exasperation in his voice.

"Fine! I will!" Kyria shouted back at him. They were only inches from each other. Alex cleared her throat.

"Look, it's been a long day," she said, "we're tired and I get where both of you are coming from. Kyria, I don't like trusting the formerly evil fish any more than you do, but I don't see a lot of other options. Be honest, do you have a better plan?"

Kyria wrinkled her nose and grunted. Alex could tell she didn't but didn't want to admit it.

"I didn't think so. My dad used to tell me we don't make the world, we just do the best we can with what we have, and God willing that'll be enough."

"He was a wise man. I would have liked ta have met him," Kyria said, relenting the point.

"He was. Now let's get some shuteye. Death lightning and doom waves await!" Alex said in a chipper voice.

They all looked at her and replied with a half-hearted "hooray." They took turns sleeping, but between the storm and the mission at hand, no one could get more than thirty minutes.

The storm passed within two hours and the group made ready to leave. As Alex opened the door of the tavern, they found the moonlit streets of Damonfall empty. Even the drunk who had fallen in the pile of manure had stumbled his way home (a trail of manure-laden footprints led to a hut on the edge of the village). Alex made her way down to the docks, and her friends followed.

Alex had never been a fan of heights and tried not to panic on their way down. The path was barely three feet across with no sort of handrail or rope between Alex and a several-hundred-foot drop to the rocky shoals below. The rain made the path slick, and it was slow going. Near the bottom, Alex saw Sullas making the final preparations for launch. They were almost at the docks when a single pebble hit Alex's head and she looked up. Above her all along the cliff face, a large group of pride assassins moved silently down the cliff, using metal claws to find hand and foot holds.

Stifling a scream, she tapped Kyria's shoulder and pointed up. Alex and the group moved farther down the ramp at a quicker pace, but it was too late. By the time they reached the bottom, a large war party had formed. They smiled cruelly, gripping axes and daggers tightly in their paws. Sullas had hidden behind some riggings, and they seemed unaware of him for the moment. Alex turned back, but the assassins had swarmed onto the path behind them. They were trapped.

The one at the front of the group spoke. "Poor little thralls. Come all this way just to die. We take the female with golden hair. Others die." the lion's voice, like the others Alex had heard, was a condescending sneer. He also shared the pride's unilateral commitment to monologuing.

The assassins moved in from the front and back, closing in the pinscher trap.

Thistle grabbed Alex's shoulders and spoke in a hushed tone to her.

"Well, m'lady, I promised to get you to the Eastern Watch or die trying. It looks like I shall only keep one of those promises. Live well, Alex Winters. It has been my honor. I should have liked to have seen baseball at least once..."

Before Alex could process what he had said or stop him, Thistle raised his mace and charged headfirst into the group of assassins, moving with a ferocity and grace Alex had never seen. Instinctively the group ahead of them dodged to one side, clearing the path to the ship Ahrun pulled Alex and Kyria towards the boat. Alex screamed and fought him, but in her mind, she knew it was only a short window of time Thistle had bought them. She relented and ran onto the ship, tears stinging her eyes.

Alex reached out with her mind, but her powers were nowhere. She had never wanted them to show up more, but it made no difference. As she reached out and screamed, there was nothing but the sound of the wind, which seemed to laughed in the face of her rage and agony. She screamed and pressed her mind to the point of breaking, but nothing came.

Sullas wasted no time launching the ship, whose sail caught the wind and propelled it forward. Several assassins leaped from the docks, but they were too slow, and Thistle was keeping them busy. He had killed several but was being quickly overwhelmed. Thistle locked eyes with Alex one last time and smiled, and then he was gone. She looked away and collapsed on the deck sobbing.

The ship quickly struck out towards the east, and Alex's heart shattered more with each passing moment. She had known the dangers of her journey, and so had Thistle, but nothing prepared her for this. The cost had been too high. The ship drifted on the winds in an eerie silence, the hole in her heart growing larger as the storm-riddled horizon loomed closer and closer in the east.

19

Shadows in the Water

The storming sea churned around them, but Alex heard nothing. Stinging salt rain lashed at her face, but she felt nothing. She stared out into the uncaring steel colored sea, but she saw nothing. The world was a mute tapestry of loss and regret. The emptiness poured into Alex's soul like ice water.

Kyria was swinging her daggers at the air cursing, and Ahrun sat in quiet contemplation. Sullas busied himself moving about the deck adjusting riggings and sails. The ship was moving at a quick pace, but the height of the waves was growing as they traveled deeper into the sea. Alex couldn't even get up. She had never felt more useless. The one time she could have saved someone, she failed. She had made fire appear from nothing. She had caused tools to appear out of nowhere. She had barbequed plant demons. She had made the impossible possible. And yet her friend still lay dead on a dock.

The weather grew increasingly foul as the ship sailed deeper into the Heart of Storms. Lightning was thick, and came down in splintered arcs, slamming into the water. Even the air buzzed with electricity. Alex strained to keep her balance against the railing as the ship bobbed up and down against the towering waves. Sullas manned the rudder, while Ahrun took the wheel. They managed to mostly keep the ship out of the path of the larger swells, but it was treacherous going.

The group slept below in shifts throughout the night. Alex found the motion of the ship somewhat melodic and she drifted in and out of sleep. Kyria seemed less enchanted by it and spent most of the time hurling over the side. Ahrun didn't seem to move or sleep but kept steadily at his post.

By morning the ship was being tossed about like a rag doll and Alex was on deck with everyone else trying to control it. They narrowly avoided one swell after another until finally, they reached a patch of calmer sea. The waves died down and even the churning black clouds receded into lesser gray monsters, brooding on the horizon. There was enough wind to keep the sails filled, but it didn't seem like they were traveling in a hurricane anymore.

Alex ate lunch with the others around mid-day, and they sat in silence. No one had anything to say, leaving only the eerie howling of the winds and the tumult of the distant waves.

By the evening they had drifted into a much calmer part of the sea. The ocean was silent glass where their ship drifted but around in every direction storms raged relentlessly. Alex assumed it was the eye of a tempest.

That night Alex tried to sleep. After hours of tossing and turning, she finally gave up and wandered on deck. She stared up at the stars, which were crystal clear and reflected perfectly on the water below when she noticed Kyria standing beside her. Sullas stayed silently at the helm, careful to keep his distance.

"It's no' yer fault ya know," Kyria said.

"I didn't say…" Alex trailed off.

"Ya didn't 'ave ta. I see tha' look in yer eyes. I did the same thing when I lost my father. We weren't close then, so I doubt ya noticed,

230

but the "what ifs" nearly ate me alive."

Alex spoke but the tears were coming back into her eyes. "I just don't understand. I'm supposed to be this all-powerful magus, but I couldn't do anything! I watched him die, for me. First your dad, now Thistle, I'm not worth it!" As she spoke, the water below rippled with a steady stream of tears.

"Don' ya dare say tha'," Kyria replied in a quiet whisper. "My father an' Thistle both knew what ya were, and what ya might do someday. They bet their lives on it. I know ya don' see it in ya, but they did. Lets no' sully their memory with the notion that they were wrong." Her voice was a matter of fact and blunt.

"But I couldn't... he was right there..." Alex stammered.

"Ya can' save everybody, Alex. No matter how hard ya try people die. I learned that with my father, and now ya have ta. Aquillon's a cruel place, but it's a good teacher. We can only do the good we were put here ta do. No more, no less. Their work is over, yers is jus' beginnin'," Kyria stared pensively at the horizon. Alex saw the glimmer of a tear on the edge of her eye, and Alex figured she wasn't one for sobbing. Far beyond the most distant waves, the first ghosts of morning light were dancing on the skyline.

Alex choked back another sob. "But what if I'm not strong enough? What if it was all a fluke, and they died protecting someone who wasn't what they thought?" she asked.

"Then they died for what they believed in. Short o' living a long, full life, I don' think either of them ever wanted anythin' else. In fact, I think goin' out in a blaze o' glory was exactly what tha' noble knight wanted. Ta die with honor."

Alex nodded in silence as her tears rippled in the sea below. "Thanks," she said, sniffling, "I needed that."

Kyria nodded. "Well, someone's gotta keep things going around here, an' I don'..." She never finished her sentence. A violent lurch rocked the ship, and every plank shook. Ahrun ran on deck, and he drew his weapon. Alex looked around for the source of the disturbance but couldn't see anything.

The hull shuddered again with another great quake as something violently pulled the ship. Alex looked down and realized the water was black shimmering, and she couldn't see anything, even inches below the surface.

"Guys, is this normal?" she asked in a panicked voice.

Ahrun ran to the side and looked over.

"Gods preserve us..." his face turned white, and that terrified Alex. If Ahrun was afraid, they were in serious trouble.

Sullas glanced over the side of the deck. "This cannot be!" he shouted, "She is far out of her part of the deep!"

Ahrun drew his sword and Kyria armed herself.

"Anybody want to tell me what we're dealing with?" Alex yelled.

They had no time to respond. The surrounding sea frothed and churned. Fast as the nearby lightning, countless gray and brown tentacles shot out of the water and gripped onto the ship. They pulsed and undulated with sea water and a slimy ooze that covered everything they touched. Ahrun went to work severing them but they grew back almost as fast as he could cut them. Kyria tried to fight back, but the ship was being pulled in every direction by the forest of tentacles and maintaining balance on deck was easier said than done.

With a violent lurch, all the tentacles pulled the ship back towards a huge shadow in the water. It rose as they moved towards it. When it had fully cleared the water, Alex screamed in horror at the most hideous creature she had seen since she arrived.

A woman's head, old and haggard, glared at them from putrid green eyes. Her disjointed mouth hung several feet below her face, moving independently of her head. Within it, rows of serrated shark teeth moved about. Below her neck, all trace of humanity ended. A long neck, like a plesiosaur Alex remembered seeing once in a dinosaur book, led down to a bloated torso floating in the water. Spider-like legs extended down into the depths and from every side of her, tentacles extended towards them. In the center of her torso a giant hole filled with serrated teeth rotated in circles. Alex recognized that part of her. She had nearly been pushed into one in the Shelhyle forest.

They continued desperately to hack at the creature's tentacles, but they continued to grow back as they pulled the ship and closer to the maw. Sullas had thrown old harpoons at the creature's head but its tentacles swatted them away easily. As they got closer, a horrific stench of rot and digestion overwhelmed Alex. Deep within the maw, fish, sharks, and even some muradae were being slowly digested. Even if she wanted to abandon ship, the surrounding sea was being sucked into the maw and she wasn't a great swimmer.

"What on Aquillon is that thing!?" Alex asked.

"It's," Kyria said, but a tentacle knocked her prone before she could finish.

"The Lady of Hunger," Ahrun finished her sentence, before being slammed down by the back end of the same tentacle.

"Fantastic," Alex shouted back. "How do we kill it?"

"Foolish thrall. I am eternal. I *am* hunger. I am the void which swallows the world." The words were not coming from the creature's mouth but from the surrounding sea as the Lady's tentacles pulsed and vibrated. "I am…"

"An annoying blather mouthed manatee who I am in no mood to deal with," Alex yelled back, cutting her off. She grabbed a metal ball anchor and hurled it into the maw with more force than even she thought she had. It flew straight into the maw and shattered one tooth from the inner row. A deep howl of pain echoed around them.

"I don't know if we can kill it," Alex said to the other three, "but we can sure enough hurt it, and that's a start."

At that, her friends and Sullas stopped chopping tentacles and threw various projectiles at the mouth of the creature. It tried to swat them away, but the opening was too wide. Every missile shattered a tooth which shot forth geysers of blood. Eventually, the demon closed the maw, and the water stopped pulling forward, giving them a break.

They all breathed a sigh of relief as the creature sat motionless for a moment. It stirred again, this time with more purpose. Alex felt the tentacles pulling the boat in opposite directions, and cracks and splinters erupted along the deck and the hull.

"She's pulling us apart!" Sullas yelled, "I have to brace the hull or she'll rip us in half!" He went about frantically trying to secure the deck and the hull with patches and other quick fixes, but it wasn't working. The ship was coming apart quickly. A massive fissure burst open midship and Alex ducked down, covering her eyes, to avoid the hailstorm of splinters. The ship had only minutes to live.

Alex looked around the deck, desperately searching for a way out. Then she noticed an old metal sheet, used for patchwork but discarded, and she had an idea. It was a mad, wonderful idea, but in survival situations, those kinds were usually what saved everybody.

"Kyria," she shouted, getting her friend's attention. "I need a boost," she continued, pointing at the old metal sheet.

Kyria looked at it for a moment and then smiled. "Tha's crazy," she replied in an amused voice, with a supportive smile. Rushing to the edge of the deck, Kyria grabbed the metal and pulled it over herself, bracing her weight against it.

Alex had her ramp. The ship was drifting closer by the minute as its integrity withered. Alex breathed deep and focused, her battle senses roaring around her. *You just need one good shot Alex, just one.*

Alex waited patiently, even though every instinct in her body told her to go. After a few seconds that felt like a painful eternity, she saw the opening. The Lady of Hunger dipped her head for a moment, exposing a large section of her neck, and her tentacles relented. Drawing her scimitar, Alex sprinted forward, placing one foot in the shield and using her momentum to launch her forward off the deck straight towards the monster.

She saw the neck, and it was thicker than she had expected. It didn't matter. She focused everything on one perfect strike. All of her hatred, all of her rage, all of her sadness over the loss of her friend, she unleashed in one perfect downward cut, slicing through the creature's neck in a fluid motion, all anguish, and fury capped off with a savage cry against the uncaring sky. Her timing was perfect. Just as her blade cleared through the creature's neck, the ship drifted below her and she fell onto the deck.

The headless neck lashed about wildly, spraying black liquid everywhere. Its torso listed about before bubbling and sinking beneath the surface. The tentacles relinquished their vice grip on the deck and the hull floated free of the creature. Sullas wasted no time in unfurling the sails which caught a breeze and they were moving.

"She will not stay down for that long, but we have bought ourselves some time," Ahrun said in a grim voice.

"She badly damaged the ship. If it moves at all, we should be lucky," Sullas said, adding to the overwhelmingly cheery mood.

"Well, anyone you walk away from," Alex muttered, trying to find some measure of victory. They worked for the better part of an hour patching and nailing and sanding until they had patched most of the ship's cracks and holes. The ship moved, but the water it had taken on slowed it. Sullas worked diligently below to empty it, but the work was tedious and there was only one bucket.

After another hour they had finally moved at a decent speed, and the weather held, being only surly and not all out terrifying. Alex noticed that wherever they sailed, the cone of calm weather followed them. For a place called the Heart of Storms, Alex thought it was suspicious.

She figured the Yang would catch up with the Yin soon enough and their good fortune would balance out.

Alex breathed a sigh of relief they finally had a moment of peace. She sat against some old fishing nets and closed her eyes, hoping for a moment of peace, but it didn't come. Every time she closed her eyes, Thistle was always there, giving her that last gallant look before the pride assassins overwhelmed him. She instead wandered below.

Below deck, Kyria had found a soggy cot and was getting some shuteye. Ahrun appeared to be meditating. As she passed, his eyes opened. He smiled sadly at her.

"I am sorry about your friend. I truly am." There was sympathy in his voice born of shared experience. Alex was sure he had lost plenty of friends over the years.

"Thanks," she said. "I guess I really thought I could do it all. Fight the Court, save everybody. I was a fool."

"No, you are human. Humans have always dreamed bigger than they could accomplish. It is no fault, but rather our greatest strength," he said in a calm voice.

"How do you do it? How do you keep going after all these years? After all that you've lost?" she asked.

"My order swore me in as a paladin right before the Fall. Everything I knew, the Court destroyed, and I lost when they sealed everyone's memories. I lost everything so I suppose over the years I avoided getting close to anyone because I would eventually outlive them. I didn't want to lose anything else. Even when I was in Alcrest, I fought for the people, but I never walked among them, never really knew them. I don't know if that's helpful," he said with a wistful sigh.

Alex nodded. "It is, in a way. I haven't lost anyone since my dad. I never let myself get close enough, on purpose. Hermit by design I guess," she said and chuckled. "Then when I came here, I had to make friends, had to get close again, to survive. I just wasn't ready to lose him."

"We never are, but he died how he wanted to live. An honorable man," Ahrun said.

"It doesn't make it easier for the ones left behind. It doesn't make it..." Alex sobbed quietly, and she felt Ahrun's hand around her shoulders. She continued to cry, letting the grief out until there was nothing left. She felt herself slipping into a deep sleep, free of dreams and thoughts of Thistle.

The morning came with a shudder that Alex knew all too well. She ran on deck, her weapon drawn. One massive tentacle gripped the ship and coiled around the hull. Far out from where the slimy thing protruded from the water, a bubbling mass was rising from the surface and Alex knew what it was before she saw it.

Alex's friends hacked at the tentacle helplessly, but it was like trying to cut down a redwood with a steak knife. Instead of many tentacles, they had merged as one infinitely thicker one, with tendons like irons and skin of thick wet leather. Even where they cut into the skin, the flesh below did not move or bleed.

With a crunch, the tentacle twisted and squeezed and cracks formed anew across the deck. At that moment the Lady of Hunger surfaced, having regrown her head. The Lady leered at Alex as if to say, *you took your best shot, but you missed. Now you're my lunch.* Alex felt the ship moving backwards towards the maw that opened in the demon's chest. Once again it sucked seawater and creatures backward in the current, the ship along with them. Alex was out of ideas. She had beaten the monster once, but it wasn't enough. Evil, it seemed, never really died on Aquillon, but just got back up again for an encore performance.

The ship was only a few feet from being swallowed up into the monstrous maw. Alex, Ahrun, and Kyria raised their weapons to fight.

Alex screamed in anger, telling herself that she'd at least hurt the beast before the end.

But it never came. From nowhere, and nothing, a massive bolt of lightning split the sky and slammed into the Lady of Hunger. Her vile body pulsed with energy as the current surged into her. The lightning sustained itself for a long while, far longer than it seemed possible , and finally, there was a popping sound and the body of the demon exploded violently. The ship buckled violently under Alex's feet and without warning, she felt herself thrown high in the air. She eventually landed several dozen feet away in the water. The head landed next to Alex, and she watched with satisfaction as it sank, eyes rolling and tongue flayed out.

The surrounding sea began to churn and Alex watched with alarm as the waters around her began to swirl into a vortex pulling downward. Alex struggled against it, but it didn't matter. She saw the others swirling around her and shattered bits of the ship. Finally, she gave up and allowed it to drag her under until finally, the current vomited her up onto a rocky island.

She took moments to regain her bearings. As she looked up, she saw the funnel spiraling upwards towards the surface of the sea. Around her, she saw her friends wheezing and sputtering out water. Kyria seemed the most tired, having fought the hardest (this didn't surprise Alex). They were all lying on a rocky island at the bottom of the ocean. Nothing surrounded them but water, trapped in the vortex. Alex finally looked forward and saw a creature on a brine and barnacle ridden throne smiling at them, and it was not a pleasant smile.

20

The Last Living God of Aquillon

A lex gazed up at the creature in the throne. The creature was massive, at least ten feet tall and composed entirely of electrical current. Thousands of small lightning bolts coursed over it and through it, making it nearly impossible to discern its true anatomy. A crown of jagged sapphires rested on its head and cold, glowing green eyes watched her intently. From a gap between the current, brilliant teeth made of shining pearl gleamed at her in a smile that was far more malevolent than friendly.

Even the air buzzed with current and Alex could feel her hair standing on end. The current wired her senses and from every side of her, she felt the energy coursing through her veins. Her companions had awakened fully and were on their knees, though Alex couldn't tell whether it was of their own volition.

"So…" the being spoke. Its voice was a thousand live wires hissing and popping, like living energy given voice and sentience. "The girl who jumped through time; this is a rare occasion." Alex realized he was talking to her.

"Actually, my name is Alex Winters, so nice to meet you and thanks for saving us," she said, trying to sound casual and friendly.

"Al.. ex… Winters… interesting." It played with the sounds of her name like they were foreign words. "As for saving it, do not grow so bold fleshthing."

Alex sighed. First thrall, now fleshthing. These names were getting worse, not better. Pretty soon she would miss thrall.

"I have not decided what to do with it yet. It is ten thousand years and more since a fleshthing was in my eyes. Your kind have not improved much." It sounded bored like it was visiting a new restaurant that its friends had raved about, but was finding it to be a bit of a disappointment.

"Well, then why save us?" Alex asked.

"Save…? Its words are strange and stupid. I don't like them," the creature replied.

Alex felt a painful jolt of a current run through her and she screamed. Kyria tried to run to her, but she an invisible force bound her to the ground. *Ok, speak nicer to the lightning beast,* Alex mentally noted.

"You called me the girl who jumped through time. Why, may I ask?" she said, trying to be more polite.

"The fleshthing thinks it can ask the questions. Curious. Has its species grown bolder in the last thousand years I wonder? No. This one is just stupid and doesn't know who it speaks to."

Alex waited for it to finished talking to itself, and spoke again. "Well, if you had bothered to introduce yourself…" but it cut her off.

"No, no. I will ask the fleshthing questions," the creature said.

Alex waited.

"Why was the Lady of Hunger trying to eat it?" the creature asked.

"I mean, it seemed like it was trying to eat everything, but I think the fact I've made a habit of irritating the Court has something to do with it."

The being's eyes opened wider.

"It is enemies with the Court?" it asked.

"I am, yes," she said.

"Then I was right to save it, for now," it replied, seeming proud of itself.

"Let's be fair, I've introduced myself. Wouldn't it be far more civilized if I at least knew who you were?" Alex asked.

"An ant may not know the name of the bird that eats it, but what does it matter?" the creature said, sounding bored.

"So, you're going to eat us? I think that might cross the line of civility, don't you?" Alex asked.

"No. Is metaphor. This fleshthing is stupid. Perhaps was wrong to save it. Perhaps let bloated whale eat it? No. Whale too fat already," the creature said, vaguely motioning to a whale suspended above in the whirlpool. Alex had to agree. The whale was fat enough.

Kyria was growing impatient. It was only ever a matter of time before Kyria's temper got ahead of her brain. Alex needed to be quick.

"Then perhaps," Alex said in a sweet, placating voice, "you could be so kind as to grace us with your name?"

"It finds manners. Fine, it speaks to Ahazi, the Lord of Storms," it said.

Ahrun's eyes grew wide, and Sullas visibly shrunk away from Ahazi. "You cannot be Ahazi," Ahrun said bluntly. "He died in the Fall. It is common knowledge."

"It is wrong as it is stupid. I thought it would be smarter for a fleshthing that has such a good memory. It is only common knowledge because the Court made it so. The Court could not kill. Only banish. Now Ahazi lives here, but still, I take my revenge. None of their ships cross my prison! I destroy all!" As Ahazi said this, lightning brewed around his crown. He paced back and forth now, regarding each of them, his eyes growing wilder.

"So ya been down here for a thousand years?" Kyria asked.

"It is observant. Yes, I am imprisoned here these thousand years. But I saw that fat, ugly cow entering my sea, chasing you, I killed the cow, once fleshthings had proven themselves strong. Ahazi does not favor the weak.".

"Well, if you're so powerful, how did the Court banish you?" Alex asked, trying to bait him into her trap.

It worked. Darkness fell over the island and the air grew thick with energy. Ahazi's power was everywhere and every breath Alex took was full of current.

"Fleshthing would do well to learn respect. I am no demon. I am god of living lightning, lord of all storms, bringer of hurricanes and sinker of ships. All the seas are my domain. I am the last. My two brothers the Court killed. My sister they corrupted. I alone remained strong. It is a breath in eternity's mouth. I am eternal, and I will snuff it out." As Ahazi spoke, thunder rolled through his words, bolts of lightning served as exclamation points.

"So. if all you say is true, it should be no difficult task to help us on our way then? A simple gesture really," Alex said, continuing staring piously at the ground.

"What it says is true. But I would not help it unless I wanted to. I know it has power. I know it is on its way to see Magi. It proves it is worthy. Save its friends. Then I help it," Ahazi said with what looked like a wicked smile

Ahazi snapped his fingers and two bubbles of water crashed in from the whirling vortex of water around them, covering Ahrun and Kyria's heads. They clutched at their necks but could not remove themselves from the swirling globes of water, kicking and squirming as they drowned. Panic and fear and anger gripped Alex all at once, as she was released from the bonds of whatever invisible force held them down.

She considered attacking Ahazi, but it seemed like a foolish waste

242

of time, and it might provoke him to kill them all. If this was a test, the object was to pass, and there was no way around it this time. Alex focused, trying to clear her mind but everything was so busy inside her head. Thoughts and emotions collided, and she had trouble stringing even a coherent thought together, much less figuring out how to get her powers to work. She tried desperately to think of all the times they had.

They had come to her when she needed them most, but not when she wanted them. She tried to focus on that, the need, pure and elemental as if her power was breath and she might drown without it.

"Hurry fleshthing," Ahazi taunted, "time is up soon and then other fleshthings will be dead."

She ignored him and focused on the need. She isolated each factor outside of her control, each errant thought, each chaotic emotion inside herself and put them away, focusing solely on the need. There was no water, there was no Ahazi, she even ignored the gurgling sounds of her friends dying. The world became still, and there was only Alex and her inner self.

When Alex was younger, she had watched a documentary about Buddhist monks who could slow their heartbeat down so low they could breathe underwater for much longer than a normal human. She felt like that now. The only sound she heard was her breathing, the only thing she sensed was her pulse, slow and steady. There was a stirring within her, from the deepest part of her. It was a place of shadows and dust, a space inside her soul where nothing but her deepest self lived. From that dark place, her power came rushing in; a sea, surrounding her in a torrent. Even Ahazi's power seemed like the echo of memory, and she disconnected from her surroundings.

She stood slowly and turned to her friends who had nearly spent their oxygen. Extending a hand, she pulled back, and the power responded. The water sucked itself away from their heads and splattered harmlessly on the ground in front of her. As they gasped for breath she turned to Ahazi,

"Now are you satisfied?" Her voice was not her own, but something much older, and deeper. It was a voice that echoed power, that was as old as the world itself. She felt herself swirling with power and for a moment, she was not Alex, she was something else. And then the moment passed. Like a great storm, the energy faded and Alex was herself again, but the effort had tired her. Her shoulders slumped and she could barely stand. Kyria stood and caught her wearily, being barely able to stand herself.

"I am pleased. I knew such a trick would work. It has done well, this fleshthing," Ahazi said, smiling and clapping.

Alex really wished she had even an ounce of power left within her to smack him in his stupid face.

"It has done well, and Ahazi will do as he says. Behold," He extended his arms and from the swirling vortex, the pieces of the Sullas' ship flew from the water and Alex watched as the ship regrew itself. Barnacles grew from the cracks, acting as a sealant to keep the hull together. Finally, when the ship reassembled, it sat at the edge of Ahazi's island, just outside the funnel of water, which had reversed course and now moved upwards towards the surface.

"Can I ask you one more question?" Alex said.

"It may," Ahazi said.

"Why help us? You don't seem that interested in humans, or our problems. What's in it for you?" A little voice in the back of her head was screaming something about a gift horse, but she was curious. It made no sense.

"Fleshthing still doesn't understand. Even Ahazi is part of the wheels of fate. It would always come here, and Ahazi would always help. I have seen the great game, and I know my place in it. Besides, help it, help Ahazi. I have grown bored in prison. If it destroys the Court, perhaps Ahazi goes free. If it dies, no bolts off my back," Ahazi said, roaring with laughter at his own joke.

Alex rolled her eyes and ignored him. "What do you mean I would always come here?" she asked.

"If it does not understand, I cannot teach it. Begone, away with you. It will take weeks for the smell of fleshthings to go away as it is," Ahazi bellowed, making a shooing motion towards the ship.

Alex needed no further prompting and left while she was ahead. She boarded the ship. As soon as the last of the group was aboard, it moved up the water funnel. Halfway up, however, it took a turn for the unexpected. A large tunnel of water opened up, and the ship veered left into it. It alarmed Alex at first, but she didn't imagine Ahazi would have gone through all the trouble of saving them and testing her just to drown them all. He was capable of that had it been his intent.

Alex leaned against the railing, feeling more and more like Alice going down the rabbit hole. Sullas moved about the ship inspecting it for damage and grumbling about the barnacles. They did an excellent job holding everything together, but he wasn't fond of their look. It seemed odd to her for a slimy eel creature to dislike barnacles, but the fact that Alex was on a ship with a slimy eel creature at all was odd enough.

Alex was squeezed into a hug from behind. She yelped, and turned to find Kyria hugging her, which was the strangest thing she had seen all afternoon.

"Well, this is new," Alex said with a bemused chuckle.

"Shut. Up." Kyria muttered. "I just wanted ta thank ya for saving me. I really thought I was goin' ta die back there."

"While I won't be hugging you," Ahrun said from behind them, "I owe you a staggering debt of gratitude."

Realizing that another human was nearby, Kyria shed herself from the hug in a hurry and stood nonchalantly nearby, braiding her hair absentmindedly.

"I'm not losing anyone else," Alex said. "From here on out, nobody dies. Ever again. Or at least for a long time, and of nothing other than old age."

Her friends smiled and laughed as they took in the scenery. The ship moved like it was on a track, flying through the water at speeds that seemed absurd. Alex looked below. It surprised her to see the water moving in opposite directions. The surrounding tunnel composed itself of water moving in a circular pattern, like the wheel at the end of a funhouse, but the water the ship floated on moved forward in a river. It seemed to defy physics, but Alex imagined being a god had its perks, and apparently ignoring physics was one of them.

As they moved beneath the surface of the ocean, the diversity of life beyond the tunnel of water fascinated Alex. Brilliantly colored schools of fish swam through coral reefs the size of cities. Mysterious ruined cities popped up every so often, encrusted with barnacles and mollusks. It was hard to tell, but through the shimmering water, Alex could almost swear she saw faint images of people moving about.

"What are those?" she asked Kyria.

Kyria wandered over. "No one really knows. I heard the old folks call 'em the Seaward Cities. Ruins o' the height o' the empire, when humanity stretched out o'er every inch of Aquillon, or tha's what the old legends call em.'"

"Are those ghosts?" Alex asked

"Aye. Spirits o' them that were in the cities during the Fall. They sunk, and their spirits trapped forever beneath the waves. The Seaward Cities run all over Aquillon. They're rarely explored, and after destroying them, the Court found no use for them, so they lie abandoned in the depths," Kyria said.

Alex remembered the ruins off the shore the Drowned Coast she had nearly slammed into. It seemed like a lifetime ago now, even though it hadn't even been two months.

Changing the subject, Alex turned to Ahrun, who was sharpening his sword on the edge of some barnacles. "So where are we going to find this waystone," Alex asked. Despite its importance, Alex had somewhat forgotten about the mission. The events of the past several days had pressed it from her memory, but she felt ready to focus on it again.

"As I have told you, my order shares our memory. I have the memory of every paladin who lived after the Fall," he began.

"How does that help? I thought they have sent nobody to the Wyld Places since the Fall," Alex said.

"Lucky for us, that's not so. During the Fall itself, and for a time after, what remained of the order sent several expeditions to the Wyld Places, in search of the Eastern Watch for aid. The expeditions never returned, and we presumed them dead."

"An' this is helpin' us how?" Kyria asked.

"Besides having access to all of my brothers and sisters' memories from Aquillon itself, I can also see the remnants of my brothers and sisters' work in far lands. We call them fragments, like traces of memory for us to find. I know only that we were on the trail of a waystone, and I can trace fragments of past expeditions back to it."

"Nifty trick," Alex replied.

"It is indeed nifty," Ahrun said with a sad smile.

"Have ya seen these fragments as we've traveled?" Kyria asked him.

"I have. I can't speak with them, but it is some comfort to see my brothers and sisters again, if only for a moment," his voice was distant and lonely.

Alex felt for him. In his own way, Ahrun was an orphan, and his disconnected nature made more sense to her. He was a man who lived with one foot in the past, surrounded by ghosts and memories. Alex had often wondered about the far off looks he had given them as they traveled together, but they seemed to make sense now.

From the lack of light in the water above the ship, it seemed to be night. Alex, Kyria and Ahrun shared what was leftover of some soggy meat in Kyria's pack, and tried to get some sleep. It came easier than Alex would have thought, given their bizarre surroundings. In the morning the ship was still on its path, and it seemed not to deviate at all. Alex wondered how many miles they had traveled, but there was no real way of determining that.

Near mid-day however, Alex felt the hull creak and she noticed they were rising instead of going forward. After what seemed like hours, Alex braced herself as the ship shot out of the tunnel of water and landed on the surface. She considered it a minor miracle that the ship didn't break apart.

Alex and the others blinked for a while as their eyes readjusted to full sunlight. They were a hundred feet from the shore of a new land. A brilliant white beach, free of rocks and boulders, led into a dense jungle of strange and beautiful trees. It differed completely from anywhere Alex had yet seen in Aquillon. As Alex watched, a massive beast moved through the underbrush, and even from this far out she could hear the felling of trees, and the destruction the mighty creature wrought as it passed. Alex took a deep breath.

After nearly two months of travel, she had arrived on the shore of the Wyld Places.

21

Where Gods Do Not tread

The ship surfaced around midday, but it took Sullas another hour to find a suitable place to dock. Razor sharp rocks jutted up out of the water along most of the beach, but he eventually found a small stretch where they put down anchor.

"Goodbye, my friend," Ahrun said as he clasped hands with Sullas. "Perhaps we will meet again, in some other place."

Sullas smiled, which Alex hadn't seen him do the entire voyage. "A fair journey to you, my friend. I hope you find what you seek."

Alex walked over to him. "I'm sorry I distrusted you. Thanks for everything!"

Before he could respond she hugged him. He may have been a slimy eel demon, but without him, they wouldn't be here, and he had risked everything for them to make it safely to their destination. None of this made hugging a slimy eel demon any less disgusting.

He seemed stunned but smiled back at her. "I hope you are what Ahrun thinks you are. And I hope you give the Court what is, as you humans say, coming to them."

Alex chuckled nervously. "You and me both, pal, you and me both."

Kyria was slow to approach Sullas and didn't say much more than, "well, thanks I guess. Try no' ta die on yer way back."

Alex knew she felt terrible about being wrong, and the things she said in Damonfall. Sullas knew that too, and her simple words brought a smile to his face. He wrapped her up in a slimy hug before she could protest or run away. She wriggled free and punched him in the arm, giving him a death glare, but smiled as she turned her back and walked away. Alex chuckled to herself, having apparently taught the first demon in Aquillonian history to hug.

They all disembarked and waded onto the beach. As soon as they were clear, Sullas dropped his sail, and the ship moved. The wind was brisk, and before long he and his barnacled ship were a speck of white sailing into the western horizon.

"Do you think he's the only one?" Alex asked Ahrun.

"The only one to defy his Lord or Lady?" he asked.

She nodded.

"I hope not, but I suspect he is. He but advances his own doom, and that kind of selflessness is rare, even in humans.".

Kyria cocked her head. "What do ya mean?"

"What do you think will happen to him when the Court falls, and the Hands are dead?"

It took Alex a second, but she slowly understood. Lesser demons could not live without their masters, comprising their essence. The moment the Lady of Deep Waters died for good, every muradae would die with her, including Sullas. Alex marveled even more at his courage and felt now in hindsight that her few words were not enough. For as long as she had been alive, on Earth and in Aquillon, people never stopped surprising her, and that included eel-faced demons.

Sullas had given Alex any supplies he had on board, but it wasn't much, save for what was in her packs. They had even lost Koga's charm. She silently hoped the stories were true and that the Court wouldn't chase her all the way out here. "I think we should hunt up some food before we get going," Alex said.

"A fair suggestion. I will need to meditate to attune my essence with a nearby fragment," Ahrun said.

"How do we know we'll find the right one?" Kyria asked.

"Of the expeditions the Order sent to the Wyld Places, only two ever reported finding leads on a waystone. It will admittedly be a process of some trial and error, but at least, we will not have to concern ourselves with the Court. I do not think they would send an expedition here under any circumstances."

"Well, that's a plus," Alex said.

"Right, except if this place scares the Court enough ta avoid it, I can only imagine what kind o' lovely critters we'll bump into," Kyria muttered, rolling her eyes.

"Well, let's let the man get to meditating, and we'll go find ourselves a small to medium size critter for dinner," Alex said, gathering her pack and scimitar. Kyria shrugged, and they walked off the beach, leaving Ahrun to his meditations.

It took forever just to find an entrance into the jungle. Twisted roots and thorn bushes the size of elephants blocked the entry of anything smaller than a dinosaur, but after keen searching, Alex spotted a small path that led into the underbrush and they entered the jungle cautiously.

As soon as they entered, Alex turned and tied a length of rope to herself and a tree. As confusing as it looked from the outside, the jungle was a green nightmare from within. Palm fronds formed an impenetrable wall of verdant armor around trees that stretched upward and outward in all directions. Holes riddled the path and spiked roots someone (or something) had honed into a series of deadly pitfall traps made travel less than safe. At one point, Kyria nearly fell into a yawning cavern through a tangle of vines that looked like solid ground. Alex grabbed her hand and pulled her back at the last second.

If navigating wasn't hard enough, the level of extrasensory input from the forest was almost enough to drive a person mad. All around Alex, life teemed and surged, as if unbound by law or predators. Lizards the size of pit bulls skulked through the low-lying branches of trees above, and odd looking ape-like creatures swung over top, paying Alex and Kyria no mind. Massive swarms of mosquitoes and flies buzzed everywhere and a myriad of other insects created a cacophony of sounds.

Then there was the heat. Gone were the balmy climes of Aquillon, replaced instead by steaming humidity. Alex had been out scouting for less than an hour and she was drenched in sweat. Behind her, Kyria breathed heavily, stopping every few feet to wipe sweat from her eyes.

Alex stumbled upon a stream that wove throughout the jungle floor and they gulped water down greedily, as well as filling their canteens. Following the stream deeper into the jungle, they found a clearing and Alex saw Kyria motioning for her to remain quiet. In the clearing ahead a single deer stood grazing from a tall stalk of red grass that sprouted from a root.

Kyria crouched down and Alex followed, careful not to disrupt or disturb the surrounding foliage. Alex pulled out a hunting knife and gripped it by the blade, preparing to throw it. At the moment , there was a colossal crash and a massive claw swooped down into the jungle. Alex looked up and stifled a scream as she watched several story high lizard gulp down the deer.

It gulped the entire creature down in one swallow and came back down onto its claws with a thunder that rocked the entire jungle. Its leg was nearly the size of the clearing and Alex and Kyria dropped prone at once. The lizard which appeared similar to a Komodo dragon curled its head around to see if any other yummy snacks were nearby.

Alex held her breath as the massive forked tongue of the creature probed around them, nearly touching Kyria's leg. Satisfied that it had eaten everything of reasonable size and tastiness in the area, the beast moved deeper into the jungle.

Alex looked over to Kyria, whose face had gone white. "So, that's why nobody ever comes back from the Wyld Places?" Alex stammered.

Kyria nodded blankly. "Yup. Giant lizards, an' gods know what else."

"Should we go back?" Alex asked.

"Nae. I'd rather get eaten by a giant scaly thing than die o' hunger. I'm sure we can find somethin' tha' great scaly beast 'asn't eaten yet," Kyria said, still looking shaken.

The only good thing about their close-call with Godzilla was the monster had cleared a path deeper into the jungle. Alex and Kyria followed it to a riverbank where several more deer were drinking. Kyria wasted no time killing one with a well-aimed throw and hauled it back into the underbrush to avoid it being snacked on by something bigger than her. Kyria showed Alex how to skin the creature and before long they had a clean kill, ready to roast on a fire. Alex felt slightly bad. She never had much of a stomach for hunting, but she figured she was well within the demographic of people who needed to hunt.

Alex's string had run out a while back, but she found it easily enough, and they had returned to the beach before nightfall, no worse for wear (excluding almost being eaten by a giant grub that was hidden inside a log). Alex was grateful to be back on the beach where they could at least see anything that was planning on coming after them.

Ahrun finished with his mediation and in the intervening time, he had started a roaring fire and establish a rudimentary camp. Alex waved to him.

"Honey, we're home!" She said this with a smile, setting the deer carcass down on a nearby log. He gave her the same look he always did when she used what he and Kyria had dubbed Earth-speak. Alex chuckled to herself all the same.

"Well, we found the grub. Ya manage ta' find any ghosts?" Kyria asked. As she spoke she set up a spit and pushed large chunks of meat onto it. After a while, it sizzled and pop and Alex's mouth watered.

"I located the nearest fragment. It is some distance from us, but we should be able to get there within a day's hike," Ahrun said nonchalantly like he was describing a walk in a pleasant meadow.

Alex and Kyria exchanged glances.

"Well, it might be more than a day, but I suppose that's progress," Alex said.

"It is," Arhun said. "I realize the going will be difficult, but once we find the first fragment, it will only be a matter of time before we can track down the location of the waystone."

"Right, if Godzilla and friends don't turn us into lunch," Alex said with a rueful chuckle.

By now the deer was cooking and almost ready. They all waited in silence enjoying the fire. Alex realized how long it had been since she had felt the simple joy of a fire. The whole time she had been in Aquillon the focus had been stealth, but now at least they could enjoy the quiet. Somehow dealing with giant prehistoric monsters seemed less frightening than the Court. There was no malice in a giant creature trying to eat you. It was just the way of things; nature playing out as it always had. Alex wondered if that was how the Court saw it, how they found justification for themselves. She didn't care. They had killed her friend. They were going down.

After a hearty meal, they all fell asleep pulling at them, and Ahrun agreed to take first watch. Alex curled up under a blanket from her pack and let the sway of the palm trees and the crackling of the fire lull her to sleep.

Her sleep was deep and undisturbed. It seemed as if only minutes had passed when Kyria woke her. Alex sat up on a log, allowing Kyria to return to her blanket. She took no time to fall back asleep. Alex sat in silence, listening to the sound of the ocean. The fire died down and she was left to her thoughts.

It was quiet, and she missed Thistle's snoring. She remembered how his snout would vibrate with each chorus of snores, and their absence deeply saddened her. She tried to keep her mind on other things. Still, she felt small and lonely, even though her friends were close. She tried to think of what her dad would say. She could almost see him sitting on the log next to her.

Once, when she was twelve, they had gone camping in Oregon and camped out on a beach like this one. They stayed up all night talking and counting the stars. She missed him now more than ever, on the edge of a world she barely understood, facing a task she barely felt adequate enough for.

"Listen, kid," she could hear him say, "the world is a tough place and we're just small people. You can only do what you can do, but the question isn't what you can do. Never has been. It's how are you going to do it? All you need is a plan, and everything in the world becomes about as complicated as doing the dishes. Just need a plan." Granted, he had been talking about her algebra class (math was evil, and she had always hated it), but she felt better remembering his words. He had always known just what to say, and she would have given anything to have him here with her.

She felt hot tears running down her cheeks as the first pale streaks of sunlight glimmered on the western horizon. The sun rising in the west was another thing she hadn't processed, but on the long list of strange things she wasn't used to in Aquillon, solar anomalies were somewhere near the bottom. She heard the other two stirring, and she wiped her tears away. *Now isn't the time for feelings and tears. Now is the time for not getting eaten by giant death lizards,* she told herself.

It didn't take long to break camp and before long they were on their way into the jungle, following Ahrun's lead. Alex could tell Kyria noticed her puffy eyes, but thankfully she said nothing. Focusing on the task at hand and moving forward was comforting to Alex. Her head was a busy place lately that she'd just as soon stay out of and focusing on the mission helped.

As Ahrun led them into the jungle, it appeared they were following a map only he could see. Here and there he would stop to overturn a rock, check the trunk of a tree, or look at an overly large fern as though it might talk to him (to be fair, it wasn't the most unreasonable possibility in Aquillon). By midday, he seemed to be onto something.

"So, what does it look like to you, following these fragments?" Alex asked him, deciding to break up the sounds of the jungle with a little conversation.

"It is hard to describe," Arhun said. "Imagine following a visual echo. I see a footprint here, or a handprint there. Sometimes even a full blow silhouette if I'm lucky. The fragment is a complete memory, but leading to it, I only see echoes. They grow stronger as we grow near".

She nodded. "But how we know it's the right one? There were two expeditions that might have found the waystone, but we don't know which one."

"We just hope to get lucky," he replied with a smile.

Kyria and Alex both exchanged skeptical looks and giggled.

\#

The morning's hike was a crash course on the vibrant ecosystem of the Wyld Places. Everything grew in abundance here, and the only natural law seemed to be that of good old Darwin; survival of the fittest. The plants that grew were taller and healthier than Aquillonian plants. They took thirty minutes to walk around a fern that had grown to the size of a two story building.

The fauna was equally fascinating, and none of it had tried to eat them, which was a big plus in Alex's book. Smaller animals made their way through the underbrush, and the large ones dared to put their heads above the tree cover. They saw a giraffe looking creature with three heads that moved through the jungle, grazing as it went. It noticed them and camouflaged instantly. Later that day they saw a pack of leopards that had spots that shimmered and changed color to match the surrounding jungle. Fortunately, they paid Alex and her friends no mind, seeming to be after bigger fish. Everything in the jungle was equipped to survive perfectly. It reminded Alex of Shelhyle, and she marveled at the splendor of nature unbound, undeterred by man or demon.

This forest was different though. Shelhyle had felt dark, like corruption from the Lady of the Wood polluting it. This one did not. It seemed clean and free, unconcerned with the corruption across the sea. That fact made it no less deadly, but at least it felt clean.

By the late afternoon, they had arrived at the end of the trail of invisible echoes Ahrun was following. The jungle trail bottomed out at an old campsite. A wide berth of the jungle was clear-cut and burned for long-term engagement. Everything seemed ancient and delicate. The remains of a stone wall ringed the edge of the encampment and one rickety guard tower constructed of palm wood remained to watch over the ruin.

As soon as he stepped foot within the camp Ahrun fell to his knees gripping his skull tightly. Alex and Kyria turned in alarm, but he waved them off.

"I am just a bit overwhelmed. It has been many years since I beheld a complete fragment. Do not aid me or it will pollute the vision!" he insisted.

Alex did as he asked and set about exploring the camp. Several skeletons lay strewn around the camp, ripped into a variety of shapes and arrangements. Without further investigating it seemed like something had overrun the camp, dooming the few paladins who had remained to guard it. Vines from the jungle had consumed most of the camp, and only a few tents made of sturdy material seemed still usable. Alex helped Kyria get a fire going while Ahrun continued battling with the vision he was trying to process.

By nightfall Alex huddled around a pathetic-looking fire. The ruins of the camp were far more eerie than they had been in the daytime, and Alex and Kyria sat closer to each other. They nearly screamed when Ahrun walked out of the darkness and took a seat.

He barely looked himself. Even in the firelight he seemed pale and his eyes looked haunted and distant, like a soldier that has seen too much. He sat for a moment in silence before speaking,

"Forgive my gaunt outward appearance. The stress of the fragment was almost more than I could bear." His voice was weak, and speaking seemed to strain him.

Alex nodded. "It must have been a lot. This place is putting off terrible vibes, so I'm sure it wasn't pleasant. Didn't you say you shared the memories of your order? Why even put yourself through the strain?" Alex asked.

"Some things I can remember easily, but the more distant the memory, the longer it would take to recall. I did not know these paladins, and this was a very long time ago. It would take, well...much longer than we have to retrieve the information. The fragments are much faster," Ahrun answered.

"Well," Kyria said, "I don' mean ta be a touch indelicate, but did ya have any luck tracking down the group tha' came looking for the waystone?"

"I have seen a way forward, and many other things," Ahrun said with a shudder.

"So, we know where the waystone is?" Alex asked, her curiosity getting the better of her empathy.

"Not directly, but yes, I found something. We are standing in the last camp of the Order, established five hundred years ago," Ahrun said.

"Wow, it's really well preserved for its age," Alex said.

"Fragments have a way of preserving a place. Without the fragment, this camp would fade away and the jungle would consume it.".

"I see. You were saying?" Alex asked.

"The Order established this forward camp with the goal of locating the expeditions that came before it, which they sent in search of a waystone. They failed and never returned, but one sent a letter claiming to have found it," Ahrun said.

"What were they hoping to do with it?" Alex asked.

"Study it. Take it back. That part is less clear. Whatever the Order intended with it, they did not focus on it because it is not as strong as other parts of the fragment."

"So, where do we go from here?" Alex asked.

"They sent out a scouting party to find any evidence of the other expedition. That was when something overran the camp. The guards fought valiantly, but they were no match for the raw strength of the creatures, they were…" Ahrun began stammered his words and his eyes went wide.

Alex gripped his shoulder and squeezed. "You don't have to tell us," she said with a smile, "no need to relive it again."

"My thanks," he said, returning the smile. "I think from here I can follow the fragments to the other expedition. We can make our way to the waystone tomorrow."

"For now, we sleep," Kyria commanded.

They drew straws and Alex got last watch again. She drifted off to sleep uneasily. There was something in the ruins. She could feel its presence looming just beyond where the firelight died, and she knew they were being watched. She just wasn't sure by what.

The night's rest seemed to do Ahrun some good, and in the morning he was more like himself. They struck out, leaving the camp behind and Alex was glad. The place had a seriously creepy vibe going on.

The trail grew harder and harder to follow as they went deeper and deeper into the jungle. It seemed to Alex the deeper they went, the life they encountered became more hostile, and better equipped to survive. The deer near the beach had looked like any deer someone would find munching on a garden, but here the deer were strange, alien creatures. They had multiple eyes and outward chitinous armor covered their hides, that looked like it would bend Kyria's hunting knife if she even tried to throw it. The deer were not skittish or shy, and did not budge when they saw Alex, but looked back at her as if to say, *try it, I dare you.*

Ahrun halted and kneeled down, clearing vines away from a small patch of earth. Alex and Kyria looked down at what he was digging away at and the pale eye sockets of a skull greeted them. As Ahrun unearthed more, it was clear it had been a paladin (Alex recognized one symbol on its armor from Ahrun's sword), though the body was in bad shape. Puncture holes riddled the torso, and something had crushed the back of its skull. Alex gulped as she looked at the remains. This paladin had not met with an unfortunate accident; he or she had fallen prey to something vicious.

"We are close. This brother found the first expedition, but he never made it back to camp. There is something I don't understand," he examined the body further, "it is like someone killed him," Ahrun said with a puzzled look on his face.

"That's what it looks like," Alex said. "But who would have killed him? Nobody lives out here, right?"

Kyria shook her head. "There are no records o' people settlin' in this area. They say the empire tried to colonize, but it always ended badly."

"Whatever he found, someone didn't want him to share it with the Order," Ahrun said darkly. "Unfortunately for his killer, he left a strong memory. We should be able to follow it back to the expedition."

"Good, the sooner we find this stone, the better," Alex muttered. "I get a bad feeling that whatever killed him might still be out there."

"That was hundreds o' years ago," Kyria replied skeptically.

"Maybe, but there's something evil in this jungle. I feel it. I don't know how, but I feel it," Alex said, shivering despite the heat.

As they traveled farther down the trail, the heat of the day beat down with brutal, unrelenting oppression. Alex was covered in sweat, as were her friends, but they were lucky enough to find streams here and there to take on water and wet their faces. Ahrun finally pulled aside a large palm to reveal their destination. Alex breathed a sigh of relief.

The trail let out into a large opening in the jungle, at the base of a cliff. Vines and flowers had consumed most of the cliffside and it extended up quite a distance. Water cascaded down from a river that ended at the top of the cliff into a large pool nearby. A large camp of stone structures hollowed out of the base of the cliff and sat sheltered from the heat of the day. It reminded Alex of cliff dweller structures she had seen on a trip to Arizona. In the center of the village, a large hole yawned into a black void below.

Alex felt Ahrun grip her shoulder painfully tight. She turned to see what the matter was and saw that a vision had taken him. He slumped over, gripping his head and mumbling nonsense. She looked at Kyria, who sighed.

"Well, we best leave 'Ser Faints a lot' ta his vision. This looked like a good place to camp, if nothin' else," Kyria said.

Alex nodded, but she felt something else here. It was like the camp from before, but worse. The air here seemed saturated with a presence of deep and terrible intent and she was at least mostly sure it wasn't just the stifling humidity, although that felt downright evil.

Alex poked around the ruins in search of something useful, while Kyria made camp and watched over Ahrun. The huts seemed to pre-date the equipment left by the paladin expedition, and there were strange carvings etched into the walls of a great creature being worshipped by small creatures (presumably humans). Inside each hut, more skeletons in paladin armor lay strewn about, but these were more disturbing. They were each in bedrolls, or what remained of them, anyway. It appeared as though something had ambushed these paladins at night and killed them in their sleep. Alex shuddered to think what could take out an entire camp of paladins. She had seen Ahrun fight, and she hoped that whatever had killed a whole group of paladins died a long time ago.

A groan of pain from Ahrun interrupted Alex's survey of the village. Running outside, she went to him and knelt beside Kyria who was sponging his forehead with a damp cloth. His eyes were barely open, and he looked far worse than the last time the vision had taken him. His muscles seemed strained, and the color had left his face completely. He appeared he was trying to say something, but the words weren't coming out. Finally, he spoke,

"We should not have come here. I see now the pain and the horror that this place contained. I was a fool not to have seen it. I should have listened to my gut..." he was shaking his head.

"I don't understand, is the waystone here or not?" Alex asked, confused.

"It is, but the Eastern Watch hid it somewhere they knew no one would ever recover it from. A place of primal evil, where even good men go mad. A place no mortal should tread, where no power on Aquillon should go." As he spoke, his eyes opened wide, and Alex saw the fear in them. Raw terror, as she had never seen in his eyes, transfixed on a single point. The pit in the center of the village.

"What evil? It can't be tha' bad after what we've been through," Kyria joked, punching him in the shoulder.

"There were evils that walked these lands long before the first man walked upright and before the Court came. Evils that looked upon the stars when they were new. Now comes the vision upon me, and I was a fool not to heed it. I once asked a wise elder of my Order why we never sent more expeditions, and she told me, "Ahrun, there is a darkness in the Wyld Places that no light can expunge. Tread not there, for no god can save you if you do. I was a fool, I have led us to our doom!"

Alex could see him unraveling fast and he tried to bolt into the jungle, but she and Kyria stopped him. As they did, Alex saw his eyes following something behind them. Turning around, she saw a man climbing out of the pit. She knew now what had killed the paladins, and why she felt a presence watching them from the shadows.

He wasn't much taller than Alex, but his skin was dark, blackened with coal and soot. Scars of ritual carvings ran the length of his body and in his hands, he gripped massive cudgels made of stone and wood. A terrifying animal mask made of a large skull and animal fur covered his face. Aside from that, he wore only a filthy loincloth. Out of the eye sockets, his eyes, riddled with madness, gleamed malice and hatred at them. He had a wide smile of sharp, crooked teeth, painted black.

"It is too late," Ahrun mumbled, "it begins."

"What is tha'?" Kyria asked. Even her voice trembled.

"Come, children, the master calls!" The creature snarled. "Come on down to the night and we'll gobble you up, to eat your light." His voice was the sound of gravel and bone breaking, a shrill hiss.

Great, Alex thought, *a rhyming lunatic.* "All right Dr. Seuss, just go back down in your little hole. You're outnumbered," she said, sounding more confident than she felt.

"Fear is the only response. I hear the drums in the jungle call for blood. Drums, drums, drums," he said in a wild scream.

He raised his cudgels up and charged. Alex narrowly dodged him and drew her scimitar. She couldn't attack back because all she could do was dodge each strike. They grew stronger, and she felt the earth shake as the great stone weapon smashed into the jungle floor. He swung his weapons wildly in every direction, making a sneak attack from Kyria impossible. He attacked and defended on all sides leaving no gaps.

Alex was tired, but she saw an opening. A small palm frond rested precariously over a hole in the ground. She wasn't sure how deep the hole was, but it would slow him down at least. She lured him back until finally she hopped back over the hole and he fell into it with a cry. The hole extended down into the untold darkness below, and he held himself carefully. She walked over to him.

"Clever girl, clever. Drums for me, drums for you, drums for the master! Drums and blood!" He laughed a wild cackle as he spoke.

"Well, if you're looking to kill us, I'm afraid you'll have to get in line, pal," Alex replied. She kicked his head, and he fell all the way through the hole, laughing into the darkness below. His laughter echoed for a long time after he had fallen out of sight. She did not hear him hit the bottom, he simply fell until she couldn't see him anymore. She returned to Kyria who was helping Ahrun to his feet. He seemed somewhat recovered.

"You good?" Alex asked him with a raised eyebrow.

"I believe so. The evil that happened here was a lot to process. My brothers and sisters never had a chance. Slaughtered in their sleep, by those things."

"Are they humans? I thought there were no humans in the Wyld Places," Kyria said.

"No men we know of, but evil things often draw men to the darker corners of the world. Here is no different. I don't know who this master is, but his followers found the waystone and used it to lure the paladins to their deaths," Ahrun said.

"You said the Eastern Watch placed it here," Alex replied.

"They did, but they knew it would draw darkness to itself. Powerful artifacts have oft been known to draw evil as a flame draws a moth. They most likely buried it within the ground here and these tribesmen and whatever they worship found it. I sense greater darkness at play here than some madmen in the jungle," Ahrun said, pointing to the pit.

"So, we have to go down there and find it. And by down there, I mean the scary monster filled hole where the crazy murdering psychopath came out of?" Alex asked with a sigh.

"It seems that way," he replied.

"Well, I guess we'll descend in the morning," Alex said.

"Hate ta burst your bubble, as you say Alex, but we need ta go. Now." Kyria's voice was brimming with panic, and it didn't take long for Alex to figure out why. Far beyond the clearing, something was rustling through the underbrush and Alex heard them, thundering in the distance. Drums. Drums in the jungle.

22

Darkness Deep, Where Creatures Sleep

A lex had to move fast. Dealing with one of them had been difficult, and there wasn't any way of discerning how many were about to crash through the jungle into the village. Kyria went about hacking vines off the cliff and Ahrun helped her tie them together into rope. Alex had some rope left in her pack, but not enough.

Alex peered into the pit and the darkness of it pulled her in. It extended for an endless time into the gloom but far below, a small platform of wooden planks extended outwards. She tied her remaining rope onto a nearby root and waited for the others. When they had assembled enough vine into rope, they joined her. Alex went first, slowly descending on her rope into the pit. She moved down the walls, using rocks and ledges as she went to lower herself. One poorly chosen step and she would fall back into the void, and she didn't want to play trust fall with her rope.

The other two followed, slowly at first, but as the sound of drums grew louder, they quickened their pace until all three of them were standing on the platform below. The platform was old, and the wood creaked under their weight. Alex heard murmuring above, so she moved into the tunnel that opened up on the side of the platform. Kyria followed and Ahrun brought up the rear.

As Alex walked through the tunnel, a vast array of morbid carvings covered the walls and every fifty feet a torch illuminated the way forward. The air was dank and old, and the presence Alex felt earlier was nearly stifling. There was something else down here, something old, and Alex sensed them getting closer to it. She wanted to ask her friends if they felt it, but they seemed unsettled enough and she didn't want to make it worse.

As Alex walked, the tunnel sloped down periodically, sending them deeper into the ground. The tunnel was carved stone, and wide, with enough space for two or three people to walk side by side comfortably. It was clear to Alex that whatever made it was not a human in a loincloth, though she saw remnants of humans living in the tunnels.

Alex halted. Kyria and Ahrun nearly slammed into her and they gave her an annoyed glance. They looked ahead and quickly realized why she had stopped.

In front of them was a large chamber. Alex looked around, amazed. It was hundreds of feet high and rounded out into a massive sphere. The walls of the chamber were perfectly smooth and all around it, carvings and runes decorated them. A long stone ladder, carved into the wall, led down from the tunnel to a small stone village which sat next to what appeared to be a huge nest. From the distance, Alex couldn't tell what made the nest but she had a bad feeling she already knew. A gust of wind shot through the tunnel behind her and she heard angry voices.

"We need to keep moving," she told her friends, "we are definitely not alone down here."

Ahrun and Kyria nodded, and they all moved down the ladder. Alex gripped the ladder tightly and climbed down. It was terrifying. The rungs extended only inches from the wall and they were smooth and hard to grasp. One bad step or slip of the hand would have resulted in a long fall with a very short stop. She moved as fast as she was able but the voices and the drums were growing louder.

Finally, Alex and her friends reached the base of the ladder, just as the voices reached the top. Alex looked up and saw five more men and women, dressed just like the one she had fought in the village above. They pointed and shouted angrily, but she couldn't tell what they were saying. Alex imagined it was something like, *kill them and feed their bodies to our diabolically evil master, ha ha ha.* Clichés were just as terrifying if her enemy meant it.

"We need to deal with them. We can't keep running. This tunnel will end eventually and I *really* don't want to be down here long enough to meet whatever lives in that," Alex said, pointing to the nest.

"Fine, but we need a plan," Kyria replied.

"They have the numbers, but maybe," Alex trailed off as she looked around the chamber for ideas, "we can use that village…" She looked up.

The group of six was traveling slowly down the ladder, not looking anywhere but forward. "We can surprise them in the village and take a couple out and make it a fair fight, as we did outside Alcrest."

Ahrun nodded. "We are short on time, and it seems as good a plan as any."

"Aye, let's get on with it," Kyria said with a shrug.

Alex made her way to the stone village quickly and each of them hid inside a hut, within sight of one another. After an eternity of tense waiting, Alex heard the villagers reach the bottom of the ladder and they spread out. Finally, one made his way into the village. As he entered the center of the ring of huts, Kyria threw a pebble at him and waved with a smile. The wild-man raised his cudgel and charged, but didn't make it far as Alex's scimitar embedded itself deep in his ribcage. He fell over and didn't move.

Soon enough two more entered the village and Ahrun quickly took one out while their attention was on Alex, who ran through a quick recitation of the chicken dance. Before Ahrun dealt with the second one, the tribesman shouted in a strange guttural language and the others noticed and charged towards the village. Ahrun quickly dispatched him, but the jig was up. They'd have to fight the remaining two head on.

The tribesman attacked much like the one above, wild and unpredictable. Alex had trouble defending against each strike and could do little but jump out of the way of each massive blow. There was a moment between each attack though and she sensed a pattern she used to her advantage. Each time the wild-man paused she placed a well-timed slash against his side or a swift kick to his head. They were only minor wounds, but as he attacked relentlessly, they wore on him. Finally, he paused a moment too long between attacks and Alex took advantage, bringing him down with a quick strike.

Alex looked over and saw that Kyria was still dealing with hers. As he swung his cudgel at her, she dropped to her knees and brought her leg sweeping under him, sending him to the floor with a crash. At the moment before he recovered, she pounced on him, plunging her knives into his chest.

As the adrenaline in her died, Alex was sick. She had killed demons on Aquillon, which somehow seemed less heinous, but she hadn't killed a person. She had pushed the villager down the hole earlier, but this was different. Her own hand had killed a person. She doubled over, riddled with guilt and nearly threw up. She felt Kyria's hand on her shoulder. "We didn't 'ave a choice," she said reassuringly.

"I know, but I'm not... not used to killing people," Alex said.

"As well you shouldn't be. You have a good heart Alex," Ahrun said. "To kill another person is an inhumane action. And you never get used to it. It would concern me if you did."

Alex felt slightly better and stood up.

Ahrun continued, "besides, if you had seen the atrocities these people had committed, you would have no remorse. They were more beast than man." As he said this, he grimaced and spat. As Alex recovered, he walked over to one of the fallen villagers and removed his mask. Alex heard him gasp and curse loudly.

Alex called over to him, "what is it?"

"I had suspected but hoped it was not true. These are my brothers. Paladins of the Seventh Dawn, fallen to madness. They are all that remains of the first expedition. They lured their own brothers and sisters to their doom. Why, I do not know."

It was Alex's turn to comfort him. "I'm so sorry, I know this is hard."

Alex and Kyria gathered him up into a tight group hug before he protested.

"What drove them crazy?" Kyria asked.

"Hard to say. This is the den of something old and evil. In such places, men can lose their wits. The power of what dwells here can stain a person's soul. I know you sense it."

Alex nodded. "It's like a weight on my chest, and it gets worse the deeper we go."

"Then we should be quick about our business. The longer we delay, the worse the toll will be, and the greater the chance the creature will return. Even our combined wits will be no matter in the face of such an evil," Ahrun said in a grim voice.

Alex didn't argue, and she searched the area for a way forward. She couldn't find any exits. After an hour of searching, she cursed with frustration and returned to the village center. Ahrun was standing over the bodies with his hand held out, chuckling to himself. "So simple..." he said, trailing off.

"Care to share with the class?" Alex asked him.

"These men may have been mad beasts, but they were once paladins, so they left a fragment when they died. One moment," he said.

Ahrun meditated. After a time he opened his eyes. His face had gone pale and his eyes blazed wildly.

"What did ya see?" Kyria asked.

"Horror beyond imagining. I know what lived here. I also saw where they hid the waystone. We should retrieve it and move quickly to get out of here. I am unsure when the last time the creature who lived here used this burrow but it may return at any time so the quicker we can escape, the better." Ahrun visibly shuddered as he spoke.

"That makes two of us. So where is this shiny magic rock?" Alex asked.

"That's, as you say, the bad news," Ahrun said, pointing towards the nest.

"It's buried deep in the big nasty's nest, isn't it?" Alex asked with a sigh.

"An' we need ta go an' get it from the depth o' the nest, mos' likely rousing the beast out o' some slumber?" Kyria said, with an equally aggravated sigh.

"That's more or less the situation," Ahrun said with a resigned grimace on his face.

As she neared it, Alex's worst theories came true, and she saw that thousands of bones made up the nest. Most were from animals, but here and there a skull or a ribcage surfaced in the ocean of death and marrow. They reached the ridge of the nest and peered into the crater below. At the base , the weight of a massive creature had crushed the bones, several hundred feet wide. At the exact center, a deep hole radiated the foul energy and Alex nearly choked being this close.

"Are either of you feeling this? Super gross…" she said, trailing off and making a disgusted face.

Kyria and Ahrun shook their heads, looking at each other confused.

Great, Alex thought, *I'm now being choked by invisible voodoo energy that nobody else can see or detect. Fantastic.*

"So, I'm assuming the waystone is in that hole," Alex said.

"Absolutely," Kyria said with manufactured cheeriness and pluck. "Where else would it be?"

"The Eastern Watch was wise to bury it here. Nobody in their right mind would come looking for it," Ahrun said.

"Well, that makes us the perfect crew or magnificently mad fools to get it!" Alex replied, mimicking Kyria's gusto.

Ahrun gave them both a disgruntled frown and proceeded forward. It was slow going as Alex made her way down the bone horde. Some bones were razor points, hewn sharp, and others were facades of holes that riddled the nest. They were only ten to twenty feet deep, but potentially fatal if stepped on by an unsuspecting climber. Then there was the fact that climbing on a pile of bones was disconcerting and in Alex's words, super gross. As she climbed down, Alex found some bones that hadn't been picked clean and her hand would grip something gooey and squishy. It took a lot of nerve not to scream and let go, but death, as always, acted as a successful deterrent to rash actions.

After what seemed like an hour of climbing down and only five near-death experiences, Alex reached the base of the nest. She was barely breathing and she relied on Kyria for support as she hobbled to the edge of the pit. The energy was tangible now, radiating out black tendrils like veins of polluted, vile magic. Alex sensed her energy being sapped with each step, and the energy pressed in on her throat, as real to her as a clenched hand squeezing the life from her. As she stood at the base of the pit, it took both Ahrun and Kyria to support her and her vision blurred. Alex wasn't sure why her companions weren't feeling the effects of the energy, but she wasn't able to concentrate on anything.

"Almost there, kid," Kyria said, "don'cha go dyin' on me now. I'm no' haulin' your rump back up tha' ladder."

Alex chuckled weakly. "There you go again, being all sappy. Buck up, softy."

Staring into the pit Alex saw only darkness at first. Then the stone appeared gradually, but Alex wasn't sure it wasn't a hallucination.

"I see it," she called out.

"I see nothing, where are you looking?" Ahrun said, sounding perplexed.

"Got nothin' here," Kyria responded.

"Really? It's right there!" It flabbergasted Alex, but slowly realized they truly couldn't see it. She pointed towards the stone, which came more and more into focus as time passed, but they shook their heads, exchanging confused looks.

"Perhaps your connection with the Watch makes you able to see it," Ahrun suggested.

"Maybe..." she trailed off. This was a problem. The stone looked too heavy to lift on her own, and she really didn't know how they would bring it back out of the evil death pit if her friends couldn't even see the stupid thing. Alex extended her hands and concentrated on the stone, hoping something might happen. She sat for several minutes looking immensely foolish. Finally, she got angry and muttered to herself, attempting to focus her aggression on the stone. She had marched halfway across a steaming jungle, all the way across the world, nearly died more times than she could count, and lost a good friend, and now this stupid stone had the gall not to appear. She let all of her anger flow through her and something inside switched on, as it had when Ahazi was drowning her friends. Energy surged around her and she directed it towards the stone. It glowed red.

The vile energy slowly dissipated. It appeared whatever hex the Magi had placed on it, was waning in the presence of Alex's abilities.

Without warning, a small set of glowing eyes opened on the stone, as did a mouth, which wasted no time in twisting itself into a crooked smile that reminded Alex of the Cheshire cat.

"Ah, no need for the anger dear. I am here!" The stone announced itself as though it were a great hero descending from on high to rescue her. Its voice crackled like a roaring hearth.

Alex quickly glanced at her friends. "Guys, I'm not the only hearing the talking rock, right?"

They looked at her, and to her relief, they shook their heads, dumbfounded.

"Narry you worry my dear lady! I have enabled these lesser forms of life to perceive my glorious voice so they may bask in their own inferiority. You are magnanimous to travel with such creatures!"

"Aye, thank ya yer ladyship," Kyria said with a humble curtsy. Alex thought Kyria's sides might explode from suppressing the laugh that was trying to engulf her.

Alex scowled at her and returned her attention to the talking stone. Red runes glowed around the circumference of the stone and they glowed as it spoke. Alex spoke first.

"So, is this a genie in the lamp situation? How does this work?" Alex asked.

"Ah, I see you are uninitiated! Still, the gift flows through you. I would not deign to speak with a lesser being." Its eyes drifted scornfully towards Kyria and Ahrun. Kyria appropriately stuck her tongue out at it.

Before Kyria got in a fight with the rock, Alex continued the conversation. "Let me be more clear: how do we use you to get to the Eastern Watch?"

"Use me, I well, I don't, I never..." the stone seemed to sputter. It took some time to collect itself from what seemed like a grave insult. "I apologize, your phrasing seemed, brusque, and it is many years since

I dealt with an uninitiated magus. There is a certain level of decorum shown relics of my pedigree." Alex couldn't be sure, but it seemed like the stone was preening.

"To answer your question, I can transport you to the Sanctum, and your servants, if that is what you wish," the stone said.

"Great, simple answer to a simple question. I love it. C'mon guys, I think we're finally in the clear!" Alex said with a smile.

They moved to the center of the pit. The stone hovered over the pit just close enough to touch. They all reached out and grabbed ahold of the stone, waiting for something to happen. Nothing did. They waited for a moment longer, looking at each other. An astonishing amount of nothing continued to happen.

"Well?" Alex asked the stone, trying to conceal her irritation.

"Well, what? You can't expect me to perform under these conditions," the stone said indignantly. "Do you have any idea how long I've been down here? I need the sun! I need fresh air! I need a space to breathe!" it said in what sounded like an angry voice.

"Yer a rock! What in the blazin' abyss would ya need tha' for? Just transport us already," Kyria said in an exasperated voice.

The runes flared, and the stone pulsed with energy. Alex felt it radiating from it, and she tried to cut it off at the pass before they all got turned into fish.

"A very nice rock! And a very helpful rock! And if you need air and sun to work, we will take you there!" As Alex said this, she desperately pleaded to Kyria to stop antagonizing the stone. She wasn't sure what it was able to do, but the last thing she needed was it getting in a huff and shutting down.

"No! I will not be spoken to like that by some filthy, lowborn, no good, pond scum! It will apologize or there's no deal. I would never shame my masters by bringing such a rude little creature to them!" the stone said.

275

"Why ya prissy little… I'm gonna turn ya into a pile of pebbles ya useless…" Kyria grabbed the stone and squeezed it but yelped when it shot lightning out at her. Their shouting match echoed around the dark chamber and Alex looked around nervously.

"Look, we can work this out! But I really think we should keep our voices…"

Before she finished, a howl that chilled Alex to her core rocked the chamber. In all her life, even the time she had spent on Aquillon, she had heard nothing like this. It was an ancient noise, like something that had crawled out of the fabric of a primordial world, made of pure terror and death. No natural creature made it; it was too horrible, too savage, too far removed from the realm of gods and mortals.

"Down," Alex finished in a voice that wasn't hers. It belonged to her eight-year-old self, the girl who still jumped at shadows, and needed a night light. Her friends looked pale, and it muted even the waystone. "Guys, I think whatever lives in this pit knows we're here and we need to be scarce. Like now," Alex finished.

Nobody was in a mood to argue, even the waystone. Alex looked around. From the sound of the roar, the creature was coming from the other end of the chamber, although no tunnel was visible. That way was no good, and they would never make it up the ladder by the time the creature arrived. Alex was caught in the bottom of the nest with the giant evil beast that lived there making quick progress towards them. As she glanced around, she saw the village of stone huts.

"We need to get to the buildings," she said to her friends. "And you," she said angrily to the stone, "you are coming with me whether you like it or not because there's no chance you're ever getting out of here without us!" The stone did not argue. Alex pulled it towards her. As she did, it shrank until it was the size of a fist.

"I have adjusted the space ratio of my composition for enhanced traveling!" it said, sounding impressed with itself.

The beast roared again. It was getting closer. The walls shook with every step it made towards them,

"That's wonderful, but now is really not the time!" Alex said.

Alex made her way to the huts and ducked inside one, followed closely by her friends. Just as they did a great bellow shook the chamber, followed by a crash as the sound of rocks exploding rocked the hut. The sound came from the back of the chamber. Whatever this thing was, it was powerful enough to dig through solid stone. Alex's heart pounded so fast she was afraid someone would notice. She closed her eyes and waited.

The creature was huge, by the sound. Every step it took rumbled the chamber and a foul stench followed it, gagging Alex. She choked, but she realized the others were fine. The energy that had nearly suffocated her earlier wasn't coming from the pit or the stone. It was coming from the beast. She saw black tendrils of it whisping inside the door. Whatever this creature was, it radiated pure malice and raw hatred in a tangible form.

They remained silent as the creature prowled about the chamber. Alex heard it sniffing around. As it made its way over to the nest, it roared in fury, throwing bones into the air as it searched for something. Then she realized it was looking for the stone. She really hoped the creature couldn't track it.

After a while of searching, the creature settled into its nest, deciding apparently that the intruders had left. That, or it was cleverly waiting for them to come out so it could chomp them down as a snack. There wasn't really any way to be sure. Alex put her head out of the opening of the hut they were hiding in and looked around. From the top of the nest, she could see the ridge of the creature. It was as massive as it sounded, running several hundred feet long, and nearly as many wide. From where she stood, only the top of the creature was visible.

Great spines stood up on its back, rising and falling with the creature's breathing. Each spine was as tall as a fully grown human, and they gleamed a razor's edge in the cavern's gloom.

Alex motioned for her friends to follow her lead, and they slowly made their way out of the hut. It was a thousand feet or more to the ladder they had come in on, by Alex's rough estimation. They would have to be silent, however. One noise and the creature would be on them, and even Alex doubted that her powers would get them out of that mess.

They snuck across the cavern, prioritizing silence over speed. As they did, Alex took in the creature. The scale of the beast was incredible; even for Aquillon, a land of demon lords and mythical beasts, it was impressive. Whatever it was, it was ancient and lived in a land without law, save for survival of the fittest. If there was something in the Wyld Places scarier than it, Alex didn't want to run into it.

Arriving at the ladder they shuffled up it quietly, Alex taking up the rear. As she moved up the ladder, it was tempting to look back down to get a clearer picture of the creature, but something stopped her. There were some things that humans weren't meant to see. Perhaps it had driven the first expedition mad, perhaps not. Alex didn't want to chance it and her gut told her it was a bad idea. Her gut rarely failed her, so she listened to it.

Alex made it to the top of the ladder, arriving without incident. Kyria turned to look back down, driven by the same curiosity inside Alex. Alex grabbed Kyria and turned her around.

"Don't. I don't think you want to see what's down there," Alex said.

Kyria shrugged, and they moved forward. Alex pulled the stone out of her pocket and it hovered in her hand as they walked.

"So," she said, "can you work now? And don't even think of asking for another apology. It's water under the bridge." It looked as though it was about to say something pithy in retort, but she was in no mood and gave it a foul look, and the stone thought better of saying it.

"I will help, but I need to be under an open sky to function. My core directional matrix is completely out of synch down here. I could try to send you to Sanctum, but you'd as likely land in a whale's stomach as your intended destination," it said matter-of-factly.

"Fair enough," she replied.

"Although an apology would be nice…"

"Don't start with me!" she spat.

The stone clammed up with a pouty look on its face.

They finally reached the entrance shaft and thankfully Alex's rope and the vines were still there. Some rocks had shifted about from the vibrations of the beast entering the chamber, but the rope was intact. Alex put the stone in her pocket, and grabbed her rope and climbed.

She took a long time to get up the rope. Still, she could tell her strength had grown in the months she had been on Aquillon. Back home, she never would have been able to pull herself up to a shaft, but she moved up all the same, inch by inch. Ahrun and Kyria made it to the top first. Alex could have sworn she heard a muffled shout, but the sounds of the jungle were near now and she figured it could have been anything.

Alex was eager to make it to the top and finally put the mission behind her. She felt so close to the truth now, a truth she had been seeking since the moment she came to Aquillon. It seemed like a lifetime ago now. Alex concentrated on the climb and finally reached the top. The climb had drenched her in sweat as she pulled herself over the lip of the hole. Maybe the Eastern Watch had figured out the mystery of indoor plumbing, Alex hoped. She'd sell her soul for a shower.

As she stood it took a moment for her eyes to adjust to the brilliant sunlight overhead. Once it had, her stomach fell, and she cursed herself for not paying more attention. Men and women in fox masks surrounded them. She took a moment to remember them, but she finally did. They had narrowly escaped the Fox's Guild outside of Felwind when they met with Maggie. Alex had forgotten about them entirely, mostly because there had been other terrors to focus on. Apparently, the Fox's Guild hadn't forgotten her.

Kyria was being held by two burly looking men but was still squirming and kicking against them. Ahrun looked worse for wear and had put up a struggle from the blood running down his face. They had disarmed both of her friends.

From the center of the group, a tall woman walked over to Alex. Alex looked around, trying to think of a way out, but the Foxes hopelessly outnumbered them. Even if Alex knew how to use the waystone, she wouldn't be able to take her friends, and she wasn't going to leave them. She wasn't losing anybody else. She knew that for a fact.

The woman regarded Alex with a cold smile and spoke.

"Alex Winters, you're a hard woman to find. I respect your tenacity," the woman's voice sounded bored and aristocratic."When the Lord of Long Shadows realized you were special, I told him his moronic foot soldiers couldn't handle tracking you down. If only he'd listened, I wouldn't be in this steam drenched wasteland. Ah well, we're here now, and my employer wishes a word with you."

"Why not kill us?" Alex demanded angrily. "I promise if I can escape I will. Why not just kill us and get it over with?" She was sick of the games.

"I am not at liberty to discuss my employer's motivations. And I know you will try, my girl. It would disappoint me if you didn't. Now, we'll be taking those things from you." She snapped her fingers and two guards roughly relieved Alex of her belongings. Alex tried to concentrate on her powers but she couldn't. It was like trying to think while being surrounded by a thousand buzzing insects.

"We're leaving! Pack everything up and make the prisoners ready for transport." She turned back to Alex. The fox mask she wore obscured her features beneath the mask, but she flashed Alex a cat-like smile. "Come, dear, we must away. My employer has waited long enough to meet you."

The guards bound Alex's hands and tied her to the end of a wagon. He separated her friends and attached to their own wagons. Large horses drew the wagons and with the crack of a whip they began their journey into the jungle.

Alex cursed herself for not being quick, she cursed the stone for not working, and she cursed her rotten luck. As they made their way deeper into the jungle, all Alex could do was dwell on her failures and wonder despondently about what the Hand of Seven could want to talk about. She vaguely hoped it would be to issue a formal apology for being such a jerk, but Alex doubted her luck would be that good. Luck had never been in her favor , now less than ever. So, it left Alex to be pulled by her wagon and wonder what lay in store for her and her friends.

23

A Den of Foxes

Alex had heard the term death march before, but she had never seen it in practice. The pace of the Foxes was brutal and unrelenting. They moved quickly through the jungle, led by trackers in lithe outfits that moved like shadows through the trees above her. Their faces were dark, painted with animal blood, earthen clay and other substances that obscured them from the sight of predators.

Their captors only gave Alex and the other prisoners water at sparse intervals. Every muscle in her legs screamed in an ocean of agony as the march wore into its first day. Her friends fared no better. The guard had beaten Kyria twice, once for mouthing off, and another time for biting a nearby Fox. Ahrun had subsequently been beaten for knocking out the guard who was beating Kyria. The guards seemed to hold back, however, as if on orders not to use too much force. The other prisoners were not as lucky.

Along with Alex and her friends, several chain gangs of miserable looking slaves trudged behind other wagons, baking in the day's heat. She didn't want to know what the slaves' purpose was, but the guards took any opportunity to abuse them as they traveled. The Foxes may have been human, but they were no better than the demons they served.

Around midday, the caravan stopped at a small pool of water that ran off from a nearby river. The other slaves gathered water, but the guards gave Alex water and food and allowed her to rest. The breaks also gave her time to think. She needed to plot an escape plan, but the situation limited her options. The Foxes were careful to keep Alex and her friends separated, and even now her wagon had stopped far away from either of theirs, making a covert conversation impossible. Still, she had to try something. She figured escaping would be even harder when they got wherever they were going.

A thunderous crash interrupted her thoughts (and everything else) in the jungle, close to their location. Everyone paused, looking around nervously. The underbrush rustled, as whatever had made the noise headed their way. The woman in charge calmly walked over to one of the slave gangs and pulled them by the collar until they stood near the edge of the clearing. Alex slowly realized what the slaves' purpose was, and her stomach churned.

A massive bird, like a stork with feathers of shining armor and legs like tree-trunks, emerged. The creature looked over the caravan and spotted the slaves, who cowered before it to no avail. It pulled the first slave up, taking the rest with him, flailing in the air like a wriggling fish on a line. The woman turned with a satisfied smile and made a motion with her hand that seemed to mean *wrap it up and move out*, because the caravan quickly got its affairs in order and moved deeper into the jungle. Alex tried to ignore the sound of crunching and screaming but she couldn't; it was too horrible and bone-chilling and she felt sick. Alex glowered at the woman who walked ahead of the caravan without so much as missing a step. This woman was living, breathing proof of how evil the Foxes Guild was.

As they traveled, the jungle somehow got hotter. For the first few days, the temperature and ecology of the jungle stayed the same, but on the third day, things changed. The caravan was deeper in the jungle now and the plants and animals had become far more savage, and cruel. Here, only the most cunning and lethal creatures survived, devouring all others. A deer with two heads and serrated teeth pulled a Fox guard into the bush as they walked, and Alex couldn't pretend she felt sorry. Still, the existence of a man-eating, two-headed deer didn't bode well for what else might lurk beneath the shadow of the trees.

On the fourth day, the jungle became less dense, and Alex could see the open sky again. It was impossible for her to tell what direction they traveled in, lacking a compass or even a passing knowledge of Aquillonian stars, which were a solitary source of beauty in the otherwise unrelenting nightmare. They radiated down like shining diamonds every night and Alex looked up at them and wondered how far her home was. Alex didn't notice any familiar constellations, so very far away was the best answer she could come up with.

The past days had brought no useful ideas to Alex in the way of escape plans, and no opportunities to speak with her friends. She was grateful that they were being spared, though her heart broke for the poor wretches on the other wagons. The Foxes had used several more of them as diversions for the jungle's giant monsters. Kyria and Ahrun seemed to have stayed out of trouble, but several of the guards looked worse for wear. Alex wasn't sure, but she could have sworn she saw Kyria push one into a hidden hole in the ground, but it may have been dumb luck. Either way, fewer Foxes was a good thing.

On the fifth day, Alex's luck changed for the better. A giant centipede-like insect pulled the horse that was carrying Kyria's cart into the ground. It pulled the horse, the cart, and nearly Kyria into its nest when the horse stepped on a patch of leaves that concealed a hole. There weren't any other wagons without prisoners, so it forced the guards to tie Kyria to the back of Alex's wagon. Alex noted that the surrounding guards doubled, but they were paying more attention to the jungle than her, given that hungry jungle critters had now scooped up five guards for lunch.

"Glad to see you've made it and haven't been eaten by anything," Alex said to her friend with a smile.

"Likewise. I don' know how much longer we have ta go, but with any luck, we'll be alone soon enough if these cretins keep gettin' gobbled up," Kyria said with a gleeful smile.

"Quiet! Keep moving," the guard nearest to them chided and brandished a whip. Kyria gave him a death glare and lowered her voice.

"Any idea where we're headed? The guards around me have been tight-lipped about our destination," Alex said, being careful to keep her voice at the level of a whisper.

"I'm no' for sure, but I reckon we've been marchin' north for a while," Kyria nodded toward a nearby moss covered tree with a grin, "an' headin' out o' the Wyld Place toward the Foxes' Den. It's the guild hall where these lunatics operate out of. "It's in the Eastern Marches, pretty much the last patch o' land as can rightly be called Aquillon."

"So, we need to get out of here before we get there or…" Alex trailed off.

"Or bad things happen," Kyria said with a grimace.

"All right, plan, plan…we need a plan," Alex muttered to herself. The only bright glimmer of hope was that the waystone would be able to teleport them to the Eastern Watch, even if they were marching back toward Aquillon - if they could get to it. That was an elephant sized "if" at this point.

She couldn't think of anything in the way of an escape plan, but after an hour they rounded a bend in the path and she heard the roar of a waterfall. Ahead of them, a ravine stretched out, tearing a scar through the jungle. It looked like an earthquake might have made it eons ago, but the jungle had reclaimed the land. Vines ate the cliff line on either side of the ravine and trees and bushes sprouted from roots deep within the rocks. The scene was picturesque, but one detail, in particular, had Alex's mind buzzing with possibilities.

The ravine offered no natural crossing points, but nature had provided one in the form of a fallen tree. A towering palm, two wagons in width spanned the gap, providing ample, if unstable, passage across. If the goal was to pick off Foxes, there wouldn't be a better time.

As they neared the waterfall, the sound roared like a great beast, and the noise was enough to obscure conversation between Alex and Kyria. They took advantage and spoke freely.

"You thinking what I'm thinking?" Alex asked her friend.

Shining a mischievous smile at her, Kyria said, "way ahead o' ya. It's a long way ta the bottom. It'd be a cryin' shame if some o' our foxy friends slipped on tha' bridge. It looks terribly unsafe!"

Alex had to restrain herself to keep from smiling too much. As they neared the trees, the path along the ravine became narrow, and Alex concentrated on her feet. The edge of the wagon wheel traced the edge of the canyon dangerously and Alex breathed deeply, trying her best not to freak out. Kyria walked behind her and pulled a root up with her feet which caught the guard behind her, sending him screaming to the bottom of the ravine.

"What's that?" Another guard was quick to make his way over. "What happened?" he demanded angrily, snarling in their faces.

"A," Alex said, "your friend should have been watching where he was going. Clumsy and stupid I guess. B. Your breath is awful. Do you eat garbage regularly? Please, stop talking because I'm afraid I might pass out and fall down there, and then you'd be in trouble," she said with a witty smile.

He seethed but still seemed under orders to leave her alone.

"Move out! Everyone, watch your footing!" he shouted, shooting them one last foul look before making his way back to the front of the caravan which moved on seconds later.

Their wagon made its way to the edge of the tree bridge and the forward guard climbed to the top of the tree. The exposed root system was massive, at least fifty feet or more high, and just as long across. It took nearly an hour to rig a rope system and then the guards slowly pulled horses and wagons up to the bridge. As the sun set over the eastern horizon, they pulled the last of the wagons up to the top of the tree where the caravan waited to move out.

They had freed Alex and Kyria of their bonds to climb. Once they arrived at the top, Alex spotted a horse that looked especially skittish of the height, and they moved behind that horse's wagon and tied themselves to it. When a guard came back to secure them he gave them a curious look, but moved on, apparently deciding not to ask further questions.

As the caravan meandered across the trunk, Alex bided her time. Near the center, Alex shot Kyria a look and stopped moving. Alex dropped to her knees and clutched her side, groaning in pain, mimicking cramps. Several guards moved over to Alex.

"Get up! We can't stop here, keep moving," one said brusquely.

"I can't! It hurts too much! My delicate female sensibilities are giving out from the heat," Alex protested, hamming it up as much as possible. She thought she heard Ahrun guffaw from somewhere further up in the caravan.

The guards looked at each other, somewhat baffled what to do when the leader approached them with a scowl beneath her fox mask. "You absolute idiots! You can't tell she's stalling for time? If any of you imbeciles make it back to the Den, I swear you'll wish you hadn't! Where's the other one?" She began frantically looking for Kyria, but it was too late.

While Alex was putting on her best damsel routine, Kyria freed herself from the poorly tied restraints and snuck up to the horse that led her wagon. The creature was frightened already, not being a large fan of heights, so Kyria didn't have to do much to set it off. Bringing her hand back, she smacked the horse's rear as hard as she could while making a hissing sound she hoped sounded like a snake.

The trick worked. The horse reared back, ignoring all attempts by its driver to bring it under control. As the horse bolted forward, the wagon rocketed into a large group of Foxes pushing them from either side of the bridge into the gloomy ravine waiting below. In his frantic attempts to calm the animal, the driver did not notice Kyria pocketing his dagger. She slipped under the wagon and cut Alex loose just before the animal bolted forward.

The guards surrounding Alex seemed frozen in time as a grenade of panic exploded across the bridge as other horses grew frightened and tried to flee. Alex took advantage of the chaos and slammed into two nearby guards, who fell screaming into the gaping canyon below.

The woman was not as slow as her guards and had drawn her weapons, moving closer to Alex and Kyria as wagons reeled past them. Alex wasn't eager to hang around for a fight. Most of the convoy was being brought back to order, but there was a small window for escape which was narrowly closing and Alex wasn't about to miss it. Ahrun had used the chaos to free himself and was running towards the other side of the bridge. He called his sword to him as he ran.

By the time the three of them had nearly cleared the bridge, most of the remaining Foxes were in hot pursuit. Despite Alex's war of attrition, nearly thirty remained. The expedition had come prepared to deal with them.

They were close now, nearly to the other side but then Alex saw something she really wished she hadn't. In the diversion, the last wagon of slaves became caught up in the chaos, and now hung over the ravine, and was being held up only by a series of branches which cracked and splintered under the weight. The slaves reached out to her as she passed them. They were trapped inside a metal cage and which would fall over the ravine in minutes. Alex stopped and Kyria and Ahrun stopped.

Kyria yelled at her. "Are ya daft? We need ta' move faster, no' slower, in case tha' wasn't clear!"

Without speaking Alex pointed to the slave wagon dangling in the branches.

"But we don' 'ave time, we need ta..." Kyria stopped herself mid-sentence. It wasn't an argument she would win, or even one she wanted to win. Alex would not leave the slaves to die. It wasn't an option, no matter how close rescue was. Climbing down onto the branches, they assisted the slaves out of the cage, one by one, until the last member of the chain gang was standing on the bridge next to them. As Alex and her friends pulled themselves up, they realized Foxes surrounded them.

The guards quickly apprehended Alex and her friends and shoved them to their knees. Alex felt a swift boot in her side and an explosion of pain followed as several guards kicked her, taking their frustration out on her. She tasted iron as blood pooled in her mouth. Alex spat it out at them in defiance.

"Enough!" The woman in charge was shrieking now. "Don't kill her or all of this will have been pointless!"

After they stopped Alex looked up at her, blinking away tears and recovering from the pulsing and throbbing in her side. She didn't think they had cracked any ribs, so that was a plus. The woman stood over her and removed her mask. Underneath, a woman in her late forties glared at her from amber eyes that dripped with malice and resentment. Her hair was black and silver, cut short.

"Clever little insect, aren't you? I can see why you survived this long. Thought you'd run, but had to stop and play the hero?" As she spoke Alex saw a mania in her eyes that glimmered like a fire, and it frightened her, though she kept her face resolute. "And giving up your escape for what? Some slaves? That's what makes you weak! You haven't got the stomach to do what you needed to do! It's why nobility always loses. It's why humanity will always lose."

"You can justify it however you want," Alex said, hatred glowing in her eyes, "but you're a coward, and a traitor, and you always will be. I might die, but at least I'll know I tried. You'll die and be forgotten. Just another lackey." She spat blood in the woman's face as she said it. It was almost worth the savage fist to the face that knocked her in the jaw moments later. The woman smiled, the mania increasing in her eyes.

"And in the end, you heroes are all the same. Noble and pointless deaths. You got yourselves captured, and for nothing. The lives of these slaves are worth nothing, and I care nothing for them. I want you to know you wasted your time and your one chance of escape spent for nothing."

The woman grabbed the slave at the head of the group and hurled him off the bridge, dragging the other five with him. Alex screamed and tried to run at the woman, cursing her. "I'll kill you," Alex said, screaming. She fought through several guards who assaulted her as she ran, but she was eventually brought down.

"See. Pointless. All of your fighting, and all the death. It means nothing. You can't fight us. You can't fight the Court. You can't win." There was a smug tone of finality and victory in the woman's voice as she spoke.

Alex struggled against the guards. She swore she'd get revenge on this woman, no matter what else happened. The woman made the sign for them to move out and they pushed Alex forward with the sharp edge of a sword. The guard separated Alex and her friends again, this time placing at least five guards in between each, and the death march continued.

The next several days were brutal. The guards drove them relentlessly and only given two breaks for water a day, and one for food. Alex felt like she was broiling in the heat and she wondered if just giving up might be easier. Then she remembered the slaves tumbling down the ravine and the promise of revenge she made. Alex felt a surge of raw hatred and anger pulse through her and kept walking.

Her communication with her friends was limited to a few glances here, and a word passed quietly there, but they were kept heavily under guard. The woman had been right about one thing; whatever chance they had of making an escape had vanished the night of the bridge.

The only bright bit of luck was that the Foxes had not yet paid any mind to the waystone. It lay discarded and unexamined with a large pile of their belongings. To its credit, the waystone hadn't so much as glowed or cracked one remark since their capture. If they were going to get out of this mess, the waystone was their last chance.

The jungle thinned out as they traveled and finally stumps and grassland replaced trees. The caravan entered a large valley, clear-cut of any vegetation taller than a man's boot. Alex realized now why the woman had been so nonchalant about sacrificing the last of the slaves to make a point (aside from the fact that she was a horrible, horrible person). They had arrived at the Den of the Foxes, where they did not need to fear the great beasts of the jungle. And besides, they had more than enough slaves to make up for the loss.

Slaves worked the land in droves and they drew massive carts of fruits and vegetables in on great wagon teams to the Den. Around the imposing stronghold, a large array of farms dotted the landscape. It seemed like nearly any plant life could take root here and prosper, and the Foxes had created a self-sustaining farming commune in the jungle.

The Den itself was an immense construction of red stone and wooden pylons. A single wooden set of doors bound with a massive iron bar was the only way in or out. Overseers and taskmasters with cruel, barbed whips littered the surrounding area, and Alex shivered despite the heat, getting unpleasant flashbacks of Alcrest. Humanity could still be as warped and awful on Aquillon as it could be on Earth.

As Alex moved closer to the Den, the suffering increased. Everywhere she looked slaves were being abused and left to die where they dropped from the heat of the sun. Her anger boiled as they walked, and she was grateful when they finally reached the massive gate that led into the Den.

The fortress itself was impressive in scale and nearly impenetrable, or at least appeared that way. Now that they were close, she saw dozens of small holes in the wall, just big enough for an archer to aim a crossbow out of. A contingent of pride stood guard outside and they growled at Alex as they passed. Kyria had been right. They were back in Aquillon; back in the Court's territory.

As she walked into the fortress, Alex's stomach squirmed in knots and she sensed an oppressive presence in her mind. The Lord of Long Shadows was here somewhere. She didn't know how she knew, but she knew. The walls were dripping with his dark energy.

Inside the stronghold the light was dim, provided by glowing torches on the wall. They were not burning, nor were they connected to anything, so Alex assumed demon magic was at play. A long hallway led them into an antechamber where an old man scribed furiously on a desk. He seemed, from what Alex could see, to be working on an invoice of sorts, but it was a language altogether unfamiliar to her. She realized it was the first time she had seen writing in Aquillon, and as she stared at it, the letters shimmered and transformed into English. It was an invoice of slaves. Reading foreign languages was apparently one of the various manifestations of her powers. She also realized that she probably hadn't been speaking or listening to English. No time to focus on that now though.

As he looked up from his desk, the old man scowled at them.

"A costly venture, Valari," he said, grumbling at the woman who led them.

"The board discussed this and approved my mission," she hissed back. "Their bounties will be more than sufficient to replace the resources spent. Just process them and I can be on my way. I stink of slaves and jungle, and I don't plan to meet the Lord that way."

"We will see," he said. "I will do the calculation for the cost of your mission later. Now then, a processing form." He rifled through drawers on his desk and pulled out a long piece of parchment. It was already filled out partially. "Inventory: two slaves and one tribute," he said to himself as he wrote . Alex saw Kyria's nostrils flare, but she kept her temper in check.

As the old man finished filling out the form, Alex looked around, noting each detail for an escape. She saw the guards take their belongings to a small room behind the antechamber, and Alex noticed that they didn't lock it. That would help them later. Images of foxes hunting and motifs of their patron animal filled the antechamber. A large chandelier of antlers burned overhead and three corridors branched out, each leading to a series of rooms. A Fox guard came out of one room and she saw the glimmer of heaps of gold and jewels behind it. The Court had paid the Foxes Guild well for their atrocities.

At the end of each hall, a spiral staircase led above and below. Alex saw slaves being led below, and Foxes moving up into the second floor. She was pulled down the hall to the left.

"Slaves down to pit A. The flaxen-haired one goes above to meet the Lord," the old man said.

"No!" Kyria yelled and kicked as they pulled them apart. Guards

293

swarmed on her and beat her.

"Stop! I'll go, just don't harm them," Alex said desperately. She pleaded to her friend with her eyes, and they both stood down. "Later," she mouthed silently. She would see them again, they just needed to stay alive.

The woman said nothing, but the old man shouted at the guard. "Enough! Haven't you idiots lost enough slaves for one mission? Leave these two be!"

They stopped hesitantly, looking at the woman, who nodded with a sneer.

The guards shoved Alex down the hallway on the left. She noticed them take Kyria down the center hallway and Ahrun to the right. The Foxes seemed to have learned their lesson about what happened when Alex and her friends were left together for too long. Alex gave her friends silent goodbyes, and she swore to herself she'd see them again. She just had to survive whatever was coming next, but given the circumstances, that seemed like a tall order.

Alex trudged down the hall, in no hurry to be wherever they wanted her to be. As she ascended the spiral stone staircase, she tried her best to see what was on the floors she passed. One seemed to be a chemist's lab, as indicated by a flare of flames and the smell of sulfur that erupted out before they slammed the door in her face. The next was a counting house where accountants kept records of ill-gotten gains. They ran about like ants milling in between tunnels of a colony. There were so many of them, Alex figured the wealth of the Foxes Guild must have been vast, spanning even beyond the treasure horde she had seen below.

Alex finally arrived at the top floor, which was mostly empty, save for some administrative looking personnel moving between offices. As she passed, they seemed unconcerned with her and focused on their business. The most interesting detail of the entire stronghold was the lack of guards. While Alex saw a small presence on each floor, overall, there seemed to be more guards on the outside than the inside. It seemed a critical miscalculation that Alex definitely planned on using to her advantage.

At the end of the third-floor hall, a door led into a wide open room. It was mostly empty except for a large window that looked out over the surrounding farmland, and a banquet table. Every kind of appetizing food covered the table from end to end. Plates of smoked meats steamed next to cheese platters and every kind of fruit. Crystal jars of water leaked condensation onto the table below. Alex's mouth watered but she didn't trust it. Nothing in Aquillon had been easy or simple, and she imagined food was no exception to the rule. Even if it was delicious, tasty food.

Near the banquet table, a small table with fresh clothes waited. A clean blouse and a pair of traveling pants sat harmlessly waiting for her to put them on. The guards left her and she changed out of her filthy travel-worn clothes. It didn't seem all that likely the clothing was a trap, and she felt beyond gross.

At the other end of the hall, a massive door sat ominously. After a while of waiting, she heard the door open slowly, and she paused, her hand reaching for a weapon she didn't have, her heart thundering in her chest. Alex knew what waited on the other side of the door. From the darkness, he emerged.

He was a lion, like the Pride she had seen, but larger than any of them. He stood nearly to the ceiling, and he walked towards her with powerful strides. His entire coat was black, and out the darkness of his mane, two red globes burned where eyes would have been. He wore fine golden armor that covered every inch of him and in his hand a wicked scythe gleamed in the torchlight.

The sculptors outside Alcrest hadn't done him justice, but how could they? From every stride, he exuded power and control. It was as though the surrounding air sat still, not eager to anger him or behave out of line. His eyes regarded her coldly, and she felt him looking at her and had to fight the urge to run. Cold fear pulled at her entrails and she felt alone. His power washed over her, and she felt his authority radiating from every surface.

There was a deadly silence in the room and Alex could barely breathe. After what seemed like forever, he finally spoke. The Lord's words flowed easily in a calm and restrained voice. His voice was smooth and crisp, like an old-time Hollywood actor.

"Ah, Alex Winters; finally we meet. We have much to discuss."

24

The Lord of Long Shadows

The tension in the room was a lightning storm, and Alex was in the center. The Hand of Seven walked back and forth, letting the tension build.

"I took great pains to arrange this meeting, girl; spared no expense. Please, eat," he said, motioning to the table of food.

Alex stood motionless, keeping her distance from both him and the table.

"Come now, girl, I have no wish to kill you. Do you really believe I didn't know where you were this entire time? Could I not have killed you a hundred times over? That meddling ape's charm gave me some trouble, but the Foxes' Guild was more than happy to work around it, for the money I paid them," he said. As he spoke, his hand rested on his scythe.

Alex stayed where she was. Every word he spoke beguiled her more and her wits left her. Even his words dripped with the power of command, and she longed to do what he asked, despite her mind fighting the charm. It was a strange thing she thought to herself; to be so powerless to the pull of words from a creature she hated. It made his power no less potent. Still, she resisted and held her ground.

The Lord seemed annoyed as he spoke, hoping his power would have weakened her by now. "You are strong, but now is not the time for that. Now is the time for words. Actions may come later, but at least will you sit with me? We have much to discuss."

It seemed harmless enough to sit, so she did, and he followed, taking the tall chair at the end of the table. He held out his hand, and it expanded to fit him and seemed more a throne than a chair. The Lord sat, seeming more relaxed as he carried on.

"So. You have traveled far, and I as far to match, just to meet you. Tell me, how did you come to this world? You are not of it, I am sure at least of that much. Your essence betrays you for an alien." His words were smooth as honey. They pulled at her, whispering in her ear to give in, to relent.

"If you haven't figured it out by now, *cat*, I'm not answering your questions," she spat her response at him. It seemed to her to be unreasonably hostile, but she had to keep up her defenses. His words pulled on her mind like a drug and they were becoming more and more reasonable.

"Come now, girl, no need for such hostilities. I seek only a calm, respectful discourse. Truly there can be no harm in this. Tell me how came you to our world." His question was more insistent now, and with greater urgency. She could no longer resist, but she tried at least to obscure her truth in riddles.

"I fell through a door, into the sea," Alex barely heard herself. Her words flowed out of her and she felt unaware like her attention was being pulled elsewhere.

"Interesting. Well, if you will not be plain, I'll not press the issue. Tis' a pity I did not intercept you before you fell in with that riff-raff you travel with. Such misguided people," he said, shaking his head.

Alex realized this was the first time she had heard a demon refer to humans as anything but thralls.

"Why? I would never support you! I've seen what you really are!" Alex was shouting at him, although it was a front. She didn't mean it. No matter how much her brain hated him, she fell more and more under the sway of his words.

"Have you, girl? I think not. You know only what people have told you of me, most likely the Old Guard. They have no true conception of what I have in mind for this world. Even if they did, they would never share it. It conflicts too much with their propaganda," the Lord said.

His argument seemed all too plausible, and yet she knew it was a lie. Or was it? Alex's

head was hurting as she weighed the plausibility of the lie with what she knew was true.

"You're lying..." Alex murmured.

"Am I? Consider that you only know what the Guard has told you. Nothing else. If they are your only source of information, how can you know it to be the truth unless you hear my side?" His words were a soft purr, and Alex felt them seeping into the gaps of doubt in her mind.

She found no valid argument to present but replied, anyway.

"I know what I have seen! I saw the suffering in Alcrest, in Vandlehaven, everywhere in this world, I've seen what your Court has created - misery and suffering!"

"True, but is it possible they have guided you on a path that would show you only what they wish you to see?" he asked.

Alex nodded, even though she didn't want to. What he said made too much sense, and even now her memories of those places faded. Maybe it was a trick? Some elaborate scam to convince her to join the resistance. With every word he spoke, the Lord of Long Shadows made more sense, and she yearned for the truth, or at least his version of events.

"Suppose I believe you? What of it? What explanation could you offer?" she asked. Her voice was indignant, but no longer defiant.

"You will see! Ours is a divine mission of providence most high. The gods sent us to rule these people because they need peace, order. Before we arrived, chaos ruled, pure anarchy. We have given them structure, purpose. Now all of humanity works towards a great and noble goal!" As he spoke his voice rose to a crescendo and Alex almost agreed with him.

"Then why do people all seem so miserable? And you speak of anarchy, but what of the empire that existed before the Court?" Alex asked.

The Lord considered her question and replied. "Well, we are not unlike their parents, and when children act out of turn, we punish them. Is that not so where you come from?"

Alex nodded.

"As for their empire, it is vain fantasy. It never existed. When the Court arrived, they were nothing more than warring tribes, all but begging for a leader. At first, all was well. Once we put away the rebels and dissemblers, we accomplish much. But soon discontent swept over some as they forgot all we had done for them," the Lord said.

"And the slaves in Alcrest? What was their crime?" she asked, pressing him for more information.

"Those people were but a few who would distract the whole from our glorious mission. Each only interned there for a length of time as fit their crime. I assure you we routinely free people, you simply didn't stay long enough to witness it," he replied.

There was a congenial quality to his voice that put her at ease. Alex felt her shoulders relax and her plans for escape faded in her mind.

"And what is this glorious mission?" Alex asked.

"That we will show ourselves worthy of the world the Gods have given us. Picture a vast shining empire of citizens, not slaves. We would be glorious if only we stood united under a common vision. If only more humans would see it how the Court does. Already there are prospering cities of gold, where my kind and humans walk hand in hand."

The Lord extended his hand and above her floated a translucent image of a city. It was as he said, humans walked free next to the creatures she called demons, but there was no animosity. The city was peaceful.

He had proven his words true, and Alex abandoned her foolish notions of resistance, but one question still plagued her mind.

"I still have one more question."

The Lord nodded, waiting attentively.

"Why not kill me outright? If I've caused you so much trouble, why meet with me and discuss all of this?"

He chuckled a soft, rolling laugh. "I wanted to talk to you first. Since you wounded the Lady of the Deep some time ago, the rebels see you as a hero. They hold you up as a beacon of hope for their cause. Killing you would accomplish nothing; it would simply martyr you. I wanted the chance to speak with you and convince you that ours is not the side you want to fight. The Court of Hours is the rolling tide of history, and every man must play a part." He paused.

"I see," Alex said. "Well, I don't see why anyone would argue with that. Now what?"

"I offer a choice," He extended his hand and chanted until a portal of swirling energy opened near the end of the room. As the energy cleared Alex saw her trailer in the woods, exactly as she had left it. Alex's heart fluttered, and tears welled in her eyes as the image plunged her into a sea of homesickness. It had been so long since she had seen Earth, and she longed to go back where things made sense.

"I know well the magic used to bring you here, even if I know not the purpose. I offer you a way home. Go back to your own kind and this will all be but a dream. Return to your old life. Or..."

The Lord of Long Shadows extended his other hand and an image of her in armor on a warhorse at the head of an army appeared, hovering above the floor. "Be my general. The people have heard of you and believe in what you represent. You can show them that enemies can make amends, that peace in our time is possible. What's more, I can show you how to use your abilities for good, in a way the greedy magi would never be able to. With your help, I can lead these people to a new age of order, and prosperity!" He sounded so genuine, so kind, Alex felt stupid for ever questioning him.

Alex looked at the image of herself and had an equal compulsion to join the Lord. Everything he said made sense, and she could do real good. She would end the suffering of so many people. She would be a hero. Both options pulled at her, and it seemed impossible to make a choice. Something still nagged at her though, like a thorn in her mind. She took several moments to quantify it in the form of a question.

"Before I decide, I have one more question."

The Lord nodded.

"What about my friends? What happens to them?"

He frowned, gritted his teeth, and replied in a curt voice. "In either case, they stay here. They cannot return home with you and they cannot join me; they will distract us from the work. In a noble cause, we must all make sacrifices," he said.

Sacrifices; Alex couldn't get that word out of her mind. It reminded her of something, and she was overwhelmed with sadness. It seemed like a distant memory of some long-forgotten thing, but as soon as he said the word, she couldn't stop thinking about it. A face materialized in her mind, chopping through the fog and coming into focus. She had forgotten something, and it was roaring back to her now.

"Your choice, girl, make it now! I cannot hold this portal for long.

What are you doing?" He spoke now in a terrible growl. His voice had lost all its charms and was angry and terrifying.

"I forgot something..." Alex said, slowly shaking her head.

"Enough of this! Make your choice! The portal is collapsing," he roared, his voice gripped by panic and urgency.

"You made me forget," she retorted, glaring at him. There was no fog now, and she knew what she had forgotten. Thistle. Alex had forgotten Thistle. Her friend had given his life so she could keep on fighting, so she would make it to the Eastern Watch and free Aquillon. She realized now how hollow the demon's promises were. He had lied to her, and she had fallen for it. Anger and rage swelled in her chest and a dangerous calm washed over her, and power surged all around her.

"My Lord," Alex said. Her voice shook with unchecked rage and every word quaked with anger. "I considered your offer, but you neglected one detail. One life. It was nothing to you, but it was something to me. More than something, it was a person. A king, and decent, and noble person. You killed my friend, you son of a bitch. So, take your offer and go to hell!"

At that moment, power swelled within her as it never had before and she released it all in one primal scream that shook the walls. A fire erupted from her hands in a molten blade that shot towards the great lion, searing the air as it flew. It pierced his eye, and he roared backward, grabbing at the seared flesh. The demon lord doubled over, the remains of his eye oozed out in molten fire and boiling flesh. Alex saw the flesh try to reform, but it could not.

"Mulling wretch! What did you do? I will tear you apart and strew the ramparts of this stronghold with your entrails!" He spoke with a distorted and horrible voice as if the real creature that hid behind the visage of a noble lion was speaking.

Before she could respond he charged at her, and she waited to dodge.

Unfortunately, her powers had gone as quickly as they had come and she was now facing a ten-foot tall demon lion that was very, very angry. As satisfied as she was about blinding him, a half-blind lion with a scythe was probably just as dangerous. Before he could reach her though, the room shook with an explosion in the far wall as a giant flaming rock burst through into the room. The impact shattered the windows, and the Lord turned in surprise.

From outside the stronghold, the sound of braying and screaming filled the room, as if thousands of angry goats were attacking. Alex craned her neck up to see what was causing the clatter. The sound was, in fact, coming from a large army of goatmen which had assembled outside the Den. They wielded axes and swords and armor for battle. There must have been a thousand at least. Every hundred feet of their battle line, a large siege engine stood to fling flaming boulders at the stronghold which shook with every impact. At the center, a massive ram walked back and forth. The ram was white but covered in blood that seemed still wet. His eyes glowed red, and he was screaming.

"Come out, brudda! Witness what I done wrought!" The large goatman screamed in a manic voice.

The great lion shouted back. "You idiot! What are you doing here?"

"De' Lord O' Wrath done come for blood! Too long ya have been denyin' me and my

Akari sweet war. Ya done neglected me Akari the chance for blood! Too long ya done held our hand back. Watch as I take what is mine!" His voice was a terrible goat cry that sounded like war drums. He turned to his army.

"Come my brood, children o' da blood. I gone call a war!" The ram's voice echoed, and the goatmen went mad.

They charged in a chaotic wave and fell on the Fox guards without mercy. Another flaming missile struck the room and collapsed the door of the room, and a large part of the ceiling. Alex wasted no time making her escape. The Lord of Long Shadows charged at her, but as he did, a large flaming chunk of the ceiling collapsed on him. He roared and his rage was still in her ears as she escaped the room. The lion's hateful eye, burning with vengeance, was the last thing she saw.

Alex needed to move. She doubted the big cat was dead, and when he worked his way out of there, he would be in a very grumpy mood, and she would be extremely dead.

She had to get to the bottom floor. The stronghold seemed solid, but at the rate, the goatmens' army was attacking, it would fall soon, and Alex had no plans to be nearby when it did.

25

A Reckoning of Fire and Wrath

The Foxes' Den had descended into madness and chaos long before Alex reached the base of the spiral staircase. As she ran down the steps, the enraged roar of the demon lord above followed her, motivating her to keep moving .

Each floor she had passed on her way up a short time ago was on fire, and swarming with guild members trying to rescue documents, move piles of gold coin, and save what wealth they could. The siege had obliterated chemical lab, presumably from when a fireball from outside had interacted poorly with the chemical compounds in the lab.

As Alex reached the bottom, she saw the massive door to the stronghold had splintered and fractured, with a great fissure running all the way down. Rabid goat warriors tried to clamber their way inside, but a large contingent of the Fox guard was holding them off for the moment.

The farther away she got from the demon lord, the less his power affected her. Alex's head cleared and her memories rushed back. She looked down the other hallways and walked down the one she remembered Kyria being taken. She paused, remembering their supplies, and the waystone, were inside the small room.

By some miracle, the storage room was intact. Alex clung to the shadows and stayed on the outskirts of the room as she approached the door which led into the storage room. Most of the guard focused their attention on the invading army of goat demons, but there were some patrolling the room and Alex knew she couldn't afford to be discovered. It would only take one to sound the alarm, and then they would overrun her.

She hid behind a large, shattered pillar as she waited for two to pass by her.

"Bloody monsters. They're gonna regret this once the pride gets here," one said angrily.

"I've never understood why Seven never wiped out the Akari," another asked. "Nothing but warmongering thugs. Wait, what was that?"

Alex nearly cursed as she realized she had shifted against the broken pillar, causing a single chunk to fall to the ground beside her. It was barely audible above the cacophony outside, but the guards heard it. They approached her pillar and Alex readied herself for a fight. She might take the two out, but she wasn't sure if she could manage it before they alerted the others.

As they rounded the pillar, they saw her and grabbed for their weapons. Alex caught one with a vicious right hook and he crumpled in front of her. The other one swung her sword at Alex but she ducked under it and snared the woman with her legs, bringing her down into a sleeper hold. She held it until the woman stopped moving and Alex stood up, breathing heavily. Feeling fairly pleased with herself, she turned to continue sneaking across to the storage room when she looked across the hall and realized with alarm that there was another guard staring right at her. He reached for the horn that hung off his belt.

Moments before he could blow it however, a blade came sailing through the air and lodged itself in his back. Alex nearly screamed in surprise. Looking at the blade itself, she recognized it; it was Ahrun's. He emerged out of the shadows and retrieved his blade, bending down to clean it on the dead guard's cloak.

Ahrun ran over to her. She raised an eyebrow, and he answered her unasked question.

"My blade always finds me," he said, grinning. "Turns out it's harder to keep prisoners in their cells when they have weapons. Who knew?" he said with a smirk.

"Nifty trick. You should teach me some time," Alex said with a chuckle.

"It might take some time, but for now we need to go. I can't make this body disappear and there will be other patrols," he said.

Alex nodded and snuck her way over to the storage room, Ahrun bringing up the rear and watching for other patrols. Alex saw the sword-sized hole in the door and chuckled. Inside the room was a massive collection of items from every walk of life and profession. Alex deduced that they must have been the belongings of slaves who the Foxes had processed recently, and not yet sold. Fortunately, their pile was near the front and in only minutes they re-equipped themselves and were to escape. Alex checked, and to her great relief, the waystone was still in her bag where it had been.

Taking it out, the stone whirred to life and glowed with energy.

"About time," it chided angrily.

Alex gave it a foul look, and it resigned itself to grumbling.

"Are we leaving soon? This place stinks! Terrible energy in the air. And being handled like some, possession! I declare, I've never seen this poor treatment of a waystone since well, ever!" it said in a whiny voice.

Alex ignored it and put it back in her pack. Having recovered her scimitar and secured the waystone, she was ready to find Kyria and get out of the place before it collapsed altogether. Leaving the storeroom, they proceeded down the left hall to the stairs that led down to the darkness below. The shaking was getting worse and the sounds of battle were clear; the Foxes were not winning. Alex turned to Ahrun.

"How many guards did you have to get through down there?" she asked

"The guards were far more numerous on the upper floors than they were in the pits. It should be simple enough to free Kyria," he said.

Alex nodded. Still, her guard was up because nothing was ever as simple as, *Go into a dark hole in the ground and rescue people with no issues* on Aquillon. There were always issues on Aquillon.

Alex descended slowly into the darkness of the slave pit. Ahrun was right. There were few guards in the lower levels, but the suffering was still terrible. The stairs ended on a suspended walkway that hung in the air above a great void. Every hundred feet a metal ladder led down into the darkness, but a spiked cage at the top prevented anyone from coming up. Far below in the darkness, hundreds of people were milling about in holes that looked like animals had dug them. At the end of the pits a large tunnel opened, but the Foxes had sealed it with a great metal door. Alex shuddered as she looked down. She wasn't sure what was more repulsive; that these pits existed, or that humans had built them.

Even from the air, Kyria wasn't hard to spot. She sat on a large boulder surrounded by a group of unconscious guards. They may have been dead, Alex wasn't sure. She reached the ladder nearest to Kyria's pit and Ahrun sundered the lock closing the spiked cage around the top. He carefully removed it and set it down on the walkway. Then he climbed down into the pit, and Alex followed.

As she moved deeper into the pit, the air became foul and full of acrid smells. Sweat and blood and other less pleasant things mingled together into a choking miasma and she could barely breathe. It shocked her the slaves could survive at all. Jumping off the ladder near the bottom, they encountered two guards who drew their weapons and charged them. Alex ducked underneath the sword of one, but the spear of the other caught her in the leg and cut through her thigh. She yelped in pain but returned the attack and brought the spear-holding guard down with a ferocious slice of her scimitar. Ahrun caught the sword-wielding guard from behind and cut him down.

There were no other guards within sight so Alex proceeded to where she had seen Kyria from the air. As she and Ahrun moved through the pit, the slaves avoided them. As Alex looked at them, they scurried to avoid even eye contact. These people were broken and had been for many years. She felt the spirit of defeat hanging heavily over them, and even though they could have overwhelmed the guards, someone broke their minds. The slaves believed themselves powerless, so they were.

Arriving at the end of the pit, Kyria jumped down from her rock and waved to them jovially. A guard from the pile groaned, but she picked up a nearby rock and slammed it into his head.

"What took ya so long? I finished with these eegits an hour ago! They jus' kept sendin' 'em in twos until I guess they ran out." She shrugged and grinned happily. "If it 'adn't been for tha' annoying cage I would 'ave made it back before now. I guess we should be takin' our leave o' these charming abodes," she said.

Alex and her friends walked back to the ladder, but as Alex looked around at the slaves she paused. Ahrun and Kyria stopped, looking back at her.

"We can't just leave them," she said. "I know we have to go, but this is worse than even Alcrest. If we walk away from this...what are we fighting for?"

Neither of them argued. The suffering in the pits was too great to ignore, even with the mission at stake.

"How do we go about getting them out?" Ahrun asked. "We'll never get them all up these ladders in time. Besides, the stronghold is a war-zone, if it's even standing at this point."

"I heard some o' the guards talkin' about an escape plan for the merchandise, an' I don't think they were talkin' about gold marcs," Kyria said.

"So that gate must open up somehow," Alex speculated. "Maybe a mechanism upstairs?"

Ahrun and Kyria nodded. "Were the other pits set up like this?" Alex asked Ahrun.

"Neigh identical, down to the last horrible detail."

"All right, then we go up and find out how to open them," Alex said.

Finding the nearest ladder, Alex ascended back out of the pits and went back into the great hall of the Foxes' Den.

The situation had degenerated in the time that they were below. Where the door to the stronghold had been, a massive smoldering hole billowed smoke. Everywhere Alex looked, the battle raged and Akari warriors fought with Fox guards. Flames consumed everything and the heat from the many fires across the hall was nearly lethal.

Avoiding any conflict, Alex led the group along the back wall until they arrived at the spiral staircase that went up into the center section of the middle hall where Ahrun had been. Alex led her friends up the winding staircase, stopping on the second floor. An explosion had blown the door off, and the bodies of the coin counters littered the hall, so Alex figured this wasn't it. The Akari had taken nothing; their only interest was in slaughter and mayhem. Alex shook her head, and they continued upwards.

The next floor seemed more promising, so Alex explored it. She moved down the hall which she could tell was a maintenance hall, as the only bodies seemed to be slaves who knew the workings of the fortress. A trail of bodies was here too, and it was clear the Akari didn't distinguish between civilian and combatant. Alex moved down the hall and her friends followed.

"This is horrible," Alex muttered as she went.

"Such is the will of the Lord of Wrath. I'm sure you can guess his vice. To him, there are only the strong and the weak, and he takes no prisoners." Ahrun said.

"I thought the Lord of Long Shadows controlled the court," Alex said.

"Aye, he does, ta a point," Kyria said, stepping over a body. "He's the most powerful o' the Court, and has the most territory, but there are always bids for power, an' the Lord of Wrath, he jus' enjoys killing. Don' matter what."

"The enemy of my enemy I suppose," Alex said, shaking her head.

"It wouldn't be the first time we've taken advantage o' one o' their squabbles," Kyria said with a wicked smile.

At the end of the hall, the door was open slightly and inside, Alex found a room of moving cogs and great mechanisms that ran inside every wall and throughout the stronghold. Strange letters labeled several great levers with writing Alex didn't understand, but the letters shimmered into English after she stared at them for a moment. Both were labeled, "Livestock Holding Pens." Alex bridled at the name but motioned to Kyria and they pulled the levers, which released quickly, and a great rumbling came from the base of the Den.

"Let's go make sure that opened what I think it did," Alex said.

They took a while to make it back down to the pits, but the fighting was mostly over. The Akari were mopping up the last of the Foxes. The demons were far stronger and better equipped, and more numerous. Alex wanted to make sure the slaves escaped the compound, as the bloodthirsty monster would kill them armed or not.

When they arrived at the pits, Alex smiled when she saw the light of the outside world streaming in. The slaves hadn't moved. She looked at Kyria, who shrugged. Ahrun shook his head.

"These people don't know what to do with themselves. The Foxes Guild has enslaved them so long, anything else is frightening. I saw much of this in Alcrest. We should talk to them," Ahrun said.

Alex nodded. "On Earth, we call it being institutional syndrome. They may need a push, I agree."

Alex wasted no time making her way to the bottom of the pit where she found a large crowd gathering around an older man who was speaking to the slaves. He glared at them angrily.

"Outsider! You have brought much trouble!" He said in an angry growl. "The masters will be cruel with us when they see someone open their doors! We did not ask for this!"

Alex inhaled deeply, before replying. She had to be patient with him.

"Look, we're just trying to help. Your masters are dead! You are free. I've seen what they do with you people. Take back your lives!" Alex was trying not to shout, but she couldn't let them stay here. "Besides, the roof will collapse any minute and you'll all be dead. The Den is burning."

"You lie! The masters are strong and they will return. You are a charlatan! My people, we must wait here for our masters to return!" They shifted uneasily, as if unsure of whom to believe.

Alex stopped talking to him and turned to address the crowd. "You have more power than you think! They only enslaved your mind. You can be your own people and never be used as bait to feed jungle beasts again!"

The slaves looked at each other and murmured. The slaves in Alex's convoy clearly weren't the only ones who had been fed to jungle beasts. The foreman felt the people shifting against him and tried one last appeal.

"We cannot abandon the masters now! They need us! There will be much suffering! There will…"

The slaves had already streamed out of the pit. Alex and her friends led them out, pausing at the edge of the tunnel. Outside the stronghold, the battle still raged and the surrounding farmlands were a chaotic, fire-drenched wasteland. Alex turned to the people and addressed them.

"Get yourselves to the treeline and hide there until the Akari have left. There should be enough supplies in the Den to rebuild. Take this land back for yourselves!" she said.

There was a silence, and they inundated Alex with hugs and grateful handshakes. She waited for the slaves to make their way across the battlefield into the trees, where they made their best effort to blend in. Once they had made it safely, the slaves from the other pit made their way across, apparently deciding that they would rather take their chances as one large group.

"All right, now we can go. Do you think they'll be ok?" Alex asked her friends.

Kyria nodded. "These people are resilient. They've worked this land for gods know how long. I think they're goin' ta be jus' fine."

Ahrun nodded in agreement. "I concur. You've done real good here, Alex, the kind that isn't measurable. These people owe you more than just their lives."

"Owe *us*," Alex corrected him.

"Well, I don' know about ya fine, fancy folks, but I'm ready ta get gone from here, pleasant as it has been," Kyria said cheerfully.

"Agreed. Let's blow this popsicle stand," Alex said.

Ahrun and Kyria looked at her in confusion. Alex sighed and chuckled. Goal number one, once this was all over: invent the Aquillonian popsicle.

Alex reached in her pocket and retrieved the waystone. It glowed to life, grumbling.

"I'm sure no one cares, but it was stifling in that pocket!" it whined.

"Yer right, rock. No one cares," retorted Kyria.

"I'm going to transport you to the moon," it snapped back.

"Seriously, you two! You," Alex said, looking at the stone, "pipe down!" She looked at Kyria, "and you! It's a rock. Stop letting it get under your skin. Let's just out of here.

"No," the stone said sulkily.

"What do you mean, no?" Alex asked, trying her best not to throw the stupid thing in the nearest fire.

"Too much smoke. I need to be somewhere clear to geolocate for my locational matrix to work." It turned to Kyria, "in stupid peasant language: Smoke bad. Stone no work."

Ahrun grabbed Kyria's arms as she tried to grab it.

Alex looked at it in disbelief. "Do you have anything in mind, Mr. Particular?"

"Well, excuse me for having standards and not transporting you into an active volcano by accident. Well, one of you would be an accident, anyway. The roof of this building would work fine."

"Anything else you need to work properly?" Alex asked with an annoyed sigh.

"Some peace and quiet and not being surrounded by idiotic lesser life forms would be nice, but I suppose I can make due," it said with a sneer (or whatever the glowing stone face equivalent of a sneer was).

"I'm sorry I asked. C'mon," Alex said, sighing and shaking her head.

There was still heavy fighting in the fields, where the last of the Fox Guild was attempting to hold back a sea of crazed Akari. As it seemed like there was lots of death that way, Alex backtracked to the ladder and go back up into the stronghold. Inside, the last of the Foxes were being crushed between two fronts of Akari warriors. Keeping to the back of the wall, Alex navigated to the stairs. Ahrun was the last one to start up the stairs when they heard the scream.

A single Akari, drenched in blood was screaming at them and drawing others away from the Fox guard. Soon enough a swarm of warriors charged, screaming in horrible goat noises and swinging their axes in the air. They rushed the stairs, bucking horns with one another to be the first to chase their prey. Alex and her friends quickened their pace with screaming death charging behind them.

As she reached the third floor, Alex ran down the corridor, hoping to find some roof access. Fortunately, a ladder at the end of the hall led up to an open grate through which sunlight streamed in. Unfortunately, the Akari had caught up, moving faster and seeming in an even worse mood (if that was possible), probably because they hadn't killed anything in the last several minutes. Alex didn't want to break that streak and continued up the ladder, followed by her friends, followed by the raving goat warriors. Thankfully, their cloven hooves weren't ideal for climbing ladders and they took some time to master the concept. Ahrun pulled himself onto the roof and closed the grate behind him forcefully.

The rooftop was thankfully clear of angry goats or Foxes. Alex took the stone from her pocket and it glowed, blue this time instead of red, which Alex desperately hoped was a good sign.

"Ah, fresh air at last. I am glad you could at least accomplish that simple task. Perhaps there is some hope for lesser life forms," the stone said, eyeing Kyria in particular.

"I swear by all the gods, I'm gonna kill it!" Kyria said, fuming.

The waystone ignored her and continued. "Now if you'll allow the normal two-hour period, I will summon the…"

"Two hours!" They all shouted angrily at it, and even Alex wanted to crumble it to dust.

"But, I suppose I could skip a few steps. It'll be a rough portal, but for the three of you I guess it'll do," it said with what sounded like a sigh.

"How. Long?" Alex demanded angrily.

"Only a few minutes. Now allow me to compute or none of us are going anywhere," it snapped back. As its face faded on the stone and it cast energy on the floor. There was a humming sound and runes flashed over the waystone.

Alex exhaled. Despite the Akari pounding on the grate, Alex felt like they might finally be leaving. Then, nearly the moment she had the thought, she instantly regretted having it. A colossal roar ripped through the upper ramparts and the Lord of Long Shadows landed with a thud on the roof, having jumped up from the floor below through a new hole in the roof, courtesy of the Akari war machines.

"I swore I would drench these ramparts with your entrails, whelp! Now you have doomed your friends. I will keep them as slaves! Their torment will be never ending." The demon lord said, screaming each word with uncontained fury.

He charged and Alex turned to the waystone.

"Please tell me you're almost done!" she pleaded.

It raised an eyebrow, or what looked like one, and said, "You can't rush genius, but since you asked; one minute. I can't make it any faster, so don't ask!" It shut its eye and resumed casting its spell.

Alex turned to her friends. "We don't have a minute, but I have a plan. Run back there." She pointed behind the grate that was just barely holding back an army of angry goatmen. They ran behind it and turned to face the demon lord, who was only feet from them. Alex could feel his power and his hatred surging towards her in waves. Fear washed over her, but she stood strong.

Hold, Alex. Hold.

The demon lord drew closer.

Hold, Alex. She steeled herself. The wrong timing and this plan would fail and they would all be dead.

Closer now, so close she could smell him and her heart raced in her chest like a war drum. *Hold, Alex.*

The demon lord was on them now and as he charged the last several feet, he raised his scythe high; it gleamed golden death for her and her friends. At the last moment, Alex ducked down and pulled the pin out of the grate. An explosion of motion followed as the Akari surged forth, directly in the demon lord's path. Seeing him, the Akari forgot their intended target and screamed a war cry before jumping onto him. The Lord of Long Shadows roared in fury and protest, hacking the Akari down several at a time, but it didn't matter. They were a sea of wrath and madness and they overwhelmed him quickly.

Altogether ignoring what was going on around it, the waystone announced, "Portal opening in the nearby vicinity. Please enter it quickly as it is unstable."

Alex glanced over the nearby rampart and a glimmering blue portal hovered in the air, several feet from the edge of the rampart. She wanted to yell at the stone for not summoning it closer to them or, the roof itself, but there wasn't time. She extended her hand, and the stone floated to it and she ran for the portal, her friends in tow.

Behind them, the demon lord screamed in primal fury and rushed towards them. Several dozen Akari held him down, but his demonic strength and rage drove him forward. The roof shuddered under them as an Akari siege weapon struck the floor below and it collapsed into the fiery remains of the Fox's Den below. Alex ignored all of this and threw herself into a dead sprint. It was only a short distance to the edge of the rampart. The demon lord was close behind them now, and she could hear his roars. She ran, compelling her legs past where exhaustion would have prevailed, past what seemed to her to be humanly possible, for death was behind her, and salvation ahead of her. Reaching the edge of the rampart she jumped, placing all of her strength and faith in one final leap, hoping it was enough.

Her friends jumped as well and the last thing she saw was the Lord of Long Shadows falling into the collapsing roof, covered in screaming Akari warriors. His eye locked with hers for one final moment, and she felt his hatred singe her soul. Just as he was about to fall, the Lord vanished in black smoke, and the Akari that were on him fell screaming to their deaths in the fiery inferno below.

Alex reached the threshold of the portal and felt herself being pulled in. The portal warped her senses and the feeling of time left her altogether as she floated momentarily in a dark, starless void between places. Just as soon as she had entered it, it pulled her to the other side and she landed with a hard thud on the ground, her friends not far behind. As soon as she heard the portal close behind her, her body gave out, having nothing more to give.

All that mattered was that she had made it, and her friends had too. Everything else could wait.

26

At The Doorstep Of Sanctum

Alex returned to consciousness slowly and cautiously, as if her body feared that bringing her back all at once would be too much of a strain on her mind. Hazy images flashed across her fluttering eyes as the world slowly put itself back together. When she finally awakened, the first clear image she saw was Kyria and Ahrun smiling down at her, next to a fire they had built.

"Welcome back to the land of the living, Alex Winters," Ahrun said pleasantly.

"We almost thought ya was a goner for a minute. Which would 'ave been a cryin' shame, because ya really have ta see where we are," Kyria said.

Alex smiled at them and sat up, slowly. Her head was pounding and every muscle in her body screamed in raw agony. She could barely sit up, and when she moved her legs, they may have as well laughed at her for all the good her effort did. She decided that for the moment sitting was all she could accomplish. None of that mattered though as soon as she looked around.

Alex wasn't sure if her jaw literally dropped, but she imagined theirs had too so she didn't feel too foolish. They sat encamped on a raised plateau. All around them the jungle encroached, held back by a shimmering barrier. In the distance, a massive tower, wide as a city, and as tall as the Empire State Building, loomed against the dark horizon.

The plateau extended for several miles in all directions from the tower, and around it on the ground, great runes glowed like crop circles, illuminating the area surrounding them. Imposing statues towered across the landscape of men and women in flowing robes and heroic poses, keeping watch over the night. The entire plateau was silent. Not a single sound from the jungle crept through the barrier, and Alex felt very much at peace. It was a stillness that settled her soul, and for the first time in her journey, Alex's mind felt clear. None of this, however, could keep her eyes off the sky.

Above them, a clear void of stars hung in the heavens and she could see far out into space. Gas clouds and galaxies gleamed, and it seemed like there was nothing between them and the sky above. It was mesmerizing to look at and gave the plateau an unearthly feel about it. She could see the surrounding jungle, but the plateau felt removed from the world around it, existing outside time and the cares of the world.

Kyria's voice broke into her thoughts. "It's incredible," she said, her voice filled with genuine awe. "When I was a little girl, Rex would tell me stories about this place, but honestly, even his fanciful exaggeratin' doesn't do this place a lick o' justice."

"Many a paladin gave their lives in the pursuit of Sanctum. I feel only fortunate to fulfill their noble quest," Ahrun added.

"Yeah, I guess I wasn't ready to get here. Doesn't seem real that after all this time, now that we're finally there," Alex said in a dreamy voice.

"All journeys must end, but many have their beginning in another's end. I don't know what the Eastern Watch has in mind for you, but I sense this is not the end of our journey together," Ahrun added sagely.

Alex stared at him. It was often easy to mistake him for a young man given his physical appearance, but beneath it, there were millennia of wisdom.

Kyria grinned. "I reckon not," she said. "I've no intention o' gettin' rid of ya now, temptin' as it might be."

Alex nodded. "Well, I guess we'd better go see what these mystics want with me. I'm ready for some answers."

"An' breakfast! For all their mystic power, I'm gonna break heads if they don' have some eggs and a bit o' bacon," Kyria demanded in a mockingly serious voice.

Alex and Ahrun fell into fits of laughter, and Kyria wasn't far behind.

Packing her things up, Alex prepared for the final leg of the journey. The sky was dark, but she felt fully rested if sore. She suspected time didn't work the same here. Setting out towards Sanctum, the group found an old path that led down out of the hills onto the plateau itself. It fed into the main road which led straight to the tower.

As they walked, Alex reminisced about her adventure and took a final moment to remember Thistle and his bravery. Reminiscing helped ease the growing tension brought on by the unknown. With each moment, the tower grew nearer and more ominous, representing the end of a journey, and the answer to a question she desperately needed. Dwelling on the past for at least a few moments longer made the uncertainty of the future more bearable.

Alex smiled as she thought of all they had seen together. It seemed like a lifetime ago she had first fallen into the sea and escaped the Red Fleet. She laughed to herself as she thought of her first meeting with Thistle, and their narrow escape of the Golden Host along the old eastern road. It all seemed so distant. Kyria spoke of her last memories of her father, and times of the guard long gone. Ahrun told them stories of his past, and the grand adventures he had seen.

Still, the air of uncertainty hung thick around them, and Alex couldn't shake the deep and portentous feeling that clung to her like a coat one size too small.

They neared Sanctum and the scale of the tower left them all in muted silence. Well, except for Kyria who wisely observed. "Holy Gods thas' a big tower!"

"Astute observation there, Captain Obvious," Alex teased.

The tower seemed to extend forever, and as they neared it, Alex couldn't wrap her mind around the vast scope. It seemed like a monument of another age, before mankind, built by something greater and older than any human eyes had ever seen. There were no windows at all, and only one door that led in. It was a massive wooden door, a hundred feet high and twice that length. The road ended at it and Alex stood before it, feeling tiny.

Blue torches burned on either side of it but there seemed to be no handles or knockers on the door itself. Alex looked over to her friends and raised an eyebrow. "I guess we should knock?" she asked.

They looked back at her and shrugged, having no more useful suggestions to offer. Alex clenched her fist, breathed deeply, and knocked.

The sound of her knock seemed almost comically light and Alex was sure nobody heard it, even if they had been listening. Still, she waited; she didn't want to seem rude or pushy, and she wasn't looking to make a bad first impression with people who could probably melt her with their minds.

After a torturously long time waiting Alex went to knock again but stopped when she heard a deep cranking of gears and mechanisms from somewhere behind the door. All three of them backed up giving the door a wide berth. The door opened several feet; only a crack given its impressive stature and a single figure walked out slowly.

The figure was a small woman, dressed in shimmering blue robes.

Her brown hair danced in an invisible breeze and she smiled at them with a sad smile. Her eyes were icy blue crystals and her face was beautiful but worn as if by years of care and worry. She locked eyes with Alex, and Alex's heart raced, though not from fear.

"Hello, Alex. I'm so glad you made it." As she spoke, tears welled in her eyes and she beamed with joy.

Her words were like a bolt of lightning passing through Alex's heart and she nearly fell to her knees, but Kyria caught her. A thousand things swirled in Alex's mind as she wrestled with a truth that came to her, which was altogether impossible and possible at the same time. It was a truth that seemed too strange, too wild to be true, but she knew in her soul it was. Memories rushed back to her from a time she had long since forgotten, memories of a woman saying goodbye to a man and a tiny girl. Her eyes welled with tears she had never thought to shed and she looked back at the woman, barely able to speak or make eye contact. She responded in a single word which was as much a question as a statement, and as she spoke it, the whole of her existence reverberated in a single moment of impossible truth that danced outside of time.

"Mom?" she asked, her voice breaking.

The woman nodded and Alex collapsed into her outstretched arms and all the rest of the world faded into nothing as she sobbed. Alex felt her mother's hand on her head stroking her quietly, and her mother replied to her question in a soft voice, nearly a whisper.

"Welcome home, my darling girl. I have so much to tell you."

The End.

www.ingramcontent.com/pod-product-compliance
Lightning Source LLC
Chambersburg PA
CBHW051609100726
47898CB00001B/287